9670 6658

Also by Belva Plain

LEGACY OF SILENCE
HOMECOMING
SECRECY
PROMISES
THE CAROUSEL
DAYBREAK
WHISPERS
TREASURES
HARVEST
BLESSINGS
TAPESTRY
THE GOLDEN CUP
CRESCENT CITY
EDEN BURNING
RANDOM WINDS
EVERGREEN
FORTUNE'S HAND

AFTER THE FIRE

AFTER THE FIRE

Belva Plain

First published in Great Britain in 2000
by Hodder and Stoughton
A division of Hodder Headline
338 Euston Road London NW1 3BH

This edition published 2000
by Doubleday Book Clubs in Australia and New Zealand
by arrangement with Hodder and Stoughton.

ISBN 1 876590 30 0

Printed and bound in Australia by McPherson's Printing Group.

AFTER THE FIRE

PROLOGUE

In a house where women are gathered for a meeting of *Mothers Without Custody*, she searches the room with anxious eyes as if some answer might be hidden there for her. It is a neglected, cheerless room in which, with its gray curtains and wilted amaryllis that pleads for water, the very air is thick with sorrow.

The desperate, poor immigrant whose husband has fled back to India with their two daughters sits with her face in her hands, for she has neither the means nor the worldly knowledge to pursue them. The fashionable woman, with the coral scarf and the handsome earrings, has lost her twelve-year-old boy to the charms of his father's lakeside mansion. The recovered alcoholic pleads in vain for a second chance.

To them and to all of them her heart goes out. Still, there is never any pain as piercing as one's own, she cannot stay here for another minute. Quietly she rises and goes outside into the muggy summer noon.

From the top of the hill where her car is parked she looks down at the rooftops below and thinks about the random cruelties that may be hidden under any one of those roofs. Strange — or not so strange — that, standing at a window in Paris not very long ago, she had the same thought . . .

Chapter One

Solid in status, circled by wide lawns and lavish shrubbery, the house stood where the outer suburbs met the countryside and the road wound toward the Berkshire hills. The land rose in ripples. In the morning the rising sun washed the hilltops in hazy pink light; at day's end the afterglow, lingering above them, lay like a scarlet stripe between the dark land and a foaming grey sea of clouds.

On such an evening, Hyacinth put aside the sketches and charcoal on her desk to gaze with pleasure at the scene. Except for the faintest rustle of leaves in the warm September air, it was quite still. And at the open window she too stood quite still, in awe of the evening.

A mood, one of those that in occasional self-mockery she called her 'poetic moments,' had overcome her. Yet the mood ought not to be mocked, especially now when she was so incredibly happy. So secure, contented and loved, so incredibly happy!

Abruptly then, she heard voices. Her parents, following their custom, were sitting on the open porch below. She had never eavesdropped and was certainly not about to do so now. But she had heard her name.

'Hy is twenty-one,' Dad said. 'She's not a child anymore.'

'Hyacinth is twenty-one going on twelve.'

'You amaze me, Francine. Here's a girl, an A student, only one year out of college, and already interning in one of the finest museums in the country. And,' he went on in the proud, earnest tone that a father assumes when he is boasting about an only

3

daughter, 'she's an artist! She'll make a name for herself. Wait and see.'

'I'm not talking about academics. I'm talking about emotions. Haven't you noticed how she walks around with a smile all the time? I wouldn't be surprised if she was already planning a wedding. Oh, I'd like to ship that fellow to Australia, or Tierra del Fuego, or anyplace.'

He pulled the desk chair to the window and sat there dumbfounded.

'What have you really got against him? All right, so you haven't been enthusiastic about him, and that's your privilege, but why so vehement? Why?'

'He'll break her heart Jim, that's why. He's a chaser. I see it. I feel it in my bones. Right now he's having a struggle to get ahead, but once there, he'll drop her. I don't trust him. He'll chase after women, and women will chase after him. He's too gorgeous. He ought to be in Hollywood. Hyacinth's no match for that kind of business.'

'For God's sake, your imagination is running away with you. He's certainly faithful enough. Three times every week, plus every weekend.'

'I don't say he can't be sincere at the moment. It's possible, after a fashion. She certainly has qualities that you don't find everywhere you look. Deep intelligence. Taste. Dignity. And she so obviously adores him. That flatters a man.'

'I still say you're making a mountain out of a molehill.'

'Jim! I'm talking about humiliation. I'm talking about heartbreak. He's not for her. He's not!'

Hyacinth's heart hammered in her ears. Not for me? What do you know about him, or about me either? You know nothing about my life.

'She's so good, Jim. A genuinely good human being.'

'Yes, yes, that she is.'

As clearly as if she had been sitting down there on the porch with them, Hyacinth saw their faces: her father's pale eyes, so much like her own, reflective, looking off into the distance; her mother's darting eyes, bright and blue, with the two vertical lines between them that appeared whenever she was alert or emphatic.

4

'I don't see it at all, Francine. He's agreeable, well-mannered, smart, medical school, medical honorary society. Pretty desirable, if you ask me. And the fact is, I rather like him.'

'Yes, he's likable enough. But I tell you again, he's too shrewd for her. She's a total innocent. What does she know about the world? Or about people? The only men she's gone out with are college boys and maybe a couple of artists she's met at her job. And not even many of them. Gerald's taken up practically all of this year.'

The best year of my life. The year that's changed my life.

'She's a typical artist, a student, a loner, and always has been.'

'A lot of people are artists and students and loners. A lot of remarkable people.'

'Yes, and they are often the ones who get hurt the most.'

'Well, if you feel this way, why don't you talk to her about it?'

'Talk to her? For all her sweetness she can still be stubborn as a mule when she wants to be, can't she? Do I have to tell you? How long have we been asking her to stop smoking? And has she stopped? It's odd, too. She doesn't look like the type to go around with a cigarette in her hand.'

Should she run downstairs now and confront them with her outrage? But she sat there, unable to move, and waited for more.

Dad spoke quietly. 'You're getting yourself all worked up.'

'What shall I do? Sit calmly watching a man get what he can out of my child?'

'What do you mean by "get what he can"? Sex?'

'Who knows? But there are other things beside sex.'

Dad persisted. 'Such as?'

'Look around. What's bad about this house? Pretty comfortable here, isn't it? He noticed things, too, the few times he was here. He kept looking around. I saw him.'

'Well, why wouldn't he be curious? It's only natural. He's lived poor all his life, and he's up to his ears in debt to the university. It's not like you to be so critical. It's not like you to be cynical.' There was a sigh in Dad's voice. He hated argument.

'Not cynical. Realistic.'

'Let's go inside. The mosquitoes are out.'

5

But Francine was not finished. 'Don't be misled by Hy's brains or her energy or her ambition. At heart, she's a bookworm. Give her a book or a new CD, and she's happy. Her wants are simple. She's simple. And that fellow isn't. They don't even like the same things.'

Dad laughed. 'How much chemistry did you know or like when you married me?'

'That was different. You were Mr. Honorable, Mr. Salt-of-the-Earth. And you still are,' Francine said softly. She gave a small, rueful laugh. 'She's soft, like you. Not like me, Jim.'

'Well, we've been a great combination anyway, haven't we? Come on in with me. This is a big, useless fuss about nothing. Believe me. And even if it were as serious as you say, there wouldn't be anything we could do about it.'

The screen door slammed below. Night came falling out of the sky. Still Hyacinth sat, trembling in the dimness. She had been wounded, degraded and insulted.

What cruel things to have said about Gerald! He was so gentle, so thoughtful — so *decent*! Decent, you would say if you had to sum him up in a word. He worked so hard, and had been given so little. Yet he never complained. He was happy with even the smallest pleasure that came his way, a book on his birthday or an occasional dinner at this house.

I should go right down there and defend him, she thought fiercely. What am I waiting for? But her legs were weak. As water is sucked out of a basin, so all the energy she had possessed an hour before had drained away.

There was no use trying to do any more work this night, so she lit a cigarette, cleared the desk, putting away the charcoal and the folio of sketches. After a while she undressed and lay down on the bed.

Fear came suddenly. Oh God, if anything should happen! Could anything happen? If Gerald were here, he would hold and comfort her . . . So she lay, while her mind drifted back and back.

How clearly she remembered their first meeting, the place and hour, the first words, and even what she had worn. She had worn a raincoat, the day had been raw, and the museum's parking lot was a puddle of mud. She had started down the hill and was passing the university when, through the rear-view mirror, she saw a young man standing in front of the medical school, unprotected against the downpour by either coat or umbrella. He was clasping to his chest a bundle of books in a plastic bag, and he was soaked through.

She backed up. 'Need a lift?'

'I'm waiting for the bus. It goes on the hour, but I think I've just missed it.'

'You have. It's ten after. I'll take you where you're going. Climb in.'

'Thanks, but I'm heading the other way.'

'No matter. You can't stay out in this.' You wouldn't want to leave your dog outside in such weather, so cold, with winter in the air.

'I won't refuse. Just as far as the next bus stop, then. That would be great.'

'You don't have to wait for the bus,' she said as they neared the covered shelter. 'Where do you live? I'll take you.'

'Hey! I live in Linden. No, drop me off here at the stop.'

She had never known anyone who lived in Linden. It was a factory town with a railroad bridge and truck traffic, a place you barely glimpsed and skirted as you passed on your way to some-place else. And it was a good ten miles distant.

His books were still pathetically clutched to his chest. She had hardly seen his face, half-concealed as it was between tousled wet hair and hunched, sodden collar. Now she looked: It was a nice, respectable face.

'We'll go to Linden,' she said.

He protested. 'Oh no, I can't let you do that.'

'You can't not let me unless you jump out of the car.'

'Okay, then.' He smiled. 'Gerald's my name. What's yours?'

'Hyacinth. I hate it.'

Now why had she said that? Always apologizing for the silly name! It was a habit that ought to be broken.

'Why so? It's a gentle name. It goes with your face.'

Gentle. What an odd thing to say!

She was not feeling gentle right now as she lay, remembering, with all this pounding in her head.

'My car's stalled. It's thirteen years old,' he explained. 'I hope it's just a dead battery.'

'I hope so.'

An uncomfortable silence fell. Apparently it had the same uncomfortable effect upon him, because he broke it.

'I'm a fourth year med student, finished next May. Are you a student?'

'I graduated last May. Now I work.'

'Out in the world already. I've got three more years to put in, maybe four if I do a fellowship after the residency.'

'You sound sorry.'

'Not really. I love what I do. It's just that I'm in kind of a hurry to earn and be on my own. What do you do?'

'I was an art major. Now I'm an intern at the museum, conserving old or damaged art. And I paint and have a studio at home.'

'All kinds of ways of making a living; conserving damaged art – that's one I never thought of.'

'It's more than "making a living." It takes a lot of skill.'

She should not have answered him that way. It had sounded arrogant, and she hadn't meant it to. So she softened her words with an explanation. 'We get paintings and sculpture from all over the country, things that have been badly restored, or not restored at all. Right now, I'm removing varnish from an 1870 oil portrait that's turned all yellow.'

'Sounds interesting.'

'Oh, it is. I love it, but I have a lot to learn yet. Repairing tears – it's nerve-wracking.'

'Sounds like surgery. What I'm hoping to do.'

It was a funny thing about conversations. If you don't return the ball but let it drop, people think you're unfriendly. So you must quickly think of something to say. Though why should she care whether this stranger thought she was unfriendly or not? Nevertheless, she continued.

8

'This is a nice place, one of the best state universities in the country, they say.'

'It is, and I'm grateful to it. But if I could have gotten as good a loan from someplace out west or down south or anywhere new, I would have gone there instead.'

'I wanted to get away, too, but I have three older brothers who've done it, and I knew my parents hoped I'd be the one to stay home.'

Another silence fell. After a minute or two, he broke it again. 'This is a great car.'

'I suspect it's my reward for staying home.'

Yes, surely it had been a reward, her little red car, her shiny toy, a reward like the summer art course in Italy. Just in time, she stopped herself from saying so; you didn't mention European trips to a person on scholarship.

'They're making a real cultural center out of this old mill town, aren't they?' he remarked. 'I hear the museum is really famous.'

'It is. Have you never been in it?'

'No, I don't know anything about art.'

'It's marvelous. You should visit it sometime.'

'Maybe I will.'

The windshield wipers were barely coping with the rain. As the car lurched roughly over potholes and labored dangerously through a gush of high water, it was a struggle to stay on the road. Conversation lapsed until they reached the turnoff to Linden, where she asked for directions to his house.

'It's on Smith Street. Middle of town. I'll show you.'

When he got out and stood thanking her, she had her first full sight of markedly noticeable height, bright black hair, vivacious eyes and a firm, oval face. Anyone, man or woman, would look twice.

'I can't thank you enough,' he said earnestly.

'You talk as if I'd done something extraordinary.'

'Well, you just did.'

She drove back down the street of dingy shops interspersed here and there with the wretched relic of a fine colonial Massachusetts townhouse. Here, shoes were repaired, newspapers bought, meat sold, and hair barbered; above them, behind fire escapes, tired curtains hung at dreary windows. The sight of these in the now-slackening rain was curiously sobering to her.

Gerald. He hadn't even told her his last name. And she remembered now how even in the privacy of her mind, she had been so hotly ashamed of her own absurd thought: *He is the kind of man I could love.* And that after just twenty minutes!

'You never know what tomorrow will bring,' Granny always said. She made good use of clichés. 'You won't have to be told when you meet Mr. Right.'

Perhaps Granny really did know a thing or two. For only two days after the rainstorm, she had become aware while at work that heads were turned toward the door behind her; looking about, she had seen Gerald peering into the room. His lips were forming words.

'May I come in?'

Flushed and disbelieving, she was unsure of an answer, but he had already stepped in.

'I took your advice about visiting the museum,' he said.

'We — we're working here,' she replied awkwardly, thinking that people would not like this intrusion.

With an olive pit she had been polishing an ancient bronze Buddha. She remembered it well, the great, airy room, the northern light, her trembling hands on the treasure, and Gerald looking at her.

'I understand. I'll wait for you outside. I only wanted to see you again,' he said.

She remembered everything . . . Quieted now, and purged of the evening's rage, she looked up at the shadowed ceiling and smiled.

Chapter Two

But anger, in the morning, surged back.

He's too shrewd for Hy. He'll break her heart. He'll chase after women.

So violently did she brush her hair, that her scalp stung. He'll break my heart? No, it's you who's doing that, Francine, you.

'Why do you call your mother by her first name?' Gerald had asked.

'Because Francine likes it,' she had explained.

Her real name was Frances; of French extraction some four generations or more ago, and even though she couldn't speak a word of the beautiful language, she loved to appear French. Probably she felt that Frenchness went along with her beauty.

Hy's indignation mounted. Every irritant, every grievance that naturally accumulates among people living together under the same roof, all the stifled and relatively trivial offenses, rose up now to flood her mind. And she spoke aloud: 'Because you were a runner-up in a statewide beauty contest, you expected your daughter to go as far or farther than you. Oh, I understand clearly! I know I've been a disappointment to you. I'm too tall and angular, gawky and thin. I don't run with the Saturday night crowd as you did when you were my age. Nor have I ever been an athlete, or not enough of one to captain the women's swim team or play basketball in the intramural games, as you did. You're not really interested in my paintings. You'd never say so, but I know what you think. Yes, you love me. There's no doubt of that, and you've been a good mother, but you are disappointed in me all the same. You alone. Not Dad, nor my bosses at the museum, and certainly not Gerald . . .'

The house was quiet. Suddenly she wanted to flee from it before anyone should wake up. There was no way a person could possibly put on a normal face after last night. And dressing quickly, she went on stocking feet toward the stairs.

The walls there were lined with family photographs. Thousands of times she must have passed them, yet today something compelled her to pause in spite of haste to look at these people again. Here now was a nineteenth-century gentleman wearing a high starched collar; here was a 1920s girl wearing a bell-shaped hat. Who were they, really, behind their composed and amiable semismiles? Are we at all alike, they and I? Here were her older brothers, George in white with his inevitable tennis racket; the other two at their respective weddings with their lacy, proper brides. George, Paul and Thomas they were, all handsome duplicates in male form of their mother. They were not like Hyacinth, not at all.

'You give them sensible names,' she had many times complained. 'Then you name me *Hyacinth*. It's idiotic. Whatever were you thinking of?'

'They had to have those dull names,' Francine would explain with remarkable patience, one had to admit, 'after two grandfathers and one uncle killed in the war. So when you arrived, I wanted something beautiful for the only daughter I would ever have. I wanted the name of a spring flower.'

For an otherwise intelligent woman, Francine could say absurd things. In some ways, she really was a trifle ridiculous. And such a judgment about one's own mother was, at the very least, discomforting, like having a sharp pebble in one's shoe. But when absurdity turned into cruelty like last night's, it was no pebble.

When she had started the car and reached the fork in the road, she stopped. Where to go? It was Saturday, and Gerald was taking today and tomorrow to study for a test on Monday. The conservation center at the museum was officially closed except to senior independent workers. The obvious choice then, the only choice, was Granny's house.

You could always open your heart to her. She was as soothing and strengthening as – as hot oatmeal on a cold Monday morning. Even her house, on an old street in the heart of the old, original town, had a comforting welcome with its wraparound porch, wooden lace and flowers in season, tulips, hollyhocks and asters, against the backyard fence. In that house, Granny had been born and married. Most probably she would die there, too, but also probably not for a long time. She was as strong as she looked, a woman at peace with herself. You could never imagine her striving for popularity or worrying over what 'people might think'! It was known to all but never mentioned, that Francine and Gran had little love for each other.

A fragrance of sugar and cinnamon filled the hall when the front door was opened. Hy sniffed the air.

'Baking already? It's just past eight.'

'Apple pies,' Granny said, 'for that shut-in couple down the street. I try to bring them something on weekends. Come on in. Or do you want the porch? It's warm enough.'

'The porch is fine.'

'Then wait till I get my sewing. I'm making a quilt for your brother's baby, squares and circles in pink, blue and yellow, to be on the safe side.'

You never saw her with empty hands. Maybe it was some Puritan heritage that compelled her to keep moving, or maybe it was just nervous energy. And thinking so, while Granny settled herself with her work on her lap, it seemed to Hyacinth that she herself had more than a bit of that nervous energy.

'I never thought I'd live long enough to be making things for a great-grandchild. Do you like it? Honestly?'

Hy considered the subject. 'Not quite so much pink. Pink ought to be no more than an accent, I think.'

Tilting her head from one angle to another, now Granny considered. 'You know what? You're right. You always did have a good eye for color. You should think of making something for the new baby, too, an heirloom from Aunt Hyacinth. You haven't forgotten how to hook a rug, I hope.'

'It's been a long time, but I haven't forgotten.'

'No, of course not. You have golden hands, Hy. I tried to teach your mother, but she wasn't interested.'

No, you could never imagine Francine sitting still over any painstaking work, or spending hours in a kitchen, either. She liked being out of the house, working for charities and good causes, of which she was often the organizer; or else she was competing in a sport like tennis or golf, at which she was often the winner. Francine had to win things. She had to run things and lead people.

'Tell me about your work,' Granny said pleasantly. 'Your father tells me you're in one of the country's best conservation departments.'

'That's true, but I'm only a beginner. It takes years of training before you can be entrusted with a painting worth a few million dollars.'

'You'll be making a name for yourself with your own paintings one day. That was a splendid study of your dad taking a nap.'

Hy was pleased. Indeed, it seemed to everyone who saw it that the picture was a very fine, very sensitive portrait.

But Granny was regarding her intently. After a few more casual remarks, she suddenly interrupted her.

'Why have you really come here so early this morning? There must be something serious on your mind.'

Having come to ease herself by pouring out her complaint, Hy wished she had not come. It was such a shabby story after all, a mother and daughter at odds over the daughter's lover! But she sat up straight, told the story, and concluded, 'I'm sorry. I shouldn't expect you to take sides. I should not involve you. I should have kept it to myself.'

'Not if it makes you feel better to speak out. I'm always here for you, Hy, you know that. I have only one piece of advice, though. Don't make an issue about what you overheard. There'd be nothing gained except more hard feelings. Pretend you never heard anything and go about your business. Has he asked you to marry him?'

'Not yet, but he will.'

'And you'll say "yes"? You're sure you ought to?'

'Of course I'm sure. I love him.'

'Your mother's a pretty smart lady, you know.'

This observation, coming from this particular mother-in-law, astonished Hyacinth.

'She and I don't always have the same opinions about things, as you've probably noticed.' This was spoken with a wry smile. 'Still, perhaps you should think about what she said. Of course I know nothing about your young man, but I do know that marriage is not a picnic and you had better know what you're doing.'

For the first time ever, Hy was receiving no comfort here where she had expected to find agreement and indignation on her behalf.

'You're annoyed with me, Hyacinth. You wanted me to say something else.'

'Well yes, I guess I did.'

'Cheer up. The sky hasn't fallen. Tomorrow will be a better day.'

The old-fashioned clichés, usually rather amusing and endearing, were at this moment neither.

'Take a pie home. I made three of them.'

'We're all dieting,' Hy said shortly.

'Such a fuss about a few pounds! And you as thin as a stick. Doesn't your mother feed you people anything but salad? Don't you ever do any cooking yourself? You should. I've taught you enough. Take the apple pie and a chicken casserole with it. I've more in the freezer.'

She didn't argue. The simplest thing was to accept the food because it would be thrust into her hands anyway. So she gave thanks, got into the car and drove slowly down the street, unsure of where to go next.

A sense of defiance, lonely and chill, overcame her. In no mood to go home, in no mood to see any friends, she stopped the car in front of the library. It was as good a place as any in which to hide out for the rest of the day.

When Hyacinth went home, Francine's car was not in the garage, and that was a relief, however temporary. Dad was probably in the garden planting spring bulbs, and that, since she did not feel like talking to anyone, was good, too.

Upstairs in the room that had once belonged to George and was now her studio, she closed the door and surveyed her work. For some minutes she stood, trying to see it with impartial eyes, to judge proportion, perspective, shading, brushwork, all of it. Every teacher had praised the snow scenes; studying them now, it seemed she had truly gotten the feeling, the dream-like silence of falling snow. She looked again at the portrait study of her father. It was *true*. It seemed to her that she had caught the essence of him.

Ever since the chemical plant had been downsized, forcing him into retirement, he had grown older and quieter. He had always been quiet, but now his eyes were heavy-lidded, even when he was cheerful. Yes, it seemed to her that she had caught the essence of him; here he was, ready to be framed.

And suddenly came revelation: Her work was good! Whatever else might befall her, her work was her strength. It would take her freely through the world. It would be foolish to let anything sap her confidence in herself and her future. Why then had she wasted this whole day in sorrow?

From the yard below there sounded the whir of the old hand mower that Dad employed to tidy edges. And she called down to him.

'Hey, Dad, I'm home.'

'I thought I heard the garage door. Your mother's still out. Where've you been all day?'

'Places. I stopped at Granny's, and as usual, she gave me food. That chicken thing with shrimp that you like. And I'll make a tossed salad.'

'No, we don't need one. You work hard all week. Take the day off.'

'For Heaven's sake, a salad's no work.'

'Okay, I'll set the table on the porch. There'll be just enough time to eat and finish before dark.'

Plainly, he enjoyed these domestic moments with his daughter. She sensed that the shrinkage of his family, George at a bank in Singapore and the two married sons in business together on the west coast, was more painful for him than he would admit, even to himself.

When she had assembled the customary heap of greens, to which she had added some unexpected sprinkles of strawberries and chopped walnuts, she placed it in a handsome Wedgwood bowl that was kept in the dining-room cabinet for display. Dad's eyebrows made two startled V's when he saw it.

'Using that?'

'Why not?'

'Well, it's a treasure, an antique—'

'All the more reason to enjoy it ourselves. I believe in everyday pleasures, not in keeping them for company. Isn't it a pleasure to look at that perfect blue?'

Dad was silent for a moment. 'The man who gets you is lucky, whoever he is,' he said then. 'Smart, successful, independent, and still domestic enough to make a person want to come home and stay.'

Now Hyacinth was silent. Had she not decided and had Granny not advised her to say nothing? Yet now, of their own accord, her words flew. 'Whoever he is? You really do know who he is, don't you? I heard you both last night, Dad. Or I should say, I heard Francine. I didn't mean to listen, but I couldn't help it.'

'I'm sorry. Awfully sorry.' Dad sighed. 'I didn't agree with her, as you heard.'

'I should hope not. She said horrible things.'

'But still, listen to me. Your mother's opinion is worth respect, no matter what. It comes with the best, most loving intentions. I don't have to tell you that.'

'It was cruel. It was nasty. Wanting money and chasing after women – she doesn't even know Gerald, for God's sake. She was so vehement. You said so yourself. Vehement, you said.'

'All right, I did. But try to understand that she's only expressing her fears. She sees you possibly making a mistake. She's a mother, protecting her child.'

'Child? Me? Twenty-one years old, self-supporting, in a wonderful job?'

'All true. But you haven't mentioned that you're also rather stubborn, Hyacinth.' Dad's smile was a bit rueful.

'When you know you're right, you have to be stubborn. I'm defending Gerald. He's being misjudged, and I love him.'

'Well. Just don't be too much in love too soon, if you can help it. Time takes care of many things.'

Bury your differences, smooth them, and eventually they will disappear. Platitudes. A nice way of saying nothing.

'I hope you won't let your indignation run away with you, Hy. It would only lead to argument and would solve nothing. Certainly not right now, while the fire's still hot.'

'I know, I know. Granny said the same thing. I'm not foolish. I don't want a fight. In some ways, I'm a lot like you.'

'If Gerald is the man you say he is, and I believe he is, your mother will believe it, too. Just don't be in a hurry.' Dad looked at his watch. He wanted the discussion to end fast, before Francine should appear. 'Anyway, you're not getting married tomorrow, so there's no rush,' he was saying, just as Francine came out onto the porch.

'I'm late,' she said. 'I didn't expect so much traffic going home. And the fashion show took forever. What you have to endure if you want to raise money! We cleared sixteen thousand dollars, believe it or not, for the Children's Hospital. I really knocked myself out over this luncheon, I can tell you that.'

'You don't look knocked out,' Dad said. 'That's a nice outfit.'

The grey tweed suit was simple and would have been quiet were it not for the jade green scarf so skillfully fastened over neck and shoulders. When she raised her arm to push a black sweep of hair from her forehead, silver bracelets glistened. Framed by the doorway, Francine made a picture. Hy gave it a title: *Woman with Silver Bracelets*. For all her modern dress and manner, she also had the poise and polish of what Sargent would have labeled *Portrait of Francine*.

'My goodness, what a beautiful table! And the chicken dish – it looks like your mother's, Jim. Or is it yours, Hy?'

'No, Granny's. I was there this morning.'

'Well, this is a feast. The food was awful today, so I'm starved.'

Loquacious as always, Francine spoke brightly, gliding from one topic to another, and certain that they were waiting to hear her.

'I don't believe it's been two years since Tom's wedding. Did I tell you that Diana phoned yesterday to thank us for the anniversary present?'

'I forget what we sent,' Dad said.

'A copper coffee urn, really stunning. Large enough to serve fifty cups. They're giving a lot of parties to help the business. I'm so proud of Tom. It's a good thing, too, that Diana is very sociable. Which reminds me, Hyacinth, I passed Martha's house and saw a truck unloading chairs for the party. Her mother was at the lunch today. She said they expect a houseful. What are you going to wear?'

'I'm not going.'

'Whyever not?'

If a voice were a ribbon, Hy thought, you could distinguish the threads in those words: alarm, impatience and a trace of exasperation.

'It'll be nothing but a great big bash, and I never like them.'

'But you need friends, Hyacinth.'

'Don't I already have plenty?'

'But these are particular old friends. They're neighbors. And you've known Martha since grade school. How can you snub her now?'

'I'm not "snubbing" her or anybody. Do you think she cares whether I come or not?'

Francine pushed the half-eaten dessert away and returned her voice to gentle patience.

'Maybe she does care. You don't want to hurt her feelings.'

Hurt her feelings! Impossible! Martha moved as smoothly through the world as if she were gliding on ice. In an odd way, come to think of it, she resembled Francine herself. She could be her daughter. 'I don't want to hurt anybody's feelings. But I have other plans, so I couldn't accept anyway.'

Nobody spoke. Dad, watching this exchange, poured another cup of coffee and stirred it uselessly until Francine did speak.

'I thought I heard something when I came in about "not getting married yet." If it's true, I'm glad about it, but does it have anything to do with turning down Martha's party?'

'Yes, it does.' Hy spoke steadily. 'I would rather be with Gerald.'

'Well, take him to the party.'

'It wouldn't work out. He doesn't fit with that crowd.'

'Why not? What's wrong with "that crowd"? They're perfectly decent young people as far as I can see.'

'I never said they weren't decent.' The reply was sulky. Feeling cornered, Hyacinth would have liked to walk out of the room.

'So? I don't understand all this.'

'It's hard to explain. It's subtle. Subtle differences among people, that's all.'

Oh, can't she see that all I want – we want – is to be alone? We hardly ever have any alone time. No place except a seedy motel. And you talk about Martha's unimportant party.

'Subtle differences. Yes, there are. And you are wasting your time by giving all of it to one man. You need to get out more among groups and observe those subtle differences, instead of spending every free hour with him.' Francine was losing her struggle against impatience.

'On Gerald, you mean.' Now anger rushed back. 'You might as well know that I heard everything you said last night.'

'Oh, Hy, you promised,' Dad cried, putting the cup down so forcefully that coffee slopped onto the table.

'I'm sorry you did,' Francine said. 'I'm truly sorry. But I can't help what I feel. I'm not telling you never to see Gerald. I'm only afraid you will get too deeply involved. I may be all wrong, but I don't think so.'

There went the worry lines on her forehead again. They were absurd, theatrical and absurd.

'I already am deeply involved,' Hy said.

And now their eyes joined in a long significant look. Each was recalling an afternoon's encounter no more than a month ago.

'I have to ask you Hyacinth, you'll say you're twenty-one and it's your life, which is true, yet parents don't lose interest simply because a person is an adult – but are you sleeping with him?'

This had been the ultimate humiliation. 'Not yet,' she had lied, and enjoying the freedom to taunt a bit, however politely, had added, 'Not yet, although he wants to.'

'Of course he does! And of course you are! Just don't let him play with you! You may be twenty-one, but you don't know everything. Sex isn't a game.'

Hyacinth said fiercely now, 'This talk is all about your hating Gerald, Francine. That's all it is. I can't believe the things you've said. It isn't like you to be so unkind.'

'I never said I hated him. You are so stubborn, Hyacinth!'

'Dad's already told me that once today.'

Francine glared at Hy. 'Well, you are.'

'Weren't you stubborn when you were in love with Dad?'

'There is no comparison, Hyacinth. None at all. We knew each other well. Our families knew each other. We were part of the same community. There was nothing sudden about the affair.'

Hy kept looking at those tiny vertical lines between her mother's delicate eyebrows; they were the only lines to mar her perfect skin. *Skin like milk*, Dad said.

She's always so sure she's right, Hy thought, replying quietly, 'It's not the suddenness that you mind. It's that Gerald's not "part of the community." It's that he lives alone in a room in Linden.'

Francine gasped. 'Is that your opinion of me? If it is, you should be ashamed. Are you hearing this, Jim?'

'I am. Yes, that was unfair, Hyacinth. The last thing anyone could accuse your mother of being is a money snob.'

Well, probably it was unfair and untrue. And yet the things she had said about Gerald and this house—

She apologized. 'I'm sorry. I shouldn't have said it. I'll only say that for some reason or other, you don't like him. And that is totally, unforgivably mean of you.'

For a mother and daughter, they were too often at odds with each other. Now they were at an impasse.

Once again it was Dad who broke through the tension. 'You're both letting your emotions run away with you, and that's a great pity because you are both reasoning people, and you love each other. So here's what you do. Both of you, drop the subject. Right now. I don't want to hear it again, and I mean that. None of us really knows the young man all that well to have any worthwhile opinion anyhow. You may tell him, Hyacinth, that we would like to see more of him. If he's sincere, he'll welcome the invitation. And now, let's finish this pie in peace.'

Chapter Three

'Thirty miles one way to see an art movie,' Francine asked. 'Is it worth it in such weather?'

The objection was pleasantly spoken, and coming as it did after two or more weeks of calm, was pleasantly received.

'It's only rain.'

'Look out of the window.'

A violent wind racked the trees, whipped the lowest branches far enough to graze the ground, and snapped them back.

'It's the last day,' Hy said, 'so it's our only chance to see this picture. It's supposed to be marvelous.'

'You have to drive so far out of your way to pick him up in Linden.'

'Because I'm the one with the good car. We can't depend on his. Don't worry about me. It's not as if they were expecting a blizzard. We'll take our time getting there, have something to eat after the matinee, and be home a little late.'

On the screen, a pair of lovers stood watching a sailboat approach the curve of a blue-green bay on the Tyrrhenian Sea. They were standing close, hand in hand. A breeze blew the girl's cotton skirt above her bare knees.

Gerald pressed Hy's hand. 'Let's get out of here. We don't need to wait for the end, do we?'

'It's so beautiful,' she whispered. 'I like to see the fadeout.'

'You can imagine it. I'll give you a better fade-out. Trust me.'

The Highway Motel stood between an abandoned warehouse and a vacant lot littered with rusty machinery. A large sign, conspicuously placed, and now brightly lit in the waning afternoon, advertised rooms with television and video. They had been here so often that Hyacinth was sure the desk clerk must recognize them.

Gerald shuddered. 'Disgusting, dirty place. God knows I should be used to them. I've lived in one long enough.'

'It's not really so dirty.'

'There goes my Hyacinth, looking at the bright side.'

'Why not? I've brought a nice quilt from home. It's in the trunk, wrapped up so nobody'll know what it is, although it's none of their business if they do.'

Gerald chuckled. 'You think of everything.'

'I think of you. I think of you all day.'

They went inside. She had no idea what name he had written in the book and did not ask. That, too, was nobody's business. When they closed their door and locked it, she undressed the bed, laid the quilt upon it, and began to undress herself.

'Feel my heart. Feel how it's thudding,' she said.

'To look at you, such a refined young person, so ambitious and so serious, no one would ever guess what else you are. I know I didn't guess it.'

'So why did you come to the museum that day looking for me?'

'I don't know. Why does a man seek out a woman? You interested me very much.'

'Wasn't it love at first sight? Don't laugh. It happens, and not only in fairy tales, either.'

'All right. Call it love at first sight. Oh, come here. Get under this quilt with me.'

After their brief sleep and the familiar peace that follows completion, they lay watching the rain slant across the gray window.

'How it rained the day we met,' Hy murmured.

His neck was soft to her lips. She wanted to lie like this, never to move, to be here for all time, to be one with him forever. A tremulous swell of emotion filled her breast; a gladness and a tenderness that she had never known before. She felt her heart's strong rhythm.

In the hall, loud voices rang and a door was rudely slammed.

'What a dump this is,' Gerald complained.

'I don't mind it. We're both here. Isn't that enough?'

'No. We deserve better.'

A vague sadness was thickening her throat with the lump that precedes tears. From somewhere came the memory of a saying: *After coitus, man is sad*. Why should that be? Is it fear that the rapture will never come again? The sensation that we have when we hear immortal music? Is it the feel of a June day, flawless and once gone, gone forever? Or the fear that he does not love her as she loves him . . . She clung so tightly to him that he felt her wet eyelids on his shoulder.

'I don't know . . .'

'I was only teasing before when I pretended not to believe in love at first sight,' he said.

'Tell me what you love about me.'

'I love your grave charm, your spirit, your talent, your voice, your hot blood, everything. Hyacinth, darling, you worry too much.'

She said unexpectedly, even surprising herself, 'We must be completely honest with each other, you know.'

'Well, aren't we? I don't understand.'

'Sometimes I've hesitated to say . . . some things are not easy to say . . . my parents would like to know you better . . . We are seeing so much of each other.'

In the semi-darkness on the bed, his smile was invisible, but she heard it in his voice. And she sat up, turned on the light and looked at him anxiously.

'You're not angry?'

'No, no, of course not. They're only behaving like parents. Parents of daughters.'

'Dad thinks it's great that you're going to be a doctor. As a chemist, a scientist, he appreciates doctors. And he really likes you besides.'

'I know he does. And I know your mother doesn't.'

Hyacinth felt the prickle of heat in her cheeks. 'Oh, she—actually, we haven't discussed you. To begin with, she's not as talkative as Dad is, so she and I – I don't mean that she and I don't get along, but what I'm trying to say is that she can be very positive, and I'm rather stubborn. I know I am, so I sometimes avoid getting into discussions—'

She had digressed from the subject. She was inexcusably clumsy, and she stopped just as Gerald put his hand up to stop her.

'What you are trying to tell me, very tactfully, is that I should not be hurt when I don't get a hearty welcome from her. I understand. But I've known almost from the very first time that she does not approve of me.'

'I had no idea. I never thought—'

'You said we should be honest with each other, didn't you?'

'Yes, but – What happened? What did she say?'

'She didn't say anything. She has an expressive face, and I read people rather well. A doctor should.'

'I'm sorry. Oh darling, I'm sorry! She just doesn't know you, that's all it is. She'll be the first to admit she's wrong. She's very fair that way.'

'If you'll tell me what she objects to, I can try to change it.'

How could she tell him what Francine had really said? And not able to look him in the face, she made a half-hearted attempt. 'She thinks you will not stay with me, that I should not depend upon you.'

'But of course that's crazy. I shall simply have to disprove her.'

'You're sure you aren't angry?'

'I'm sure.'

The whole business, this ugly suspicion, was a humiliation for both of them. She had been reckless to bring the subject up at all. And now, from head to foot, her body burned with the shame of it.

'Don't look so miserable, Hy. Come here and see yourself.'

In the bathroom before the full-length mirror, they stood naked together.

'You're spoiling your pretty face with that frown.'

'Is it really pretty?'

'You know very well it is.'

Straight shoulder-length chestnut hair fell alongside a nicely symmetrical face with grave eyes and high cheekbones below a broad, smooth forehead.

'You could be really lovely with more makeup,' Francine often said. 'There's nothing wrong with you except that you look too quiet.'

'Your face shows character,' Granny said, refuting Francine. 'You don't need to put a lot of stuff on it,' meaning obviously that Francine used too much 'stuff.'

This amusing recollection now caused Hyacinth to smile. She thought then how odd it was that her self-confidence should vacillate so easily between its highs and its lows. Though maybe everyone's does, and they simply don't talk about it or even admit it to themselves?

'Do stand up straight,' Francine said. 'Tall women like you can fall into the habit of slumping. You must watch out for round shoulders, especially when you're with a man who's not tall enough for you.'

There was surely no need to worry about that with Gerald. Here he stood, this miracle of a man who turned people's heads, and he was all hers.

'You're trembling,' he said. 'Let's get some clothes on. It's freezing in here. And it's late, almost midnight. We'd better start. And don't worry about anything, certainly not about your mother and me. Just smile and leave it to me. She will approve of me, I guarantee it, and sooner than you think. She might even learn to love me.'

Chapter Four

The fire crackled and snapped. It glossed the brass fender and flickered over the rosy Persian carpet.

Gerald stretched and sighed. 'Bliss. Perfect bliss. Falling snow outside, peace and beauty inside.'

Hyacinth was seeing the room with his eyes: the books, the crystal horses on the mantel, and Francine's flourishing potted gardenia in the window bay. With his memory, she was also seeing his room, which she had once visited: a dim box filled with the noises of house and street, rank with the smell of frying grease, crowded, cramped and lonely.

In a sense during these last months, they had entered each other's lives. They had come to know each other in ways beyond sexual love, in ways that no amount of sexual love by itself could ever provide. It seemed to her that she was feeling an increased tenderness in Gerald, a thing quite apart from passion.

He said, 'I love your hair.'

'Too straight. I should take more time to curl it.'

'No, don't. When it's smooth this way, the light glows almost red over it.' And he stroked her head.

The gesture was proprietary, as if he had a right to prescribe, as when a husband asks a wife to please him. The intimacy touched her heart as when he would caution her against salting her food, or driving too close to the car ahead.

Dad had been so right when he had required her to bring Gerald here every week. Gradually, almost uneasily at first, he had begun to fit into the life of the house. The two men were most definitely compatible. And even Francine, although far from enthusiastic, had a very different way with Gerald, seeming to accept him without critical gesture or word. No doubt she was sincerely examining the situation.

'What a wonderful room,' Gerald said now. 'The whole house is what you think of when you use the word "home." Is it always so tranquil?'

'Now it is. It surely wasn't when I had three brothers here. It was mighty noisy. And still we all miss them.'

'That reminds me, your father told me last week he hadn't played a real game of chess since they left.'

'I know. My mother and I both try, but we're not good enough. He wins too easily and it's no fun for him.'

'I think it would be nice of me to propose a game again right now.'

'Yes, why don't you? He says you're a great match. I'll sit here and look at this gorgeous art book you gave me. You really shouldn't have spent so much. You really shouldn't.'

'Why not? You're worth it, I think. I'll go get your father.'

They had planned to walk to the great pond this afternoon, but snow had already started to whirl in the wind, and it had been a better idea to be here where they were, while it whirled on the other side of the window. The chess game proceeded in the usual silence of deep concentration. For a while, Hy looked toward the two bent heads, the black and the mottled grey. And watching them, she began to feel a soft, almost sleepy contentment.

An odd thought came, one of those foolish images that pop up out of nowhere: this one, for instance, of colored marbles in a jug. Shake the jug, and they all change places! Now what if I had not been reared by *that* particular man; would I be what I am? Very probably not. Almost surely, I would not have met *that* man! And here we are, each linked in some fashion to the other two, as well as to Francine, who is upstairs making calls for one of her charities. A jug of marbles . . .

She opened the book and read half a chapter about the neo-Impressionists. But she was reading the same words over and over without absorbing their sense; she was leafing through the rich illustrations without seeing them. Her mind had veered away from the room and the moment.

A few months from now, a major turning point would be reached. Gerald was seeking a hospital residency. Where was it to be? And what of her? Nothing definite had yet been said about their future. Was it not strange that nothing had been said?

Yet they had been making full and free confessions to each other, had spoken of painful and sad things, of embarrassing and confidential things dredged up from the secret corners of memory.

Gerald had told her about his mother, who had died of Alzheimer's disease after long suffering. She knew that he too had suffered this tragedy, along with the family's poverty, and that he had perhaps not been brave enough, as he put it, 'to take things more like a man.'

She had felt free to tell him the most silly trivia, laughing at herself while she described Martha, down the street, as her 'nemesis', ever since the fourth grade when Martha had taunted her about her name. 'You surely don't look like any flower,' she had said. Martha had had waist-length braids and no braces on her teeth.

They had even talked about past lovers, of whom Hyacinth had had none. 'I've never loved anybody before you. They were all only friends, the boys I knew.'

And he had replied, 'I've had my share of women, maybe more than my share, but they were none of them like you. They were all meaningless. Can there be anyone like you, Hyacinth?'

Simultaneously, now the two men rose from the chessboard. Gerald bowed. 'I bow to a master,' he said gallantly.

'Nonsense! We're not halfway to the end, and I'm fighting hard. I only got up because Francine's standing in the doorway. That means dinner's ready and we have to break.'

Hyacinth had made most of the dinner. Francine had done the marketing, set the table and peeled the vegetables; it was a fair division of labor today, since the one loved to cook, and the other did not. The season's first tulips flopped gracefully, as tulips do, in a blue glass bowl. The fragrance of herbs rose from a beef ragout that was surrounded by browned potatoes and carrots. A green salad lay at each place, and twin decanters were filled with a fine red wine.

'A feast!' exclaimed Gerald.

'Hyacinth is not only an artist, but a first-rate cook.'

She flushed. A person might think that this father was trying to advertise his daughter, for goodness sake! But no, Jim was too forthright for that, and too innocent of wiles. He was merely being affectionate.

Now he amended his remark. 'Not depriving my wife of any laurels, either.'

Francine smiled. The smile was almost too small to be called a smile, being merely a touch at the corners of her mouth, merely enough to make a dimple in each cheek. She wore a dark blue dress and no jewelry but diamond studs in her ears. When she moved her head, they winked. Today she was being reserved. She wanted Gerald to do the talking, Hy knew. She was watching him, waiting for something – for what? – to reveal itself.

Yet you could not fault her behavior. It was only if you understood Francine very well that you would be able to guess what was happening inside her head as she sat there so correctly and courteously. So perfectly. Perfect even to her fingertips, which were pale pink.

Hy looked at her own hands. She had forgotten to scrub off the ocher paint from yesterday's work. No amount of showering ever seemed to clean stuff from her fingers. And suddenly, she felt oppressed. There was something artificial about this occasion, a feeling that had not been present during the chess game.

'Yes,' Gerald said, replying to Dad's question, 'I'm very sure. We had a neighbor who'd been wounded during the Korean War. They had to rebuild his face. It was fascinating to me, a marvel of science and art, what they did. I knew almost at once when I saw him that that was what I wanted to do with my life.'

He spoke precisely, as he did everything with precision,

whether slicing an apple, folding a sweater or, as now, laying the knife at the top of the plate, parallel to the edge of the table.

Dad inquired, 'How long does it take to be certified in plastic surgery?'

'Three years at least.'

'So then,' said Francine, 'you must be looking for a residency right now.'

'Yes, I've sent out a good many applications.'

'You will want a first-class teaching hospital.' And when Gerald nodded, she added, 'There are none around here. The local hospital would hardly do for you.'

'That's true.'

They were sparring over Hy's head. Of course Francine is glad that he will have to leave here. Why does he never talk to me about it? What is behind this?

'At least they pay you fellows these days,' Dad said. 'Years ago, interns and residents were expected just to be grateful for the opportunity to learn.'

'They pay, but not very much, especially if a person has debts.'

'Ah, yes. You owe the university here for their loan,' Hy tells me.

'And I still owe for the care of my mother before she died.'

'You're an ambitious young man. And responsible. I take my hat off to you.'

Hopeless, thought Hyacinth.

As if he had sensed her mood, Dad changed the subject to the tulips. 'So nice of you to have brought these flowers. Makes you think spring can't be far away.'

Now Gerald addressed Francine. 'They reminded me of this yellow wallpaper. I always think this room, and this whole house, belong in a magazine.'

A desultory conversation passed across the table. Hy barely heard it. A lump of cold fear lay in the pit of her stomach.

'What do you say we go in and have a brandy?' suggested Dad. 'You can practically feel the wind-chill seep through the walls.'

'You all go,' Hy said. 'I'll clear the table and load the dish-washer.'

He's going away, God knows where to. Am I to wait three years? He will find somebody else.

Gerald said promptly, 'I'll help you.' And turning to Francine, 'Don't worry, I know that goblets don't go into the dishwasher. I'll be very careful of them.'

He was trying so hard to please! But why should he care about Francine's opinion if things were coming to an end?

'No,' Hy said, contradicting him, 'I'll do it myself. Go finish the chess game with Dad.'

When she looked around from the sink, Francine was standing in the doorway regarding her with a faintly sad expression on her face.

'I'll do the goblets for you,' she offered quickly.

'Eight goblets, water and wine for goodness' sake! Why is everyone making such a stupid fuss about them?' Hy blurted. And an instant later, aware of her own brusque tone, she blurted again, 'Sorry. I guess I'm tired or something.'

'Not tired. Worried,' Francine said gently.

'I'm not at all worried. Why should I be?'

She was not going to open any space for the discussion that her mother probably wanted.

'I don't know why you should or should not, Hyacinth. That's for you to tell me if you want to. If you think I can help.'

'Only if you have changed your opinion about him.'

Part of her wanted to cry out: 'I'm afraid. I wish somebody – you or somebody – would tell me what to do. I don't know whether I should ask him first, or wait for him to ask me first. In there at the table listening just now, he even seems strange to me. I don't know—'

'My opinion is still that Gerald is very charming and intelligent. He speaks well. He tries to please, and as I've said from the beginning—'

Jim shouted from the hall. 'Francine, come in here and invite Gerald to stay overnight. He thinks it'll be too much trouble. But the road is a sheet of ice. You'd have to be crazy to get into a car in weather like this if you didn't have to.'

'Of course. It's not trouble at all to have you stay. We have plenty of room.'

Gerald hesitated. 'I've got work at home, paperwork due Monday.'

'You can leave here by noon tomorrow,' Jim insisted. 'The roads will have started to melt by then. And you'll still have plenty of time to do your work.'

'You're very kind, but really. I've driven on ice before—'

Hyacinth stood there, alone under the light in the center of the hall, waiting. Why are you begging him to stay? He doesn't want to. Can't you see that?

But Dad had decided. 'Go on up, Hy, and show him George's room.'

They went upstairs. 'You didn't want to stay,' Hyacinth said, 'and you shouldn't do it if you don't want to.'

'You're angry at me,' Gerald said in some surprise.

'Yes. Or no, not angry, but hurt. You had all these plans that you were just describing, and you've never said a word about anything to me.'

'I was going to do it today, but I lost my nerve. I didn't want to spoil the day.'

'Spoil the day? What do you mean?'

'Sit down, and let me explain.'

She sat down on the bed and stared at his moving lips. He was about to say something that would shatter her. She knew it. And she sat up tall, waiting.

'I wanted to tell you this when we were alone. I already have a residency, two of them, as a matter of fact, and both first rate. But unfortunately, they're both in Texas.'

'And why is that unfortunate?'

'Well, it – it's not exactly a cheap or easy commute to Texas, is it?'

His words, which usually flowed easily, came awkwardly. His smile was wan.

'Go on,' she said.

Opening his arms wide and breaking into a lament, he cried to her, 'I've known about this for the last two weeks, and, Hy, I haven't dared to ask. Will you wait for me? I've been so afraid of your answer. But will you?'

Then the facts struck her. 'You mean we can't see each other for the next three years? What are you saying? Why?'

Softly, he put his arms around her rigid shoulders and softly replied, 'One word explains it. Money.'

'But you said they pay you.'

'You're forgetting that I also have debts.'

'You can't mean this,' she whispered.

'Darling, I do. I have to.'

'You always tell me that a week away is too long.'

'And so it is.'

'Yes,' she whispered, 'there must have been something in the air tonight, some poisonous premonition. When we were at the table, I looked at you once and felt such pain. Do you understand? And I was angry, angry at the world. I didn't know why. It was as if somebody had died or gone away forever.'

'Not forever,' he protested.

'None of this makes sense. Other couples manage. Do you think I'm going to stop working, for Heaven's sake?'

'It's not that simple. Unmarried, I get a room at practically no charge. Married, I don't.'

'I never said anything to you about marriage, did I?'

'Well, what else would we be doing?'

'Staying together. Being together.'

'No. I'm not going out to any hospital like that. I go either singly or with a proper wife, like everyone else there. No halfway measure.'

'So then this is a proposal?'

'Very definitely a proposal, with a proviso. We'll have to wait.'

She looked at him in dismay, in despair.

'Here,' Gerald said, taking a notebook and pen from his pocket, 'let me show you in dollars and cents so you'll see what I'm talking about.'

She watched his moving hand with its delicate blue veins and fine oval nails, this hand that knew every curve of her body. Her mind, in panic, was already leaping ahead of his additions and subtractions. Dad, she thought, he will help. He's not a rich man, but he will.

'There has to be a way,' she said. 'I'll ask my father.'

'For money, you mean?'

'Of course.'

'I can't do that. I can't ask for money from him, of all people.'

'I don't expect you to do the asking. It's only natural for me to be the one. And why do you say, "from him of all people"?'

'I should think the answer is obvious. The humiliation—'

'—will be mine, not yours.'

'Well, I'll feel it. It's about me, after all.'

'You weren't humiliated when you accepted the money from the medical school.'

'There's no comparison. That was a loan.'

'Then make this a loan. You can repay it when you start your practice.'

There was a long silence, until with great reluctance Gerald responded, 'I really don't like the idea.'

'But I like it.'

He smiled. 'So now I'm finding out why they say you're stubborn.'

She smiled back. 'All of a sudden, I'm feeling normal again, now that I know this has only been about money. I thought— Oh God, I thought you had changed your mind about me.'

He laughed. 'You're crazy. You're really crazy.' Then seriously, 'This whole business may not be as easy as you seem to think it will be. You can't have forgotten your mother's opinion of me.'

'That was months ago! Besides, if Dad wants to do it for us, he'll do it, no matter.'

There was another silence until Gerald broke it again. 'Well, ask then. I certainly can't.'

Often that spring, Hyacinth thought how on some far day she would look back on this time as old people do, as Gran did, endlessly reminiscing about that season of hopes fulfilled, when everything, kisses, tears, champagne, good wishes, white dresses and flowered hats, all come into bloom.

'I'm very thankful that I can do this for you,' Jim declared on that night when it all happened. 'It will free your spirit, Gerald, to forge ahead with your work. There's nothing like a too thin wallet to distract a man.'

'So it is an established fact,' Francine observed, 'engagement, commencement, wedding and off to Texas?'

'Two weeks after graduation,' Hyacinth said, now flushed and pink with a joyful heat.

They were in the living room. The fire was low, and the music, to which Jim had been listening when she had come to interrupt him, was also low; the Verdi *Requiem* would be forever afterward linked to this event.

'I would like both of you to know,' Gerald said at once, 'besides how grateful I am, more than I can ever say, that I shall not be taking Hyacinth away from you. She's told me how you miss your sons, so I promise that after my training, we will come back here and we will stay. Doctors don't move around, anyway. I'm going to remember,' he added, this time speaking directly to Francine, 'or at least I'm going to try to remember, not to call Hyacinth "Hy." She tells me you hate it.'

'That's all right, Gerald. You must call her whatever she wants. I'm really not such an ogre, you know.'

Her smile this time was gracious, and her embrace warm. What she was thinking, Hyacinth could not imagine. Certainly she could not have been taken too much by surprise. And too, very probably, she had changed her mind about Gerald. At the very least, she must see how he was trying to please.

These last weeks of the term before commencement, when his calendar was nearly empty, might have been purposely arranged to let him fit himself into the life of the house. The spring was exceptional, a long stretch of cool, green weather after a hard winter.

Jim was establishing a new perennial border on the shady side of the house. Together he and Gerald searched through gardening manuals for flowers that would thrive there, bought seedlings from the nursery and worked outdoors together through the lengthening evenings until dark. Rarely had any of Jim's sons given him quite as much time and attention as Gerald did. They painted the lawn chairs, went fishing, shopped for a new barbecue grill and set it up.

A lovely peace filled the air. At the turn of the road lay a stretch of woods whose owner had no objections to innocent users of his land; here Hyacinth and Gerald took long walks, sat on a log and held long, searching conversations in a silence and serenity that were an astonishment to him. It seemed to her that they were growing even closer now, and in a new way.

At Granny's house one night they let themselves be deliciously over-fed. Afterwards, they were regaled with tales of the old days when the town was surrounded by grand estates with their prize cattle and private railroad cars; of the chauffered Pierce Arrows on the shopping street; of the band playing 'Over There' in 1917. Before they left, Granny brought forth gifts knitted by herself: a sweater, one for each, a matching dark blue pair. Hyacinth had felt uneasily that Gerald might be bored, for Granny could sometimes talk too much and for too long about things that interested her and might well be of no interest to anybody else. But no, he had found her 'most delightful, a dear old lady, a "character."'

Everything was organized by May. On a glorious morning in perfect sunshine and with stately tradition, from 'Pomp and Circumstance' to the prideful presentation of diplomas, Hyacinth through shining eyes saw Gerald receive his degree: Doctor of Medicine. Afterwards at home he was introduced to all obligatory relatives and friends. Later in the evening he was even shown off to Martha the Nemesis and the rest of the 'in crowd' when, seemingly by accident, Hyacinth strolled with him past her house. They all made introductions; Hy, observing Martha's mild but undeniable surprise, embarrassed herself by her inner conflict between a sense of triumph and a sense of her own foolishness for giving a damn what other people thought.

Preparations for a small marriage ceremony in the garden were then in order. The brothers bought their plane tickets. Hyacinth selected the wedding dress while Francine ordered the engraved invitations. A few gifts had already arrived, and thank-you notes were sent. The journey to Texas had been carefully mapped.

It was Dad who suggested, who in fact insisted, upon the party after the ceremony. 'It's all right not to have a crowd at the service if that's how you feel, but you'll regret it if you don't have some celebration afterward. And besides, after living in this neighborhood, going to school here all your life, it's unfriendly not to include people. What do you say, Francine?'

Surely you would have expected her to be the party instigator? Still, she was promptly agreeable. She had been nothing but agreeable, if perhaps a trifle quiet – or was that Hyacinth's imagination? – since the snowy night on which Jim had opened his heart and his pocketbook to Gerald.

'Well, you know how I love a party,' she replied. 'Hyacinth, you must give me all your ideas about the decorations and the menu and the guests. I need to get busy right away.'

Often Hyacinth came to the brink of asking her what she really thought about Gerald now that he had become such a familiar in the house. But each time she drew back; since Francine never brought up the subject, almost surely it was because she had changed her mind about him – how could she not have changed it? – and was ashamed to remember her original mistake. It was far better to forget the bad beginning.

Hyacinth was feeling the sweetness of life.

Chapter Five

They had been dancing all afternoon, whirling to the music of a very good five-piece band. A floor had been laid on the lawn and an awning prepared in case of rain, which happy to say was nowhere in sight. All round stood a scalloping border of small tables, each with its starched white petticoat and taffeta bows. At one of them now sat the family, momentarily at rest and watching the dancers.

Jim was 'in his element,' to use one of his own frequent expressions. He used it now.

'Watch that Gerald swing. He's in his element. And watch Hy keeping right up with him. I never knew she was that fine a dancer.'

Francine was pensive: 'I suppose there must be much more that we never knew about her.'

'Quiet little baby sister,' George said. 'The first one in her class to get married! I would never have predicted it. He's quite a guy, too. Very impressive. And let me tell you I meet a lot of impressive guys in the global banking business.'

Granny agreed. 'Yes, isn't he a charmer? I fell in love with him myself the first time I saw him. As I told Hyacinth once, marriage is a very, very serious business. But this one is going to be splendid. She's going to be so happy. I see it. I feel it in my bones. How about you, Francine?'

Of course Hyacinth has told her what I said about him that time, and now she wants to pin me down to a yes or a no. It will surprise her to hear that I am moving toward a yes. At the least, I haven't found anything to criticize in him during all these past months.

'Yes, I do think so,' she said.

She prayed and she hoped, hoping now that she had not done too much damage in misjudging this man whom Hyacinth so adored. She prayed that the memory of her drastic words might fade completely away. There in the bright afternoon, Francine grew solemn. How easy it had been to rear those three young men who had now gone back to whirl on the floor! Never had she been baffled by any one of them. But Hyacinth? I suppose I annoyed her a good deal, she reflected. I know I did. She worried me, and we bickered far more than we should have done. But I only wanted her to be happier, and livelier. I only wanted her to be something she couldn't be!

'Look at her,' Jim said. 'She's opened up like a rose.'

Francine's eyes were already following her daughter. Her head was flung back in laughter, her short veil was floating, and her feet were flying. She was dancing with a fellow who worked at the museum. Friends there had sent an original and pleasing wedding gift, a set of photographs, most beautifully framed, of the Shackleton expedition to the South Pole. Hyacinth had her own kind of friends.

When Gerald cut in, she stood up on her toes to reach him, and kissed him on the mouth. And again her feet flew. Her veil floated, and she was radiant with love. She had indeed opened up like a rose, as Jim had just said.

He, too, was beaming with happiness. 'A perfect party, darling, my efficient wife. Perfect as always. I'd love to catch you once forgetting some little thing. Just one thing, once.'

'Well, you've caught me now. The decanters are close to empty. I'll run in and make sure I've remembered to tell the waiters there's more wine in the garage.'

When she returned, she brought a message for Granny. 'The cooks want to know where I bought the cookies and what they cost. They're interested.'

Granny laughed. 'Oh Lord, those are my old spice cookies. They're an eighteenth-century recipe from a Williamsburg cookbook, or maybe it was New Orleans. I don't even remember.'

'Well, there are hardly any left, and you must have made two hundred at least. But, Jim, didn't Gerald say they want to start by six o'clock? Then they should be changing now – where is Gerald? I don't see him.'

'He went inside a while ago,' Granny said. 'Too much wine, maybe. Too much excitement.'

'Well, I'll go ask him what he wants. The band is flexible. They'll stay or quit, whatever we like.'

The house, except for the busy kitchen, was otherwise silent as she walked through it. Then she thought she heard voices above, coming from Hyacinth's little studio at the top of the stairs. And she went up, calling, 'Is that you Gerald?'

'Yes, here I am. I've been showing Hy's— Hyacinth's work to her friend, Martha.'

A dart of anger struck right to Francine's heart. What was the meaning of this? Martha had a vivid white smile for Francine, who had to look twice to recognize her. She had been working and living in New York; her light hair was now blonde, expensively so, with gleam and without roots.

Martha exclaimed, 'All these years we've known each other and I never had any idea that Hy was so talented. This one of her father – it's absolutely superb! And the still life, the fruit, is perfect.'

'It's sold,' Gerald said. 'One of her friends at the museum is buying it. And her grandmother is buying the watercolor of this house to give George on his birthday.'

'I never, never knew! But Hy is so modest. She always was, all through school and college, so modest.'

'That she is,' Gerald said.

'Well, she's an artist. They're not like other people, are they?'

Francine was scolding herself: Don't be an idiot. What on earth do you think they were doing up here, arranging a rendezvous? Still, it doesn't look right, walking away from the party together. They both should know better.

That girl does know better. She feels her power over men and loves to use it, even as casually as this. Oh, didn't I know? But once I had Jim, I never used it, and there's the difference.

'I adore this snow scene,' said Martha. She was taking her time to comment on the pictures, thus to emphasize the earnest purpose of this visit to the studio. 'You can really feel cold, can't you?'

Thoughts that Francine had long stifled now rose like an emergent weed that has, despite much effort, not been eradicated after all. Wasn't it a French philosopher who had written, or was it simply a folk saying, about 'the one who loves and the other who is loved'? Hyacinth loves. Hyacinth gives her heart and soul, without guile, because she has no guile. Blunt-spoken and honest, she is one of nature's innocents. Of 'street smarts,' she has none.

And standing there at the window, Francine gazed down at the happy, noisy party below. All of a sudden it was a throng of agitated bees buzzing around one another. Morbid thought! Is that what it's all about, struggling to get on top? *Of course he knew Jim would come up with the money . . . He played it well.*

Gerald spoke to her. 'You were calling me?'

'Yes. I remembered what time you two plan to start, and I wanted to remind you.'

'Thanks. I was coming right down.' He turned to Martha. 'Look at Francine. Isn't she beautiful?'

'Absolutely beautiful. And she doesn't grow older, either.'

Putting his arms around Francine, Gerald kissed her cheek. She had always observed his expressive eyes. At this moment they were gentle and deep with empathy.

'You're worried. Your last baby's leaving, and of course you're feeling sad. But please try not to be too sad. I promise to make her very, very happy.'

How do I know he will not? I have no right to revive my morbid thoughts. I am looking for trouble. I must be careful to guide and guard the way I think.

'I'm sure you will,' she said.

The red car, its trunk filled with new luggage, stood ready in the driveway while the farewell crowd waited for the bride and groom to appear. Francine and Jim, in the forefront, were feeling the moment of departure, the departure of the last child, just as Gerald had said. From behind came voices.

'Didn't Hyacinth look lovely? And so happy that she sparkled.'

'What about him? Isn't he something to look at, too?'

'Are they going straight through to Texas?'

'No, they're going to tour for a couple of weeks before he starts work, the Grand Canyon, the Tetons, the big sights. He's never been west, but she has.'

'She's been everywhere, or almost.'

Yes, we did what we could to feed that curious bright mind, thought Francine. And not a scrap of all we gave was ever wasted on her, stubborn little creature that she was—

'Mom,' said Hyacinth.

She was dressed for travel in jeans and thick sweater; a chill wind had risen. No proper going-away suit for Hyacinth!

'Mom, I want to whisper something, please. Listen. I'm so thankful that you and Gerald . . . No daughter could ask for a better mother than you've been. Forget any stupid thing I ever said to you or about you. Please. This is the most perfect wedding anybody could dream of. Oh, you know what I want to say. I'm feeling teary, so I have to stop.'

'Darling, I'm feeling teary, too. Be well, both of you. What is that old Irish saying? May the road—'

'May the road rise up to meet you,' said Jim, 'and may the wind be always at your back.'

'Here we go!' cried Gerald, holding the door for Hyacinth. 'Climb in.'

'Into my lucky car. Only, today it's not raining.'

He took the wheel, they both waved, and a few seconds later the lucky red car was gone.

Chapter Six

Coming home sometimes in the late afternoon, Gerald would pause in the doorway, shake his head, and speak in wonder.

'I never thought my life could turn out like this.'

'Neither did I,' said Hyacinth.

She was feeling like a queen in her domain. The apartment had been fitted out with every possible comfort and convenience; the furniture, solid and simple, was made to last through a lifetime and beyond, for Francine and Jim, who had provided the wherewithal for it, had believed that quality in the long run was economy, not to mention the fact that it gave great pleasure.

The shelves were already crammed with books and music; flowery fabrics and a lacquered screen that George had sent from Singapore were lively; the ice-blue kitchen, freshly painted, was tidy with its rack of copper-bottomed pots; then came the most precious bedroom, yellow as a daffodil and soft under foot where one of Granny's largest, best and oldest hooked rugs had followed them to Texas.

From every window they looked out at another view. From the little kitchen the end window faced the wide, flat earth of Texas, an empty vista on which in the far distance there rose an unexpected cluster of skyscrapers, some of them completed and some still but a framework of steel beams. The side window, when open, brought in a breeze from the grave of cottonwood trees across the street. The bedroom windows lay above some young persimmons that, so Hyacinth had been told, would in the fall turn from glossy green to yellow; at the moment they were merely dusty and drooping in the one hundred degree heat. The front room looked out upon the teeming highway that every morning took them past gated communities of lavish houses behind lavish stone walls, past lavish malls into the heart of the city where Gerald worked at a hospital and Hyacinth worked at a small art gallery nearby.

There had been no opportunities at the area's museum. With rueful amusement, she had reported to Gerald that its tiny amount of restoration work was always sent to the museum at home! So the next best choice for her was the gallery. It was interesting enough, and the hours left time for her to do some watercolors and sketches on the kitchen table, where she was usually at work when Gerald came home.

Never had she known him to be as exuberant, in such high glad spirits, as he now was. Absorbed in the life of the hospital, he was in awe of a surgeon who could rebuild the face of a child born with half a nose, or could restore an arm that had been mangled in a machine. Half laughing at himself, he was in awe of his own certainty that he, too, would learn to perform these miracles.

For such a man after a day of tense concentration, the quietness of home must be precious. Hyacinth was touched by his appreciation of small things, the good supper as well as the pretty table at which they ate it; he remarked the flavor of freshly brewed coffee and the pattern on the cup, too. He praised her for every attention she gave him.

One night he looked up from the text he was studying and said abruptly, 'I'm feeling the permanence.'

'What did you say you're feeling?' she asked.

'The permanence. I've never lived more than two years in any one place, and not often as long as that.'

Hyacinth had also been reading, but his words and his soft expression moved her to rise and put her arms around him. 'We're permanent,' she said.

'I was thinking about your mother today, about how far she's come from her first impression of me. Now I feel that I have a friend in her. And you should be having very tender thoughts about her, too.'

'I have tender thoughts about everyone.' Hyacinth spoke solemnly. 'I wish that everybody could have what we have. Maybe it sounds naïve, but honestly, I sometimes feel as if I loved the whole world.'

She was hardly so naïve as to believe that 'loving the whole world' was anything other than an epiphany that would appear, rarely, and disappear, as moods do. She was also not naïve enough to believe that the first glory of the honeymoon could remain unmarred.

You were bound to discover that you had, after all, not known everything there was to know about each other. Considering the dozens and dozens of habits, memories and tastes that constitute a personality, how on earth could any human being expect to find his duplicate in another one?

For instance: There was the time when she had wanted to see an opening exhibit at the museum and Gerald had refused to go with her.

'It's only a half hour's drive,' she had argued, 'and those paintings are on loan from the National Gallery. You don't want to miss it, do you?'

'To tell the truth, I do. I really couldn't care less about paintings, Hy.' He had looked sheepish. 'I just pretended I cared.' Continuing, as he saw how startled she must have appeared, he said, 'You should be flattered. It was only my way of getting to you.'

For instance: When she was cooking, and she did seem to be doing a good deal of cooking, she liked to listen to music on the kitchen radio. One day, catching his grimace when he came home, she asked him what was wrong.

'It sounds like a lot of loud noise to me.'

She answered mildly, 'It's beautiful. It's Mozart.'

'I suppose you come by it rightfully. Your father was always listening to that stuff.'

'I guess I do, but I'll turn it off when you're home.'

Standing there with a spatula in her hand, her feelings were mixed. In one sense, she was a very little bit annoyed, while in another, she knew she had no right to be. For this was his house, too, and if this kind of music annoyed him, he should not have to hear it, should he?

Well then, they had different likes and dislikes, that's all. The only surprising thing was that he had concealed his for so long. But marriage, at least now at the start, was bound to reveal a series of surprises, until through long years, two people have finally grown together, or, she told herself more realistically, have *almost* grown together.

Secluded honeymoons cannot last indefinitely, either. Living as Gerald did in the heart of a great, busy hospital, he had made many friends. Hyacinth had had no idea how sociable he was. Gradually, their apartment became a Saturday night gathering place. Plainly, she saw that he had already won a position of leadership in the group; his mind was respected and his personality was alluring. In a subtle way it had expanded before her eyes.

Recognizing his enormous pleasure in all this, she was touched. Their apartment was his pride, for most of the other young couples were, as they themselves described it, 'camping out,' and also, 'eating out.' Here on the other hand was fullness of color and comfort, along with appetizing refreshment.

'They never get food like yours,' Gerald said.

'Well, you can thank Granny. She taught me.'

Hy, too, took pride in being the hostess at these lively evenings. Yet after a while she began to wish that there were not quite so many of them, or that she could take more of a real part in them. For the conversation rarely led away from things medical, veering from serious subjects to simple gossip about somebody who happened to be absent. Most often, then, she found herself there as a silent observer, a listener and watcher, following the interplay of temperaments, a rivalry between two men or an incipient attraction between a man and a woman.

'You're curious about the world, aren't you?' Gerald had once remarked. 'You notice everything. Thinking, thinking, all the time, trying to figure it all out, aren't you?'

Yes, that was true. She did notice things, and very carefully, too. As the seasons progressed through fall and their first winter, she formed opinions about every one of these frequent visitors. And since it was her nature to like most people, at least to dislike very few, she had taken a dislike only to one, a doctor named Elizabeth and called Bettina. She was not a classic beauty, but she was startling, and she knew it. How could she help but know it, or that she was no favorite among women? It was only to be expected. At their very first meeting she greeted Hy with this remark: 'So you're the wife of that beautiful man! You should have heard the nurses the day he walked in! He's going to have a fabulous practice, oh yes! He has an irresistible charm, along with his brains.'

Charm, indeed. Before their marriage, Hy had never seen Gerald as a member of any group, and so it was a new experience to hear tones of voice and see facial expressions that she had never before heard or seen. He had a different laugh recently, an infectious chuckle, and in his eyes a new, mischievous, knowing twinkle, as if his beholder and he had a secret between them.

Then on an effervescent evening not long afterward, Hy heard a woman's voice at her ear. 'You're very patient. Patient and tolerant.'

Startled, Hy followed her glance to where Gerald and Bettina were standing and had long been standing together in the hall.

'But I suppose you're not really bothered. Bettina will never leave that fat husband of hers, or even risk any real fun on the side. He's positively loaded, and she loves the life he gives her.'

Hy, feeling a furious flush mount to her cheek, answered stiffly, 'I'm not sure what you mean by patience and tolerance.'

The other woman, an occasional member of the group, gave a casual shrug. 'Just sitting there and letting him humiliate you is what I meant.'

She had had too much to drink, and Hyacinth walked away. 'I do not feel humiliated,' she said, wishing that the whole lot of them would go home.

She was confused. Was it really a humiliation? Was she being a prig, a foolish prude? Was she having a rebirth of the old 'Martha' syndrome? If so, she must put are end to it . . .

Much later, when she had brushed her teeth and readied herself for bed, the incident still rankled. Dressed in transparent violet silk, a typical gift from Francine, she went to the full-length mirror, lifted the gown and examined herself. Her body was slender, yet well curved; her face was pleasing enough, but she was undistinguished. When she appeared, heads did not turn as they turned toward Dr. Bettina.

Gerald stepped through the door and laughed. 'What are you doing, posing there? Satisfied with yourself, I hope?'

'That's not the question. Are you satisfied with me? That's the question.'

'Hey, what's your problem, Hy?'

'I'm comparing myself with – with that woman Bettina.'

'Oh, for God's sake!'

'We need to be honest with each other.'

'I thought we always were honest.'

'Oh,' she cried, 'jealousy is so – so *low*! It humbles me.'

His eyes darkened, met hers, and held the look. This look of his, earnest, beseeching and a little sad, she recognized.

'Darling Hyacinth, I'm sorry if I've hurt you, but you're being very, very silly. As if anybody could measure you against a total zero, a clothes horse, a cheap flirt! Come on to bed. Don't be an idiot. Come on, or I'll drag you in. It's going on one o'clock.'

For long minutes she lay with her face buried in his shoulder, in the beloved flesh, while he murmured into her hair.

'Dear Hy, so sweet, so smart and such a fool. An innocent. Isn't that what Francine calls you?'

She was filled with yearning. Her heart, her throat, her whole body wanted to blend with his, to become one with him.

'I would die for you,' she whispered.

'No, no, don't say that.'

'Yes, I would. Do you remember that woman on the *Titanic*? Straus was her name, Mrs. Straus. They wanted to put her in a lifeboat, but she wouldn't go. She wanted to die with her husband. I would have done that, too.'

'And I would have pushed you into the lifeboat. So that's enough of that talk. You know what you and I need?' His hands, warm and strong, pulled at the silk skirt. 'Take this fool thing off, will you?'

...

Chapter Seven

It was a mild afternoon in their second fall, so different from the chill, brisk weathers of Massachusetts, that Hyacinth talking on the telephone to Moira had needed to remark as usual on the difference.

'They call it cool weather. It's down to eighty. Can you imagine? And football has started very, very seriously. The rivalries are like France against Germany in a world war. But it's all such fun. People are so informal here, so friendly, even in a big city. Oh, and I've learned all the words to "The yellow Rose of Texas"!'

In this mood of well-being she entered a doctor's office; and half an hour later she left it, overwhelmed by surprise and wearing an uncontrollable smile.

'No method is a hundred percent reliable,' the doctor had said. He, too, was smiling. 'June is a good month to have a baby, before the worst of the heat, if we're lucky.'

Obstetrics, she thought, must be for the most part a happy specialty. She seemed to be walking on springs, bouncing with every step. Or she seemed to feel bubbles in her chest, popping in effervescence like the champagne cork and the laughter that comes with it.

It was only four o'clock, which left two hours to contain her excitement until Gerald would be home. She wanted to sing, or stop some passerby, anyone at all, to tell the amazing news. One would think that civilization must come to a halt because of this baby. They had not planned to start a family until Gerald's stint at the hospital was over, and now this! But never mind; this baby was simply in a hurry to see the world. And she walked on, observing babies in carriages and strollers as she had never done before.

She had to buy something, had to commemerate this day. So she went on a spree, and when she returned to the parking lot, her arms were full of her purchases: a gigantic stuffed panda, a bouquet of asters, a bottle of real champagne, and a little cake.

Once home, she remembered that tomorrow her parents were coming. They were on the second leg of their visits to their sons and grandchildren. Next year at this time they would have another grandchild to visit. We should get a better camera. This cake is too small. How could she have forgotten about tomorrow? In the morning she must run out and get another cake. Or maybe bake one if there was time. Home baking was always better, more welcoming. And another bottle of champagne. Hurried, disconnected thoughts like these went rushing through her head, while she set out the plates for supper and arranged the asters.

'What's this?' asked Gerald at sight of the panda, who was occupying a corner of the sofa.

'Guess?'

'Another baby in your brother's family?'

'Well, not exactly. Not in his immediate family.' And she began to laugh.

He stared at her. 'What are you talking about?'

She was enjoying the suspense. 'I saw Dr. Lilly today.'

'Lilly? Ob-gyn?'

'Of course. Oh darling, it's to be in June! I wasn't sure enough about it to tell you without first hearing it from him. But it's true.'

Gerald took off his jacket and laid it precisely as always, without causing a wrinkle, across the back of a chair. For a moment he said nothing.

'Are you so absolutely stunned that you can't talk? You remind me of those funny old movies where the wife breaks the news and the husband faints, and—'

'Stunned? I guess I am. This isn't exactly the most convenient time, is it?'

His face! His lips drew a thin, mean line between his cheeks. She could not take her eyes away from it.

'Are you sure?' he demanded. 'Was Louie positive?'

'That's a funny question. Of course he was.'

All her strength was flowing out below her knees. They shook, and she sat down at the table, still clutching the asters.

'I don't understand,' she said. 'I thought you would be so glad!'

'Well, I'm not. Not here and now. Be sensible, Hy. The timing couldn't be more inconvenient. I've got almost two more years before I finish here, this apartment is too small for a crib, a carriage, wet diapers, and – for God's sake, let's do something about it and wait till the right time as we planned. For God's sake, please.'

Her heart was pounding so fiercely that she could hardly speak. '"Do something?" What can you possibly mean?'

'Don't talk like an ignoramus, will you? This innocence of yours gets to be a little too much sometimes, a little too cute, Hy. What do you think I mean?'

She had such a queer feeling of unreality! *Is this happening?* she thought. I don't know how it can be happening, these words coming from his mouth. He of all the people in this world. He.

'An abortion,' she whispered. 'You're asking me to do that.'

'It's only the timing, don't you see? It's all wrong, it doesn't fit. We can have kids later. Be reasonable, Hy, instead of sentimental.'

'"Sentimental?"' She repeated. 'My baby – our baby. And now you don't want it. And I'm "sentimental"?'

She burst into tears and, jumping up, slammed so hard against the table that the champagne bottle fell and shattered on the floor.

'Watch out! Don't step on the broken glass,' he shouted.

'What the hell do you care about broken glass? You don't love me! If you did, you would love our child, too. You wouldn't ask me to kill it. We're young, we're healthy, we're not starving, we're not in a concentration camp! An abortion – my God, you should be ashamed! How can you—'

Gerald closed the window with a bang. Temper! Temper again. 'The whole neighborhood doesn't have to hear this.'

'I don't give a damn whether it does or not! Let everybody

know that my heart's breaking, that you're breaking it. Let the whole world know what you are.'

'Wait a minute, calm down, Hy. There's no sense—'

But she had already run to the bedroom. The door crashed and the wall shook. Weeping and shaking, she dropped onto the bed; then suddenly queasy, she ran to the bathroom to be sick. When she went back to the bed, she lay in a fog, in despair, as if her very heart had collapsed.

Hours later, when she awoke, the room was dark. She was still dressed in her sweater set, and Gerald was asleep at the farthest reach of the enormous bed. For a few moments she stood there looking down at him. So you marry in total trust, and then one day, in one minute, the total trust is breached and what you're left with is only bitter, bitter anger. Quietly she went out and undressed in the bathroom. Her eyes were slits between swollen lids and pale, puffed cheeks. Her face was hideous. If only there were some way of calling Francine and Dad not to come tomorrow! But how, and with what excuse? It was impossible.

But no, nothing was really impossible. She spoke aloud to herself; 'Nothing. It's simply a situation that has to be met. Somehow.'

'A washcloth soaked in ice water will help,' Gerald said.

He was standing in the doorway. Perhaps her slight fumbling had awakened him or perhaps he had only pretended to be asleep.

'I'll tell you what will help. My return to the place from which you so joyfully took me. What is that poem of Robert Frost's? "Home is where, when you have to go there, they have to take you in." But it will only be temporary. I can manage alone. I and my baby can manage. We don't need you.'

'What time does their flight get in tomorrow?' he asked, ignoring her words.

'Four-fifteen. Does it matter?'

'Of course it matters. You can't go looking like this, and you can't let them stand there waiting.'

'It's not your problem. They're my parents and I'll go for them.'

'That's ridiculous. I left the afternoon free for their visit.'

'Oh, you care so much, about them, don't you?'

'I want to give you another hour and a half to get your face back to normal before they see you.'

'What are you saying? That you think this horror can be kept secret?'

'To begin with, it isn't a "horror." It's a thing that can be discussed with reason if you'll only try. But we don't have to greet them with it the minute they set foot at the door. That's all I'm saying.'

'Don't lecture me. I hate that harsh voice. If it weren't for the baby that's growing in me, I'd want to die tonight, or murder you.'

'Hyacinth, will you listen to me? And for God's sake, for the thousandth time will you throw the godamned cigarette away? I'm sick of seeing it.'

'Then don't look at it. Let me alone. I don't know you. I don't want to know you.'

There was no other place to sleep than in the bed. The night had turned chilly and, shivering from dampness and tension, she lay long with open eyes watching light flare in and out as clouds moved over the moon. Whether he slept or not she neither knew nor cared.

Yesterday's asters, retrieved from the floor, were on the table. On either side of them stood the crystal candlesticks that Jim and Francine had just brought. Hyacinth had made her father's old favorite chicken-and-shrimp dish. She had iced the celebratory champagne and Gerald had poured it. Francine had reported on all the brothers and their children; in her scarlet blouse and her pearls she glowed. She never has any trouble, Hy thought. It was all very familiar, all very cozy. Or, to be accurate, it would have been so if she had not still been wavering between telling them now or waiting to write or telephone to them later after they were home.

Conversation ranged from their grandchildren who, like most grandchildren, were extraordinary, to George's transfer back home from Singapore, to Paul's new house. It was Jim who did most of the talking. Francine, unusually quiet, seemed to be glancing more often than necessary at Hyacinth.

'We were thinking,' Jim said, 'only beginning to think that our house is getting too large and empty for us. Of course, I love my garden. We both do. But if we could find a smaller house with the same outdoor space and if maybe you folks when you come back east were interested in our house, we might do something about giving it to you.'

'It's a beautiful house,' Gerald exclaimed. 'An incredible gift!'

'It's far too early to talk about it now.' Francine's intervention was pleasant and practical.

'Well, of course,' Gerald said. 'Right now I'm in another world.' And he launched into an account of his daily routine, which appeared to interest them. He spoke in his usual vivid fashion.

'It was a totally unnecessary accident – no seat belts. He went through the windshield on the passenger side. I can't begin to describe his face. Can you imagine a whole life to be psychologically transformed after that? A young man with everything to live for? You can believe I was shaking in my shoes when Grump – that's Malcolm Grumboldt, chief of the service – told me to take over. Of course he was right at my elbow and he would have stopped me in a second if I'd been doing anything wrong. But, thank God, it went well.'

'Don't know how you do it,' said Jim, admiring his son-in-law. 'When was this?'

'Yesterday afternoon.' Gerald smiled. 'My nerves were still twitching, even when I got home.'

And that, thought Hyacinth, is for my benefit. Shall I say it now?

Francine was still examining her. 'Is there anything wrong with your eyes? They look awfully tired, or swollen or something.'

No, not now.

'I seem to have developed an allergy. It's nothing much, just comes and goes.'

'Oh, tell them,' Gerald intervened as if he were coaxing. 'All right then, if you won't, I will. Hyacinth is pregnant and hasn't been feeling one hundred percent.'

Her startled stare asked him what trick this might be. And then came the gasps of delight.

'Darling!' cried Francine. 'Why didn't you say anything? Why, that's marvelous!'

Gerald said, 'You women, so they tell me, like to keep it secret until you're sure everything's all right.'

Then came that dreadful, uncontrollable flush again. It burned its way up Hyacinth's neck. What did he mean by this? And she waited for him to go on with an account of their quarrel, their fight, their break. But he did not.

Jim, rising to kiss her on the forehead, became emotional. 'There's something about a daughter's having a baby that's different somehow, although it shouldn't be, I guess. Oh, your grandmother will be so pleased to be a "great" again.'

Francine, having kissed Hy, remembered to kiss Gerald, too. 'Lucky baby,' she told him. 'Not everyone's child in these days has such good parents. Now, Hyacinth, will you let me buy the layette? I love to shop for baby things.'

She loves to shop, period. What am I supposed to say now? And Hy sat there in dismay.

'Now you'll really have to stop smoking,' Francine said.

Her smile was loving. It had been a long time since she had, even casually, criticized anything about her daughter, her hair or makeup or smoking. And Hyacinth understood that that had been because she was so pleased, so grateful that the marriage had turned out to be wonderful after all.

Gently, sick at heart, she replied, 'Of course I will. I threw away every cigarette in the house the moment I knew. I intend to take good care of this baby,' she added, with a straight look at Gerald.

Then there were questions about another apartment, about a larger car to replace the little red one, and whether to buy or lease it, an hour's worth of kind and loving questions.

'We have a long time to wait,' Gerald said at last, 'although Hyacinth has already made some preparations. Where's the panda? Go get it, Hyacinth.'

So she had to bring out the clumsy thing which that morning she had stuffed away on the top shelf in the hall closet. Humming and singing the 'Blue Danube' waltz, Jim circled the room, and everyone except Hyacinth laughed, everyone except Hyacinth had more champagne, and everyone said what a wonderful day this was, until it became time to take the parents back to their hotel for the night.

'Come ride along, Hy. We're flying home early in the morning, and we won't be seeing you for a while,' Jim urged.

But Francie contradicted him. 'Let Hyacinth stay here. I think she's tired.'

'I am, a little.' I'm not tired, Hy thought. I'm torn to pieces, that's all.

She was putting the cream cake into the refrigerator when Francine followed her with a question.

'Are you all right, Hyacinth?'

'Why yes. Yes, I'm all right.'

There, as always whenever Francine was resolute, were the two vertical lines between her eyes. *No, not now. Write to them.*

'You and Gerald – you get along well together, don't you?'

It was a mother's prerogative to ask, wasn't it? And some sort of answer was required, wasn't it?

'Oh, we have our little spats,' she admitted.

Francine was judging her. For a moment she seemed to hesitate. Then cheerfully, she agreed. 'Little spats. Yes, it would be pretty queer if one didn't.'

Hy was in bed when Gerald came back and stood in the doorway.

'What was the meaning of that talk at the table?' she asked as she sat up.

'That I had been thinking things over and realized that I was terribly wrong. I'm ashamed, and I'm here to apologize.'

'Yes? What changed your mind so suddenly?'

'It's not sudden. It was my first response yesterday that was sudden. There wasn't any thinking behind it, no thinking at all. I'd had a hard day, as you heard. I was tired, which is no excuse. I couldn't possibly, now that I think about it, couldn't possibly have meant what I said. That's why I'm apologizing.'

He looked as if he were in pain. Everything was all mixed up.

Her eyes began to fill, and she didn't want *that* business all over again. Angrily she wiped them with the back of her hand.

'I've made you suffer,' he said.

'That's true.' When he moved toward her, she put up her hand. 'No, not yet. Do you really want this baby? Because if you don't, you know, I'm going to have it anyway. Without you.'

'I'm ashamed,' he repeated. 'Hy, please. Please understand. I beg you. I panicked. I was thinking about time and money and everything. But now, yes I do want it. All the way back from the hotel just now, I've been thinking how we'll manage it. There's space enough in this room for a crib. He – she – won't be much more than a year old when we leave here, and then we'll have plenty of room. The carriage can go in the hall. It'll be a tight fit, but that's not important. Oh Hyacinth, forgive and forget! Please, darling, you can forgive it and forget it. You know you can.'

Given time, thought Hyacinth, a cut heals. The injury that first bleeds red becomes a white scar and ends as a faint indentation in the flesh.

Her boy was born with no trouble at all before the dawn of a fine June morning. After a welcome sleep, she woke to feel noon; the sun glittered and the public golf course in the park across the road was already filled. People dressed in primary colors were dots on the green as in a Breughel landscape, she thought with pleasure. Close to her window a locust tree was dripping a rain of creamy blossoms. And in the nursery down the hall, slept a husky baby with a crown of black hair.

'A handsome boy,' the nurse said when she brought him in to Hy's room. 'He looks like his father already.'

'Gerald, Junior,' said the father. 'We'll simply call him Jerry with a "J" so there'll be no confusion.'

The name was not Hyacinth's choice, but what's in a name, as she of all people had to remind herself. The important thing was that Gerald was already rejoicing in his son. He was jubilant.

'Look at him! Look at the long legs! And what a pair of

shoulders. A beautiful head, too, for a newborn. You can see the bone structure even now.'

As Hyacinth fed the baby, he sat there watching the process while shaking his head as if in disbelief.

'Mother and child. What a picture. Most common sight in the world, yet always new, always a miracle. Well, I hope life will be good to him. Your parents were thrilled, weren't they?'

'Oh, yes. Francine had been wanting a boy after all my brothers' daughters.'

'I think I've got some real news for you, Hy. Grump – excuse me, I guess I really should say Dr. Grumboldt – knows we plan to go back east, so he gave me a contact that might be just the thing. He's a tremendously successful man who did a residency here ten or twelve years ago. He's got a crazy name. Listen to this: Jack Arnold Ritter-Sloan. Anyway, he's a very nice guy, Grump says, good natured, easy to get along with, a real business getter besides being a top-notch surgeon, bit of a spend thrift but that's his business. In short a very bright guy. Grump wanted to keep him here, but he just suddenly decided he wanted to leave and be up and left. Now he's so busy back east that he needs an associate. Top quality only, Grump says, and I might be just the right man.' Gerald paused. 'Let me tell you, Hy, Grump doesn't often give compliments.'

Her mind went back to the day when she had given a lift to a forlorn young man alone on the hill in the driving rain. New mothers tend to be over-emotional, and I, she thought, was always over-emotional to start with. She had to smile at herself.

The months rolled around the calendar, and things happened as things do while big changes loomed ahead like tumbled summer clouds in a blue sky. Jerry laughed, rolled over, sat up, crawled and stumbled on two feet. He was strong, vigorous and sweet. He throve. When his eyes flashed mischief, as they often did, he was more than ever a duplicate of his father. Often Hyacinth, as she watched over him, reflected on what his advent had done for his parents. She had never thought that, except for some minor vexations and a few crucial hours in the past, they could ever know greater harmony in marriage. But this tiny boy, this life that was half his and half hers, had brought it about.

Gerald was comical. He bought every conceivable toy from age six months up to a bright blue three-wheeler that Jerry would not be able to use for at least two years. He bought a cowboy hat and western jeans the size of a dinner napkin. For Hy's birthday he surprised her with Jerry's photograph in a handsome old frame. And for Jerry's first birthday, he corralled every doctor who had a toddler for a cake-and-ice-cream event on a great lawn in the park.

'I want him to have everything I didn't have,' he said.

The apartment was cramped. All their fine presents, from Granny's handmade rugs to Francine's ornaments, were put away for safety's sake. One could barely move around without stubbing a toe or bashing an elbow. And it was all wonderful.

Somehow Hyacinth was still able to do a little painting while Jerry napped in the afternoon, or in the evening after bedtime. Far from being worn out, she was exhilarated. She painted cottonwood trees, a distant skyscraper rising alone on the vast flat land, and made a pen-and-ink sketch of the apartment house so Jerry might have a memento of his first home.

She even sold some paintings. The best of her work was a copy of the photograph, the gift of her friends at the museum back home, of Ernest Shackleton's stranded ship in Antartica.

It was Gerald who urged her to take it to the gallery where, although she no longer worked there, she had a warm relationship.

'Somebody's going to buy this,' he said. 'You've done it right to a T, the dark ship tilting, about to fall into smashed ice and white waves. It's great, Hy.'

It hung in the gallery for less than a week before a boy bought it for Father's Day. The price was almost a pittance, but as Gerald said, that was not the issue.

At the start of the final year in the residency, acting on his own advice, he flew back east to meet Dr. Ritter-Sloan. There was no sense in waiting until they moved to the area; supposing then that the two men should be incompatible, too much time would have been wasted.

When he returned, he was enthusiastic. It had gone well. Long into the evening they set talking across the supper table. 'We liked each other at once. Arnie started right out with first names. He's very friendly, and considering his position, unusually modest. You'll like him, Hy. The practice is larger even than Grump described. It's in a handsome building that Arnie designed himself. And the town is actually a small city, only a two-hour drive from your old home.' Gerald's eyes glowed with pleasure in the telling.

'Wait till you see the offices,' he continued. 'I don't even want to think about what he's got invested in equipment. And that's all money I would have to spend – borrow, I mean – if I were to open a solo practice.'

Hyacinth wanted to know more. Was he married?

'No, he's never been married.' Gerald grinned. 'Maybe he likes his good times too much. He's twelve years older than I am, but oddly enough, he acts younger. Yes, you can see that he likes his good times and his luxuries, racehorses among them. He rides, he travels and he has an apartment in Florida.'

'He doesn't sound like anyone I've ever known.'

'I imagine so, but I still think it's a great deal for us. I think he wants to take it a lot easier. That's why he wants me. He's promised me a full partnership after one year if he's satisfied. And he will be,' Gerald added. 'I know my work. Yes, I'm so sure that I've taken a one-year lease on a house, a great house only twenty minutes from the office, with option to buy.'

'Oh,' she cried. 'You never even phoned me!'

'I had no time. It was take it or leave it. You'll love it, though. I guarantee. It reminded me, the minute I saw it, of your parents' house, only a trifle smaller.'

She was astonished. 'How can we ever afford anything like that?'

'You've forgotten. I'm going to be a full partner. You needn't be doubtful about the house. I know your taste, and I'm telling you that you'll love it. If you don't, we won't buy it and that's a promise.'

Clearly, he was thrilled with the turn that his life was taking, and Hyacinth was thrilled with him.

* * *

This time the red car pulled a fair-sized U-Haul behind it. As they were about to start the motor, Hyacinth remembered the camera, and a neighbor kindly took their picture in front of the building that had been their first home. There they stood, the tall pair and the little boy who barely reached his father's knee, smiling for their posterity, as for themselves in their faithful old age.

Hyacinth was moved by this departure.

Gradually, without being aware of what was happening, they had blended into this place. Now at the moment of parting she noticed that the young persimmons on the southside – a particular species found only in Texas, according to the man who tended them – had grown at least a foot. On the west side where a couple of years ago you could drive past cattle grazing across a few thousand acres, another cluster of office towers was rising. Even in this sizzling heat, with the temperature rising toward the noontime zenith, you could feel the energy in this place.

Friends grouped around the car to see them off. Somebody had given Jerry a miniature ten-gallon hat, which he refused to let go of. The resident staff at the hospital had given Gerald and Hyacinth each a pair of splendid cowboy boots with a card attached. 'You'll make a hit with these in Massachusetts', it read.

So at last the moment arrived. The engine started up, the car moved down the street and onto the highway.

'We were so happy here,' Hyacinth said as they rounded the corner and took the road to the east.

Jerry slept or babbled in his car seat while his parents traveled to rollicking music northward through Arkansas, crossed the Mississippi at Memphis and sped through Tennessee to the Great Smokies. On the third day they rolled through the Shenandoah Mountains and down into Pennsylvania, nearer and nearer to New England and home. Just as the journey away had been a grand adventure, so now was the return.

At the end, they arrived at a wide main street with maples and prosperous shops on either side, passed a fine Gothic high school, a pond in a cool green park and an imposing hospital. Beyond lay more grand old trees and the to-be-expected comfortable white houses with colonial fanlights over the doors.

'So,' said Gerald. 'So here we are. What do you think?'

Familiar was Hyacinth's immediate reaction. The house was friendly and unpretentious; yet if that were not a contradiction, it had elegance. And there, sitting on the doorstep, were Dad, Francine and even Granny, who, with perfect timing, had come all the way across the state to greet them.

'And Arnie, too,' cried Gerald. 'Now that's a real welcome for you! I'd never have expected it. Didn't I say you would like him?'

Arnie stood discreetly apart from the family greetings, the hugs, the questions, and the fussing over Jerry. When all this was past, he stepped forward to be introduced, exclaiming, 'Gerald, you didn't tell me what a pretty wife you have!'

A playboy, was Hyacinth's impression. His thick, greying hair was styled in waves. His jacket was tinged with purple. In her quick, inquisitive fashion, she also saw that his oddly copper-colored eyes were kind. This playboy was harmless. Gerald, when later she would give him her assessment, would be amused.

'I got hold of a couple of men to unload this evening for you,' Arnie said. 'They'll put up the beds, do whatever you need tonight. And there's a great deli in town. They don't usually deliver, but they'll do it for me because I'm a good customer. So you'll have something to eat tonight, too.'

'Arnie,' Gerald said, 'you're too much. Everybody should have a boss like you.'

Arnie's hand wave dismissed the compliment. 'And I opened an account for you at the bank. Your first two weeks' salary is in it. I figured this lady will need plenty of cash to shop for the house here after coming from three rooms in Texas. Come on, let's tour the house. You'll want to stretch your legs after a day in the car. Tell me, how's old Doc Grump?'

They went inside, down to the cellar, through the first floor, up the graceful staircase, and through more rooms that Jim admired.

'Nice square rooms. I always like that.' To Gerald he whispered, 'Short of cash? I'll be glad to help out if you are.'

'No, thanks for the offer, but we'll be fine.'

Francine and Granny agreed that the house would be really lovely. They liked sunny rooms.

'So cheerful. You can have flowering plants at the windows all winter.'

'Plenty of wall space for pictures, too,' Gerald said. 'We'll have them covered one day. Did I tell you my wife's an artist, Arnie? She's sold quite a number of paintings, making a name for herself.'

Arnie's enthusiastic response made Hyacinth uncomfortable. She wished Gerald wouldn't always boast like that.

'As soon as you people are settled here, you'll come over and see my place. I'm in one of the new condominiums near the golf course.'

'So you're a golfer, too,' Francine said. 'That's my sport.'

'One of them,' Jim amended.

'No, that's the funny part, living across from a golf course and not using it. I keep a couple of horses. Get out to the stables as often as I can. Greatest sport there is. This little fellow here – now as soon as he gets to be five or so, I'd get him a pony if I were you. Start early. It's a lifetime's pleasure.'

'Well, what do you think about Arnie?' Gerald inquired later.

Jim was dubious. 'I should be frank, so I'll just say I have a few doubts. He's – I don't know quite how to express it, but—'

'What you mean,' Granny said tersely, 'is that he doesn't talk as a doctor should. Times have changed, I know. Manners and tastes have changed; even so, I also think—'

Gerald interrupted to ask Francine what she thought of Arnie.

'I liked him. He's somewhat flighty, of course, and you should keep that in mind, but I sense that he would never hurt anybody, and that's what's important, the most important.'

Gerald nodded. 'I'll take your opinion any day, Francine. You're a very competent judge of people.'

'I'll tell you something,' Gerald said to Hyacinth some weeks later. 'Arnie's not altogether what I had expected. He surprised me. There've been big changes in medicine since he finished his residency twelve years ago, and he hasn't kept up with them. For instance – it's not the most important thing, by any means – his noses all look alike. I'm not saying he's incompetent, of course he isn't, but he's certainly not the best, and he knows it, although other people don't.'

'I wonder why he doesn't do anything about it?'

'I don't think he cares. He spends half his energy on his business interests and his pleasures. Mercedes Toadsters and God knows what else. He's already begun to leave the tougher cases to me. Well, so much the better. I like this town, I'd like to buy this house and stay here. Agreed?'

Hyacinth had made up her mind about that before the first week was over. She worked quickly, and before a month ended had finished her scheme for the furnishing of the house, to be done piecemeal, according to income. Arnie had most generously offered, had almost insisted, on lending them a substantial sum. But Hyacinth had refused it.

Already she had made friends in the neighborhood and had enrolled with one of them in a music appreciation group that met twice a month.

And now again she had a spacious studio at home. In it she went to work with a hopeful heart. Although there was no place for further study within a reasonable distance, it had to be remembered that many of the world's great artist had never had lessons.

Arnie's costly building stood on one of the best streets. The office, replete with the latest medical equipment and decorated where appropriate with the finest furnishings, occupied two floors. Seeing Gerald there for the first time and meeting him once at the hospital wearing his surgical gown, Hyacinth felt a vicarious glory. At last he was where he deserved to be.

Only fools walked through the world believing that they were in a rose garden. Yet there were moments when she could almost believe that it was so.

Emma Louise's birth, a week after Jerry's third birthday, was one of those moments. She was another copy of her father, and although he had hoped for a boy, he immediately fell in love with her.

'She's beautiful, and she won't go through life with a ridiculous name like mine,' said Hyacinth to Francine, who had lovingly made some typically 'Francine' suggestions.

The little family prospered beyond any reasonable expectations. Often on Sunday afternoons as the children grew, Hyacinth would sit on the back terrace reading while they played with Gerald, for it was important that he have his private times alone with them. Then she would raise her eyes from the page just to listen and look again at the scene.

The baby voices chirped and shrieked, commanded and begged. 'My turn, Daddy. Pick me up first. You promised. Why can't I? Oh, that was great! Swing me again, Daddy! Again!'

She supposed that this was as close to perfection as one could find on earth: the cloistered, leafy boundaries of the private space, the jolly red and blue toys for climbing and swinging, the agile young man with his healthy children, all of it so safe and *permanent*, to use a word that they had used more than once before.

Suddenly there comes a moment when it is apparent that the garden is not flourishing as it had been doing. Subtle changes were altering its bloom. A cold spell? A hot spell? Too much water, or perhaps not enough?

They had small, fretful tiffs. Out of nowhere, it seemed, Gerald had been developing a new sardonic manner, and he was too often irritable. Pondering the matter, Hyacinth concluded that they were moving too fast. Gerald was a full half-partner in the practice now, doing more than half the work, which did not seem to bother him. He had all the prestige and responsibilities that went with the position: the busy surgical service at the hospital, and the member-ship of the fund-raising committee. In addition, partly as a result of these and partly because he was very popular, an active social life had begun to fill their evenings. They were always being enter-tained at other people's full houses, or doing the entertaining in a full house at home.

Naturally, she was aware of Gerald's high standards; they had been evident from the very first days when he had railed against the ugliness of the motel where they had first lain together. He had become more meticulous now, paying detailed attention, when they had guests, to everything: to the menu, the table service, and to Hyacinth's dress. She, too, had always taken pleasure in doing these things well, but although reluctant to admit it, she was also beginning to wish for less crowding of the hours, for a return to the more private life that they had enjoyed before Jerry was born.

'He pushes himself too much. You wouldn't believe his schedule,' she said to her good friend Moira.

'Hy, take it from me. He doesn't work any harder than you do. Let a man try running after two kids, cooking, caring for this big house, and Lord knows what else, beside all the parties you give. See how that suits him! And you still make time to work in your studio. When do you sleep, for Heaven's sake?'

Moira had a blunt way of talking, and Gerald did not like her. 'What the devil do you see in that woman?' he demanded.

'She's kind-hearted and loyal, and we speak the same language.'

'What language is that?'

'Oh, music and books, I suppose. She has interesting opinions.'

'Well in my opinion, a woman that homely should stop talking so much.'

'She's not "homely," Gerald. And that's a horrible thing to say. I want you to be nice to her. We're giving them a dinner for their anniversary.'

'My God. Why?'

'Because they had one for us, that's why.'

'Can't you give a present instead? I have no patience with them. The woman's an idiot, and he's not much better.'

They gave the dinner and Gerald was coldly polite to the couple, more cold than polite. After everyone left, Hyacinth had an argument with him, the first intense one in a long time. It was made up the next day, of course, yet it troubled her greatly. Gradually, she began to be aware of having tense moments when there was no reason to, when for example, she was at the supermarket or even working peacefully at the easel. And she was frightened without knowing why.

One afternoon she was at work there, when Arnie came to the door.

'Gerald's been trying to reach you,' he said, 'and the operator said your phone's off the hook.'

'I know. I noticed it a few minutes ago. Emma plays with it sometimes, and that's what must have happened again. Is anything wrong?'

'No, he only wanted to say he won't be back till very late. I pass near here on my way home, so I said I'd deliver the message. I see you've been painting. There's a green smudge on your nose.'

Poised in the entry, Arnie seemed to be waiting for an invitation to come in, and she gave it. She had only good feelings toward him, recollections of pleasant things like all-male excursions with Gerald and Jerry to ball games and fishing ponds. For a while now he watched her fill in a cluster of distant trees at the far back of a harbor view.

'That's a nice picture, Hy. Will you sell it?'

'I'll always sell when I get the opportunity,' she replied ruefully. 'The problem is that I don't get it often.'

'I don't know much about art, but your work, all the stuff here in this room, looks top-notch to me. Maybe I ought to own a couple of paintings. You've been in my place, so what do you think? Something over the fireplace where I have the mirror?'

'You could surely have one there. It would be a good spot.'

'So how about you and Gerald stopping by to take a look? See what colors will best match the furniture. You have a big choice here.'

'I'd be glad to, Arnie,' she said, being both touched and amused.

'Say, what's that lighted cigarette doing in the ashtray?'

'Uh-oh, I forgot. I put it down when you rang the doorbell.'

'I didn't know you smoked. I never saw you.'

'I haven't smoked in years, not since before Jerry was born. And now just a week or two ago I started again. I don't know why.'

'That's pretty dumb, Hy, if you don't mind my saying so. I gave it up fifteen years ago, and Gerald never even began, he tells me. We don't think we'd enjoy lung cancer that much.'

'You're making me feel guilty.'

'So why are you doing it?'

She hesitated. 'I can't explain it, even to myself . . . Please don't tell Gerald, will you?'

'All right, I won't. But he'll find out, you know.'

He was looking at her so intently, with a serious concern unfitting his familiar personality, that she was startled and looked away.

'You must know what made you begin again when almost everybody including you has stopped or is trying to stop.'

Arnie was persistent, and she knew enough about him to know that he would not give in until he had some sort of answer.

'I get tense sometimes, and a cigarette soothes me.'

'Why should you be tense?'

'Isn't everybody sometimes?'

'Ah Hyacinth, answering my question with a question! That's a lawyer's trick.'

'I'm sorry, but it's the best I can do.'

'You're a lovely woman. I can't explain it exactly, I've known a lot of fascinating women, but nobody like you. You're different.'

It's funny, she thought, that's what Gerald used to tell me, the exact words.

'I don't like to see you unhappy, Hy. When a person is tense, he's unhappy. And you don't deserve to be. You mustn't be. You're married to a remarkable man. My God, he did a burn case last week that you wouldn't believe! I almost couldn't believe it.'

Arnie stood up, and with his hand on her shoulder, continued in a manner almost fatherly. Yet there was also a frank admiration in the manner that, although entirely respectful, was not fatherly.

'I've watched you for almost four years now, and I'm going to tell you something: You underestimate yourself. I'm going to tell you something else, too, and I give sound advice. You and Gerald need to get away. Between work and children, you've never had a real vacation together. You need two weeks in France, or Italy, or wherever you like, and you should do it now. God knows you can afford to. Take a week to make arrangements, pack some new clothes, and be gone. No, don't argue with me. I'll tell Gerald tomorrow. No, don't thank me, either. I'm in a hurry. I'm late.'

From part way down the front walk he called back to where

Hyacinth still stood in astonishment. 'And throw those cigarettes away!'

'It's a pity you have to rush off right now,' complained Francine. 'If you could postpone it for a few weeks, you know we'd love to stay here with Jerry and Emma. But Diana's having surgery, and we've promised Tom to go there.'

'That's what happens when you have so many grandchildren,' Jim said as he tied the loose bow on Emma's pigtail.

They were a charming sight, the grandfather and the little girl sitting together on the big wicker porch chair. In a way, Hyacinth thought, I would just as soon stay home. But in another way, she felt a need to go. Arnie was probably right; they had been housebound for a long time.

Jim worried, 'I hope they won't miss you too much.'

'They'll be fine. Jerry's a tough little man, and Emma loves everybody. It's only two weeks. They'll be in good hands.'

'Are you sure this woman is responsible?' Francine asked.

'She's thoroughly responsible. Sandy's been working at the office for the last three years. Gerald thinks the world of her.'

'Is she young? I'm asking because you always wonder what kind of boyfriends the young ones may bring into the house while you're away.'

'She's the quiet type, not the kind who runs around. You can tell. She's plump, with a pretty face, but in a few years she'll be fat, poor thing.'

Francine laughed. 'Some men like the plump ones.'

'Not I,' Jim protested. 'Slender with a few curves is my taste.'

Exactly so. In her scarlet slip dress Francine stood at the railing watching Jerry and his friends in the yard.

'Look at that boy's curly head! Some women would kill to have hair like that, wouldn't they? What on earth are you doing with a cigarette, Hyacinth?'

'Smoking it, Francine.'

'Well, you shouldn't be.'

Nagging again. Taking up where she left off years ago, As if I were still nineteen.

'Ah well, ah well,' Jim began, and was interrupted.

'Look at her, Jim. Don't tell me you haven't noticed because I know you must have. She hasn't relaxed her muscles in hours. Let your shoulders drop down, Hyacinth. They're all hunched and tensed. Even your jaws are clenched. You worry me. I've tried since yesterday to keep my mouth shut, but I can't help saying that I don't like what I see.'

It was on Hy's lips to retort, 'Then don't look,' but on second impulse, she said nothing. The criticism was loving after all.

'Leave her alone,' Jim said quietly. 'Hy's old enough to take care of herself. Don't let's spoil this perfect afternoon.'

'All right, all right. I'm sorry, Hyacinth. I didn't mean to spoil the day. Isn't that Gerald's car?'

'Yes, he's home early to spend some time with you and maybe start work on his suitcase. First trip to Europe. He can hardly wait.'

Chapter Eight

In the rental car with the top down, fortified with maps, Hyacinth's fairly fluent French, and a delightful breeze, they traveled out of Paris to the places that tourists go to see: the grand palaces, Versailles, Fontainebleau, Monet's water lilies, châteaux and gardens like living tapestries.

'It's a dream,' Hyacinth said with a laugh. 'Dream's not an original word is it? Still to me, this is all so beautiful that it could be a dream, and I'm in love with it.'

'But you've seen it before.'

'When I was twelve. What did I know when I was twelve? Now I would come here every year if I could. Yes, like a dream,' she repeated.

'So you're happy. I'm glad.'

'Who wouldn't be happy? Look at those gorgeous poppies growing wild, like common daisies at home. And in midsummer you can see acres of sunflowers tall as a man. I still remember them.'

They drove on between the fields. A popular song came over the radio, and Hyacinth, hearing the refrain, sang along in French. Gerald turned to her with a smile.

'You're a cheerful person, Hy, you're good company.'

'You are, too,' she said, meaning it.

Why, I am feeling like myself! Myself! she thought in surprise. The fog, or whatever it was that had been smothering her, was gone. Suddenly she realized that she had not wanted a cigarette for the last two or three days. Arnie had given fine advice. They had really needed to be away together, away from work and house and children, much as we love all that. We must do something like this again, must refresh ourselves, if it's only to take a weekend in the city or at a country inn.

'We're staying at another lovely place tonight,' she said. 'I showed you the picture, didn't I? It's a nice drive from Chartres, not too far. Wait till you see Chartres, Gerald. It's one of the greatest cathedrals in Europe, some say the greatest. There's a wonderful guide there, a real scholar, who writes about it and lectures all over the world. He explains its history and the stained glass windows—'

'I guess I can look at a window and figure it out by myself.'

She glanced at him. He was driving, so that seeing only his profile, she was unable to read his expression. After all these years, she was still sometimes unsure without looking whether a remark was meant to be facetious or not.

'We're early enough to walk around the town,' she suggested. 'We can have a good lunch and still be in time for the tour.'

'How long is this tour? Not too long, I hope.'

'You can leave at any time you want.' She was puzzled. 'I'm sure very few people do, though. I've read his book, and it's fascinating.'

'To tell the truth, I'd like to get back to Paris. We only have a couple of days left, and we should get in some more night life, get together with those people at the hotel, do some shopping – we haven't even bought any gifts to take home.'

Why he should want to leave this enchanting countryside and get together with a group of tourists at the hotel she could not imagine. She had learned of course, and especially during these last few years, that he was far more gregarious than she was, but even so—

Nevertheless she said agreeably, 'Our Paris room's reserved again, and we can be back in no time. We'll make an early start in the morning.'

'I was even thinking we might go back today. Maybe just have early dinner at the inn and forfeit the overnight. I'd be willing to start back now if it weren't for your wanting to see this cathedral.'

'I do want to. We're almost in sight of it. You can see the two spires in the distance.'

Gerald's words had taken some of the exuberance out of her mood. But no doubt it was self-centered to expect that he should share all her enthusiasms, anymore than she ever shared all of his.

The lecturer was a superb teacher. The season having just begun, the crowd was still of a comfortable size, and along with it, Hyacinth followed him. Down the great aisle they moved to the transept and apse, then retracing the distance on the opposite side, arrived at last to the resplendent rose window where, to her astonishment, stood Gerald tapping an impatient foot and looking bored.

'So you left us,' she cried pleasantly.

'I thought he would go on talking all night,' Gerald said.

'I'm sorry. I thought you would love this.'

'I guess I don't fall in love with everything as easily as you do.'

'Fair enough. Let's drive to the inn, have another marvelous dinner, and then back we go to Paris.'

During the last hour, the sun had abruptly disappeared. It began to drizzle, and they put up the top. On the winding, unfamiliar roads Gerald had to drive slowly, while Hy watched the map and the signs.

By the time they reached the inn, under furious rain, the dinner hour had already begun. In a dining room not much larger than what one might find in an aristocratic mansion of the eighteenth century, Hyacinth started the conversation.

'Gerald, do look at the portrait over the door, the man with the peruke and the lace cuffs. This might even have been his house.'

'It might.'

The mushroom soup was smooth and rich, the bread was warm, and the wine, although she was hardly a connoisseur of wines, must be, she thought, extraordinary. Gerald was enjoying it.

'Wonderful food,' she said.

'Oh, very.'

'Gerald, are you angry about anything?'

'Angry? Why should I be?'

'You shouldn't as far as I know. But you do seem put out.'

'Well, I'm not. I'm just tired, driving all day and now this miserable rain. We can't go back to Paris tonight on these unfamiliar roads.'

Dim lights on the driveway revealed a wild, windswept night, bringing a picture to her mind.

'It rained like this the day we met. Do you remember how fierce the wind was? I could hardly hold the car on the road.'

'Damn! This had to happen while we're stuck here in the middle of nowhere. Nothing to do but go upstairs to bed.'

Nothing to do but lie together in that charming room, all snug and safe without a care, while the storm beats outside.

I don't understand, Hyacinth said to herself. And for no reason at all except perhaps to have something to do, she looked around the room.

A little family, a couple with three children, sat directly in her view. The children were sweet, French and well behaved. The wife was just an average woman. But the man had a remarkable face. Bulky and square, it was not like Gerald's, a classic face that anyone would talk about, but it had something else, an expression that brought her back to look at it again. It was the way he was gazing at his wife. There was such tenderness in that small crinkle of a smile! It brought an answering message from the wife, as if they, too, had some knowledge between them that was their secret, and only theirs. Then he reached over and for a moment covered her hand with his own.

'What are you staring at?' Gerald inquired. 'What's so interesting?'

'Was I staring? That's awful of me, I didn't mean to. They just seemed so nice.'

'Did you notice that she has no chin? A little surgery would improve her.'

'He loves her, anyway.'

'Ah, you still do notice things! That I didn't see. How can you tell that he loves her?'

'There are ways . . . Tell me, do I need any surgery?'

Gerald regarded her carefully.

'You're examining me as if you had never seen me before.'

'No, actually you don't need it. You have good bones, a trifle angular, but good. No, you're all right.'

'Just dull,' she said.

He laughed. 'Ah Hy, stop fishing for compliments.'

'I don't always have to fish. Arnie admires me. I get fine compliments from him.'

'Arnie! He's got women all over the place. Kentucky, Florida, every place. Wherever there are horses, he has a woman. Women.'

Her hands were trembling. Blinking her eyes so that no moisture would show, she fumbled in her handbag for a cigarette. Before she had lighted it Gerald cried out, 'What, again? Oh well, what's a little long cancer? Of course, you might remember that you have two children.'

Dropping the cigarette, she stared at him. 'All right. But why, why, why don't you tell me what's wrong between us? A blind man could tell that there is. I have a right to know. Am I boring? Ugly? Mean? What?'

'Nothing's wrong! For God's sake, Hy, nothing. Eat your dinner. Have some more wine.'

I don't understand.

In bright sunshine the next day, they raced through Paris. Hyacinth was barely able to keep up with him; from the Etoile down to the President's palace, across the river and back to the Place de la Concorde, they rushed through the shimmering afternoon.

'You need to be young in this city,' he said, and then to her astonishment, 'I am already too old.'

'Why that's nonsense!' she cried. 'Old at thirty-four?'

'No. This is a city made for youth, for youth that has leisure and means.'

He is feeling sorry for himself, sorry about all the years when he did not have this, she thought, and was angry at his self-pity.

'I'm going to visit the hospital,' Gerald said. 'A man at home gave me the name of somebody who'll show me around.'

'Fine. I'll go to the Rodin museum and meet you later.'

She was forcing cheer that she did not feel even on reaching the museum, so filled with treasures. And, half seeing them, she walked about feeling heavy and cold.

Then suddenly something struck her as if she had been stabbed: a small sculpture of a man with a joyous young woman raised high in his arms, as one picks up a laughing child. '*Je suis belle,*' she read. Yes, of course. *I am beautiful when I am loved.* And for long minutes she stood there looking at the faces, the wonderful young bodies and the gladness.

After a while, she went downstairs and out through the lovely gardens. To be in Paris, of all the places in the world, and to be so troubled! To feel so lonely! She walked on. At a shop window filled with children's clothes, she stopped before the prettiest little dress she had ever seen, white linen, unadorned except for a band of roses appliquéd from neck to hem. There were rosy shoes to match. Emma would love those shoes. They did not have her sizes, but they could have them by tomorrow.

'Positively? Because tomorrow will be our last day. The next morning we fly home.'

Yes, they would have the dress and shoes by late afternoon. And all the way back to the hotel, she kept thinking about her children. For the first time since they had left home, she felt a painful longing for their faces, for Jerry's merriment and Emma's curiosity. With all her heart, she longed for her children.

They had their dinner. Gerald had missed the man at the hospital, so had spent the time buying gifts. Punctilious as always, he had chosen appropriately for Hy's parents, for Arnie, for Emma and Jerry and the people in the office, and for Sandy, in appreciation.

They went to a nightclub with the Americans whom Gerald had met in the hotel lobby. And sitting there beside her husband, Hyacinth felt again the loneliness that had corroded the afternoon. He and the other couple were enjoying everything, the crowd, the bustle, and the prance of the naked women. Pretending to be one with the mood, she feigned pleasure. But truly she found no fault with any of this; people were entitled to their tastes. If only she could know what Gerald really wanted, she would willingly give it to him.

What could be wrong? Another woman? Was that absurd, or was it not? It was absurd; he had everything, her ceaseless love, his work, their children, their home, everything. And she sat there twisting her rings, the wedding band and the precious diamond chip he had bought with his first month's pay.

'Well,' he said in their room that night, 'just one more day. I could turn around and come right back here again next month.'

'I didn't think you loved it that much.'

'Who, me? What makes you say that?'

'You haven't been very jolly these last few days, Gerald. Haven't I been asking you why you're so morose?'

'Morose? You mean because I didn't enjoy the tour at Chartres?'

'Of course I didn't mean that. Please, please don't dodge the question. Answer me: Is it anything I've done? Be honest with me.'

'No, and no, and no again to your silly question.'

'Do you swear it?'

'Yes, I swear it.'

Lamplight fell upon the bright black hair and on the dimple in the chin that softened the intensely virile face. She thought of the sculpture she had seen that afternoon, and without intending to, made a sound that was part outcry and part sigh, blinking the tears back, although not before he had seen them.

'What's the matter with you, Hy? What is it? Oh, I hate to see you like this. If it's my fault, I'm sorry. But there's no reason, you're imagining—'

She ran to him. 'Pick me up and carry me to the bed the way you used to do. I love you so . . .'

Later, while Gerald slept his usual peaceful sleep, she lay awake staring through the darkness at the outlines of the marble mantel, of flowers on a table, and of luggage, the best fine luggage, waiting in the corner. She had wanted affirmation, and he had given it, or had at least pretended to. Can there be, she asked herself, an impersonal way of doing what is so personal? Why yes, of course there can be. It is as if you did not care who lay there with you.

Quietly, she slid out of the bed and went to the window. It was very late and traffic in the grand place had slowed. Lanterns bordered the bridge that stretched across the river. On the other side stood stately public buildings, presenting to the world the face of dignity, that face which human beings present each day to one another. But beyond these, and all through the great pulsing city in the little spaces where men and women lived together, there are myriad others beside Hyacinth who, in a different language from hers, are crying her same cry, baffled by loneliness and a fear of falling.

Francine's telephone call came before breakfast in the morning. 'Jim died. He slept away without warning after dinner last night.'

Chapter Nine

Too many things occurred during the following six weeks for Hyacinth to think very much about herself, so that the time in Paris receded abruptly into a distant past. The present loomed large. Poor Granny, the invincible, having reached her limit with this totally unexpected loss of her second son, had gone to a retirement home. Francine, at the insistence of her sons, had left for a long vacation trip with them through the northwest and Alaska.

'Don't worry about her,' Gerald said. 'Francine will get along. She's strong and very smart. She always was the brains of your family.'

Rather shocked, Hyacinth protested, ' "Brains!" And my father had none, I suppose?'

'Very different. He was an intellectual, a gentle soul. But Francine is smarter. Smart enough not to let it show too much. I wouldn't want to be on her list of enemies.'

This remark, along with other idle bits and pieces of the recent turmoil and tragedy that accompany a death, was in Hyacinth's mind on that morning in late summer when she received an anonymous telephone call.

'You don't know me,' a woman said, 'and in a way I'm ashamed of what I'm doing, not giving you my name. It's dirty and cowardly. I've been putting this off for weeks. But suddenly just now, I decided I must. It's about your husband, and a woman.'

The hand that held the phone shook so much that Hyacinth had to brace it with the other hand. 'What are you saying? Tell me who you are.'

'I can't. I really can't. Please understand.' The voice was soft, even trembling. 'I'm not an acquaintance of yours, you've never even met me. I only know you by reputation in the community. I know you're a good woman with a nice family. I've had troubles of my own, and I just can't bear to see yet another woman being spat on, as men do. That's all. I thought if I told you what's happening, you might be able to do something about it before it's too late. The woman works in your husband's office.'

The telephone clicked off. Hy put her head down on the desk. Dirty and cowardly, people say, and yet there was something in the manner that rang true.

'I don't know,' she whispered.

When she raised her head, the room seemed to swim in a circle. It took a few minutes before she was able to steady herself and call Moira. She would put everything aside and come right over. You could trust Moira.

They sat on the porch steps. When Hyacinth had spoken her few words, there was a long silence. Sweating, hot and cold, she waited.

Then Moira spoke slowly, not looking at Hyacinth, but out across the sun-browned grass.

'I've known it for quite a while, Hy. The one who minded the children while you were in France – she's the one. I knew it before that, and I've kept asking myself whether I should tell you. I'm guessing that Gerald knows I know, and that's why he doesn't like me.'

'How did you find out?'

'Are you sure you want to hear all this? What good will it do you?'

'I have to hear it. Tell me.'

Moira sighed. 'Things get around. People talk. One woman's husband is a doctor, and his office nurse is a friend of that one, of – of Sandy. Somebody saw Gerald in the car with her, leaving the shore on a Sunday. Somebody saw – oh, what's the use? They've been seen, that's all.'

'So everybody knows, except me.'

Now it was the trees that moved slowly in a circle, tilted against the sky. Hyacinth stood up, leaning against the doorframe.

'Are you going to be all right, Hy?'

Moira's kind face was so anxious that it seemed she was the one who must cry.

'No, I feel very weak, that's all. No strength.'

'Go in and sit down. Oh, I'm sorry, I'm so sorry. You don't deserve it. Are you sure you're all right?'

'Yes, really. Really, Moira.'

'Are you going to tell him?'

Hyacinth smiled. 'I'll have to, won't I?'

'Do you want me to stay here with you?'

'No, thanks. I have to get moving and take care of the children.'

'I'll take them home with me. They can stay for supper. Don't worry about them.'

'Thank you. Thank you for everything, Moira.'

'A dirty, anonymous phone call,' Gerald said. 'And you take it seriously? Some malicious woman is envious of you, someone sick in the head who has nothing to do but spill venom.'

'She wasn't like that.'

'Like what? What do you know about her? This is ridiculous, and I'm surprised at you.'

It would be wrong to involve Moira, so Hyacinth said only, 'Other people know. The woman said I could ask about your being seen in a car with Sandy.'

Gerald laughed. 'Well, well! Sandy is a valuable employee, and still I'm not permitted to give her a lift in my car now and then? That's immoral, I suppose.'

'It was on the road to the shore.'

'Her mother lives on the road to the shore. And where on the road, anyway? It's fifty miles long, for Pete's sake. Don't you see how ridiculous this is and how insulting?'

A small, persistent part of her mind, wanting to believe him, was holding hard against the larger part that knew differently. And she was so, so tired. It had been a long day since morning, probably the longest day in her life.

'Come, let's get something to eat,' he said, kindly now. 'I have to eat fast and get back to the hospital.'

'I meant to cook something, but I didn't. These are just left-overs. Hamburgers left over.'

This was not the dinner to which Gerald was accustomed. But he only said cheerfully, 'Good enough. Stay there if you're not feeling well, and I'll heat them.'

When they had eaten, she went to fetch the children at Moira's house, Gerald helped bathe them, and together they read to them before putting them to bed. Then they went downstairs, Gerald to watch a ball game and Hyacinth to sit with an unread book and a whirl of thoughts.

Surely he could not be thinking of divorce. If only for those two asleep up there, those two whom he adored, he would never do that. And surely, if he had such intentions, would a man like Gerald, so critical, so fastidious, even dream of replacing her with somebody like Sandy? She looked across the room at him. No. The very idea was ludicrous.

Well, suppose he had been doing a bit of flirting. Face it, Hyacinth, you've seen that before, as long ago as Dr. Bettina in Texas. You may not like it, of course you don't like it, but you've seen enough of life to know that no harm need come of it. This whole business could be nothing but trumped up gossip that spreads and swells and fools even intelligent people like Moira. It happens often enough.

The next day was Sunday, a pleasant, routine morning with pancakes and bacon, the newspaper, and a child's game of croquet on the lawn. In the afternoon, Gerald had to go to the hospital, which was neither usual nor unusual for him on a Sunday.

But suddenly, after having placated her doubts, or having thought she had done so, Hyacinth began to feel them again; the reasonable words of the stranger on the telephone and the devastating words of Moira sounded quite clearly in her ears. And so, in the late afternoon, she called the hospital and learned that Gerald had not been there all day.

When he came back, they had their dinner and put the children to bed, as always. Never would they argue in front of Jerry and Emma. But she was furious when she confronted him.

'You were not at the hospital today.'

'What do you mean?'

'What I said. Don't lie to me. I called up and found out.'

For a few seconds, she let him try for an answer, and when none came fast enough, she attacked him.

'Where were you? Out with that Sandy woman?'

There was that ugly line again, the tightened mouth of Gerald's scorn, very seldom seen, it was true, but when seen, dreaded.

'As a matter of fact, I was with her this afternoon. I decided that the gossip you described might perhaps be very harmful, not as ridiculous as I first said it was. So from now on I shall give her no more lifts to her mother's house, even though I may be going that way. There will be no more rides to the Main Street stores, even though they're on my way home. It's outrageous. But if this is what evil-minded people make of such innocent behavior, we'll simply have to change our behavior. And that's that.'

Hyacinth stared at him. Did he really expect her to believe this flimsy nonsense?

'You must think I'm retarded, Gerald. Tell me, then, why you had to lie about going to the hospital. You could have told the truth to me instead of what you're telling me now.' Trembling as she had done yesterday in the presence of Moira, she clutched the back of the chair where she stood. 'Oh, I've seen how you bask in women's flattery. I've—'

'"Bask",' he mocked. 'How literary.'

'Yes, *bask*, like a cat lying in the sun. Not that there's much harm in that. It's only natural male vanity, I suppose. Many times I could have complained, but I chose to ignore them. I never thought—'

She had stung him, and now he responded. 'The wronged wife! So that's your pose. "Many times." Why didn't you speak up instead of suffering so nobly in silence?'

'I didn't want to make an issue of it. We had a marriage, Gerald, a real one. We have children.'

'Thanks for telling me. I forgot we have children.'

'Yes, I guess you do forget when you climb into bed, or wherever it is that you have your fun.'

'Go on. Some people do enjoy torturing themselves, don't they? You must be mighty insecure to shake like a leaf because your husband is friendly to some young woman. And in this case, a hard-working young woman who took good care of your children. Well, you always were insecure. Too bad you had such a beautiful mother.'

She could not speak, nor could he. The cruel blow, the unspeakable, now spoken, had horrified them both. He looked stricken.

'I'm sorry, Hy. I didn't mean that. It isn't true. It was crazy. But you made me angry. This is all crazy. I'm sorry, awfully sorry.'

Biting her lip, Hyacinth controlled herself. 'Get out. Go to her, or to anybody. Go anywhere. I don't care.'

'Yes, yes, let me out of here, too.' He clapped both hands to his head, groaning, 'Take a walk, take a ride. Anyplace.'

An hour later, having settled the hastily summoned babysitter, Hyacinth went to the garage. Gerald's car was gone. Very likely he had fled to the office; there was no safer place for them to meet than in their familiar surroundings after dark.

In her pocket she had his duplicate key ring with which to silence the burglar alarm. In her handbag was a miniature flashlight to guide her up the stairs to the room where they would most likely be. On her feet were the sneakers that would not spoil the surprise.

Half a block away, where it could not be seen from the building, she parked the car beneath the cover of trees. The short street that was so cluttered by day was now vacant, and so quiet that her tread on a twig was alarming. Like cotton batting, clouds smothered the night sky, and the scene was as eerie as something out of *Sherlock Holmes*.

A weak beam from the street lamp fell upon the graceful façade of Arnie's 'little gem.' For a moment or two, with the key in her sweating hand, Hy stood facing it as if to make a final decision; then having made it, she mounted the shallow steps to the entrance and turned the key.

The main hall was without any obstacles that could cause a

noisy bump or stumble, so that she moved easily and without sound to the room where they were most likely to be. It was vacant. Aware of her hammering heart, she went from room to room, through consulting rooms, surgeries, record rooms, x-ray cubicles, everywhere, keeping the flashlight low to the floor. Where were they then?

At *her* house, most likely. But she lived with a sister. Yet what difference would that make? The sister might well be no better than she.

She! I never harmed her. I was good to her, yet now she takes my husband. She destroys me. My children. My home. My life.

A dreadful rage such as Hyacinth had never known now swelled in her chest. It seemed to be flooding her with hot blood whose salty taste was in her mouth. Think. Think. Up and down she walked, back and forth, trying to focus her thoughts on some sort of action. She lit a cigarette, and then another one, and kept on pacing.

Here was the desk where Sandy sat. Here were her tidy tools: the telephone, a lamp, the computer, and a glass paperweight enclosing a glass Eiffel Tower – souvenir from Paris, from Gerald. As patients came and went, his door would open upon a view of her. Would they acknowledge each other's presence, or pretend not to? Most probably they would pretend indifference, for Gerald was not one to risk decorum.

The center drawer of the desk was ajar. This was where women in offices kept personal belongings, a spare lipstick, mirror and comb, tissues, and even sometimes precious letters that they wanted to have with them. She rummaged, and yes, there at the back, lay an envelope fastened with a rubber band. Inside of it was a bundle of little notes, addressed in Gerald's writing and sent to *her* home.

In the narrow beam of the tiny flashlight, his backhand script was bold. *Sandy, you don't know what you do to me. I walk these streets every day thinking of you. Why aren't you here with me? Another cathedral, a miserable rainy night in a God-forsaken country inn, and a big bed without you in it.*

Hyacinth went mad. And strangely, in her madness, she directed her hatred toward Sandy – not Gerald. *You were in my house for two weeks. You saw my beautiful children, you went snooping through all my things!* she cried. *My clothes, my books, my mail. All my secrets, my private ways. You and he have been laughing at me, and oh how you'd love to take my place, to live my sweet life! If you can you'll do it, you'll work, you'll eat away like a termite.*

Hyacinth's arm whipped out into the air. It struck the desk lamp and smashed it to the floor. It swept over the surface of the desk and cleared it of papers, paperweight, telephone and computer. All came crashing to the floor.

In Gerald's room she repeated the destruction, a paltry revenge for insult, for what he had done to her very existence as a woman. And with a spreading smile, she stood there surveying her work, imagining his face – their two faces – when in the morning they would see this wreckage.

Then fear came. If they should enter now and find her here – no, she was not prepared for that. And she fled. Down the hall she raced, down the outer steps, where she stumbled and fell on the grass, dropped her handbag, scooped up its contents, and with a painful, bloodied knee, limped to the safety of the car.

Except for the living-room lamp where the babysitter was reading, the house was dark. She paid the girl, answered a question about the injured knee, and learned that the children had been long asleep. No, Gerald had not come home.

Once in bed, she was seized with a queer sensation. It was as if, after painful effort, she had triumphed, as if she had reached the top of a mountain and now, looking down, saw how far was the fall to the bottom, how far and dark. What was to come next? With this queer sensation pressing in her head, on her bruised knee, and all through her exhausted body, she lay waiting for something to happen.

Night sounds woke her, first crickets and then the ringing telephone. It was on Gerald's side of the bed, but he was not there, so reaching and fumbling in the dark, she grasped it and took a message. If he had come home, he must be in the spare bedroom, so she went there at once.

'Get up. There's a fire. Arnie just got the call.'

'What? What?' Gerald mumbled.

'A fire. The office is burning down.'

After breakfast Hyacinth took the children to Moira's house and drove to the office. The scene was a total confusion of sightseers and vehicles. These, along with fire engines, the fire chief's car, a police car, and an ambulance jammed the narrow street. The elegant building was already a sorry reminder of what it had been, its stone walls erect but blackened, all wood trim gone, window glass shattered, and the fine wood-shingled roof collapsed.

Well, now they'll never know what I did to the desks, she thought, and was instantly sorry because poor Arnie was standing there on the sidewalk looking at the ruin of his 'little gem.'

'Oh, Arnie, what a pity! However did this happen?'

The air was clouded with smoke and filled with its scorching smell. Blinking with reddened eyes, he gave her a look of helpless defeat, so that she had a second's thought: if he were a woman he would weep openly.

'Does anyone know – I mean – is there anything left?' She hardly knew, in the face of his pain, what there was to say.

'No, nothing left. Just junk. Pieces. The place is a shell. And nobody knows anything, except that the fire alarm didn't go off. They're still poking around inside trying to figure it out. Maybe a short circuit. Probably. Gerald's in there now talking to people. I had to go out and get some air. The smoke smell sickens you. Well, there's no crying over it, is there? Done is done.'

'You were so proud of it,' she said gently. 'It was a really, really beautiful building.'

'It should have been, considering what I paid the architect. I got one of the best in the country. Wanted something classy, nothing gaudy, because this is that kind of town. Couldn't trust my own taste. The fact is, I'm not like Gerald. I don't have any taste, and I know it. Right, Hy?'

'Right about what?'

'That I have no taste. Come on, Hy, level with me. You know what I am, and I know you know it.'

Putting a hand on his arm, she kissed his cheek. She could have cried for him, and for much, much else besides.

'You can have it rebuilt,' she said. 'Can't you? It's insured.'

'I don't know. Gerald and I have been thinking anyway about that Florida business, and maybe this will give us the push we need to sell this practice and make the move. Fortunately, all our patients' records were in fireproof cabinets,' Arnie added.

'Florida? Move to Florida?'

'Hasn't he told you? I guess he wants to surprise you. We have a chance to buy a practice. Big. I mean big. Makes us look like pikers. Real old guy is retiring. We think we can swing it.'

She was shocked, and said so.

'Oh, but you'd like it, Hy. No hard winters, good private schools for Emma and Jerry if private schools are your thing, and a house can be gotten, too, a great house near the water. I surely don't want a house, so that'll be for you.'

He was waiting for a comment, but since she was unable to muster one, he continued.

'There's a load of cosmetic surgery down there. You'll be able to put plenty aside for the kids so they can stay dry if there's ever a rainy day. Not a bad idea, is it?'

'No,' she said weakly.

Changing the subject, Arnie resumed, 'This was a three-alarm fire. Can you believe it? When I got here a little after two, the smoke looked a burning city, grey and red, like a bomb attack. They were in there fighting till maybe seven o'clock. You have to hand it to those men. One of them broke his arm, and there are two in the hospital. Smoke inhalation. Bad stuff.'

Hyacinth looked up at the charred walls. Problem had been piled upon problem. Rage and grief had already overwhelmed her, and now there was this further twist of fate. She was still staring at the walls when Gerald came down the walk.

'It's a war zone in there,' he said, addressing Arnie. 'I don't think that one of those two men is going to live. The whole floor collapsed and he went down with it into the flames.'

Arnie shook his head. 'What the hell could have done this? I've heard that rodents, mice or squirrels, can gnaw a wire and set off a fire.'

'It wasn't necessarily electrical.'

'No? What then? Where did it start?'

'They can't be sure, but possibly, or even probably, in my room. When they arrived last night there was evidence of some sort of disturbance there. Stuff overturned on the floor. Or so somebody thought. But it's hard to tell.'

'But who could have gotten in? The burglar alarm never sounded, only the fire alarm.'

'Don't worry, they'll be looking into that.'

Gerald had still not acknowledged Hy's presence. Now he said grimly, 'You might see whether anything is needed for that poor fellow or for his family, Hyacinth. There's a little boy, and a pregnant wife. Here, I've written the name.'

She could not help but ask, 'Is he really not expected to live?'

'He fell a full flight into the cellar. Smashed his head on concrete. No, he isn't expected to live, and if he does, his life won't be worth living.' Gerald turned away. 'Can you go in again, Arnie? The insurance people need us.'

In the car on the way home, Hyacinth spoke aloud. 'God help me.'

Her hands gripped the steering wheel. As if it were an entity separate from herself, her mind talked to her; it analyzed and cautioned.

You did smoke some cigarettes, that's true. But you crushed them. Positively you did. You're known to be a careful person.

Yet— yet there is such a thing as an accident, isn't there? Something unintended. Something one forgets, like keeping one's eyes on the road, or turning off the gas oven. You can't condemn a good person for having an accident. Can you? Can you?

No, I'm sure I never left a lighted cigarette anywhere. Pull yourself together, Hyacinth. You had no part in this fire. But are you sure? Did you really stub them out? Do you even remember seeing an ashtray? Think. Think.

At home again, she sat down in the kitchen and drank three

cups of coffee. Beyond the window was the garden that Dad had laid out for them. If he were alive, dear, wise, reasonable, quiet Jim, he would know how to straighten out this tangle of troubles. She could almost hear his voice as he sat with Emma on that last day before the trip to France. She stood up, opened the door to the back porch and looked at the chair. Emma's Raggedy Ann doll lay on the floor, and Jerry's new two-wheeler was propped against the wall.

Home! Good Lord, shall a creature like Sandy be allowed to wreck it? Surely Gerald does not want that, either. This is an ugly but passing escapade. Men do it, but women need not let it be the end of their world. Who knows but what Jim, too, hadn't had his escapades now and then, known or unbeknown to Francine? Even in such a contented, tranquil marriage as theirs had been, it is possible.

It's strange that I could have been in that awful, jealous rage last night and that now I'm not any longer. I'm wounded, most terribly wounded, which is different.

But I'm stubborn. I've always been stubborn. When there's a storm at sea, what do people do? Batten down the hatches or trim the sails, whatever that means . . . So now I have to stand up straight and use my head. What do I do next?

Tomorrow is the first day of school, second grade for Jerry and nursery school for Emma, a big step for each. They'll need loving attention, and Gerald is in no mood to give it, so I'll just do double. This afternoon, new socks for Jerry and teeth cleaning at the dentist's for both of them. Last, dinner for this evening, a special one to show an angry man that the storm has begun to die down a bit.

With this resolve, Hyacinth went systematically through the day. But Gerald did not come home for dinner. It was late and she was already in bed when she heard him come up the stairs and go into the spare bedroom. Well, he was sending a message.

In the morning she stopped him at the front door as he was leaving and spoke quietly. 'We can't live like this, Gerald, avoiding each other. We need to talk.'

'Not now.'

'Well at least tell me about what's happened to that poor man—'

'He died. The funeral is the day after tomorrow at eleven o'clock in the church on Maple Street.' Gerald's tone was flat. 'After that we can talk.'

'Gerald! We have to do it before then. My head is spinning. We need to straighten out what you're going to do about Sandy. And what of this move to Florida?'

'Not now, I said. Let me go, I'm in a hurry.'

'Are you coming home to dinner tonight?'

'Probably not.'

'Oh Gerald, stop. This is no good at all. If you won't communicate, how can we ever—'

But he was already out of hearing.

Half the town, or maybe more than half of it, was in some way connected with the funeral. The two newspapers, state and local, each bore a front page photograph of the brave young fireman who had risked and lost his life among collapsing walls and flames. The flags on all the public buildings were at half-mast, with the firehouse draped in black. The church was filled, and people crowded the street outside.

Hyacinth, determined to act normally, arrived early enough to save two seats for Gerald and Arnie. It surprised her when Arnie arrived alone and inquired about Gerald.

'He'll be here,' she said. 'He had an errand.'

The coffin was closed. She tried raising her eyes toward the vaulted ceiling, but they always came back to rest upon the long black box. Thirty, he had been. Only six months younger than I, she thought.

'Oh, there he is,' Arnie said, 'coming in with the girls from the office. He doesn't see me. Oh well, they've sat down. Is anything the matter with Gerald, Hy?'

'Nothing but the fire and all the trouble. Isn't that enough?'

'Yes, of course the fire, but still I thought there might be something else.'

Now the organ wept softly above the stir and rustle of the congregation as the widow appeared. In her poor black dress, she came with her head down, holding by the hand her wide-eyed, scared little boy. The child was Jerry's age; the mother was ready to bear her baby perhaps as early as the next hour. And all Hy's stoic resolution dropped away like a discarded coat.

Outside, as if to match the funereal mood, the day had turned sober. A gray, blank sky the color of tin enclosed the earth, and a warm wind tore at the leaves, turning them inside out. Like a horse or a cow in the field, thought Hyacinth, I feel impending storm.

Shortly after the children had gone to bed, it broke. The first thunder rumbled when Gerald entered the little den where Hyacinth was sitting.

'As you have seen,' he began, 'the building is ruined.' And he paused.

This cold and formal manner disconcerted her. He might better have said something about themselves and the possible ruination of their marriage. Since the pause was long, she found time enough to say so. 'What about us? What about our marriage?'

'We'll get to that later,' he replied. 'First things first. I'd like to know how you're feeling after what you've done.'

'Done? What have I done? I'm not the one who's been caught with lies or who's had any secret affair, am I?' She spoke quietly, keeping her dignity. 'Every hour since last Monday, I've been thinking about this, Gerald. I don't have to tell you what it has meant to me because you must know very well. What I do have to tell you is that I'll put it behind me. Yes, you have my word that I'll never mention it for the rest of my life if you'll get rid of that girl tomorrow so we can start fresh and be ourselves again. I'm willing to do that. For all our sakes, Jerry's and Emma's, and our own, I want to do it.'

'That's not what I'm talking about, Hyacinth. I want to talk about why you went to my office.'

Curiously, her heart, instead of leaping, slowed down.

'I? In your office? When?'

'The night it burned down after you set the fire.'

'I set the fire? You can't be serious.'

'Oh, but I am. Very serious. That was not an electrical fire. Somebody was inside that building. Somebody vandalized my office.'

'And naturally, I'm the somebody because I found out about that woman. Oh, that's clever detective work. Really clever.'

'Sarcasm won't help, Hyacinth.'

'Listen to me. If you think somebody was there, you should question your employees. You have five of them and they all have keys. It's outrageous that you should accuse me.'

'They have all been questioned. The police and the insurance investigators know what they're doing, Hyacinth. And they all have valid excuses for that night. Ironclad.'

Each repetition of her name struck a blow. And yet her heartbeat was still slowing. Perhaps it was winding down to stop.

'So send them to question me also. I don't care. This is too stupid. No, it's not stupid, it's evil. Evil, Gerald.'

'Do you really think so?'

'Of course I do. I haven't been near your office since before we went to Paris, for God's sake.'

And God forgive me for the lie, but how else can I save myself? I didn't burn it down!

From his pocket, Gerald drew a small package wrapped in paper, took out the contents, and pushing aside some books, laid them on the table.

'Then what about these?'

Hyacinth stared. There were a powder compact, lipstick and pocket comb that they had bought together on the Left Bank near a museum. Of blue enamel, each had a narrow black band with the gilt insignia of the maker. She could not speak.

'They were on the grass between the azaleas and the sidewalk. I found them at first daylight on the night of the fire.'

Gerald's voice became surprisingly gentle. 'Nobody else knows. Nobody but us need ever know.'

Now in spite of all stalwart resolutions, tears flooded her eyes; after her usual fashion, she wiped them roughly away with the back of her hand. And still she was unable to summon a word.

'Why did you do it, Hy?'

Oh my God, that's when I stumbled and dropped my bag.

Her tears went beyond control, and she wept. 'I didn't do it on purpose! It must have been my cigarettes. I read your notes to her, and I went crazy. I only wanted to wreck her possessions, and then yours, too. I lost my mind, I tell you. Don't you believe me? I did not set any fire on purpose.'

'If I did believe you,' Gerald said, still gently, 'would anybody else? What plausible reason can you give for being in my office at night? It looks like arson, you see, and arson is no joke. It's a criminal offense.'

'Even if you didn't do it on purpose?'

'Yes, Hy, even then. You have to remember that even if you didn't do it on purpose, a man is dead as a result of it.'

She was stunned and silent as he continued.

'That makes it a felony-murder. First or second degree. This would probably be second degree.'

'What does that mean?' she whispered.

'Twenty years, perhaps, for arson, and the same for the death, to be served concurrently.'

'How do you know all this?'

'From the lawyers and the insurance people.'

'Are you sure?'

'Look it up. Find out for yourself. But don't worry. There's absolutely no suspicion of you. None at all. At least, not yet.'

She was seeing the widow's huge belly under the poor black dress. She was seeing a little boy's frightened eyes, and she was seeing herself behind a barred door.

'I want to die.'

'No, Hyacinth.'

'I don't deserve to live. I don't want to live.'

'Of course you deserve to live. You're a good person. You're a harmless innocent, as your mother says.'

'What am I going to do?' she cried, and wrung her hands. 'What are you going to do?'

'I'm going to do nothing. My lips are sealed, as the saying goes. Trust me. If I didn't care about you, I surely care about Jerry and Emma. They have a good name in the world . . . Arnie and I, especially Arnie, have put a big sum in the bank for the widow, and we, again mainly Arnie, intend to keep adding to it.'

They sat still. Gerald picked up the newspaper and began to read as if this were any ordinary, comfortable evening. For perhaps an hour, still in shock and stunned, she watched him. Then, when a restless, desperate feeling overcame her, she stood up.

'I need to walk,' she said. 'Will you come with me?'

'No, I'll wait here till you come back.'

It was almost dark. The familiar streets looked strange, foreign and unfriendly. A house looked oddly like a face; the front door was a surly mouth, and the second-story windows were mean eyes. On someone's lawn, a cat pounced with such cruelty upon a screaming bird, that she felt sick at the sight. Quickly she turned about and went home to sit on the porch in the chair where Jim had sat.

I have been going downhill for months, she thought, long before we went to Europe. In fact, that's why we went — or why I went. Arnie knew. He's a good man, and smart; he might even have known that Gerald had stopped loving me.

Now it was pitch dark. The tall clock in the hall chimed eleven, and still she sat there with her thoughts.

What have I come to? What have I done with my rage and carelessness? And before her eyes, she saw again the widow: the little boy and the unborn child walking toward her down the aisle. She saw too her own Emma and Jerry — What have I done to them?

Yes, I have been going downhill, and I've come to this. But I must climb up again, I must learn to live with this horror. I must make Gerald love me again as he did in the beginning. Yes. Oh God, please help me.

The earth, the grass, the fence, and the very bulk of the house were swallowed up now by the night, but above them the sky was bright with stars. And for some reason buried deeply in history, in myth, or in human consciousness, those ancient suns began to speak to her of courage, of climbing up from the depths.

'Come,' Gerald said, standing over her. 'Come upstairs. I will give you a pill so you can sleep.'

'You know I never take pills. I never need any.'

'But tonight you do.' And he took her hand to draw her out of the chair. 'Come up.'

'You need to pull yourself together, to get some help,' he told her the next day.

'I'm thinking how sad and bitter it is that you and I should ever need a third person to help us. But we do.'

'Not exactly, Hyacinth. I don't feel that I need any third person for counseling, since that's what you mean.'

They were in the kitchen after the children had left for school. She had been putting dishes back on the shelves. Now she pulled out a chair at the table and sat down.

'That doesn't make much sense,' she said.

'I think it does, Hyacinth.'

His use of her formal name seemed to bode no good, but she spoke calmly. 'Well, I don't think so. I'll do my best to get us past this awful trouble, this thing that I've done, and with your help, I can do it. I know I can.'

'I'll help you. I'll pay for anything you need, as I always do.'

Surely he understood what she meant and was dodging, not wanting to understand. He seemed like a stranger as he stood in the doorway, immaculately dressed, tall and too imposing for the humble background of the kitchen. *Aloof*, was the word. And *critical* was another. Cool and self-contained, and so certain of himself that it was confusing to remember him as the eager student who had come to the museum on that morning not so many years ago. When and how had this happened?

'I'm not asking for anything money can buy. What I'm asking, Gerald — I did ask — is that you get rid of that foul girl.'

'That's all the same to me, neither here nor there. It's not the issue.'

"'All the same' to you? You're not in love with her?'

'No. Never was. I'm sorry you found those stupid notes, sorry that you've been so hurt. I never wanted to hurt you. It was a stupid affair. It lasted six weeks and ended. She'll be gone by the first of the month.'

In a way, this news should have been the best she could possibly expect. And yet in another way, his cavalier attitude was a shock. And from some flash in her head, there came a sensation: In the still of the evening she stood at the window hearing Francine's voice.

Once he gets ahead in the world, he'll chase women . . . Hyacinth's no match for that kind of business . . .

'How many of these so-called stupid affairs have you had, may I ask?'

'Not many. A man does these things, you see, and afterwards he feels they weren't worth the hazard. It's just – well, you know how it is, you listen, you read, you look around the world. It's not nice, but it happens. And I do admit that I'm ashamed. Most men are.'

This is hardly a heartfelt apology or plea for forgiveness. Yet perhaps it's the best he can do. And if so, it must be accepted. Think! *He* has accepted what *I* have just done!

And silent there at the kitchen table, Hyacinth twisted the wedding ring, became aware of the habit, and stopping it, gazed about at all the dear and precious artifacts of home; the children's mugs with their names in red script, Granny's rug in the hall, and Gerald's golf clubs propped against the wall. Here was a life under construction, growing piece by piece through the years.

'We've both done wrong,' she said softly. 'But we can start again. We can be what we once were. You know it.'

He said nothing.

'No answer, Gerald?'

He sat down on the other side of the table, not looking at her but away, past the window. 'Things haven't been the same for the last year or two,' he said.

'That's true. And I've been sick over it. Sick in my heart. I've made attempts to find out from you what was wrong, but I never got more than a denial that there was anything wrong.' Still she spoke sadly, without accusation. 'Even now you sit there and you don't say anything, Gerald.'

'I'm listening.'

'All right. We've changed a bit. We've grown older. Isn't it natural to change a bit? For instance, you've become more lively than I. You want activity all the time, and people around practically every night – which is fine,' she added quickly. 'There's nothing bad about that. We don't have to be identical. We only need to compromise.'

'Maybe a separation for a while would do us both good.'

'Separation? What can you mean?'

'I only meant – in the circumstances. Just a trial, to see how we feel.'

'All this mystery!' she cried, clasping her head between her hands. 'All these things going on behind my back. Arnie tells me about Florida. You say nothing to me about it except that now you want a separation. Now, when I need your strength!'

'No, no, Hyacinth, listen to me. All I mean is a rest for both of us. We've been through a crisis. We need time to think.'

When he put his hand on her shoulder, she drew roughly away. 'A time to think? About what? When people separate to "think," it ends in divorce. Is that what you want? Tell me. Is it? A divorce?'

'Hyacinth,' Gerald soothed, raising a hand in a gesture of appeasement, 'let's calm down and talk together. Let's be civilized. It's you who just used the word divorce. But when you think about it, divorce isn't the end of life, you know. In some cases it can be a fresh, healing start.'

" 'Civilized",' she screamed. 'A "civilized divorce" – that's another modern cliché, isn't it? That's what you're aiming at, isn't it? Have you forgotten – oh my God, my God, have you forgotten how we loved each other? We were one. One mind. One body – have you forgotten?'

And sinking back in the chair, she sobbed and rocked and wept.

'This isn't good for you. You'll make yourself sick. And it won't be good for the children if you act this way. Jerry's a big boy now, big enough to wonder what's going on.'

When he reached over to stroke her head, she jumped up again and slapped him. 'Damn you! Damn you! You wanted me to abort him.'

'Control yourself, Hyacinth. We'll accomplish nothing this way. Let's talk peaceably. I want to be kind to you. The last thing in the world I want to do is to make you unhappy. But you have to listen to me.'

She was frenzied. The sky had fallen. The world had blown up. 'Do you mean it?' she cried. 'Say it right out: "I don't care about you, Hy, and I want a divorce." Say it. Loud, so I can be sure I heard it.'

'I'll never say I don't care about you, because it isn't true.'

She watched him neatly arrange the spoon on the saucer, parallel to the edge of the table. Neatly he placed the napkin to the left of the plate. These actions, in themselves correct, filled her with fury. That he could be so meticulous, so orderly, while at the same moment he was destroying their life! And with a savage swing, she tipped the table over on its side, hurling pot, cups and plates to the floor.

'Well,' Gerald said. 'Well. I see there's no use talking to you this morning, so I'd better leave our talk for another time. I'm going to the hospital. I still have patients to take care of, in case you're interested.'

'I'm not interested. Not at all. I'm interested in what's happening to my children and to me.'

'The children will have everything children need. As for you – you're unbalanced, Hyacinth. Look what you did just now. You can't call this an accident, either. You can't get away with that this time.'

'Are you saying you don't believe that it was an accident at the office?'

'No, I don't believe it, Hyacinth.'

'That I burned it down on purpose? Is that what you think?'

'Yes. You were in a jealous rage, and you took deliberate revenge.'

'I went crazy for a minute. I threw stuff off the desks. I broke things. But that's all I did!'

'That's not all. You're forgetting that a man died.'

'I'm not forgetting. I'll live with that till my own time comes. But I'm not crazy.'

'Let's not be so technical. Let's just say you're out of control. You're unbalanced. And I can't cope with that. I can't give the right care to my children, be a good doctor, and live with a woman in your condition all at the same time.'

'What do you mean by the "right care" for Jerry and Emma? That's my job. I'm the one who's home all day.'

'We'll talk later, I said.' At the kitchen door he paused and spoke solemnly. 'Hyacinth, I gave my word, and I'll repeat it. No one will ever, ever learn the truth about what you did. No one. I wouldn't do that to you or to the children. Remember that. You can sue me for divorce, for total incompatibility, irreconcilable differences, or whatever you want. I won't fight. It won't go to court. We'll simply settle. And this business will never enter into it. Now I'm going. I'm late.'

Silence fell. The house was too large, a lake without shores. She was swimming and her strength was gone, her arms and legs giving out. The walls were too close, as in a cell or an elevator stalled in a shaft with the last oxygen seeping away. She pleaded: What am I to do? There was no one dear enough to ask. Jim was dead, Gran was too old and ill, Francine's tragedy was too fresh, and even though Moira was a good friend, one still had one's pride.

Oh hello, Moira, I need to tell you something. Gerald wants to divorce me.

Get out of the house and into the air. Sit in the yard. Lie back on a lounge chair. I'm thinking I've just woken up from a nightmare. This didn't really happen. Go open the kitchen door and look. The table reminds me of a poor fallen horse that I saw, poor thing, with its four legs in the air. So it isn't a nightmare. Lie back in the chair and look up at the sky, all calm and blue. Geese come wheeling in and curving to the south. Shall I take my children and run away, run anywhere?

After a while it became uncomfortably hot, and she went into the house. The mess in the kitchen had to be cleaned. There were plenty of chores this morning, as there were every morning, all of them suddenly unimportant, but necessary. There on the table lay the blue compact, along with a pack of cigarettes. With all the strength in her arms, she hurled them into the garbage can, swearing with total strength that never as long as she lived would she put a cigarette between her lips.

'Never, never, so help me,' she repeated.

Then she lay down on the sofa in the living room. The classical station on the radio was playing a piano concerto, a piece familiar to her although she was unable to name it; simply, it was music that Jim had loved. One evening he had played it twice over on the CD, and Gerald had pretended he loved it, too. Gerald had pretended . . .

In late afternoon, the telephone range. 'Hello, darling,' said Francine. 'How are you?'

'I'm fine. And you?'

'Oh, my trip did me a lot of good. You know how I hadn't felt like going, but your brothers insisted that Jim would want me to start living again after all the crying I've done. So I went, and we talked about Jim, told some jokes about him, and I was able to laugh. I thought I would never laugh again. You should see Paul's new house. You and Gerald must take the children next summer and visit them. They have the most wonderful view—'

'Francine, you told me about it when you called last week.'

'All right, I won't fool you. I'll get right to the point. Jerry phoned me just now.'

'Jerry phoned? You mean he got the number himself?'

'Of course. He can read numbers. Gerald showed him how to use the phone, too. He called to tell me something's wrong. "Mommy's crying," he said. He heard you.'

'I was in my room with the door shut.'

'Well, he heard you.'

The further horror that her little boy was scared enough to do this and old enough to be that scared was too much. Hy's voice broke as she answered. 'Gerald wants a divorce.'

From one hundred miles away, Francine's gasp came over the wire. 'What? What?'

'He wants a divorce.'

'Why? Since when?'

'Please. It happened this morning. I can't talk now. I have to straighten up and fix some dinner. Please.'

'Hyacinth, I'm coming over. God Almighty, this is insane. I'll be right there.'

She couldn't, absolutely couldn't cope with Francine's visit now. 'No, Mom. Please don't come.' This was probably the first time since childhood that she had called her mother Mom. 'I'll be all right. You don't need to come. Please don't.'

But Francine had already hung up.

Driving at high speed through the early darkness, filled as she was with apprehension and dismay, Francine had been limp when she arrived. But this was no time to be limp; rather, it was a time for sharp eyes. These now traveled around the comfortable library to the shelves filled with books that Hyacinth had been collecting since childhood, then to the fine library steps and tall blue lamps of Danish porcelain and all the fine furniture that had been bought with Gerald's earnings.

He didn't need Hyacinth any longer. He was well on his way without her. It was as simple as that. Smooth as ever, he sat in his leather wingchair. All he needed now was a large handsome dog at his feet – an English setter or an Old English sheepdog would do nicely – and beside him a silver tray holding glasses and some rare scotch, to take his place in any fashionable, glossy magazine.

'Don't be angry with me Hyacinth,' Francine said. 'I didn't come here to take over the situation, I've never interfered for even one minute since you married, have I? But when Jerry phoned, I couldn't just sit back and do nothing, as if you were a neighbor on the next street instead of my daughter.'

Hyacinth, with her huge, tragic eyes, her blanched and devastated face, sat like a refugee in a war zone, too exhausted to say anymore.

'I know you're perfectly capable of taking care of yourself. I haven't any intention of treating you like a child, and if you want me to turn around and go home, I will.'

Neither Gerald nor Hyacinth spoke. Perhaps they had each already said all they had to say. Perhaps the presence or reasoning of a third person might clarify the air. And so she reasoned, addressing Gerald and, with effort, controlling herself.

'In an outburst of temper she upset the kitchen table, you tell me. And that's your sole complaint? While the neighborhood is talking about your affair with the babysitter? Just how would you expect a woman to react to that?'

'It's not only that. It goes much farther back, as I've been trying to explain. Hyacinth has been nervous and depressed for some time. She admits it herself.'

" 'Uncontrollable,' as you so delicately put it. If that's true, and I have my doubts because Hyacinth, in spite of a very infrequent burst of temper, has always been a rather placid, contented person, is that any reason for divorcing her? For abandoning her?'

'I'm certainly not abandoning her,' Gerald said, 'not at all. You don't let me finish.'

'Don't quibble with me, Gerald. This is too serious.'

'I didn't mean to quibble.'

He was being calm and cool, so therefore she must stay the same. But she was beginning to boil with rage.

'You see,' she said, 'there has to be a reason that reaches, as you say, "farther back." Now I strongly suspect that this affair is not your first one. So it is you who have really begun the change in the relationship that has ended in this mess.'

'This isn't about my miserable affair, for which I have sincerely – sincerely apologized.'

Hyacinth's voice was barely audible. 'And I've accepted it. That girl didn't really mean anything to Gerald, Francine. We still belong to each other.'

Belong to each other, Francine thought. Oh darling child, nobody ever belongs to anyone but himself.

'That's not the issue here,' Gerald insisted.

She must be equally insistent. 'I think it is. I think you have the seven-year itch. You're tied down here with a family, it's made you cranky, which has affected Hyacinth, and the whole thing has snowballed.'

'I'm afraid you oversimplify.'

'Then don't be so vague. By the way, what does your partner say about this?'

'He's a professional partner, that's all he is, and this is no concern of his.'

Francine, accepting the rebuke, tried another approach. 'You've been well treated in this family, Gerald, like one of our sons. I should like you to think about that before you take such a final, enormous step.'

'You mean the money? I've always been thankful. It was a godsend and I wanted to repay it, but Jim would not let me. I have every intention of giving it to Hyacinth now, in full.'

'It's not I who gave you the money,' cried Hyacinth in a swift change of mood. 'My father did. And I don't want a penny from you. Not like this. A bribe so that you can leave without any trouble and soothe your conscience? Oh, no! You were right, Francine! You were right!' She jumped up and fled from the room.

'Look what you've done to her, Gerald.'

'It's impossible to talk to Hyacinth. There's always so much wild emotion.' He shook his head. 'People divorce these days without tearing themselves apart. They agree to disagree.'

'Well, Hyacinth isn't one of those people. She married you with her whole soul, with passionate love, not a temporary – what did I say before – a temporary itch.'

'It's not that easy. You don't know the background.'

He was imperturbable, immovable, a hard man. After an hour she had made no impression on him. And forgetting her resolution, she loosed her fury.

'I predicted the "background" if you remember, after seeing you half a dozen times or less. You're a Don Juan. You change women the way a decent man changes his clothes. No, you never fooled me. She was a match made in heaven for you, my Hyacinth was, a sweet girl, refined and presentable, docile, and mad about you – until you got tired of her. You're bored with her. A whole new world is opening up for you.'

'You're a very smart woman, Francine, as I've said more than once, but this time you're off the mark. Yes, there's a little truth in what you've been saying, but there's a whole lot more than that. A whole lot that I don't care to discuss with you.'

As if to dismiss her, Gerald stood up. 'There'll be no fuss and no publicity I assure you. It will be a painless proceeding, an agreement outside the courtroom. I will pay the costs, and I will support her as long as she lives. Fair enough?'

'Fair? You bastard. And Jim trusted you! He's turning in his grave.' Francine shook her fist. 'Painless. You'll feel plenty of pain before we're through, my friend. Now I'm going upstairs to take care of my daughter, and the next time I see you, you can bet it will be in a courtroom.'

'Your mother took the children to school,' Gerald told her when Hyacinth came down well after nine o'clock in the morning.

'I overslept,' she said.

'It was the pill. You needed it. Are you feeling any better?'

'How can you even ask that?'

'Sit down and have some breakfast.'

'I'm not hungry.'

'But you need to eat. When I heard you moving around upstairs, I made french toast for you.' He got up and laid a plate before her. 'This is warm, the coffee's hot, and the orange juice is cold. Freshly squeezed, the way you like it.'

She had no desire for food, and yet the very act of seating herself was followed mechanically by the act of taking the fork into her hand. Habit, she thought; we run our lives on its greased wheels. Here we are in this kitchen together, not wanting to be together, but here because we have done it for so many thousands of mornings.

Gerald began: 'Your mother and I had some ugly words last night, and I feel bad about it. But it's hard to talk to her about what's happening without being able to tell her the whole truth.'

'You can't do that, Gerald. Francine has had enough right now. My father died on the pillow beside her. You're not to torment her with this arson talk.'

'Agreed. You have my word. How many times must I give it? Listen to me. If I didn't care about you—'

'About me? No, no. I've had an awakening, Gerald. Francine was right: I wasn't your type, if indeed any one woman could ever satisfy you.' Her words were so caustic that they seemed to burn in her mouth. 'You wouldn't have married me if it hadn't been for my father's help.'

Did I know it then, on that cozy winter evening when they played chess together? Did I know it and not want to know it?

'I'm ashamed that I have lowered myself like a jealous fool.'

When he did not answer at once, she saw that he was moved. Then he said very low, 'I never planned on a divorce, Hyacinth. Believe me. If it weren't for this fire, I would ask you, as I have asked you, to forgive me. And I would also ask you to go on together. But now that can't be, and I'll tell you why. There's talk about finding the person who set the fire. They're already looking. A cleaning woman who was at work that night in the brick building on the corner claims to have seen a car. The only car parked on the street so late. She remembers thinking that it was odd because nobody lives on that street, and there were no lights in any of the buildings. Let's hope she doesn't remember something about the car.'

Hy struggled for air. She saw herself screaming, helpless and hysterical, being dragged away to a hospital, or to a prison. And she crunched her fists in her lap.

'Fortunately, there are no fingerprints, at least so far. Debris and water may have destroyed them, I hope. But you see, you must see, that if you should become involved in this, inevitably I would be too. And there goes my reputation. What a fine heritage for Jerry and Emma!'

Still struggling for breath, Hy said nothing, and only kept looking at him. His hands, long-fingered and graceful, were resting on the table. I used to take them one by one in mine and kiss them, she thought. Once I told him I would have died with him on the *Titanic*, and I would have done it. I would. And all that was on my part, all that love, but never the other way. I see it now. I was so young then, living a fairy tale. Too young.

'You never loved me,' she said. 'I suppose I can't blame you. One can't force love. I only blame you for pretending you did.'

'It wasn't all pretense.' Gerald spoke as if he were defending himself. 'If it weren't for this fire, for what you've done, we would finish our lives together.'

'No,' she said. 'We wouldn't. I couldn't possibly stay in such a one-sided marriage and keep my self-respect.'

This was not what he had expected. He seemed to draw himself up, as if his dignity had been affronted.

'Well in that case, we should have no problem. You recall how I explained the way we'll do it? No courtroom, the whole thing uncontested, papers drawn up in the lawyers' offices, no custody argument, no trouble. We've about concluded the deal in Florida, and since the house is being sold as is, completely furnished and ready to move in, the children and I will be able to leave here by the end of next week. The legal business shouldn't take more than a few months. And I can always fly back to sign whatever needs to be signed.'

It took a few seconds for this to be absorbed by Hyacinth's overburdened brain. 'What did you say?' she cried. 'You're going to Florida with the children?'

'Yes of course.' Gerald spoke mildly. 'You don't think I can leave them here with you in these circumstances, do you? I thought you understood that I would have to have custody of them.'

A dam burst in Hyacinth. She began to scream. Over and over, her screams rang, choking terrible sounds with which a banshee or a tortured animal tears the air. Gerald ran to the window and slammed it shut. He shook her, grabbed her flailing arms and slapped her cheeks.

'My God, Hy, it's not that awful.' He was frightened. 'It's for their good. I say and swear that you may see them whenever you want. But we have to get them away from here. Can't you grasp that?'

Her teeth were chattering. Never before had her teeth chattered, nor had she had such a fearful pain in her chest. She gasped, 'You can't, you can't do this!'

'Lie down,' Gerald commanded. 'I want you to lie down in there and listen to me. But first you're going to swallow some brandy. Now listen to me. Take it, I said, it won't hurt you.'

Propelling her into the living room, he put her on the sofa and handed her a glass. She hurled it to the fireplace, where it tinkled and shattered. He poured a second glass, and this time forced it down her throat. 'Now lie there, Hyacinth,' he said, speaking not unkindly, but as a doctor might give an order to a hysterical patient.

Flattened like a rag doll she lay, thick tears draining toward her temples. Mocking voices kept repeating: Taking my children from me. Taking my children from me. They would visit her in a prison. She would be dressed in stripes. They would walk away from her in terror. My children. My life. What has happened to my life? Oh, Jim. Oh, Granny. Oh, God.

Time passed, and her tears ceased. Opening her eyes, she cried, 'What are you doing to me, Gerald? Do you hate me so much?'

'Hyacinth, I don't hate you at all. I care about you. But don't you see that it is for their sakes?' The deep, soft voice poured words meant to quiet and calm. Hypnotic in their repetition, they forced her to listen to them. Or perhaps, said another part of her brain, it is the brandy that keeps me lying here while the words flow.

'We'll do it quickly. We don't want to attract attention. It's for everyone's good, yours especially, Hy. You can't afford publicity. If they know that you and I have had troubles, they will point a finger at you. It's only logical. You don't know what clever detective work can come up with. These cases are never closed. They can open a case years hence. If I were to demand custody in court, I would have to reveal the truth, can't you see that? And remember this: It's best if your mother never finds out. She's a fighter. I admire her, but she has an idea she can manage anything. If you ever tell her, she'll get lawyers and the truth will leak to the newspapers, and that will be the end. Good God, I don't want that to happen to you! But a man died, Hyacinth. Remember that, a man died. And don't worry about the children. There's a fine private school and there's an available nanny, a nice middle-aged woman. No, don't worry about them. Now close your eyes. I have to go out. Your mother should be back soon.'

She was still lying there when Francine returned and stood over her. Now would come the quick questions, demanding to be quickly answered.

'Have you had breakfast?'

'No.'

'I saw Gerald making french toast. He said it was for you. Expecting me, I daresay, to be impressed by his kindness.'

'I didn't eat it.'

'Did you speak to him?'

'Yes, we spoke.'

'I didn't even look at him. I'll look at him in court.'

It was no doubt ungrateful of her, but she wished that Francine would go home. There would be so much talking now, and all of it useless, since it would only be circling around a truth that was not to be uttered.

'You need to have some food in your stomach. When did you eat last?'

'Lunch yesterday.'

'Stay there. I'll bring you something.'

Francine made brisk noises. Her heels clacked. In the kitchen, she clattered things. Hyacinth, recognizing the sounds, felt the start of a small, wan smile. It struck her as odd that she was able to smile right now, and yet perhaps it was not so odd: the smile was sad, a reminder of normalcy and of mundane things, like the purr of a refrigerator or the rumble of a furnace.

'I've brought tea,' Francine said, setting the tray on the coffee table. 'I couldn't find the coffee. Now eat this egg. You need protein. And I bought these muffins after I dropped the children off at school.'

'Aren't you eating anything?'

'I had breakfast where I bought the muffins. I stayed away so you and Gerald might have your talk.'

Francine's black patent leather shoe was tapping the carpet. She was nervous. But she said nothing until Hyacinth had finished the breakfast, when she removed the tray and came back with a hairbrush.

'You need a brushing. Turn around,' she commanded, and when Hy obeyed, assured her, 'This will be soothing. Your scalp's all tight. Do you know you have beautiful hair? And don't say it's too straight the way you always do.'

The pleasant tingle and the steady motion of the brush was making Hy feel drowsy again. Once Gerald had explained that, while most people are unable to sleep when they are under stress, some people escape their stress by going to sleep. Maybe I'm like that, she thought. Yes, I guess I am. *Sleep. Perchance to dream. Or never wake up.*

'Tell me, did Gerald ever tell you that your hair is beautiful? Or ever say things like that to you?'

'A long time ago, he did.'

Francine made no comment but kept on brushing. How good it would be to tell her everything, to drop it all, past and future, into her lap as a child comes home from school with his problems and knows that there will be aid for him! But she was not a child and had never wanted to be one; she had taken good hold of life until now. Now though, she was a victim . . . And before she could stop it, she gave a long, profound sigh.

Francine put the brush down and moving to a chair across from the sofa, began the parade of questions that Hyacinth had expected.

'When and where did all this trouble begin? May I ask? In Texas, or here?'

There was no sense resisting. Answer as many as you can, Hy said to herself. When you can't answer, you'll tell her so.

'If I look back very thoroughly, I suppose I can find things even as long ago as Texas. And of course one sees more the closer one gets to the now. He flirted. Sometimes he was cross with me, though never with the children. And he hasn't been very — very affectionate. I thought he was overworked.'

'I see.'

There were the double vertical lines on Francine's forehead. And in a sudden access of love for her, Hyacinth cried, 'Thank you for not saying "I told you so, I predicted it!"'

'That's all right, darling. I could just as easily have been wrong. As a matter of fact, I have been thinking most of the time until yesterday that I was wrong.'

There on the mantelpiece was Gerald's photograph, taken on the day he received his diploma from medical college. He had that faint smile with the dimple in his cheek. I don't believe I'm sitting here having this conversation, Hy thought.

'He'll pay,' Francine cried. 'You'll get the best lawyer in the state. He'll pay in every way, monetarily and in shame, for what's he's done.'

'I don't want to go to court, Mom. I don't want his money.'

'Not take his money? That's ridiculous, Hyacinth. He *owes* you. Why, he never even repaid your father for what he insisted — I remember it well — was to be only a loan.'

'Dad wouldn't accept it. You know that. Be fair.'

'Fine, let that go. It has nothing to do with this issue, anyway. And as for not going to court — that's unheard of.'

'I don't want to go. I simply don't. We'll settle it out of court.'

'Oh, what a stubborn fool you are! You've always been stubborn, but this is the limit. It's absurd. There's no other word for it.'

Hy was reading Francine's mind. Yes, based only on what she knew, it was absurd.

'All right, Hyacinth. Let's keep nothing back. Did he have anything else to propose when you spoke this morning? Anything you might not want to tell me?'

A huge wall faced Hyacinth. Up and down its length she ran, feeling its immovable stones with the palms of her hands, reaching into it for a hidden way through.

Your mother thinks she can control anything. She'll get lawyers. You can't afford publicity. These cases are never closed. Twenty years for arson. And a man died, a felony murder in the second degree. A man was killed.

'I asked you, Hyacinth, is there anything?'

Her mind had strayed so that it took another few seconds before she could meet Francine's stern eyes and reply.

'Only that he wants to take the children to Florida for a while.'

'For a while? What on earth are you saying?' Francine's cry rang through the room and would have been heard upstairs if there had been anyone up there to hear it. 'You are letting him take your children away? I don't believe it!'

It was too much. Once victimized and now to be attacked again from the other side was too much. 'Please, please,' Hyacinth implored. ' "For a while", I said. Francine, I can't talk anymore. There's nothing I can do right now. Nothing. Believe me.'

'I believe you've lost your mind. What is it that you're not telling me?'

'Nothing, nothing. I'm telling you all I can. Oh, please let me alone. I need to be by myself.'

'What is this hold that he has over you? Why, this is blackmail! Don't I have any rights as your mother? Why won't you talk to me? I'm the best friend you have in the world, and you don't trust me.' Francine bent down and tilted Hyacinth's chin. 'Look at me. You can say anything to me, anything. Have you had an affair? That's how it looks. It's all I can think of. Yes, you had another man, and this is his revenge.'

Now Hyacinth rose so that the two stood face to face. 'You're tormenting me,' she screamed. 'No, I have not had an affair. No, and no, and no. Please. Go home and let me be. I can't stand any more, I can't—'

'You're going to see a psychiatrist, Hyacinth. We have to get at the bottom of this.'

'I'm not going to see anybody. Let me alone, I said.'

'If you don't go, I'll bring one here. I'm going to find somebody before this day is out.'

'If you bring anybody here, Francine, I'll run out of the house. I wish you'd go home and leave me. Go home! Go home!'

When Francine left and the front door closed, Hy went to the window, saw her mother get into her car at the curb, get out of it again, and come back up the walk to the door, where she rang the bell. The bell was a chime, and it pealed through the house.

Hy stood with her forehead pressed against the wall. I can't stand any more, she thought. But I have to live. I have my children, and I have to live. Oh, leave me. Everybody go away, you and everybody. I can't stand any more.

The chimes pealed and pealed, reverberating through the house. After a while, they stopped.

It is all habit, she thought later, as when this morning she had sat down at the table with Gerald only because she was accustomed to sitting there. So now according to custom she began the day's chores, the tidying, the fetching of the children at school and the preparation of the evening meal. She was divided, one part of her peeling a potato, while the other part watched her, a tall, slender

woman in a plaid cotton skirt standing in a puddle of sunshine on a
green linoleum floor.

The supper was over by the time Gerald came in. He had
already eaten in town. He inquired about her mother, and upon
learning that Francine had gone home, expressed his hope that she
might be feeling better.

'It's been a terrible year for her. She doesn't deserve so much
trouble.'

Compassion, expressed as it was with such propriety, was
intolerable coming from the mouth of Gerald. Yet his words in
some way restored to Hy's ears the sound of the doorbell's chime
that morning; she saw, too, Francine's car driving away down the
street, and was suddenly filled with pity for her.

She went to the telephone. It rang and rang for a long time.
Could anything have happened to her, agitated as she had been on
the way home? When finally Francine's voice came, Hy blurted,
'I'm sorry about this morning. Are you all right?'

'The question is: Are you?'

'Well, I got through the day, and I'm here.'

'So that's today. But what about tomorrow and the rest of the
tomorrows? I hope you're giving some thought to them and
changing your mind.'

'Francine, I can't change it.'

'I have to tell you I'm very hurt. And yes, I'm angry, too, that
you won't talk about this. Whatever you've done in your private life
is no business of mine. But it can't deserve what Gerald is doing to
you.'

If only it were the affair she believes I had, Hyacinth thought,
instead of what it is. My name in the news, and my children tainted,
even though fair-minded people will say it isn't the children's fault.

'And what is he doing to Jerry and Emma? Is he merely a beast,
or is he out of his mind? I think you both are. When is he bringing
them back? And how are you going to explain divorce to the
children?'

'Oh please, Francine, don't make it harder for me.'

'When I left you this morning, I went to ask for advice. So
listen to me. If you do go ahead with this, you have to tell the

children very carefully. Otherwise, they'll have all sorts of terrible thoughts, that one of you is going to die, or that it's their fault. They'll have nightmares, or start to misbehave. You need to learn how to tell them, what words to choose – oh, this is an outrage! Will you at least do that much?'

The widow in her poor black dress. Arson – felony. A prison sentence.

'I will. I will.'

'And fight him, Hyacinth. Show your stubborn side.'

'I'll do my best.'

'Where I went yesterday, the doctor, said that if you refuse to tell me what this is about, I must stop asking you. So now I've stopped. I only want you to remember that I'm here for you. I'm angry and hurt, but I'm here.'

When she put the receiver down, Hyacinth went to the back door to look out at the yard, where Gerald was playing with the children. Jerry and he were having a boxing match, complete with feints, fists and jabs, while Emma, quite fascinated, watched from her ring-side seat on the swing.

Fight, Francine said. Very fine, except that when you have no weapon, it's rather hard to do. Still, we do not have to use the word 'divorce' just yet, no matter what Francine says. This trip to Florida can be a 'vacation.' They will stay a while and go to a new school, while Mommy stays here because – well, because she needs to help poor, sick Granny a little.

And the little while will be how little? Let me not think about that right now.

They did not see her in the doorway, where she stood drinking them in with her eyes. Jerry, showing his small fists, was jaunty and tough; above his shorts, the summer's tan was beginning to fade. Emma said yesterday, with a wise nod, that Mrs. Darty – last year's nursery school teacher, about to retire at sixty-five – was having a baby.

'Yes, she is. She is! She told me!' When Emma was earnest, her braids bobbed.

And still Hy stood there. She was having such strange thoughts, scraps of thought really, questions without answers. Would Gerald be so fond of his children if, for instance, the boy were like Moira's obese little fellow, who already weighed half again what he should? Was it perhaps his children's often-admired beauty that endeared them to him? Would Gerald have trifled with other women if—

Let us not think about that, either.

Early one afternoon, Arnie came. There were cartons of clothing in the front hall and boxes of books, all Gerald's things that were waiting for shipment to Florida.

'Finality,' Hyacinth said as she saw him looking at them. 'The house is already starting to look abandoned.

'Abandoned? Does it have to be?' And at her startled expression, of which she was aware, he added, 'I've surprised you. Maybe I should stay away and keep my big trap shut.'

He was dressed in boots and the informal riding clothes that he preferred, an open-necked, warm shirt and a wide hat that he described as 'semi-cowboy.' It crossed her mind as always that he looked twenty years younger than he was.

'Come in,' she said.

'You don't want me in the living room. I'll smell it up with horse.'

He would, but it did not matter any more whether the living room smelled horsey or not.

'Come in,' she repeated, and then, proceeding to apologize for herself, 'I'm a mess. I've been getting Jerry's and Emma's things ready. It's a bigger job than you'd think.'

'And a sadder one. I feel terrible about this business, Hy. I know I should stay out of it, only your mother phoned me when I got back from the stable just now, and that's why I rushed here. She's worried sick about you. Thought maybe I could do something. She doesn't know, and I don't know, why the kids are going and you're not going. It doesn't make sense.'

The familiar, friendly eyes made an appeal to her, as if the man, knowing that he had no smooth vocabulary, wanted to compensate with warmth for the lack.

'Arnie,' she said, 'you're the kindest person. I know you would like to help, to do something if you could, but you can't.'

'Can't patch it up? Do a little reweaving, the way you do on an expensive suit? You don't throw it the hell out.'

Bereft of words, she threw up her hands.

'You can level with me, Hy. Gerald's told me it's about Sandy. I always had my suspicions anyway, you know. Geez, I'd have expected better taste from him. Why, he's finished with her already. Piece of junk, a tramp, a big you-know-what, that's all. Ten years from now she'll be a tub of lard.'

'It's more complicated than that.'

She was wondering tiredly, and dreading, the number of times she would have to dodge these questions and fabricate explanations. First, of course, there would be Moira, who in spite of her decency and affection, would have to be given the same evasions as everyone else would get. And after Moira would come a stream of others, unless of course the unspeakable truth should reveal itself . . .

'It was a stupid affair, not worth this, Hy. Frankly, I don't understand either one of you. Gerald loves his life, his work, the kids—'

Hyacinth interrupted, 'But not me.'

'Oh yes he does, Hy. He's tickled to death over your paintings, always talking about how you're going to be famous, always talking about what a great mother you are to the kids.'

'You don't know the whole story, Arnie.'

'I know it's a mess. Your mother said Gerald called her, and she hung up. Everybody's angry at everybody. Everybody's worried. Gerald is worried about you—'

Again, she had to interrupt. 'I assure you Gerald is not at all worried about me.'

He shrugged. 'Well, I don't know. I want to be neutral. I liked you both, first time I met you, and I still do. Gerald's my partner, and a good one. I respect him. We're going to have a great thing in Florida. I only wish you'd go there, too. Why the devil can't you just buck up and go? Take a chance that it'll work out fine.'

Ignoring his question, she asked one. 'Exactly when are you all leaving? We don't talk very much, Gerald and I.'

'Week after next. Hy, this is awful, the kids going without you. Seems like a dirty deal all around. I can't make head or tail of it.'

When she put her hands over her face, Arnie was silent until she had gained control. It occurred to her that, at least for the present, she must have cried herself out.

'Whatever the trouble is,' he said, 'it can't last forever. You'll change your minds, both of you. In the meantime, I'll be in touch. I'll be going back and forth. Got to get rid of the land under the building here. It's worth a bundle. And I've got affairs in New York, so I'll be running up here and seeing you pretty often. Tell you about the kids. I'll take them to the stables down there, teach them to ride. I always promised, and now I'm going to do it. They're great, cute kids.'

Suddenly there was nothing more to say. For a moment they looked at each other. Then Arnie spoke abruptly.

'You shouldn't go to the airport, Hy. Just kiss them goodbye at the front door and run inside before they see you cry.'

'I know. Are you on the same flight, Arnie?'

He nodded and stood up. 'Well, I'll be going. I'll give you my numbers, you can call me whenever you want, every day if you want, and I'll tell you what's happening. But you don't have to worry. Gerald loves those kids. You know that.'

'I wish it was tomorrow. Do you understand?'

'Sure. I don't understand the whole business, but I know what you mean. You want to get it over with. Well, it won't be long. Only a few days. They'll go fast.'

And mercifully, they did go fast. On the final one, Hyacinth smiled and kissed her children, who were too thrilled with the thought of the airplane to care about anything else.

'See you soon,' she said as they followed the luggage to the van and climbed in.

At the end of the walk, she turned back to the house. There she stopped to read again, and yet again, a clipping that Gerald had just put into her hand: Reopening of 4-Year-Old Mysterious Case of Arson.

Chapter Ten

First, after closing the doors of Emma's and Jerry's rooms so that she would not have to look inside, Hyacinth cleaned the house. The bed, which up until a few weeks ago she had shared with Gerald, must be totally refreshed. The heavy mattress must be reversed, and she would do it even if it were to break her back. The perfectly clean quilt must be sent to the cleaners, and the pillows replaced. His clothes closet must be scrubbed; even empty as it now was, she could smell his cologne. There was to be no vestige of him anywhere, not in the garage where he had forgotten a torn old umbrella, nor in the hall closet where he had forgotten his new raincoat. Up and down through the house she went, lugging the vacuum cleaner and a basket of dusters, furniture wax, brass polish, and anything else she could think of.

Her thoughts were as frantic as her legs and arms. 'How can I live with these thoughts? Right here in town in the cemetery on Grove Street lies a man who died because of what I did. His children will grow up without him. And my children will grow up without me. How can I bring them back? How?'

The telephone rang. Oh, please don't let it be Moira again! She's tactful, she stays away because she knows I don't want to see anyone. Still, I can't keep telling her the children aren't in school because Gerald has taken them on a short vacation. She doesn't believe me. It's a stupid excuse, but the only thing I can think of. I'm not thinking very well.

It was Francine. This was the third time today. Her voice was anxious, her question plaintive.

'Are you sure you don't want me to drive over, Hyacinth?'

'It's a two-hundred-mile round trip for nothing. But thank you anyway.'

'Don't be formal with me. If I weren't able to make the drive, I wouldn't offer. You might remember that I care about you.'

Dreading another round of insistent questions, Hyacinth sighed.

'I hear you sighing.'

'You think it's that I don't want you. The truth is I don't want anybody right now. I need to be alone, to get my thoughts together, not that my thoughts are worth much.'

'What have you been doing today?'

'Cleaning house. Throwing things out, things like our wedding photograph, for instance.'

Now Francine sighed. 'Take care of yourself, Hyacinth. Call me if you need anything. Promise?'

Like a mother, Hy thought. And she thought again, she could have said '*I told you so,*' and she hasn't done it. If I had only listened to her! But then there would be no Jerry, no Emma. My babies. In his hands. 'This rage will ruin me,' she said aloud. 'I have to stop it.'

For several days she had not left the house. Outside, the afternoon glowed with primary colors. The first yellow maple leaves, a few fluttering red oak leaves, and over all, a pure, cloudless sky. Winslow Homer would paint this sky. She herself had not touched a brush or even entered her studio in weeks.

Without making any determination to do it, she sprang up, took a sweater, and left the house. There was time enough before the shops closed to get to the bookstore and send two books to Emma and Jerry. Jerry was always pleased to read to Emma. It would make him feel proud and superior. She had a vision of them sitting on the floor, or on the bottom step – but what floor, or what step? Arnie said that the children's rooms overlooked a waterway, and that the house was beautiful.

To get to the bookstore, she had to pass what was left of the office, a scorched relic, its windows like blind eyes. The shine of prosperity and authority was gone, destroyed like the fire of her first love.

A woman in passing stopped next to Hyacinth, stared and murmured, 'Horrible. They say it was deliberately set. I wonder whether they'll ever find out who did it.'

'I wonder.'

Not wanting to have any further conversation, she went on toward the bookstore. The wreckage had produced in her mind a vivid picture of a man falling through flames. The scream of terror! The agony! An ice cold shudder penetrated her bones. Yet, if I were to spend the rest of my life in prison, she thought, it would not bring him back. All this accident has done is to give Gerald an excuse for getting rid of me, which perhaps not even fully realizing it, he had long been wanting. So now he is free.

We made such a nice couple, or so I always thought, both of us in our house, at our table with guests or on the lawn with our lovely children; an enviable couple we must have been to many who were not as fortunate as we. How deceptive is the surface!

At the bookstore, still in this frame of mind, she bought an easy storybook for Jerry and a picture book for Emma that was filled with animals; many of these were horses in preparation for the promised visits with Arnie to the Florida stables.

The man at the counter was friendly and talkative. He, too, bought books for his grandchildren, he said, for they were the most valuable present you could ever give to a child. A well-spoken man, he could have been a teacher. Yet in spite of his friendly talk, he was nervous, 'new on the job,' as he explained. Observing his wrinkled shirt and shabby tie, Hyacinth was touched. What had brought him here, no longer young and still unsure of himself? She tried to imagine his life, but of course could not, any more than he could possibly imagine hers.

It was a long way home, but Hyacinth walked slowly. There was no reason to hurry. Nobody waited for her. The autumn equinox was only a few days away, and dusk fell abruptly at the end of the short afternoon, so that lights were already shining in some windows. Where no shades were drawn, you could see people in kitchens, or a dining table with chairs around it, ready for use.

Arrived at the foot of the driveway, she looked up at her own house, where no lights were lit. A queer sensation flowed through her body, a feeling of emptiness, a feeling of having no feelings, where for so many weeks past she had been churning with conflicting emotions. She had been a pot about to boil over.

All of sudden, there was nothing to do. After her fanatical cleansing, the house was antiseptic, and no single possession was even an inch out of place. The spotless refrigerator was almost empty. Women living alone were apt to neglect their nourishment; well aware of that, it was nevertheless too much trouble for her to prepare any food. So, taking a pear and an apple, she sat down on the sofa and was starting to read the newspaper when the telephone rang.

Jerry's hearty voice blared in her ears. 'Mommy! We have a puppy! Daddy took us where they have so many puppies and we picked out our own. Then we bought him two dishes, one for water and one—'

A scream interrupted the account. 'Let me! I want to tell Mommy! You know what kind he is? A tannel, he's a tannel.'

'He's a spaniel, stupid, a king Charles spaniel. That's why his name is Charlie.'

'I'm not stupid! Mommy, he's brown and white. His tail is mostly brown, and I love him.'

Her heart was pounding so! Where a moment ago there had been chill vacancy, now all was melting soft and warm.

'I'll send you a picture of him,' Jerry said. 'Uncle Arnie bought me a camera—'

'It's for me, too.'

'You don't know how to use it.'

Now Arnie's voice came. 'I'm going to show Emma how to use it, Jerry. I meant it for both of you. Let me talk to your mother a minute when you are both finished.'

She wanted to hold them on the telephone. She could have listened to them all night. And her questions flew. As soon as one was answered, she had another.

Yes, school was nice. It had a red roof. Jerry had a friend, really two friends, because they were twins, Jeff and Larry, and they were *ezackly* alike, ezackly! And Emma went swimming yesterday. Wasn't it too cold? No, it was not in the ocean, it was warm, in a pool. Didn't Mommy know they had pools in Florida?

'And palm trees,' Jerry added. 'We don't have any at home. When are you coming here, Mommy?'

'Soon,' said Hyacinth, and corrected herself, 'I'm going to try to come soon. May I speak to Uncle Arnie now?'

'I know what you want to ask,' Arnie said. 'Everything's just fine. Believe me. I wouldn't tell you if it wasn't.'

'But are you able to talk right now?'

'Yes, Gerald's still at the office. I took an afternoon off and stopped here to leave some papers for him. Yes, everything's fine.'

'Just say – do they miss me?'

'There are questions about *"when."* You understand? But contented and busy.'

'I thought about Thanksgiving. If I could come then and see them at my hotel? I don't want to go to that house.'

'I understand. Let's see what we can arrange. I always tell you that I'm neutral, and I have to be, but I'm with you too, if that's not a cock-eyed contradiction.'

'Bless you, Arnie.'

After this conversation, she cried a little, controlled herself, and returned to the newspaper in which she, an always eager reader, now found nothing of interest. Finding nothing, she went as she often did into the deserted studio, there to stand in silent contemplation of her work. There was nothing more recent than last year's picture of Francine and Emma sitting on the garden bench in front of a butterfly bush. It was the sort of scene that the Impressionists always did so beautifully, and Hyacinth was not so foolish as to rank herself with any of them. Yet as she looked with a critical eye at her own work, she knew it was good. Indeed, it was very good.

Still, in these present circumstances, nobody could expect to find inspiration or energy for art. Oh, she would go back to it! She must. But not yet, not today.

Downstairs again, she put on a disk with quiet piano music and lay down on the sofa in the den, knowing well that she had been spending too much time on that sofa, dozing, waking, fighting her fears, and struggling to find some way out of the morass.

It was cold. Soon it would be time to start up the furnace. The very thought of the long, dark winter that was approaching made it seem colder still, and rising, she went to the hall closet, where an old shawl of Granny's had been lying since her last visit months ago. The color was a dull maroon that Granny liked and Hy did not, but it was warm, not only of itself, but because Granny had made it. And wrapping it over her shoulders, Hyacinth lay down again. After a while, her thoughts began to float along with the tranquil nocturne. All the sweaters, afghans and little dresses for Emma that Granny's hands had made!

And suddenly, she remembered something else: We never went back for the dress, in Paris. Such a lovely dress it was, with roses running down the front, and the rosy shoes to match. She could still see every detail of it. With a little patience – no, a good deal of patience – she could copy it, she could make a Paris copy for her Emma.

Having sewn many a doll's dress in her time, she knew exactly how to go about it. With a sewing machine, she could have completed it in a day. But she had none, and anyway, the French dress had been handmade. If you were particular, or as some people might call it, 'fussy,' you could certainly tell the difference. The tiniest scissors were to separate each leaf and petal from the flowered cloth, and the tiniest, invisible stitches were to apply them to the fine white linen background. This was to be a small piece of art. Working several hours every day until her eyes got tired, she finished it in a week. With some surprise, she realized that it had taken all of her attention in the same way that a painting did.

Now she made a plan. She would take this dress to Florida herself, perhaps for Thanksgiving. Arnie had promised to help her, and he would arrange it. Gerald would be ashamed to make any objection to it. Francine had also mentioned a visit to the children, so perhaps they would go together. The children loved her. And if she would promise to ask no nagging questions or make reproaches, it could be very pleasant to go together.

Armed with this first ray of hope in so long, Hyacinth took the dress with her and went out to the local department store with intent to find a pair of shoes for Emma.

R. J. Miller and Co. faced the town square. Now part of a small chain, it was the place that natives of the town liked to recall as the source of their baby clothes, their prom dresses and their bridal gowns. Hyacinth, by now a steady customer, went directly to the shoe department, there to find, as she had expected, that there was no rose-colored match.

The saleslady, who knew both Hyacinth and Emma, remarked that white shoes would be better than black patent leather. 'But it's such a darling dress. Do you mind telling me where you bought it?'

'I made it. I remembered one I had seen in France.'

'You made it yourself? What a lot of work that must have been. I'd love to show it to Mrs. Reynolds up in dresses. Would you mind?'

'Not at all.' It was good, after so much silence at home, to have even a few minutes' conversation with anyone who didn't know her well enough to ask questions.

'Jerry hasn't been in school, Kevin says. Oh, Florida with his father? Do they plan to rebuild the office in the same place?'

And then Moira, very gently, 'I'm not going to bother you, Hy. Whenever you're ready to talk, let me know. Let me know how I can help you.'

'This is really outstanding,' said Mrs. Reynolds. 'I'd like the buyer to see it. She's in the office waiting for Mr. Miller. I'll ask her to come out if you have time.'

All the time in the world.

The buyer, a smart young woman in black, was also impressed. 'It has that French look. Well, not every French look these days. But it does have charm.' Stepping back, she regarded the dress. 'It's interesting. Do you realize that anybody of any age can wear it? Have you thought of doing one like it in an adult size?'

'Not really.'

'Would you consider it if I wanted one for myself?'

Hy was astonished. 'Well, I don't know. I'm not a professional, I mean— I don't know. Sewing isn't even a hobby for me.'

The smart young woman was persistent. 'It's simply caught my eye. It really has. I'm going on a cruise, and I would love to have it.'

Hyacinth was not only more and more astonished, but immensely flattered. Then came a feeling that the suggestion was quite absurd. And that feeling brought an impulsive reaction: Why not? The evenings were long. So why not?

'All right,' she said. 'Although I'm not going to make a hobby or habit of it.'

'I'll pay a top retail price. I'm about your size, an eight. And I wear your length.'

Hyacinth looked down at her old skirt, a good tweed, the kind that lasts forever.

'I'm an eight, too.'

'Good. I'm really thrilled. Will you take down all the data, Mrs. Reynolds? Addresses and all that? Excuse me, I see Mr. Miller coming in, and I surely can't keep him waiting.'

'Mr. Miller,' Mrs. Reynolds explained, although Hyacinth had not asked her to, 'is the fourth generation in the family. He used to work at the store over in Oxfield, but he's been promoted to supervise all six of the stores.' Obviously, she was enjoying this little break in the sameness of the day. And she continued, 'He's a very bright young man. A lucky one, too. With all the changes taking place in this world, the R. J. Miller Company seems to be keeping afloat.'

Out again on the street, Hyacinth began to feel foolish. With only a few seconds' thought, she had promised to do something that a few more seconds' thought would have regretted. Since when had she become a dressmaker?

But having thus gotten herself involved, there was nothing to do now but return to the shop and buy more of the materials she had used for Emma's dress. After doing that, she walked slowly around the square.

Temporarily at least, the tranquility of this old town was soothing. Time had not exactly stood still here! You might say, rather, that it had slowed. It hadn't destroyed its past. The Civil War monument stood in the center of the park that long before that war had been a public green where cows grazed. In the heart of the shopping district the Red Cross met in an old clapboard house with the well still preserved in the yard. There was a friendly comfort here, even in the dry leaves rustling underfoot, and she dreaded going home. The thought of turning the key in the front door and walking alone into the empty silence was, as always, forbidding.

Perhaps she should stop at the bookstore again and browse for something new to read. Or perhaps go into the record shop for new music. Or do both. And turning about to recross the square, she reminded herself of the times she had criticized people who spend idle hours wandering around malls and Main Streets to gaze in windows or spend money on things they do not need. Ah, but now she knew how many of them were only trying to escape whatever it was that they needed most to escape.

She was leaving the shop with two books and the sewing goods in her hands, when a man coming toward her from the opposite direction stopped.

'Didn't I see you a while ago in Miller's dress department?' he asked.

'Why yes, I was there.'

'I had a glimpse of you as I was walking in, and then they told me about the dress you're making for Sally Dodd. There is an original story for you, I thought: our customer making a dress for our buyer.'

'I'm a little bit sorry about it. I'm worried that it may not turn out all right.'

'Well, if there is a risk, it's Sally who took it, so I wouldn't worry if I were you.'

Standing there on the narrow sidewalk, they were blocking traffic. She would have walked on, but he seemed to hesitate, which brought about an exchange of names, Hyacinth for Will, and a question about her direction.

'Across the square,' she said. 'I'm on my way home.'

'So am I. Do you mind if I walk with you?'

'No, not at all. I go left at the corner on the other side.'

'So do I. I'm staying with friends on South Street for a few days before my next stop.'

She had an impression of horn-rimmed glasses and a cheerful mouth. It was a nice face, healthy and ruddy, as if he had been in sun or wind.

'I always enjoy staying here. It's got a lot of charm, old houses and so much history. Before Miller's was built – my grandfather had a dry goods store here in 1910, a two-story and attic affair – this park was three times the size it is now. And way back, so they say, it was public grazing land— Oops!'

For the bookshop's paper bag had split, dropping two books to the ground.

Will picked them up. ' "Stephen Spender." I think continuously of "Those Who Were Truly Great." Do you know it?'

'Yes. "The names of those who in their lives fought for life—" How does it go? "Who wore at their hearts—" '

' '. . . the fire's center. Born of the sun, they traveled a short while toward the sun and left the vivid air signed with their honor." '

'Are you an English teacher?'

'No. Why do you ask?'

'Because I don't know many people, especially men, who can quote poetry.'

'If anybody had told me when I was getting a Master's in European Lit that I would eventually be working in the family stores, I wouldn't have believed it. The funny thing is that a person like me is supposed to be filled with regret, or even a little shame, about leaving academia, and I'm neither. I happen to like the business. I think I'm fortunate to have this chance. Tell me, do you enjoy shopping at Miller's?'

'Very much. I'm not a great shopper, but I can usually find what I want there.'

'Glad to hear it. I hope it wasn't a brash question, but to tell the truth, it's part of my job to keep in touch with the buying public whenever I can.'

There was a mixture of earnestness and self-mockery in the way he spoke. She liked him. But then, as Gerald always had said, she liked everybody.

Gerald. The name poisoned the air. Literally. It darkened the air. It lowered gloom, which was not helped by the fact that she was now about to enter the street where the scorched ruin was being torn down.

'And what do you do besides sell, may I ask?'

'I don't sell. I'm a painter. I used to work in a museum, restoring art.'

'What kind of painting do you do? Tell me about it. I'm an art lover and an art ignoramus, both at the same time. Whenever I'm in New York, I spend a couple of hours at the museums trying to get a slapdash, fly-by-night education.'

'I don't know nearly as much as I'd like to know. I just paint what I love.'

She was staring straight ahead so as not to glimpse the ruin. Nevertheless, she was conscious of his eyes upon her. At another time, she would have felt that slight *frisson* that comes to a woman when a man gives her a look of admiration.

'It's a long time till dinner,' Will said as they came to the corner, 'and I could use a sandwich. What about you? Will you join me?'

'Yes, I'll join you. I just remembered that I had no lunch.'

The place was messy. Mayonnaise oozed from the sandwiches and the coffee slopped onto the saucers. Will smiled, took paper napkins from the adjoining table, and wiped the saucers.

'Only one waitress,' he said. 'She's rushed off her feet.'

Gerald would have made a face and probably reprimanded the woman. Am I ever going to get Gerald out of my life? she wondered. Stupid question. He is the father of my children, and the master of my fate. In half a minute, he can destroy me.

She sat up straight. Will was talking to her, telling her about his father, who had not been well and should be taking it a little bit easier, but he was a workaholic, and you couldn't hold him down—

She must pay better attention. It had been weeks since she had spoken to anyone who was neither inquisitive, nor feeling pity, nor waiting for her to produce some explanation. So this contact should have been a relief. She ought to appreciate it and act accordingly. Yet it could lead to a complication. His eyes had traveled to her hand, on which there was no wedding ring. Most likely he was going to ask when he might see her again. Strange! Because really, she looked like the devil. How can you look, when you haven't been eating, haven't been sleeping, and haven't been exercising?

Now he was being very considerate, turning the conversation away from R. J. Miller to the subject he thought she would welcome. Did she find that the museums in France were more enjoyable than seeing all the Renaissance art in Florence? And was her own work realistic or abstract?

The conversation veered to movies, with agreement on comedy, tragedy, drama, and mutual condemnation of violence. It continued after the sandwich, on the walk that remained, and came to a halt at Hyacinth's front steps. At that moment, the street lamps came on and Will looked at his watch, exclaiming, 'I had no idea it was so late! They are expecting me at my friend's house. Oh, look at that pair, perfect specimens.'

The 'perfect specimens,' small and blond, were being led on a leash across the street.

'King Charles spaniels,' he said. 'I have one at home.'

Hyacinth thought: My children have one now in Florida. And the usual dart of fear, like an arrow, pierced her middle.

'This was nice,' Will said. 'Will you give me your telephone number? Here's a pencil.'

She wrote it, shook hands and went up the steps. Without trying to see, she was almost sure that he was watching her. Thinking, some young woman is going to be lucky, she opened the door.

'No, Arnie,' said Hyacinth, 'I really can't. I never want to hear his voice if I can possibly help it.'

They were having one of their customary telephone conversations, whose frequency astounded Francine.

'Arnie is unique,' she always said. 'I can't think of any man I've ever known, including your father, who would take so much time and trouble to help somebody in a crazy situation like this. He simply has to be in love with you, Hyacinth. That's the only explanation.'

Ridiculous. Arnie was extraordinarily thoughtful, that was all.

He was an uncle figure, younger than uncles usually are, but like a good one, kind and patient.

'I'm pretty sure Gerald will agree, Hy,' Arnie said now. 'He told you that you will be able to visit the children.'

'He can just as easily say no, not yet, and I couldn't bear that.'

'Well, as I always tell you, I'm in the middle, but what the hell, you seem to be a lot unhappier than he is over it all, so I do have to lean in your direction a little bit. I'll tell him he damn well has to let you have Thanksgiving.'

'I so want to go. We can eat at my hotel, plenty of people celebrate holidays that way, although we never have in all our lives. But if you have to, you do what you have to, and I want to see them so badly that it hurts.'

'Take it easy, Hy, take it easy. You're all worked up. I'll talk to Gerald and call you back by tomorrow.'

'Thanks, Arnie. I love you for it. Francine loves you already. She wants to come with me, and though I don't need her, I think it's a good idea. The children always have fun with her.'

'Well, you have fun. Me, I've got relatives in New York. They're all old as the hills, but they're expecting me, so I'll be heading north for the holiday while you're heading south. Well so long, Hy, and stay cool.'

True to his promise, Arnie had everything arranged, the agreement with Gerald, the plane tickets, the hotel rooms with the best view of the ocean and Thanksgiving dinner complete with chocolate turkeys in a private alcove off the main dining room.

'It'll be home away from home,' he said, 'even though Florida isn't usually your thing.'

Francine, on being told of all this, could think of no word for Arnie except 'angel.'

They were loaded down with gifts. Hyacinth had baked favorite cookies in two flavors. She had bought more books, a beginner's chess set for Jerry, a baby doll for Emma, who was already maternal, and clothes for them both, including first and foremost the Paris dress.

'It feels like Christmas, not Thanksgiving,' Francine remarked, 'except when you look out of the window. Then it doesn't look like either.'

Below them lay a world of color: blue-green water, scarlet beach umbrellas, green palms, and the blazing white of sand. To the right lay tennis courts, all occupied, and to the left lay a fractional view of the marina with a bare glimpse of what must be a sumptuous, gleaming yacht. The entire scene was festive.

'I'm so happy that I'm afraid I'm going to cry,' Hyacinth said.

Francine made no comment. So far today she had made no comments at all about Hy's affairs. Not that Hy had really feared she would. Francine had too much heart in her to spoil this day.

'Let's go down and wait in the lobby, Hyacinth. It's half-past, and they might be early.'

'I hope the nanny brings them.' She was dreading the sight of Gerald, even at a distance.

'Don't worry, when he sees me, he won't stay more than a second.'

The lobby was busy, not crowded to the point at which one saw only a mass, but merely busy enough so that the space was constantly in motion. While Francine read a magazine, Hyacinth watched. Now down here among people the Florida scene turned personal, which surely was the last thing she wanted it to do, yet could not prevent. A beautiful young couple with new luggage were on their honeymoon. An old couple sitting in the corner were laughing at some private joke. A father was carrying the heavy toddler, while his wife carried the infant. And she sat there trying not to see, while the earlier joy faded.

Francine glanced at her watch and returned to the magazine. Hyacinth glanced at her own watch and said nothing. The hour passed. A half hour passed.

'Holiday weekend,' Francine remarked. 'Heavy traffic.'

'It's not that far away, Arnie said.'

'Even so.'

Nevertheless, Francine was disturbed. There went her tapping foot again, making a soft slap against the marble floor. The sound was exasperating. I'm a wreck, Hyacinth thought, scolding herself for being exasperated.

'Perhaps we should phone,' Francine said. 'Give me the number, I'll do it.'

Hyacinth watched her walk away. Everything about her was perfect, her hair, her posture, the black linen suit, the white frill around her neck, and the single gold bangle on her arm. Two men swiveled their heads to look at her. She was older than they, but even so, they looked.

If your mother weren't so beautiful, Gerald had said. So many terrible things he had said. And Francine had known he would. Odd, isn't it, that she should be so wise and yet say such foolish things herself sometimes? When I showed Emma's dress to her she said that even though she loved America, she wished she were French. Well, I suppose I say some idiotic things sometimes. Here she comes. She doesn't seem pleased.

'There's no answer. I can't make head or tail out of this. Are you sure you have the time right?'

'Francine, I've been thinking of nothing else ever since Arnie told me weeks ago.'

'Well, then there's nothing to do but wait.'

They sat without speaking. After a while, people began to enter the dining room at the far end of the lobby. It was the dinner hour. The two women questioned each other through their worried eyes.

'Can there have been an accident?'

'No. They would have called us.'

Abruptly, Francine stood up, and abruptly spoke. 'We're going to the house. I'll get a taxi.'

Hyacinth, silent as the mini malls and highway signs fled by, twisted the finger where the paired rings had been; remembering then that they were gone now, she folded her hands together between her knees and tried not to think of bicycles that over-turned, of balls that slam into an eye, of drownings— Something surely had happened. He couldn't possibly have forgotten.

'This is it,' said the driver at the approach to a stone wall. 'What's the number again?'

Francine gave it to him. At a booth outside the wall, they gave their names to an attendant and were admitted. A curving drive led past flawless lawns, tennis courts and over-sized houses, white or pink. There were lush, enormous trees and vivid flowers. Shining cars stood in driveways, and over it all there was a gloss like a reflection from the sky. Or perhaps the blue enamel sky had absorbed a reflection from below. It was all unreal, the setting for drama.

'Wait for us, please,' Francine ordered when the taxi stopped before another large, pink house. 'Get out, Hyacinth.'

She was taking charge, which was something she had carefully refrained from doing since the day of Hyacinth's marriage and departure from the home – or no, since long before that. Like an ambulatory patient being led into an emergency room, Hyacinth followed her now as she climbed the three steps and pressed the bell at an impressive double door.

A woman answered. They had evidently interrupted her work, for she was carrying a bottle of window-cleaning fluid and wearing a surprised expression.

Francine, losing no time with irrelevant explanations, began briskly, 'We've come for Jerry and Emma. This is their mother, I'm their grandmother, and where are they?'

'Why, they've gone for the holiday. Their father took them and their nurse this morning.'

'Took them away? Where to? Has anything happened to them?'

'Happened? Why no, ma'am, they went to one of those islands, the Bahamas I think it is. I forget. Left me here to take care of the house and the dog.'

Hyacinth held to the wrought-iron rail beside the steps. Her hands were limp. Let Francine lead.

'But it was all arranged. The children were to stay overnight with us at the hotel and spend Thanksgiving Day. This makes no sense. Here we've come all this way – it's outrageous!'

'I'm sorry, ma'am, but it's not my fault.' The tone was defensive, and the expression of surprise had now changed to a flicker of curiosity mixed with distaste, as if to say: *So this is the absent mother. There must be something wrong with her.*

'You would think Gerald could at least have let us know,' Francine persisted.

'Oh, he tried, ma'am. I heard him say so this morning when he went to the telephone, but you didn't answer.'

'No, indeed we didn't,' Francine replied. 'We were on the way to the airport. It's beastly hot. We've been traveling, and my daughter isn't feeling well. May we at least come inside and have a drink of water?'

'I'm not supposed to let anybody in.'

'You're not supposed to let anybody drop dead at your front door, either. Go in, Hyacinth.'

As the door was held open for them, Francine said grandly, 'Thank you very much. So now we will just sit here for a few minutes if you'll please bring the water. You needn't worry, we're not going to steal anything.'

She knows we won't, thought Hyacinth. She's already noticed Francine's diamond.

The room in which they sat was open to a sea breeze. Long windows led to a terrace. Under an enormous tree – do they have banyan trees here in Florida? – lay a big, round sandbox with scattered toys on the grass. Across the hall was a light yellow dining room, the very yellow of the one at home, Hyacinth saw, with a crystal chandelier above it. And under the curve of the stairs were a doll carriage and a pink three-wheeler. So Emma must have grown at least an inch and a half, she thought, and thought too that she must not get sick here in this place. Must not.

Having brought water on a silver tray, the woman stood before them, hesitating. With awareness now so acute that neither a ripple of the curtains' folds nor an eyelid's flicker escaped her, Hyacinth felt the questions hanging in the air between the three of them.

'Was there any reason that they had to go in such a hurry?' asked Francine.

'Well, the lady who invited them was Cherry – you know Cherry on TV? With long red hair? The one who sings with the Rub-a-Dubs?'

'I've heard the name,' said Francine.

'Well, she's a friend of the doctor's. She comes here sometimes when she's not in California. Comes to this house, I mean.' The narration had begun to flow. An entirely natural and increasingly visible curiosity was combining with pride in being the purveyor of important information. 'If you ask me, I think Doctor did some work on her face. And she's not his only famous patient. I could name – oh, I could name – of course, I don't work in his office, but when there's company here at home and you wait on table, you can't help hearing things.'

A dream, all a dream, Hyacinth thought. This house. Gerald, Jr. – 'We'll call him Jerry, with a "J".' His merry eyes. Emma, a small, alert Francine. Her rose dress in a box at the hotel. This pompous, tufted chair in the corner. The sea breeze on my face. All a dream.

Francine asked when the children were expected back.

'Late Sunday night. In time for school on Monday.'

She asked whether the children were happy.

'Oh yes, ma'am, yes. Their father's real crazy over them. And the nanny is, too. That's Mrs. O'Malley. But here, she's Nanny. Got married grandkids of her own. You should see the toys upstairs, they could open a store. The other doctor, they call him Uncle Arnie you know, he's like Santa Claus when he comes. He takes them riding. Their father bought a pony for Jerry, and now Emma's got bigger, he got her one, too, last week. Oh, those kids have everything. Name it and they've got it. It's a wonder they ain't spoiled.'

The woman at that group meeting said her boy fell in love with his father's house by the lake. It happens all the time.

'Would you like to see their rooms, ma'am?'

The question had been directed to Francine, but Hyacinth shook her head.

Francine answered promptly, 'I'd like to see them.'

'But I want to leave now,' said Hyacinth, and to herself, protested: I do not want to see the beds where Jerry sleeps his tidy sleep and Emma lies in a mound of dolls and animals.

Francine, giving her an anxious glance, stood at once, and Hyacinth, thinking, I must look frightful, rose also.

'Who shall I say was here? Your names?'

'Just say the children's mother and their grandmother were here and that we'd like an explanation. Thank you very much. Have a nice day.'

'Explanation,' Francine repeated, back in the taxi. 'You really don't think we'll get one, do you? Are you all right? You're not going to faint or do anything crazy, are you?'

'That wouldn't do much good. No, I'm numb, that's all.'

By now it was dark. The view from the car's window was a rewinding reel under pulsing lights: mall, furniture outlet, pizza parlor, used cars, another mall — all these appeared and vanished. They were almost back at the hotel before either of them spoke again.

Francine was first. 'Never in my entire life have I been in such a rage. I'm grinding my teeth. What are we going to do now?'

'Fly home, I guess.'

'Just turn around and go back after being here for six hours?'

'I surely don't feel like stuffing myself on turkey at the hotel tomorrow, do you?'

'No. Oh for God's sake, Hyacinth, if you'd only talk to me. I feel like a blind person wandering around some foreign country without speaking their language, and I'm getting tired of it. A day like this takes ten years off a person's life.'

'I didn't ask you to come along. You wanted to.'

'All right, all right. This is no place for an argument, anyway. I'm going to have some food sent up to the room. Let's eat together and talk this over.'

You wouldn't believe that a human being who was so worn down could feel hunger, thought Hyacinth, but I suppose the body wants to live even when the mind doesn't particularly care. And yet of course, of course my mind wants to. Or it would if it only knew how. And pushing the empty plate away, she looked across the table at the night sky, where stars in small islands floated upon a sea of silver-gray clouds, racing and foaming across the hemisphere. Turner could paint it, she thought, recalling his pale sunsets, all pastel mist and vapor. So much beauty, so much color and life under the vast, mysterious sky, and only man defiles it.

Francine's voice jolted her. 'You always went to ask your grandmother's advice when you needed any. Why won't you ask for mine now when you need it? How do you think I feel about that?'

'Please don't be hurt. I am not going to ask anyone for any advice. If I were going to, I would ask you first.'

'This is beyond understanding, Hyacinth. I had not planned to bring up the subject during this holiday because I wanted us to have only joy with Jerry and Emma. But now that that's been ruined, I might as well speak my mind.'

'Speak it. I won't argue with you. I'll just listen.'

'I am completely frustrated. I have to admit that when I went to another source for professional advice, I got the same advice again: Your daughter is a grown woman and if there is anything she won't tell you, then you have to let her alone.'

'That's good advice.'

'No. It's like saying, well, she's an adult, she's sixty or eighty or twenty years old – whatever – so it's her right to take poison or jump from a bridge if she wants to. Don't question her. Don't stop her.'

'I don't want to take poison or jump from a bridge, I promise you.'

'I get the feeling sometimes that you do want to. All that stops you is your children.'

Hyacinth was silent.

Francine, in agitation, got up clumsily and rattled the dishes. 'This is a case of blackmail. It doesn't take a rocket scientist to figure that out, or one of them to figure out, too, that it has something to do with sex.'

'You've told me that before. You're convinced that it's adultery. I had an affair, and he caught me.'

'Well, and if you did? It happens. You could fight that easily in court. My God! He admits his own adulteries. Why won't you get a good lawyer? Give me a good reason why.'

'I've told you, I don't want to go to court, and I haven't changed my mind.'

Francine walked to the end of the room and back. I pity her, Hyacinth thought, even more than I pity my children. Right now they are probably having a good time without any worries.

'What is it that makes you so fearful? A hit-and-run accident? Have you been caught shoplifting? Whatever it is, you need to confide in a lawyer. That's what they're for. If you'd let me, I'd find the right one for you. Your father had so many friends and contacts.'

The final wreckage. This is exactly what Gerald predicted Francine would bring about. It would all come out into the open, and it would then depend on the lawyer to get a reduced sentence for her. Fifteen years instead of twenty? With time off for good behavior?

'I appreciate it, Francine, but I already have a lawyer. Right now we are drawing up papers which I will sign.'

'Papers! Pray God you're not signing your life away. You see today how you can trust his word, don't you? He's evil. Evil! As long as he can live as you've just seen, a prince in his palace with no obligations he doesn't want, he'll see you on the streets.'

'You're wrong about money. He's been sending checks every week, sizable checks.' Hyacinth gave a short, scornful laugh. 'I send them back.'

'You what?' Francine was furious. 'I don't believe what I'm hearing. I thought you had some intelligence. A normal woman would take all she could get out of him and try for more, considering what he's doing. There'd be no limiit to her hatred.'

'There's no limit to mine,' Hyacinth said very low. 'That's the reason I won't take his money. I want nothing from him. I don't even want to touch the paper that he touched when he wrote the check. I want to forget that I ever knew him.'

'That's rather hard to do, given the existence of Emma and Jerry.'

'Please. Let's not be angry at each other. The day is bad enough as it is.'

They stood there looking into each other's sorrowful eyes, until Hyacinth broke the stillness.

'I wonder why he did this to us today. Can it possibly give him any pleasure to be so cruel?'

'You know, I don't believe he thought much about it at all. He telephoned, we had already left, so that was that. He was too thrilled about the celebrities at Cherry's place to think about anything else. He was only being Gerald, the real Gerald. Come, let's pack these presents again and take them home in the morning. Tomorrow's another day.'

Back home again, outside of the supermarket, Hyacinth came face to face with Moira, who was unloading a heaped food carriage into her car. Hyacinth, with one bag in her arm, was walking home.

'You'd think,' Moira said, 'that nobody'd ever eat again after stuffing himself on a holiday, but here I am.'

In her kindly way, she was making easy conversation, as if the two of them were seeing each other almost daily as they had done before Hyacinth's life changed.

'So you've been seeing Emma and Jerry. How are they doing under the palm trees?'

'Oh fine, Moira. They're in a very good school, didn't mind the change, we had a good time, my mother went with me, the weather was fine, just balmy—'

Lie. Why not lie? It doesn't hurt her, and it's easier for me.

'You're not sunburned, I see.'

'No, not in those few days. I never like to anyway. I'm not a sun lover.'

'Do you want a lift home?'

'Thanks, no. I need the exercise. It'll keep me from spreading.'

She stopped, ashamed of herself. What a stupid thing to say to Moira, who, still only twenty-eight, already had at least twenty extra pounds of spread on her bones! The matter with me is that I'm not thinking. I'm befuddled. And the jaunty act that I put on doesn't fool her for one minute. Go on and make amends. Make some amends, at least.

'The reason I haven't seen you, Moira, is that I've been in bad shape, not very good company. That's why I let him take the children when he moved. It's better for them until I straighten myself — until things are straightened out. It's temporary, only temporary, you understand. I should have called you to explain. You've been such a friend.'

'Don't give it another thought, Hy. Just take care of yourself.

You've had a lot of trouble, but I have to tell you that nobody'd ever know it. You look wonderful.'

'Thank you. I try. I have to get ready for Christmas, and it'll be here before you know it. They'll be flying up from Florida.'

That at least was the truth, for Arnie had made the Christmas arrangements.

'*Gerald asked me to telephone you after you hung up on him. He's been really upset. He never intended to have it turn out that way. When he left the message on your answering machine that morning, he had no idea you had already left so early. I am telling you the truth, Hy. I suggested that he make up for the mistake at Christmas. So the kids will be flying in on the twenty-third, and I'll be with them. Gerald knows, of course, that you don't want him. So just put some extra water in the soup for me.*'

'That's great.' Moira was enthusiastic. 'We'll have to get together with all the kids. Do something nice and have a good time.'

With a repetition of 'Take care,' she drove away. Not everyone, perhaps not anyone, would have let me go so easily, thought Hyacinth. She, loyal as she is, will be the one who checks the gossip the next time she finds herself in a group. Whether at a PTA meeting or a Little League game. Wherever women gather and talk about what is happening in the neighborhood, they will speculate about the strange affair of Hyacinth and Gerald; Moira will do her best to stop it; but it won't work.

Well, that's only human nature, she was thinking, when on entering the house, she heard the telephone ring. That was a rare sound so early in the day; usually at that time it was Francine, who never missed a morning. This time, though, it was not Francine. It was Will Miller.

'I phoned you the day before Thanksgiving. I didn't leave a message because I thought you might have forgotten me. Anyway, I'm in town for the day, and if you'd like to have an early dinner with me, I would like to have an early dinner with you. Will you?'

There followed a thousandth particle of time in which electrons and neutrons whirled through Hyacinth's head, and there was no solid thought, but only fragments of it such as: He knows nothing about me. What if I'm seen? I have nothing to say. I don't know anymore how one talks to a man. I'm too tired to bother. I'm burnt out. This is all fraudulent. I don't want to go.

'Why yes, how nice of you,' she said.

'Great. Since I have to get back early to Oxfield, would you mind six-thirty?'

'That happens to be my favorite time. I always like early dinner.'

'I'll come by for you at a quarter past.'

The moment after the phone clicked off, and if she had known where to reach him she would have called back and made an excuse. At any rate, it was too late now, and she was annoyed with herself.

On the other hand, it might be enjoyable, simply to avoid the long evenings in which, after being tired of reading or listening to music or watching television, tired and determined not to succumb again to fright and tears, there was no choice left but bed and the hope that she would not lie awake listening for the creak of settling wood.

Upstairs, she glanced at a mirror. Moira had said she looked wonderful, but there was no possible reason why she should. The effect of weight loss on an already slender face is not supposed to be flattering. Lingering now to study this effect, she found it on the contrary to be rather good. There were no hollows in her cheeks, yet the faint shadows underneath her eyes did seem to have made them grow larger. The long hair falling along her cheeks gave her a Renaissance look, not necessarily beautiful, but interesting, perhaps even mysterious.

'Get real. You are one big, damn fool!' she exclaimed, and was upbraiding herself for being one when the telephone rang again, surely Francine's ring this time.

They spoke briefly, as usual. A covert decision had jointly been made not to discuss the issue that lay like a burning coal between them. The reason for Francine's calls was motherly. She wanted to know about Hy's plans for the day.

'Believe it or not, I've been invited to dinner tonight,' Hy reported, and went on to explain Will Miller.

'But Hyacinth, you don't dare. That's all you need, to have Gerald find out that you're running around with men on top of whatever else it is that he's already got against you.'

Running around with men. Hyacinth felt a chill. If that were really all Gerald had against her!

'You're right,' she agreed, 'although this is totally innocent. I told you, it's only on account of that dress I made for Emma.'

'No matter. You can't be seen anywhere with another man until the divorce is final and the papers are in your hand. And if you ever want to get your—'

Children, she meant. Hyacinth, letting that pass, promised that this would be the only time.

'I don't know where he is, so I can't call it off, you see.'

'Well, go someplace where you won't know anybody. Do be careful.'

As it happened, Hyacinth could hardly have been more careful. The chosen steakhouse was in a remodeled barn half an hour's ride from town; popular in the warm seasons and on weekends, it was unfrequented now in midweek and in a drenching December rain. There were no more than three or four couples far apart in the large room. The fireplace glowed, and conversation was low.

'Very cozy,' remarked Hyacinth.

'I thought you would like it. I thought it was your kind of place.'

'But you don't know me,' she said.

'One gets a feeling about people.'

'Sometimes one is mistaken.'

'Very true.'

It was also true that, as she had feared, she did not remember how a woman starts a conversation with a new man. Once married, unless you were out in the world, you only met other women's husbands, and then your own husband was generally present. You don't *address* a man. She certainly didn't *address* Arnie, or treat him any differently from the way you would treat a kind and conscientious cousin.

He took off his glasses. 'I really need them only for reading, but when I'm at work, I keep them on so I won't lose them. I'm a great one for losing things, car keys, gloves, anything.'

She smiled acknowledgement. His eyes were deep set between prominent cheekbones and forehead. They were at once lively and earnest.

'So tell me,' he began, 'about Stephen Spender. Have you gone through the complete collection?'

'Yes, I took it along on a plane trip to Florida and return. I kept thinking all the time that there's a man I would like to know.'

'Yes, you do feel like that when you read or see anything really great. I would like to have met the sculptor who made the statue of Lincoln in the Memorial. So I know what you mean. Do you like Florida?'

'I don't know it well enough to like it or not. This was a very short visit.'

He was waiting for her to continue. And she knew that the pause was awkward. It was like one of those horrible moments at a party when a dozen people who have been talking criss-cross around the dinner table all suddenly fall silent. He was probably thinking with regret that he had misread her; the first time in the coffee shop she had been reasonably sociable, but not now. What could he know of the turmoil inside her, the sense of guilt because she was here under false pretenses?

'What is it?' he asked gently. 'I see so many changes of expression on your face. But if it's none of my business, and I know it isn't, tell me right now.'

'I'm worried,' she said, making a quick decision. 'I'm in the middle of a divorce, a nasty one, as I suppose most of them are.'

'I wondered. I didn't think anybody would live alone in a house that size.'

'Right now I am alone in it.'

If he were to ask whether she had any children, what would she say? When he did not ask, she was thankful for not having to repeat the faltering explanation of their absence that she had given to Moira.

'And so what do you do with your time while you wait for the worst to be over?'

'Well, I'm an artist, as I told you, although I am afraid I haven't been working at it lately as much as I should.'

'Understandable. Do you work at home?'

'Yes, I have a good room for it, northern light and all.'

'May I see it sometime?'

'Oh, surely. You may be disappointed, though.'

How coy that was, an arch reply that made her feel absurd, as if she had been fishing for a compliment. Words simply were not coming to her tongue.

Making no comment about that, he asked instead about the dress that she was making for Sally Dodd.

'I've scarcely begun it, to tell the truth. I wish I hadn't undertaken it.'

'But you did promise it,' he said gravely, 'and she's waiting for it.'

'I know. I'll do it.'

'In time for her cruise, you remember.'

'Yes, yes.' And she repeated, 'I'll do it.'

His eyes were so intense! Like opals, their lucid grey had flecks of green when the candlelight flickered past them. Nothing would escape those eyes; they would see through you, your pretensions, your evasions, and your falsehood. No, she would not see him again, not solely because of Francine's reason, which was a sound one, but for some other reason that she could not name.

'Where did you learn to sew?' he asked.

Glad of a changed subject, she answered promptly, 'My grandmother taught me. She's the last of her breed, I think, a totally domestic woman, born in 1910. She made an art of everything from cooking to hooking rugs. And cleaning floors, too, I shouldn't wonder.'

'I had a great-grandmother like that. I never knew her, of course, nor the other one, either. That one was different. She worked with her husband in the first R. J. Miller store. We have a dark brown photograph of that store in Oxfield, taken in 1899. The two of them are standing at the doorway, and there's a buggy parked on the street. The street is a wide dirt road in the heart of Oxfield. I wonder what they'd say if they could see it today.' Will chuckled. 'They were a great pair, or so I'm told. I guess the higher you climb on the family tree, the more virtuous the ancestors become.'

He went on the explain how the business had grown, and she paid him the compliment of listening carefully. Actually though, his account was interesting. As the daughter of a salaried chemist and the wife of a doctor, she knew almost nothing about business, how risks are taken and money is made or lost.

Freed of tension for a while, Hyacinth began to relax. Will had some marvelous stories to tell, such as for instance, the time a new salesman, not recognizing the head of the company, refused to show him a certain leather belt because 'it wouldn't be right. This belt is too expensive for you.' She liked his sense of humor. There was nothing caustic or mean about it. He had as well an appealing modesty. She had made a comment about an Indian sari shown in Miller's window, and from there the talk had drifted toward far places. He had seen Burma and Tibet. But unlike so many people who would leap to display and brag about what they had seen there, he made little of it.

He's different, Hyacinth thought. So many people are only poor, thin surface. But he has depth. And she thought again how it is when you open a new book and read the first page, you do not want to put it down until you have read it all.

They drove back through the town past Miller's windows, around the square, and into the street where Arnie's building had burned down.

Will remarked, 'I happened to be here that day, driving in very early. It was a fearful sight, the gathering crowd, the ambulance, and the flames that you could see through the broken windows. There's talk, or so I've heard, that it was arson.'

'I didn't know.'

'It was a fairly new building, too. Now you take an old firetrap like ours over there on the square, and you really worry. If I were in charge, I'd take it down and put up something with every possible safeguard. But you'd be surprised at the objections you hear. There's something about the old and the familiar that a lot of people love to keep. They find it's quaint, I suppose. Others would call it dowdy. Difference of opinion.'

Now, for the rest of the short way home, she neither heard nor cared what else he would say. She had only an awful sense of the sword suspended above her head.

At her door, Will took her hand. 'You know I want to see you again,' he told her, 'but I won't press you this minute. I hope you'll soon have your divorce behind you.'

'I hope so,' she said.

'I'll be away until after New Year's. I'll see you when I get back.'

Watching him go down the walk and get into his car, she thought as she had the first time: Some young woman is going to be lucky.

But there's no way I'll see him again. I'm sure he thinks I want to, and I'm sure most people would assume that I do, but I don't. I don't want any man, not any man, ever.

Hyacinth had set the Christmas table with the same care she would have given to a formal dinner for twelve. Four candles surrounded the centerpiece of pink and red carnations, a present from Arnie – accompanied incredibly by a magnificent Danish silver bowl to hold them – all given as casually as one might give a piece of pottery. The children's milk was served in wineglasses. From the china to the nuts and dates in their traditional bowls, the family's traditions had been kept.

Dressed for the occasion, they sat in their usual places. Jerry and Emma, she proud and pretty in the rose dress, sat at Hyacinth's left, with Francine at her right. Only the composition of the family had changed. A chair which would have been Jim's now stood against the wall. And the chair in which last year at this time Gerald had presided, was occupied by Arnie who, though not a member of the family, was surely doing his best to warm the atmosphere.

Hyacinth was also doing her best to ward off a gloomy, chilling sense of flying time: In a handful of days, in a few hours, it would all be over. The cheer was false. For two weeks past or longer, it had deluded her. Deliberate in her joy, she had fooled herself with all the 'normal' preparations, buying presents, baking and cooking, and opening the two bedroom doors that had been shut. It had begun to snow, and she had even bought new sleds, one of them for herself; they would drive out to Nod's Hill, take sandwiches and a thermos of cocoa. They would – oh, these 'normal' preparations!

When she could barely talk to them without being afraid to break down. So far, she had not done so, and pray God that when the time came for them to leave, she would not do so.

Emma was making an announcement. 'It doesn't snow in Florida. Mommy, don't you hear me? I said it doesn't snow in Florida.'

'Everybody knows that,' Jerry said.

'Who cares?'

Last summer, Emma would either have cried or become indignant at that. Now she had learned to give a scornful retort. She was preparing for kindergarten, getting ready for the real world. If you don't see a child every day, if you have to wait weeks or months, you'll be seeing a new child each time. You'll have missed everything.

'How is Charlie?' asked Hyacinth.

Emma replied, 'He doesn't weewee in the house anymore. Daddy taught him not to.'

Without intending to, Hy glanced at Francine. There had been surprisingly little mention of Daddy since the children's arrival, she thought, but each time there's been a barely visible change in Francine's face. Anyone familiar with her usual animation would know that she was being too quiet. And I was hoping she would keep up the chatter. Instead, it's Arnie who fills and refills the silences that make children restless. He did so now. 'Tell about my new horse, Jerry.'

'Oh, yeah. It's a Tennessee Walker, so big, you should see. And you know what color? Pinto. That means spots. Brown spots on white. I can't ride him, he's too big. But Uncle Arnie's teaching me to ride the pony.'

'Nanny takes me to visit the stables sometimes,' Emma said. 'And then I can get a ride. Daddy doesn't come. He likes his boat. He takes us on his boat. It has sails.'

'That's nice.' Hyacinth smiled. Boats and horses, she thought. I suppose they're only different in degree from the toys in their rooms upstairs now. We're both buying love. But never say anything against Gerald. Don't poison their minds. You will only hurt them. It's elementary. Francine knows that, too.

'When are you coming to Florida with us, Mommy?' Emma asked. 'I miss you.'

'She cried,' Jerry said. 'I didn't because I'm older, and besides, I told her we can come here to see you. Daddy said so.'

Now Emma wailed. 'But why? Why do we have to come here to see Mommy?'

Of the three adults, none had an immediate answer until Francine said, 'You see, Granny is sick, and your mommy wants to stay near her for a while.'

'Granny can go to Florida, too.'

'No, Emma. She's too old.'

'Then you stay with her. I want Mommy to come to Florida.'

Why doesn't he just die, thought Hyacinth. Just die and let the rest of us live in peace. But no, he will live to be a hundred. So, it's I who should die . . .

'I think you're getting a divorce,' Jerry said. 'That's what it is.' He was waiting for an answer. We should have told them right away. I guess we – I – thought something might happen, some magic, some miracle, and all this pain would go away. No, actually I knew it would have to be done and was only putting it off until the paperwork was finished, and then there'd be no more excuse.

'You're probably right,' Arnie said, coming to the rescue. He spoke calmly, as if a divorce were really nothing much, nothing to get excited about.

Well, in many places, it isn't. Perhaps not even for children these days it isn't. But not for my children. My children are soft.

'A lot of kids in my class,' Jerry said importantly, 'a lot of them have parents who are divorced. But they all live with their mothers. The dad comes to visit.'

Arnie agreed. 'As long as you can see them both and everybody's happy, there's nothing to worry about.'

Emma's eyes were wide and her mouth about to tremble with a sob. 'Are you happy, Mommy? Don't you want to live in our house?'

Our house. How do you answer that? Then, mercifully, inspiration came. 'We can have two houses and can take turns and be very happy.'

How am I able to do this? In another minute, I'll crack.

As if Francine had guessed how close Hyacinth was to that cracking, she stood and brightly gave an order. 'Kids, we can talk about this later. The cake is out of the refrigerator, it's got chocolate whipped cream on top, and we need to eat it right away. So each of you take his plate and help me clear the table. Your mother's done all the cooking, so now it's our turn.'

From her seat facing the window, Hyacinth saw by the street-lamp's glow that it had begun to sleet. 'Sleet,' she said, and ran not so much to pull the curtains close as to control and hide the start of tears. By his silence, she understood that Arnie was making it easier for her to hide them. Somehow, when you looked at him or heard his speech, you would probably not expect him to have such delicacy of feeling. And yet, this was not by any means the first time he had revealed it.

The dessert was superb, a specialty out of Granny's recipe book. It brought the silence of appetite and satisfaction to the table. Only Francine, who was a self-styled 'chocolate' freak, hardly touched it. When several portions had been had and the cake was devastated, she spoke.

'Hyacinth, it's been a long day, and it's late. Why don't you go up with Jerry and Emma. You have lots to talk over, while I clean up. No, don't protest.'

What she meant was: Talk to them about the divorce. I can't do it, since I really don't know anything about it, do I? And besides, it's not my place to do it. You're their mother.

Francine was even angry at the dishes, which had been part of Hyacinth's 'trousseau.' Jim had urged them on her after Hyacinth had said that they were outrageously expensive. 'But you love roses,' he had told her. Francine recalled the time distinctly, a dark afternoon, a freezing snow like tonight's. But who could have foreseen this night? Even she, with all her doubts, could not have imagined it.

'Let me help you,' Arnie said. 'I know all about dishes. I'm a bachelor.'

Gerald, too, had liked to make himself useful, at least at the start, when it was essential to ingratiate himself. But Arnie was different. She liked him.

'If you really want to help,' Francine replied, 'you can tell me, please, what's going on with your partner. Hyacinth is keeping some secret, the situation is shaky as you saw just now at the table, and I am sick with worry over it.'

Arnie gave a long, whistling sigh. 'If I could tell you, I would. I'm very fond of Hy and don't like this crazy separation from her children. It's wrong. Wrong. But I can't get anything out of Gerald, and frankly, I've stopped trying. It makes for a delicate situation, you understand.'

'I do understand. Partners don't break up because one of them is having a marital problem.'

'Exactly. Gerald's a great doctor, and' – here Arnie gave a sheepish grin – 'and he has a great social life, too. Who was that guy who had all the women? Don Juan?'

'So that's what he does with his free time.'

'You mustn't think he neglects the kids. Got to be fair and square. He's crazy about them. They have a nice nanny, takes good care of them. He likes to show the kids off. Proud of them.'

'Yes, because they happen to be beautiful, both of them. That's why.'

'Gerald would like to talk to Hy sometime, but she hangs up the phone.'

'She can't talk to him, Arnie. It would be unbearable. He has destroyed her faith and trust – or almost, because she does trust you.'

'I hope so. I would do anything to help her.'

'I wish I could, God knows, but until she tells me, or somebody does, what's at the bottom of this affair, there's nothing I can do. I think of her all alone in this house when we leave.' A cry, against Francine's strong will, came out of her throat, out of her heart and soul. 'So tender, so trusting! Filled with goodwill as she has been all her life! Even as a child, she was kind, not like most other kids, the selfish little beasts, she was always so – so decent, do you know?'

Arnie nodded. 'Sure I know. Nice guys finish last. It's always been that way and always will.'

A stand of poplars in the neighbor's yard drew dark blue shadows in parallel streaks across the unmarred snow. For a long time Hyacinth, oblivious of the cold, stood alone at the open door and stared at the slender tracks with their shadows all mathematically correct. It would be an interesting study in watercolors, she reflected.

They had gone. The house was empty without them; no more wet towels on the bathroom floor, no toys to stumble over in the hall, and no board game on the kitchen table. The house was absolutely still.

They had cried. Even the little boy, so brave in his maleness and his three years' advantage in age over his sister, had cried. He thought maybe it was his fault; had she been angry at him for being so messy? Or had Dad been angry because he teased Emma? But he hardly ever did that anymore!

'I will talk to you both on the telephone every day,' she had promised. Oh, she had promised and explained, somehow explained, told them all the right things about how they were loved; she had made foolish excuses about Gran's illness, had talked and talked them into comfort, and at last, into sleep.

So now they were gone. Perhaps I should kidnap them, she thought. I can sell this house; it's in my name. I can use the little money that Dad left me, and Francine will surely help me too, and my brothers will if I should need them. Then I'll take my children and leave the country for the farthest place on the earth: Australia, Siberia, anywhere to hide and stay.

But this is nonsense. It would be terrifying for them, and it wouldn't work anyway. Gerald would know how to get them back, and he would be so furious that he would tell the whole story. *Arson. A man died.*

As suddenly as the mercury had fallen, it rose, and a January thaw began to soften the hard, pristine snow. On first impulse, Hyacinth had begun the snow scene, but when after several tries it had failed to 'come right,' she had thrown down the brush. Her heart was not in it.

Her 'heart' was not really in anything. Her heart was the organ that pumped blood and sometimes fibrillated in a state of panic. It was quite clear that she would have to 'do something.' This was the first advice that anyone with half a brain would give her if she were to ask. Francine, controlling her own panic – ah, poor Francine, the trouble I made for her – insisted that she 'do something.' Moira, in her tiptoe, tentative voice, had done the same. And even Arnie, over the telephone, was trying to be tactful when he inquired, as he always did, what she was 'doing.'

For the present she was working on the dress that she had promised to that woman at the R. J. Miller store. Last week the head of the children's department had asked her whether she would make half a dozen more for some special customers, and she had agreed. Why not? By now the repetition of the pattern was automatic, a mindless process.

One day Will Miller came. He had cornered her on the telephone, asking whether he might drop in. There had been no way she could possibly refuse him. She had been his guest at dinner, and having accepted that, did she not owe him something in return? It was unavoidably a question of good manners.

In theory, she supposed she ought to welcome pleasant company, but in practice, in her circumstances, he was a complication to be got rid of after this one time. In an odd way, however, the small preparations that she made for lunch were energizing. The table had to be nicely set, and the house in perfect order; this was a matter of pride. She bought daffodils, a salmon steak and ingredients for salad. She pressed the linen luncheon mats that had not been used since the last P.T.A. luncheon. And she checked the house for any visible object that Emma and Jerry might have left behind; there was no reason why this stranger should know anything about her private life or her private agony.

When he appeared at the door, he did not behave like a stranger. 'Notice anything different about me?' he demanded.

'The horn-rimmed glasses are gone.'

'Right. From now on it's contacts only. I wore the horn-rims, you see, because everybody advised me to look older. Now that I'm past thirty, I need to look younger. Oh, this is a nice house! It looks like you. I rather imagined it would be like this, with outdoor colors, soft greens, all these books – you're making another dress!'

Next to a chair in the living room where they stood, she had left an open basket with her sewing. Had she done so on purpose so that he would see it? She was not sure; there had been some thread of a thought when she had put the cover on the basket, and then removed it.

'I heard from Sally Dodd. She was delighted with your dress. And now they've asked you to make some more, I hear.'

'Yes, but these are the last. Painting is my work. I need to get back to it.'

'You said you'd let me see it sometime, you remember?'

'Yes, of course. After lunch. I hope you're hungry.'

'I hope you didn't fuss.'

People who lived beyond themselves, who could never seem to do enough, read enough, hear or learn or see enough, always had things to talk about. And so, once the customary opening remarks were over, their dialogue sped along. Hyacinth contributed from what she had stored up in the attic of her mind; it was old stuff, all of it, since of late she had not been garnering anything new. But of course Will did not know that. And from the lively interest in his eyes, she knew that he was enjoying himself.

After a while, though, she saw – with that famous sixth sense – that he was nervous, though perhaps nervous wasn't the right word. Tense, then? Ill at ease? No, certainly not that. He was as fluent as he had been at their two other meetings, yet not as casual, more *hurried*. Yes, that was it, more hurried, as if he wanted to finish the unimportant preliminaries and get to something else.

Over the homemade apple tart he paused and almost apologetically inquired about the divorce. This might have been the subject he had been wanting to approach.

'Tell me. Are you getting near the end of your troubles?'

'The law moves like an iceberg, by inches.'

'More painfully, though. Not that I've had any personal

experience. The closest I've come – since we're going to know each other, I might as well tell you – is a love affair I had with a married woman. She was going through a divorce. It was awful for her, and maybe even more awful for her children. They were all still in their house, and fighting the whole time. I must make clear that I was not the cause of the divorce. The husband didn't even know about me. I say I was not the cause; what I meant was, not in any sense known to the law. But I was afraid that in the moral sense, the emotional sense, I might be partly to blame. And so I stepped out. And that, I can tell you, was painful.'

Why was he telling her all this?

'You see, I really knew that they should stay together. There were things I had been told, things I felt, that led me to believe they could work things out between them if they tried. I think people are far too casual about divorce, especially when there are children.'

He was waiting for Hyacinth to make a comment, but she was unable to make one.

'I'm not trying to present myself as a saint, Hyacinth. God forbid that I should be such a fool. I'm not a prig, nor a prude, either. But I have certain feelings, and they led me down the right path that time because' – Will smiled – 'they got together again. They've even had another child.'

Deeply moved, Hyacinth was hoping that her eyes would not fill as she replied. 'I honor you for those feelings. But they do not apply in this case. We shall not get together again. Ever.'

Why had she spoken so firmly? It would be better for him to think otherwise, so he would never come back.

'That makes it easier for you, then, doesn't it? Especially since you have no children.'

Why did she sit there toying with the apple tart, for she had no appetite, and say nothing? In all honesty, she ought to speak out. But then he, or anybody, would naturally ask about them. For was it not very, very strange when, after two fairly long sessions of conversation, a woman had made no mention, not the veriest hint of the fact that she has children?

It was her turn to say something. It must not be too obvious a change of subject, but rather an easy glide away.

'Yes, may it be over soon. But who knows? In the meantime, I concentrate on painting. I don't mean to sound important, but it's hard to find the right words without seeming to puff one's self up. The fact is that painting is the most important thing in my life. Does that sound too puffed up?'

'No, not at all. Don't you think that Zuckerman would say that about his violin? It's great that you're so enthusiastic. How about showing me something now?'

They started upstairs. Taking an idea from her old home, Hyacinth had lined the staircase with photographs, although so far there were only two, those of Jim and Francine. Will stopped to look at them. Will missed nothing. Like me, he is curious, she thought.

'You're like your father,' he remarked. 'He must have been a quiet man. Was he? Gentle and serious like you?'

At the top of the stairs a strong light poured into the hall, and under it, his scrutiny caused her to fill a sudden uncomfortable pause with the first words that entered her head.

'I can't tell about myself, but yes, he was rather quiet. My mother is different. She's the family beauty, as you can see.'

'The family beauty, you say? The only one? No, not at all. If I had to be the judge, I would choose you. The face in the photo is certainly beautiful. It has perfect symmetry. But your face is interesting. Spirit shines through it. One wants to look again at splendid eyes, perhaps a bit too large for the face, and a beautiful mouth, a chin perhaps a bit too strong – but lovely together. Yes, one wants to look at you again.'

Pleased, surprised and a trifle embarrassed at the unusual comments, she murmured her thanks and led him toward the paintings. Personal compliments might be embarrassing, but compliments to her work were eagerly and unashamedly awaited. So, allowing art to speak for itself, she stood quietly while Will walked slowly around the room.

He paused before the portraits: her old favorites of Jim in a lounge chair and Francine in a white evening dress. He looked carefully at her last year's favorite of Moira's fat little son, in which she had cleverly arranged shadows so as to make him look thinner.

He moved to the landscapes: a couple in a rowboat on a dark lake, and snow scenes in blizzard and sunshine. Slowly and carefully, he lingered before each, tilting his head or stepping back, the better to see. Here was no ordinary, polite acquaintance who, having no interest in art, would say the right things to the artist. And as the minutes passed now, a thrill of expectation mounted in Hyacinth's chest.

Last was one of her best, the still life of carrots and marigolds tossed in a gardener's basket. Oranges and yellows, some blending and some clashing, resembled Matisse's way with colors, she liked to think. A kind of daring was in it. You thought, when you put them all together, that it wouldn't work, but it did.

'At one of the charity art shows in town, a benefit,' she said, concealing her pride, 'somebody wanted to buy that one, but I wouldn't part with it.'

'Have you sold many?'

'Well, maybe a dozen.' Mentally she added up her sales. Arnie had bought two. 'Mostly to people I know. I haven't had any real exposure yet,' she explained and continued, 'but I intend to get some. It's all I want to do with my life.'

When he said nothing, she was surprised. He had turned back to the carrots and marigolds and – how strange it was! – she thought he looked sad.

After a moment, he asked a question. 'Do you go to art museums very often? I know you mentioned that you used to work in one.'

'Not just at present, but I've surely been in enough of them, the best of them. It's what I dream about. Walking into a museum someday in the future and finding something that I've done hanging on the wall.'

'In the Metropolitan or the Louvre?'

Hyacinth stared at him. Was he being serious? 'Well no, not exactly. How many people ever can expect that? You have to be a genius.'

'Well then, where do you see your work?'

'I hope to see it in a gallery, where people who know good art go to buy good art. On Madison Avenue in New York, for instance, or on the Left Bank in Paris.'

'That's a tall order,' Will said with a dubious shake of the head.

'What are you telling me? That you don't think I can do it?'

'Well, I only mean that – oh, in any field it's sometimes – it's not wise to aim too high.' Hesitating, he repeated, 'Too high,' and he smiled.

Something was wrong. Suddenly she realized that he had not shown any admiration, hadn't spoken any praise, during his slow walk around this room. Such a thing had never happened to her before.

And she decided to be forthright. 'You don't like any of the pictures. Tell the truth. I won't mind.'

He looked doubtful for a moment before answering only that he was hardly an art critic, but merely a lover of art who had done a good deal of reading – still far from an expert.

The evasion was both irritating and troubling. She had sensed enough about him to be sure of his honesty, and now she demanded it.

'Please Will, the truth, I know you're hiding it from me.'

'All right. I don't think you'll like it, but I'll say it because I like you very much, Hyacinth. So here it is: whether it's money you want, or honors, or both, this work won't get either one for you.'

She was stunned.

'You've wanted this badly, and you've deluded yourself, or other people have deluded you. Everything you have here is imitative.'

How dared he! Boldly, he stood there, sure of his judgment. Cruel and merciless were his words.

'Plenty of accepted art is imitative, that's true; goodness knows, there must be thousands of brand-new Impressionists floating around. But even they have the "something" that's hard to define, but that you recognize when you see it. It's the difference between someone who plays a Mozart nocturne recognizably, and the concert performer who plays it.'

She was devasted. If she could conceivably have ordered him out of the house, she would have done so.

He continued. 'You have everything here from Norman Rockwell's barefoot farm boys to Turner's pale sunsets over London. You have great skill. But that's not enough. You—' And then, as though he had suddenly realized what he was doing, he broke off. 'Oh, I'm sorry, Hyacinth! I don't mean to hurt you. Only to help you. In the short time I've known you, I've seen that your life is troubled, more troubled than you want to admit. So I don't want you to waste your hopes and your energy getting nowhere. I wouldn't speak this way if I didn't understand how much the work in this room – it must be several years of effort – means to you. Today is our third meeting, and on each of them you have talked so passionately about art, and that's why I'm telling you this so passionately. I would never, never hurt you, Hyacinth.'

'So what is it all good for?' she demanded. 'Shall I simply stuff it into the trash can, or shall I burn it up? What are you telling me to do?'

'Keep it for the children and grandchildren you'll have. Keep it as a hobby. Or you can probably sell this kind of thing to a department store that has an art section. There are plenty of people who buy pictures to go with the furniture.'

Bitter, shamed, and furious with Will even though it was she who had pressed for an opinion, she could not help thinking of Arnie and what he had so generously paid her for some pictures to match his upholstery. He, at least, had a heart . . .

Will really needn't have rubbed it in like this, as if he actually enjoyed being harsh. Yes, she was furious.

When he moved to touch her arm, she drew away. And then it was he who drew away, walked to the end of the room and back, threw up his arms, and lamented.

'I should be taken out and shot. Look what I've done to you! That's what comes of speaking your mind or spilling everything out without taking thought of results. When am I ever going to learn? I'll say it again, I meant well. You know I did, Hyacinth. In your heart you must know. Why would I want to make you as miserable as you are now? Why? Listen to me. If you want a career, and I don't even know whether you will want to after the divorce, you've got one at your fingertips, literally at your fingertips. Look how they've gone crazy over that dress! You need to go—'

'That was a copy, too,' she said scornfully.

'With clothing, it doesn't matter. They're all copies. Copies of copies. Saris, or lace fichus from the eighteenth century,' Will answered with equal scorn. 'What you need is design school. Learn how to cut and fit. The color sense you've got, that's plain.'

'Easy as that? Maybe I should take up ballet dancing instead.'

Will gave her a rueful smile. 'Okay. You're entitled to some sarcasm. But when you take time to think it over, I hope you'll forgive my rough tongue.'

She said suddenly, 'It's all very well to talk about design school. Even if I wanted to do it, and I don't, it's too late.'

'Of course it isn't. If you were sixty years old, it wouldn't be too late. Nothing's ever too late.'

'Let's go down,' Hyacinth said, moving toward the stairs.

From behind her came Will's question as he followed. 'Who taught you to sew?'

'My grandmother.'

'She taught you well. Sally Dodd says you have golden hands.'

'Funny. My grandmother said that, too.'

'Well, they're both right.'

In the downstairs hall, Will hesitated as though he were waiting to be asked into the living room.

People do not usually have lunch at somebody's house and depart fifteen minutes after they have eaten. Hyacinth knew very well what he expected. But he was not going to get it.

'Very nice having you,' she said correctly, and turned toward the front door.

'Hyacinth, I know you're furious. I understand it. But listen to me once more. I want to see you doing something with your life. Learn fashion design. Do it now.'

'No, you listen to me. The dress was a freak success. It means nothing. It's worthless. I have no ideas.'

'You'll have ideas, just as you did with art. You already know how to sketch. Put into cloth what you did on canvas, and I predict you'll make a new life.'

'A new life,' she repeated, not caring to hide her bitterness.

'Yes. You haven't said much about your troubles, but it's plain that something has hurt you very deeply.' Will looked about. 'This house – to be in it alone must be like inhabiting a tomb. You need to leave it behind and make a new start.'

She was unable to answer him. He had taken her only support away, had robbed her of purpose and confidence, of the very little she had left of either.

'Are you so angry with me that you won't shake hands?'

Offering her hand, she said only, 'I'm going to forget everything you said and I'm going to go right on with my work.'

Apparently Will chose to ignore this little speech, as he replied, 'Thank you for lunch. You make a wicked apple tart. I'm taking a fairly long business trip to Europe, but I'll call you when I get back.'

'Have a good trip,' she said, and closed the door.

She did not watch him go down the walk as she had done once before. If he really thought he would see her again, he was very, very much mistaken. There was a beating, a pounding in her ears. When that happens, she had once learned, you are hearing your own heartbeat. It was no wonder.

She ran upstairs to look again at the work that had been so thoroughly condemned. All the hours, the pleasure, the hopes that had gone to make these lovely things! How could he, a passing stranger in her life, come in here and wipe away all of that! Wherever she had lived, she had been the 'artist,' known and respected for her talent. Why, Gerald – even he – had recognized her for that much at least: Hyacinth, the artist.

It was too much to bear. It was being hit, hit hard, when you are already down. And Will Miller had known she was down. Hadn't he said that it was plain to see?

The beating persisted in her ears. If I should become ill here alone in this house, if I should die here, and it's possible because even healthy young people can drop if the strain is too great, I shall never see my children.

And from her throat there tore a terrible sound, like the wail of women outraged by a conquering army. There was no reason in her and nothing to restrain her as she ran to the telephone and called Gerald's number.

'You!' she cried when she heard his voice. 'You! What do you think you're doing to me? I've had enough. I want my children. I'm the one who gave them birth. They are far more mine than they can ever be yours. You're evil. You're a monster without heart. Cold. Cold. Have you any idea how I despise you? I loathe you. I would just as soon hold a poisonous snake as put a finger on you. How can you see yourself in a mirror without feeling disgust? What have you got to say about what you've done?'

'What I have to say is that you're out of control again, that's all.'

Calm, that's what he was. Another subject for a top-market advertisement. Furnishings, this time? The desk would be mahogany, a well-waxed antique, with every article on its surface in proper order.

She dropped her voice. 'I'm not out of control. I'm only asking you why you are doing this to me. What have I done to you that you should take my children away from me?'

'You know quite well that you may see them, Hyacinth. You will have that in writing before this month is out. All you have to do is give proper notice to me and—'

'And you will take them away, trick me as you did last Thanksgiving.'

'Nonsense. That was a misunderstanding.'

'A deliberate one.'

'If it makes you happy to think so, go ahead.' As clearly as if he had been sitting in front of her, she saw his casual shrug. 'You really have no complaints, Hyacinth. You must have read about couples in separate countries who can't even get permission to have their children visit them at all.'

'They're not mine anymore,' she said. 'They're yours. You make the decisions as to when I shall see them, you choose where they'll go to school, what they'll eat and wear, you watch them grow from day to day, while I—' Her voice collapsed into a sob. 'I'm sometimes a visitor and sometimes a hostess who has gifts for them. I, their mother! Their mother!'

'It's a sad situation,' he said quietly. 'It's very sad. But I am not the one who brought it about. You should look yourself straight in the eye.'

'I am looking at myself straight in the eye. And I know it was an accident, my cigarettes and my carelessness. But it was nothing more. And you know it was not.'

'I don't know anything of the sort. Was it by accident that you trashed two desks? I'm not the only person who saw the mess, the computers lying on the floor, the telephones – no, and I'm not the only one who knows about Sandy. You told me yourself, if you care to remember all this, Hyacinth, that my so-called love affair was a lively topic for the local gossips. Right here in the next town, a man was picked up when some evidence was found after five or six years, and he was then identified. Oh, he got a little time off for good behavior. *And*' – with this emphasis, Hyacinth could see Gerald's eyes widen as his brows rose – 'and there were no injuries or deaths in the case, either. So don't complain. You're well off. And you'd be better off still if you deposited my checks and went about your business.'

'Don't waste the stamps, Gerald. I shall never use ten cents' worth of your checks. With so many good people dying all over this earth, I wonder why you should still be among the living.'

'Thanks. Is that all? Because I'm busy. I don't know about you, but I have things to do.'

When he hung up, Hyacinth remained with the instrument in her hand. *Things to do.* The words repeated themselves, making an idiotic refrain in her head. I have nothing. I walk into my studio, pick up the brush and wait for an idea, but none comes. What is to become of me? I shall become a shell, with nothing inside.

On one of the first fine warm days of early spring, Gran had a stroke. Without warning and without pain, she closed her eyes. She would have been the first to say that her death did not bring with it the intense grief that Jim's death had brought. And during the lengthy prayers at the funeral services, Hyacinth's mind wandered, making loose contact between Gran's life and her own.

One after the other came before the congregation to say a few words about Gran. There was a very old man who had been an usher at her wedding; there were two distant cousins from Ohio, there was a younger woman who had been her next-door neighbor. Each of them spoke well. They were sincerely moved and as she heard them Hyacinth felt an overwhelming return of memory, the sights and sounds and fragrances of Gran and her house: the knitting needles in the basket, apples baking on the stove, Gran's lily-of-the-valley perfume, and Gran complaining to the humane society about a dog left outdoors in the cold.

The old, old man remembered things that Hyacinth had never known.

'She took in boarders during the Depression She made their meals, washed their clothes and scrubbed their floors; she had never done such things or needed to do them, but she taught herself and did them.

'When the war came and the Depression ended she helped her husband rebuild his business. When he died of cancer she took over the business and saved a nest egg for old age. She lost two sons, one in war, another war, and one not long ago, your father, Hyacinth, your husband, Francine.

'And through it all she held up her head. She never forgot how to laugh. She kept her zest for life. She lived it bravely.'

When the service was over, Hyacinth did not linger to exchange sympathy and reminiscences with the large crowd that had gathered. Heavy with thoughts, she went straight home instead, and lay awake half the night with those thoughts.

A few days later she left a message on Francine's answering machine. 'Gone to New York on business. I need time to think. Don't worry. I'm fine. I'll be back soon.'

Then she closed the front door and departed for the train.

In her room at the hotel in New York, she made a list of art galleries, twenty in all, where she would study every picture, no matter how long it might take. It would be a dizzying journey from the Italian Renaissance to the nineteenth-century landscape painters, to the first Impressionists, the Fauves, the Expressionists, the Moderns, the post-Moderns, and all the rest. But at the end, along with the dazzle in her head, some truth would speak to her and answer her question: Do I have Art within me, or do I not?

The journey lasted five days. Afterwards, she was to remember a few especially poignant moments, which in retrospect must have moved her toward her decision. One was the startling recognition of a face in a contemporary portrait of a young child lying on her mother's lap. Emma, she thought, on the day I gave her the rose dress. There was such an absolute delight in that three-year-old face, and the artist had gotten it all, the very breath of life that, while it is a joy to behold, is touched too with the moving sadness of innocence.

How could I have failed to see myself as I really am, she asked herself. Will Miller was right. My work has never moved anyone either to tears or joy. Skill I have, but never the indefinable.

And then there was the conversation at the Modern Art. Standing in front of Monet's 'Water Lilies,' a young woman said to her, 'It does something to you, doesn't it? If I ever have time after work, I go to look at pictures. Especially if you have things on your mind, they make you feel better, these artists.'

'Yes, they do.'

'You wonder what it is. What is it about these flowers? Everybody paints flowers. They paint them on greeting cards, so what's the difference?'

In Giverney, at the home of the water lilies, it had been such a glorious afternoon, and she had been so happy! But Gerald had been in a cranky rush to get it over with.

And she stood there long after the crowd had thinned, reliving that day and thinking of many things, of how those who loved her had in their loving pride deluded her, and of how she had deluded herself into thinking that her work was better than it truly was.

Will Miller would be surprised if he could know, although he never would know, that she was just probably going to take his advice. They had paid so surprisingly much for those dresses! Sewing was certainly not what she had hoped to do with her life, but how many people get to do what they hope they can do? And this was not a pipe dream. It was realistic.

On the sixth day, she was ready for her final decision. Having fortified herself with catalogs, she made her choice, got into a taxi and, before she could change her mind, enrolled at a first-rate school for fashion design.

'You're making me feel like a wayward, runaway child,' she remonstrated when she got home.

Francine scolded. 'Age has nothing to do with it. You can't blame me. Going off like that with a message about "needing time to think"! I had terrible thoughts that maybe you—'

'Committed suicide? No, not at all. You should be pleased. You've told me over and over that I must do something with my time, and you were right. So now I'm doing it.'

Francine was not that easily appeased. 'You've even upset your friend here. Arnie phoned me after calling you for three days straight and getting no answer. You need to thank him.'

Arnie, enthroned in the leather wingchair that had been Gerald's, waved thanks away. 'Your mother and I had the same fear. You might as well know the truth. I was afraid because of the kids. I thought – if you've done something to yourself – that's why I flew up here. I didn't tell anybody except to say I had business in New York.'

'I'm sorry that I've upset you all, but there's no need to fear. I would never do it. I wouldn't hurt my children like that. I suppose they're all right, or you would be telling me, Arnie?'

'Oh, they're fine. I see them two or three times a week. We belong to the same swim club. They've been having lessons there. You should see Emma—' Embarrassed, he stopped.

'Indeed, she should see her,' Francine said.

A solemn silence followed. Both Francine and Arnie were staring at Hyacinth, who was staring at the floor. Without raising her head, she felt their stare, as though they were touching her with hot hands.

Francine, breaking the silence, spoke sternly. 'This whole thing seems eccentric to me. Why don't you go back to art restoration? You loved it.'

'Because I'm barely a beginner. It takes years to become expert, and I need money.'

'Stop the nonsense, Hyacinth. You saw the house Gerald lives in. I'm sorry, Arnie. He's your partner, but he's my enemy, and frankly, I'm surprised – don't misunderstand, I'm grateful for your kindness, but still I—'

Arnie said firmly, 'I don't take sides. Gerald knows that. I'm neutral. If I could patch things up, I would feel I had done a great thing. But so far I haven't seen any signs on either side. It's all a God damn mystery.'

Hyacinth looked at Arnie and at Francine. I am separated from them both, she thought. There is a wall around me. They want me to take it down so they can get through, and I can't do it. Their words strike the wall and bounce back to them.

Arnie asked, 'What about selling your pictures? I've been meaning to ask for a couple to put in my new place. I've got a living room a mile long. I could use maybe seven or eight, depending on the size. I don't know what they're worth, but I'm no cheapskate, so you just name your price.'

'You just go upstairs and take what you want,' Hyacinth said gently. 'They're not worth much, if anything. They'll be my small way of saying thanks.'

Francine, tapping her foot, gave notice that she was more than ordinarily agitated. 'Your pictures aren't worth much, you say? But your sewing will be?'

'I think so. I hope so.'

'And on those thoughts and hopes you propose to give up your home, leave me and all your friends here, pull up stakes, and start off into the unknown.'

'You forget I've done it before.'

'There's no comparison. You had a—'

'A husband. I know. Well, I'm learning to do without one.'

'Not for long,' Arnie said. 'Not you, Hyacinth.'

Words like balls or stones kept bouncing against the wall. Francine's were well aimed.

'If you sell this house, how are the children going to visit?'

'I'll find a place in the city.'

'To give up a house like this! I'm not giving up mine. Your father always wanted it kept as a homing place. George is coming for a week in the summer with all his crew, and Tom expects to be coming east two or three times a year on business. Besides, I have friends all over, even in England, and they like to use it as a hotel. You are making a big mistake to sell this house.'

'I told you I need the money to live on in New York.'

'Permit me to disagree,' Arnie said. 'Hyacinth would be smart to sell it now. This neighborhood is going downhill. They're widening the avenue, the business section is moving in this direction, and in two or three years, this house will be worth a lot less than it is now.'

'Well, you're a clever businessman, and I'm not,' Francine admitted somewhat dubiously. 'So we might as well drop the subject. My daughter has always been stubborn, and she appears to have made up her mind.'

The hall clock struck once. It was Gran's tall clock. And Hyacinth thought instantly: That goes with me. Whatever else I leave behind, that goes; it's my lucky charm.

When it struck three more times, Arnie stood up. 'Now that I know you're all right, Hy, I'm going to leave you. But I'll be looking in on you in New York. I always have business to tend to there, so I fly up now and then.'

They shook hands, she thanked him, received a peck on the cheek, and saw him to the door.

'Yes, I tell you again, the man's a little bit crazy about you,' Francine observed.

'I don't see it at all.'

'You may not see it, but I do. I like him, Hyacinth. He's a man, straightforward and able to look you in the eye. Not that you're in a position to do anything now, but the time will come.'

'I'm not interested in him or any man.'

'You will be. You heard what Arnie said.'

'I have very little in common with Arnie.'

'I only meant that he can be of help to you. And he's so nice to Jerry and Emma while they're in Florida.'

'Yes, he's very kind, and I appreciate it.'

'He's a very clever man. You'd do well to take his advice on business.'

'I don't need his advice. I am learning not to depend on anybody.'

'Well,' Francine said. And then, 'You look tired.'

'I am a little.'

'Go out to the porch. I'll bring some tea.'

Understanding her, Hyacinth obeyed. Being a mother had nothing to do with age. Gran at eighty had mothered her fifty-five-year-old son. It was simply that Francine was terribly worried about her, and she would be a thousand times more so if the facts were ever to be revealed.

'I was thinking,' Francine said, stirring the tea. 'Since you've made up your mind about what you want to do, you should at least keep all your beautiful furniture. Take what you need for your apartment and put the rest into storage. You'll need it someday,' she finished positively.

No, never will I need it. How shall I ever have a house like this one?

'You don't agree?' For Hyacinth had not replied. 'But then you never did listen to my advice, so I should be used to it by now.' And Francine sighed.

She looked haggard. Her vertical forehead lines were so deeply carved that you could only hope they were not going to become a permanent flaw on that exquisite face. It has been a terrible year for her, and I am part of it, Hyacinth thought. With a sudden rush of sadness and regret, she reached across the little table and laid a hand over Francine's.

'Forgive me,' she whispered. 'We don't always agree. But then, so many people who love each other don't agree. Isn't that so? But I will take your advice about the furniture.'

Furniture. How unimportant in the scheme of life! She could have thrown it all away without missing it, especially this furniture, with all its past. Yet apparently, it had significance for Francine, who in her love saw it only as a guarantee that 'normalcy' for her daughter would someday, somehow, resume.

The climbing rose was gradually coming into leaf on the arbor. Faithful creature! When first snow was stirring in the gray air, it still carried gravely a last small, shriveled bud. I shall miss it,

Hyacinth thought. I was so serene on the day I planted it! And satisfied – we were so satisfied in this new house! No. It was I alone who was satisfied . . . And she sat there holding the teacup, while the season's first bee went darting and buzzing through the sunshine.

Chapter Eleven

Hyacinth, as she moved through the Institute's classrooms and corridors, was reminded of those newspaper accounts in which people of seventy or eighty are at last obtaining a college degree. She was hardly that age, and yet there was an extraordinary difference between the rest of the students and herself. They were so light and unfettered! They were too cheerful, too earnest, too ignorant of evil, too lovely in their youth, and too everything. Among them, she thought, I might be from Mars.

It was almost mid-semester before she became aware that the instructors, unlike the students, were taking notice of her. Having been so unsure of herself at the start, it was a total surprise when one of her sketches was displayed before an advanced class on drawing techniques. Afterwards, the instructor told her that she really did not need to be taking that class at all.

This bit of encouragement, she sometimes reflected, was probably the glue that kept the various parts of her psyche from coming unglued. She had, of course, a comfortable familiarity with color and form, so that although she had never been intensely concerned about clothes other than to have a natural desire to look 'nice,' the preparation of a design portfolio seemed no harder than it had once been to stand at the easel in the studio at home. Very often she brought work to the apartment, where on a card table, she laid out patterns and practiced drawing in pen and ink.

Almost always, on Saturdays and Sundays, she went to special classes. And so, by filling every moment of the week, she fortified herself against a loneliness that sometimes threatened like a tidal wave to wash her away.

Lonely in the midst of crowds is by now a cliché. Hyacinth had never lived in a place where the postman did not pause to chat for a moment at the front door, or where the checker at the supermarket was too rushed to pass the time of day. In one sense this anonymity was a relief, while in another, it gave her some rather terrifying moments. The diversity of the city, and especially of her neighborhood here on the border of Chelsea should in theory have given her many choices, but actually there was such a medley of types in her building alone, that the result was no cohesion and no real contacts other than a few friendly nods. She had nothing except humanity in common with a nineteen-year-old aspiring actress who lived across the hall with her boyfriend; nor did she have any contact with the garment workers who spoke no English; the tottering couple who had lived in the building for the last sixty-five years were in still another world.

Below her window, the street itself was in a state of change. The past remained in the form of five-story walk-ups at whose windows bedding was hung out to air and on whose stoops sat clusters of women gossiping and watching troops of children. The present and the future showed all the signs of gentrification; their brownstone fronts had been cleaned and lightened enough to show a touch of faintest pink; shops had polished brass fittings on their brass doors, and quaintly lettered signs announcing that Victorian antiques, Thai food, or secondhand books were on sale within. Over all was a bustle and haste such as Hyacinth had never seen before.

After her long days, she climbed four flights of stairs and closed her door with feelings that varied: At times the two small rooms were a shelter, while at other times they were a prison. It was not always hard to see what caused these wild swings of the pendulum. The sight of a mother walking with young children might send her running to shelter, where she need not be reminded of other people's normal lives, whereas the pleasure that came from a stimulating workshop or some words of praise so filled her with the need to be successful, to triumph over her circumstances, that she hated her prison.

Ignoring Arnie's offers of assistance, she had found the place herself. Ignoring Francine's advice, she had made no effort to adorn the two small rooms. There was a bed, there were two chairs, one in each room, there was the card table for her work. There was a kitchen, closet-sized; she cooked very little, ate very little, and grew even thinner. It did not matter. All she wanted was to get through the course of study and find a job that would pay enough to provide a place where her children could stay.

Repeatedly, she told herself that the important thing, the elementary thing, was to look forward. Backward looks are not only futile, Gran always had said; they were confusing. So on the day when the final papers were signed and she was legally freed from Gerald, she had a blinding flash of remembrance much like what is said about a drowning man's instant recall of his entire life: She saw the motel where they had had their secret afternoons under her satin quilt; she saw the wedding, their dance, the passion of her first night lying together the whole night through with his ring on her finger . . . How could all of that have disappeared? Vanished! Turned into disillusion, as though it had never been.

Yes, the only thing left was to look forward. Yet too often when sleep failed, while voices shrilled and trucks rumbled on the street outside, her mind took a short journey back to the house she had left and the wrenching last hour in which she had left it.

Only a few people had been told that she was going away. These were sensitive people, friends who asked no questions and had come only to wish her well. Moira was there, of course, along with two teachers who, assuming that she was on her way to Florida, brought little gifts for Jerry and Emma. The house painter came; when his wife had been dreadfully ill last winter, Hyacinth had cooked and frozen meals for the family, and he would never forget her.

Francine was baffled and crushed, but being Francine and very, very angry at her daughter, she was gallantly trying not to let it show. When she gave her final hug and kiss, her eyes were glistening with tears, but she had nothing to say. Had not everything been said?

Sometimes as Hyacinth lay awake hearing the bedside alarm

clock tick past midnight, she also thought about Will Miller. No doubt he would be surprised to hear that a total, or almost total stranger had taken his advice. If it were possible, she would like to tell him about it. But it was not possible. In departing she had left a false trail, and anyway, he might not even want to see her again. In any case, he would lose interest in her when, as ultimately he would have to do, he learned what an oddity she was: a woman who had given up her little children. And in the second case, she really wasn't much interested in him, either, or in any man, attractive or not.

One morning after one such restless night, she woke to find a drift of snowflakes in the air. It was still early in November, and these premature flakes were already melting into gray mush on the sidewalk. They did, however, serve to remind her of the nearness of Thanksgiving. Last year's had been a horror best forgotten. This year's was going to be empty, with no place to go. Francine was flying out west to be with the grandchildren, whose number her sons seemed to be continually increasing. Surely Hyacinth could have no desire to go there. Nor would she risk another fiasco like last year's in Florida.

Two days before or after the holiday, which Gerald would be celebrating in his customary sociable style, would make more practical sense for her. An insistent need over and above her constant yearning had suddenly seized her as she watched the snow. Already the year was coming toward its end. Months went by as fast as hours do. By the end of the next semester, Emma would be in first grade. Jerry would be in the fourth. Before she knew it, their childhood would be gone.

It occurred to her that she should ask Arnie to arrange a visit for her. It occurred to her also that this dependency upon Arnie was most unusual. Yet at the same time, it also seemed quite natural.

Flying southward, Hyacinth was continuously aware of her own mood. Almost every adjective began with an 'e': euphoric, elated and excited – but tremulous too, on the verge of tears. Determined not to allow even one tear to fall, she recited her mantra: *Head over heart,* and returned to her book. She was reading the life of Chanel, a girl who had learned to sew in an alteration shop and had become an international name.

The tale held her interest, so much so that later, in the hotel where, since Emma and Jerry were not to arrive before next morning, she had dinner alone, she surprised herself by passing judgment on all the other women's clothes. Never before had she paid that much attention to what people were wearing.

Now there's a very fine suit, she noticed, but it doesn't fit the woman. There's a lovely dress, but the color is too drab for her. Francine would liven it with a scarf; scarlet or emerald would do the trick. Now there's a dress! Handwoven silk. You can't mistake it. A few months ago, I didn't know anything about handwoven silk.

With fabric like that, she thought, with a cut that simple and a few yards of contrasting color, you could work out half a dozen fabulous designs if you wanted to: a Japanese effect with an obi in the right print, in white or black maybe; you could have a sash tied and lapped over into a tiny bustle, or a pleated flounce at the hem.

Upstairs in her room after dinner and impatient for morning, she whiled away the evening in drawing sketches on the hotel's stationery. She drew the obi and the flounce. She drew a woman in daytime dress with a large summer hat, and then the same dress worn with a small round hat. She thought of people she knew, of Moira, for instance, and how best to disguise those extra twenty pounds.

She was embarrassing herself. Who do you think you are, Madame Chanel? Well, she started with a little hat shop, decorating plain straw hats so that they looked like a million dollars, or francs. Of course, she had a rich lover, and that must have helped a little.

It was all amusing.

The next morning they arrived in splendor, stepping out of the newest, most lavish sports utility van, with their nanny at the wheel. For an instant, Hyacinth had to blink before she was sure of them. In the second instant, she saw that Jerry had grown at least two inches; there could be no doubt now, if ever there had been, that he was Gerald in miniature. Emma's pigtails were gone. Her hair hung loose and wavy like Francine's, so that in a subtle way she had left babyhood behind. They were both new to their mother. And having vowed to shed no tears, even a tear of joy, Hyacinth shed none now, even as she pulled them both together into her arms.

In the background stood an elderly seeming woman wearing a white uniform and a cheerful smile.

'You're Mrs. O'Malley,' said Hyacinth.

'Oh yes, and haven't I had a time with them this morning. They would have started at six o'clock if I'd let them. They were in such a hurry to see Mommy.'

'We brought our swimsuits,' Emma cried. 'Daddy says this hotel has a pool, and you would let us go in.'

Could she ever have thought that the word 'Daddy' would be abrasive?

She answered brightly, 'Of course. I'm sorry I never thought to bring my suit, but Mrs. O'Malley and I will sit there and watch you. Then we'll have lunch outside by the pool. It'll be fun.'

'Her name is Nanny,' Emma said.

'Nanny and I will watch you. You can change in there. Which beach bag is yours, Emma? I'll go in to help you.'

'No, Nanny will,' Emma said. 'She always does.'

'Fine. Then I'll go find some chairs in the shade.'

Nanny always does. It was such a small thing, yet it made her feel extraneous, as if she were not needed.

Having arranged the chairs, she sat and waited. The kiddie pool was uncrowded. A few young children were splashing, and a few more running while mothers warned against the slippery tiling; you could tell they were mothers not only by their appearance, but by the way they spoke. There was always something recognizable about a mother's voice.

I am looking for trouble, she thought then, reprimanding herself. I am simply waiting and expecting to be hurt. Can't you look for the positive, Hyacinth? Here they come. Here in the red trunks and the pink bikini, the little bodies, my flesh and my heart.

'Oh, no!' she cried as Jerry dove into the adult pool.

Nanny assured her that he was allowed to. 'As long as there's a lifeguard and he stays in the shallow end. Jerry's a fine swimmer already. You don't have to worry.'

'I didn't know he was that good.'

'Yes, he's a real athlete, Jerry is. He started tennis lessons last month, and the coach says he's way ahead of any other kids his age.'

'He didn't tell me, and I speak to both of them almost every day.'

That had been a stupid thing to say. It sounded positively apologetic, as if she wanted to explain herself, or show that she was, in spite of all, an attentive, caring mother.

'Oh, I know. I'm always there to remind them of the time. You must be waiting for their ring.'

They were acting, playing a role, the mother and the woman who must be – in a perfectly decent, understandable way – fascinated by this odd situation. And the mother is sitting here, imperturbable, well groomed and calm, in the groomed setting of marble, sky and pool, pretending that there is really nothing odd about the situation. Surely there must be plenty of speculation between this nanny and the other woman in the house, the unfriendly servant on that awful day. Nanny was even now stealing a curious look at Hyacinth, but catching her glance, pretended to be watching Emma, who was talking to another girl in the pool.

'Emma's the sociable one. A real chatterbox. Makes friends everywhere she goes. And people take to her, even people you wouldn't expect. Why, the other day a real grumpy-looking old man in the drugstore got talking to her, and—'

The woman was speaking as if these children were strangers who needed to be introduced to Hyacinth and described for her.

'—and so, when I told her Daddy, he laughed, got a big kick out of it. He always—' She stopped.

Fight anger and pain, Hyacinth. Keep your dignity.

'It's quite all right to mention their father, Nanny,' she said. Nanny flushed. 'I only meant she's a personality, that one.'

Yes, that's another resemblance to Francine, and it was a good thing, too. It would make life easier.

Jerry, who had also found friends, came bringing one with him.

'This is Doug. He wants to have lunch with us. His parents won't be back till after lunch. Can he have lunch with us?'

It was not clear whether the question was being addressed to Nanny, or to Hyacinth. She answered quickly, just as Nanny did the same.

'Yes, he's welcome.'

He was not really welcome. This innocent little boy was, on this one day of days, an interloper, as was Nanny or anybody who took her precious minutes away from Hyacinth. She was a prisoner here, without transportation to take the children anywhere else. She could not very well ask Nanny to go eat by herself. And then the thought came that, quite possibly, or more likely probably, Gerald had instructed the woman not to leave the children alone with their mother.

You are out of control, Hyacinth. You've got a problem.

Children's chatter filled the lunch hour. This was not at all what she had planned and longed for. And she thought of the two rooms in which she now lived. Perhaps after all she had made a mistake in selling their house. So her mind spun, round and round.

Emma said suddenly, 'I want to go riding. I'm tired of this pool.' There was something new about her voice, a petulant wail. 'I'm tired of it. The club has an ice cream bar, and this place doesn't.'

'Oh, shut up,' Jerry said. 'Shut your big yap.'

'I don't like that talk,' Hyacinth told him.

'Everybody talks like that, Mom.'

'Maybe they do, but I still don't like it.'

What was she saying? Picking on him for using a word like 'yap'? Picking on him *today*? But mothers are supposed to correct, if they do it kindly. Yes, mothers are. She was forgetting: This nanny is his mother now.

Emma repeated, 'I want to go riding.'

'I didn't bring anything for you to wear,' Nanny said. 'I didn't know you wanted to.'

Jerry protested, 'I can ride the way I am.'

'You know you can't. You need long pants so your skin won't rub sore, you need boots, and a helmet with a chin strap. You know your daddy would have a fit if you rode without one. It's the same as on your bike. And that's that,' Nanny concluded with the voice of authority.

'Can't we just drive out there to show Mom?' Jerry pleaded. 'Just to look? You would like that, wouldn't you, Mom?'

'I'd love to. I'd love to do anything you'd like.'

'It's a good long drive, but nice,' Nanny said. 'We should start now before traffic gets heavier.'

Jerry sat in front talking and fiddling with the radio dials in turn. Emma, in the middle row of seats, fell asleep. When her head fell to rest on her mother's shoulder, Hyacinth did not move; even though her body needed to change position, no such comfort would be worth the loss of that warm head so close, with the feel and fragrance of soft hair brushing her cheek.

'We're almost there,' Jerry cried. 'I know the way. Two more lights.' He held up two fingers. 'Then we turn left – no, right – and the first thing I'm going to do is, I'm going to show you Uncle Arnie's horse.'

In his excitement, he was bouncing on the seat. He had always bounced, even when he sat in his high chair.

And Hyacinth asked tenderly, 'Not your horse first?'

'Oh, both. But his first because his is bigger. It's enormous. It's a Tennessee walking horse.'

In almost every one of their telephone conversations, Jerry remembered to give that piece of information. 'I know. And Emma's pony?'

'She hasn't really got one of her own yet. She's too young. She gets rides. They have to walk it around and hold her on it. She thinks it's all her pony. But we never tell her that,' Jerry warned. 'We don't want to hurt her feelings.'

There's the goodness in him. That's really sweet, and so funny when you think of how tough he sometimes tries to be.

'What did you say about me?' asked Emma, sitting up.

'Only that you had a nice nap and we're almost there.'

Emma smiled. Her teeth would not need to be straightened. She had not kept Gerald's dimple, as Jerry had. Someone – who? – had given her a little gold heart on a chain. She had had a scratch or bite on the inside of her arm; there was a Band-Aid on it. Her mother's eyes missed nothing.

On the other hand, the mother's eyes saw nothing. It was all a blur, the passing impression of a shady lane, of some low shingled buildings, and of fields, flat green spaces with white board fences. They brought out a pony, a little creature not much larger than a Great Dane, and for Hyacinth's benefit, set Emma on it for a minute or two. Nanny clapped, so Hyacinth clapped. They brought out another pony, much larger; Jerry began a demonstration, and still there was that blur before her eyes and in her head: What am I doing here? It is all false.

Nanny touched her arm. 'Are you feeling all right?'

She came to. 'Yes, yes I'm fine.'

'I ask because you didn't answer Jerry. He's showing you how he mounts.'

'I'm sorry! I don't know why I didn't hear you. Go on, show me.'

'You hold the reins between your thumb and this finger. See? Like this, not in your fist. And you have to sit up straight with your knees down. See? Can I walk around a little? Just a little? I know I'm not dressed and I'm not supposed to, but can I, Tom?'

The young groom who held the pony was patient. He winked at Jerry. Apparently he liked him. Most people did. 'Okay, I'll walk with you once around the paddock. Then you have to get off and we won't say anything.'

'They're very nice to the children here,' Nanny said. 'I guess that's because their Uncle Arnie keeps his horse here and comes almost every day. When Jerry's in school, he usually can't come every day, so they exercise the pony for him.'

Jerry was proud as he dismounted and handed the reins to Tom. He's having a good life, Hyacinth thought. At least I have to be grateful for that, and I am.

'I didn't tell you his name, did I, Mom?'

He had told her, many times, but obviously he enjoyed repeating the name, so she told him he had not.

'King Charles is his name. Do you know why?'

'No. Why?'

'Because Charlie is a King Charles spaniel.'

'Oh. Well, that's a very good reason.'

'I thought so, too. He's a Shetland pinto.'

She had heard that many times also, but she remarked merely, 'I like his white stockings.'

'They're socks, Mom. Stockings are when they come up to the knees.'

'You know so much, Jerry.'

'I do. I do.' He nodded seriously. 'Did you know I ride on an English saddle? Cowboys use Western saddles, but I don't.'

'Well, you're not a cowboy, are you? You're an easterner.'

Nanny consulted her watch. 'If we're to beat the traffic going back, we'd better start. It's good we don't need to be on time for dinner. But daddy has office hours one night a week, you know, and tonight's the night.'

Hyacinth had quite naturally not known, but the routine and the punctilious dinner hour — barring emergency — were most surely familiar. A picture loomed, flashed, and immediately dissolved: strong, lean hands, impeccable and somehow stern, if hands ever could be stern, laying a knife and a fork in parallel order on a plate. Whether it was this image, with all its corollaries, or whether it was the awareness that the day was coming to an end, she did not know; she only knew that her supply of emotional energy was running low. What was the purpose of this day? It had only reopened her wounds. And she had no way of knowing anything about her children's wounds, if any. Perhaps by now theirs had healed over. She could only pray that they had.

'I want ice cream,' Emma announced, 'the kind with chocolate sprinkles.'

'Don't you remember the magic word, Emma?'

'I want icecream, *please*.'

'Great. We'll have it back at the hotel.'

'Do they have sprinkles?'

'I'm sure they have.'

Nanny was dubious. 'It's getting near suppertime, you know. Don't spoil your appetites.'

'It's mid-afternoon,' Hyacinth said firmly, 'and it won't hurt them if they don't finish their supper for once.'

In a polite, respectful way, Nanny was over-stepping her role. She wouldn't be doing it to any other mother or any other employer. She was doing it because she saw very clearly that she was dealing with a mother who for some mysterious reason had been defeated and cast out.

On a terrace under a breeze that rattled the palm branches above their heads, they sat in a man-made jungle surrounded by flowers. And Hyacinth, observing the children, saw that they were pleased, but not unusually so. Already they were accustomed to places like this one, this oasis of luxury.

Jerry announced that Dad was taking him to the tennis matches. He had a new racket. Emma wasn't old enough for tennis yet; she was having ballet lessons. And Dad had started to play chess with Jerry. Really there was no harm in any of this. Anyone, who could afford to, gave his children all these extra chances to learn and do. But if you had been reduced to a meager shelter, you could not afford to give them these things. As so many times before, Hyacinth remembered the woman at that group meeting who had lost her son to their father's lavish house on a lake. And she remembered – when was there a day when she forgot? – the faces of the widow and the little boy . . .

A startling question roused her. Jerry was asking whether Dad and she were divorced yet.

'Oh, yes,' she replied, quite casually.

'The papers are finished and signed, I mean?'

She was astonished. *Papers.* This generation's children knew too much, too soon. Yet how could they help but know?

Again she said simply, 'Yes.'

'Why don't you ever come to our house?' asked Emma.

Jerry rebuked her, although not unkindly. 'You don't know anything. But it's not your fault. You're only five.'

'I'm five and a half. Why don't you, Mommy?'

I'm tired, thought Hyacinth. I'm tired, and I don't know what to say.

They were waiting. And again the woman, the nanny, the stranger, gave her that curious glance.

Then Jerry answered. 'It's because Mom's sick. Tessie said so.'

'Tessie? Who is she?'

'You know. She cooks the food and cleans the house.'

Sick, thought Hyacinth. Yes, I must have looked it that day.

'Oh. Well, she's wrong, Jerry. I'm perfectly well. I had to take care of Granny for a long time, you see, and then—'

'Tessie said there's something the matter with you. I heard her. She told you too, Nanny, don't you remember? I heard you both in the kitchen. Tessie said she thought you were queer because you didn't talk at all that day when you came and we weren't home. She said you were a bad woman, and that's why Daddy went away from you. But I know that's not true. You're not bad, and Tessie is dumb. I hate her. I told Daddy.'

For an instant, Hyacinth closed her eyes. Then she heard her own voice coming as if from a hollow place far off. It seemed to echo in her ears.

'And what did Daddy say?'

'He said of course you weren't bad.'

Nanny, whose flush made two red wounds on her cheeks, interrupted him. 'You need to be careful of what you say, Jerry. I don't remember that Tessie ever used the word "bad," only "sick." Be accurate. That means not making mistakes.'

'I am accurate. I am accurate, Mom. I always remember things, don't I, Mom?'

'Yes, you have a wonderful memory.'

'Oh, he does. I know that,' Nanny said. And turning to Hyacinth, she explained, 'This is all a mistake. Nobody meant any harm. Tessie made a mistake about your being sick, too. Maybe you were that day. I don't know, I wasn't here, but you do seem very well today. Their Uncle Arnie talks about you to the children, and he's never said a word to them about your being sick, or anything. And he would have told them. He talks about you a lot.'

This woman was not fooling Hyacinth. Under the veneer of sympathy and the curiosity now verging on the prurient, there was a touch of malice, an inference that something was 'going on' and that Uncle Arnie was perhaps more to her than a mere uncle.

This kind of thing was horrible for the children. They needed to get off the subject immediately. Yet she could not help one more question.

'What else did Daddy tell you, Jerry?'

'He said Tessie should not talk like that. He said he was going to speak to her about it.'

Emma persisted. 'You won't tell me when you're coming again, Mommy.'

'I'll tell you over the telephone, darling. I can't tell you right now.'

'Then can we go to your house?'

How could she say that she had no house anymore? 'I'll tell you that over the telephone, too.'

'Why do you have to go away again today, Mommy?'

The nanny's interest was palpable. It was legible in her very expression, which said silently: *Now how are you going to answer that one?* Well, maybe you couldn't blame her. The situation really was out of the ordinary, a good topic for speculation and conversation.

'I'm going to school again, Emma, and I mustn't be late.'

'School? But you're grown up. Grown-ups don't go to school.'

'Sometimes they do,' Jerry said wisely. 'Dad told me.'

That settled the question. If Dad told him, then it must be so.

'We really should start now,' said Nanny. 'It's time.'

Promptly, they all stood and went through the lobby toward the exit and the car. Emma and Jerry went running ahead.

'Beautiful children,' said Nanny.

She might have been awkwardly trying to make amends. Or else to 'rub it in,' either one. How to know the devious path of her thoughts, or anybody's thoughts? In any case it did not matter because they would change nothing.

A few hours later as the plane rose into the evening sky, Hyacinth tried to recall those final minutes, but her mind seemed to have gone empty. She did recall that last night while she had sat making foolish fashion sketches, she had been full of anticipation. Yet today it had gone all wrong. It was not that Jerry and Emma were unhappy, for the nanny was good to them and it was plain that they liked her. Gerald, of course, adored them, so it was none of those things. It was only the cruel, undeniable truth that was slowly filling the empty space in her mind: Her children, her flesh as she always thought of them, the flesh of her heart – were slipping away. She was losing them.

Late one afternoon Hyacinth answered a knock on the door and found Arnie.

'I got no answer when I called today, so since I was coming up from Wall Street anyway, and had to pass nearby, I thought I'd take a chance on finding you home.'

'I was at class till just now. I haven't had time to straighten up all this mess. You wouldn't think a little place like this would get so messy. But come in, anyway.'

She was prattling as people can do when they are taken unawares and are already too unnerved to be taken unawares. Standing in the doorway, Arnie was within reaching distance of the card table on which her work was spread, and she was so close to his face, that she was able to catch its flicker of astonishment before he wiped the flicker away with a greeting.

'Well, stranger, long time, no see.'

'But you hear me often enough on the telephone,' she said, and smiled at him, not because she felt like smiling, but because being the kindly person he was, he deserved a smile.

'Not the same. You want to go out to dinner?'

His eye had caught the still-unwrapped delicatessen sandwich next to the bottle of Evian water, as well as the shabby bed in the room beyond. He had seen everything. I swear he can read my mind, thought Hyacinth.

'Thanks, but no,' she replied. 'Another time. This stuff that I'm doing here is due tomorrow at my second class in the morning. I'm really working hard,' she said brightly.

'Good, good. I won't get in your way. I'll stay a few minutes to rest my feet, that's all.'

Taking his seat across from her in the only other chair, he

regarded her. And she, not even raising her eyes from the pencil and paper, was aware of being under close examination.

'How've you been doing?' he asked abruptly.

'Just fine. Busy and fine.'

'Put the pencil down for a minute and talk to me.'

The tone, both peremptory and anxious, surprised her, so she complied.

'I want you to level with me, Hy. You think I don't know you're miserable? Jerry told Gerald about what happened last week when you were down there. And yesterday in the coffee shop after surgery, Gerald told me. So that's why I'm here. He was sorry about it, about the maid and the things she said. He'd like to be able to explain things to you himself. For the children's sake, it would be better for you and him to have a little friendly contact now and then, he thinks.'

Arson. A man killed. Consider yourself lucky. Get on with your life. Friendly contact.

'You can tell him for me, Arnie, that he should be ashamed of himself to give you a message like that. He doesn't mean a word of it, for one thing. And in these circumstances . . . He knows better. So please don't ask me again, will you?' It was an effort to speak, and she said no more.

Arnie made a gesture of discouragement. 'All right, I won't.' He sighed. 'Beats me. I guess nobody ever said divorce is easy. The fallout from it goes on forever, maybe, like a nuclear explosion. Me, I never married, so I guess I wouldn't know. Why I never married? Don't know that, either. Christ, the pretty women we see in this kind of practice! Maybe that's what boggled my mind. You know, plastic surgery, when I was a beginner, I thought was fixing up war wounds, accidents and stuff like that. But most of it's turned out to be making women look younger.'

Gerald, too, had had aspirations. She remembered that young man in Texas who had been born with half a nose, and how Gerald had described the awful, freakish face, and how he had been remade, given a new personality. So now it's pretty women, she thought. Well, that's all right. Somebody has to help them, too. And if some of them make extra payment to the doctor in bed, that's all right too, as far as I'm concerned.

Where has the passion gone, the passion for him that fired me from the day I first saw him until the night it exploded into a real three-alarm fire? Gone. Gone. Dead.

Arnie mused. 'Yes, yes. Too bad. I always tell you, don't I, that I like you both. And Gerald – Gerald was a find for me. My first partner was a dud. Poor handling of patients and too many botched jobs in the O.R. Lucky we weren't sued. But they're already talking about Gerald. He's the coming man down there. Top of the line, he is. Matter of fact, I'm thinking of cutting back, taking less pay and leaving more to him. Not that I'm old. God, I'm not fifty yet. But I'd like to start taking it a little more easy, spend more time outdoors with my horses.'

He was settling in for a cozy chat, and she began to feel impatience, recalling that occasionally he was given to such spurts of talk. When he gave her a long look, she had quick recall of Francine's remark: 'This man's a little bit crazy about you.' The thought unsettled her, and she seized at once on his last word to remark about horses.

'Plural, Arnie? You've bought a companion for Major?'

'This is different. I ride Major. The new one's a Thoroughbred, a beauty. He's a racehorse. I board him at the same place, though. Paid a fortune for him. You can make a fortune too, if he wins, but if he doesn't, it's still a hobby, full of thrills. You never watched a race?'

'No, never.'

It was a pity to be impatient with Arnie. For all his tough-sounding speech, his styled hair and sporty yellow silk tie printed with bridles and saddles, he had a quality of youthful artlessness that was in some way touching.

'Yes, it's an expensive hobby, but if I can afford it, why not? When I take a flyer and I win, I like to treat myself. Bought a honey of a little Mercedes over the weekend. Not quite up to a Lamborghini yet.' He laughed. 'But I always give a big hunk of the win to charity. Kids' hospitals or something. Salves my conscience.' He laughed again. 'Say, you're a kid yourself, back to school. How's it going?'

'Fine. It's interesting. I like it. I wasn't sure I would, but I do.'

'Sure. So maybe *it's* fine, but *you're* not.' Again, he stared at her. 'This is no way to live. Look at this dump. And your supper here, a sandwich from the deli. When I think of the dinners you made in that house, a queen couldn't eat better – why the hell don't you take Gerald's money? He's making enough, for God's sake. He's making plenty.'

'Arnie, you already know the answer, and a minute ago you said that you wouldn't ask—'

Waving away the objection, he continued, 'This is no place for you. Weren't you able to do any better than this even without his money?'

'I have nothing except what I got when the house was sold. I've put the money away, and I have to live on the interest income. Have you any idea what apartments cost in this city?'

'Sure do. That's why I don't have one. It's cheaper and a lot more convenient to go to the Waldorf or someplace for a couple of nights when I come here.' Arnie stood up and peered into the bedroom. 'Geez, the place is bare as a stable. Major lives better. Why didn't you bring some of your furniture, at least?'

'Why, Arnie, it wouldn't fit here, can't you see? It wouldn't belong in the first place. And in the second, it literally wouldn't fit. Neither of the sofas would get up the stairs and through this door.'

'I guess you're right,' he said almost mournfully. 'When I think. When I think of last Christmas at your house! It was sad without the kids' father, but they had you and your mother, and it was a picture, the way they looked eating chocolate cake and— What are you going to do, make Christmas for them here, for God's sake?'

She wished he would only go away and let her alone. And in spite of herself, her eyes filled so that, not wanting him to see them, she got up to look out of the window. It was past dusk, but the street was as well lit as a stage on which diverse people, shabby and stylish, young and old, the working fathers coming home, the patrons of a Chinese restaurant, and the literati shopping for antique books, all moved about their affairs. All had a lively purpose, or looked as if they did. They had somebody, husband or wife, children or friends or lovers waiting for them, or looked as if they had.

Arnie's arm went around her shoulders and turned her toward him. 'Don't cry,' he said gently.

He should not have said it, because immediately, the tears welled up again.

'I wish to hell I knew what this was all about,' he said, still very gently.

'He thinks I did it! That's why he's punishing me.'

In the next instant after she had spoken these words, and long after that, Hyacinth would have retracted them if she could. To think that she had let such shocking dangerous words slip out of her mouth! Who could say that they would never slip carelessly out of Arnie's mouth sometime?

'That you did what?'

'Set the fire. Burned down your building.'

'What?' he cried, and released her. His eyes were wide in horror. 'What? I don't believe it!'

'Yes, yes, it's true.'

And then something, some inner check occurred, and she was able to see that some amends, at least, must be made.

'Yes, isn't it crazy? When I was nowhere near the building? I hadn't been there in weeks. I was home with the children.'

'He must be out of his mind,' Arnie said. 'Why the hell would you do a thing like that?'

'Very simple. On account of Sandy.'

'Why, if anybody did it, I'll tell you, it would have been Sandy. I wouldn't put it past the cheap tramp.'

Now, suddenly, fright grew into panic. And Hyacinth, grasping Arnie's lapels, looked straight into his eyes. 'Oh my God, you won't ever tell him or anybody what I just said, will you, Arnie?'

'Of course not, Hy. Would I hurt you?'

His eyes looked straight back into hers. They were very kind.

'No, I don't think you would,' she said.

'Your mother approves of me.' He was making a little teasing joke. 'And if she does, that should be enough for you. She's pretty smart, that lady is.'

With the fancy handkerchief from his breast pocket, he wiped her eyes. 'Trust me, Hyacinth. I have already forgotten what you told me. If anyone ever asks, and nobody will – why should they? – I'll say I don't know what they're talking about. I'm thinking of those two little kids, and I'm thinking of you. This is awful. You've been very unjustly accused.'

'I don't want this to change your relationship with Gerald. The one thing has nothing to do with the other.' And recovering herself, she added with some little pride, 'I'm not a spoiler.'

'The last person in the world, Hy. The last.' Arnie threw up his hands. 'But dammit all, you can't live here. Listen to me, you've got to get a decent apartment where the kids can come. A nice place near Central Park, where they can play, go horse-back riding and stuff. Get your things out of storage, make it look like something. Has Francine seen this?'

'No. She hasn't been in New York.'

She would be shocked. Moira would be shocked. Anyone who had ever known her would be.

'Oh boy, I can imagine her face when she walks in here! No, you've got to get a decent place, and the sooner, the better. A place near the park, I said.'

'I know I need a place for my children, so they'll be able to visit me. That's why I'm trying to get ahead, trying to fit myself to earn something. But do you know what you're saying? I couldn't pay for a doorknob in the neighborhood you're talking about.

'That's because you don't know the right people. I've got a guy in mind right now, big real estate mogul. Owes me a favor. I'll get him to find you a rental you can afford. I offered before to help you, but you went ahead without me.'

'Arnie, you're an angel, but even angels don't make a habit out of performing miracles.'

'Well, this angel will. You'll see. Do I get a kiss?'

Although she was hoping for the customary friendly kiss, she was prepared for the other kind, and so was relieved when the kiss was merely a conventional brush across each cheek before he ran out and down the four flights of stairs.

From the front window she saw him standing at the curb waiting for a cab, then catch one and leap into it. He was intensely masculine, and most women would find him very attractive, she thought. But she did not find him so. They had no interests at all in common. Yet, strangely enough, he understood her, and for that she was grateful to him.

He really is a puzzle, she thought again. But then, aren't we all?

Chapter Twelve

The movers had departed three days ago, and already the place was in order. Still marveling, Hyacinth stood in the foyer, from which the entire spread, the two bedrooms, the little office or den where she might work and Jerry might sleep, these and all the rest could be seen. Indeed, she was overwhelmed. Nearer to the East River than to upper Fifth Avenue where Old Money and New Money both lived in grandeur, the area was prosperous enough to provide comfort and space. In early spring now, there were ginkgo trees greening on the street; you could walk to the river and watch the boats go by, or you could walk westward, not too far, to the great, blossoming park, where she would go on their next school vacation with her children.

In the top drawer of her desk lay a list of the places, the museums and children's concerts, and the Statue of Liberty, that they would visit. She liked to think that the very sight of that desk, and so many other familiar objects from home, would be meaningful to them and would in some way bind them closer to her again. Inanimate things had strong powers to evoke emotions. Surely, the little round kitchen table would recall the milk and cookies they had so often eaten there after school. Then there was the cuckoo clock, by which they had learned to tell time. But perhaps she was attributing to children an adult sensitivity which they did not yet have. Or perhaps, like some people, they would never have it. And if so, maybe that was all to the good . . .

Given the comparative size of the former house and the present apartment, it was inevitable that most of her possessions were still in storage waiting for that wonderful future which Francine assured her was coming. Even so, she had given away some of the choicest articles: the bed that she had shared with Gerald, the great leather wingchair with its ottoman on which his feet had rested, and the dining-room table over which he had presided. Now there was nothing here that reminded her particularly of him.

'Wait till you get it fixed up,' Arnie, with his usual enthusiasm, had said on that first day when he had brought her here to see the apartment.

Vacant then, it had seemed enormous, and shockingly expensive. And so she had exclaimed, 'Arnie! You know I can't afford this. You might as well take me to see a Vanderbilt mansion, if they still have one around here.'

He had been very patient. 'I told you, Hy, that I could make a deal. You'll pay peanuts for this – provided that you don't let the story leak out. The guy would have half a million tenants at his throat if you did. Geez, he must own a few thousand apartments. He won't miss a few thousand bucks rent here.'

'It still doesn't make any sense,' she had protested. 'It's ridiculous, the little I pay.'

'That's because you don't know anything about business. He owes me a favor, I told you. So pay your rent and enjoy it. Let the kids come and enjoy it.'

That had ended the discussion and should have settled the matter, except that of course Hyacinth herself now owed Arnie a favor, a huge one.

'And there is no way in the world that I can ever repay it,' she had told Francine over the telephone.

'Obviously, he thinks there is, and he's hoping you will.'

If that really should be the case, she thought now, I have been very unjust to him in allowing him to get such an idea. But I don't think I have been. What have I ever done to encourage him? Perhaps I should not have accepted this favor. But the temptation had been too great.

And for what must be the hundredth time by now, she looked around, feeling the atmosphere. It was so blessedly quiet here; the rooms downtown had been battered with noise around the clock; the life of the street and the life inside the old building had seemed to be taking place inside her very head. It was so blessedly light here; the sun and the night sky, equally, laid their glow on the walls and the floor.

Arnie's house-warming flowers had just been delivered, and they were everywhere. There was an arrangement on the table in the dining ell; an unidentified flowering shrub, probably rare and expensive, stood in a handsome porcelain container between the living-room windows, and on the night table next to her bed stood a tiny vase of pink rosebuds. She went to the telephone to call him at his hotel and thank him.

'You just caught me,' he said. 'I'm throwing my stuff into a suitcase to catch a night plane back home.'

'I thought you were staying longer,' she answered for lack of anything more to say.

'Hey, I'm not retired. I work. And this time I didn't have any business in town for an excuse. I came to see you moved in.'

'What a friend you are! You do far too much,' she said, meaning it. 'I'm sorry you won't see my mother. She's coming tomorrow, and I thought you might have dinner with us.'

'Your mother? Great. Good thing she never saw the other place.'

'I know. I never would have heard the end of it, would I?'

'And she would be right. I like Francine, in case you're wondering. And do you know why? Because she likes me a lot better than you do.'

'That's not fair, Arnie. I do like you. How could I not?'

'Well, well. We'll let that go.'

'I'm sorry you won't be here to dinner. I'm trying out the kitchen. It's ages since I've cooked anything.'

'Then you must be feeling better,' he said gently. 'Isn't that what it means?'

'Not really. It means that I'm learning to survive. It's either that or quit.'

'Don't quit, Hy. Never quit.'

*   *   *

Francine said as they put the last dish into the washer, 'I haven't had a dinner like this in ages. Either I eat out, or else I throw something together for myself, and I needn't tell you the result is not like your result. You're a mystery to me, Hyacinth. You always were.'

Was she going to start another harangue about the divorce and the children? Oh, please not, prayed Hyacinth. No, not this time. Her smile was fond, a motherly smile.

'And here you are, studying fashion of all things, you, the jeans-and-sweater lady.'

'Maybe I've inherited a touch of the fashion business from you. Just the smallest touch.'

Francine reached for a notebook on the living-room table. 'They remind me of your paintings, the way you did figures, your father lying in the hammock, or me in my white dress.'

'A lot of fashion people like to paint, too. Some really famous designers started in as sketchers. You show the first sketch to the manufacturer to see whether he's interested.

'Maybe you'll be one of the famous fashion people.'

The remark was fatuous. Francine had no idea of the competition, of the raw, cut-throat rivalries, the people who promise and fail to keep the promise, the businesses that zoom to the top in favor and collapse before they have barely gotten used to being on top. If I can just make some sort of a decent living, thought Hyacinth, – and thought for the hundredth time – something in a steady way, a bit more dependable than the dresses I sold to the R. J. Miller store . . . Always, always, no matter what she might be thinking or doing, at every living minute, that need was there. Without any rational basis, it was there. Even when she was taking pleasure in her work – and as she progressed and did well, it was really pleasurable – the need was there.

Often, in the middle of conversation, she found herself drifting away. Talking to someone about anything at all, her mind abruptly produced a picture: Jerry, showing all his teeth when he laughs. Or her mind asks a question: It's four o'clock. Are they on their way to the riding school?

Now she forced herself back to the moment, to the pretty room and Francine waiting for her to speak. And isn't it odd that two human beings, unless they are occupied with a book or something specific, cannot be together without talking? It is actually offensive not to talk, as if to say that one is bored, indifferent or angry.

'I bought something on the spur of the moment this afternoon,' she said. 'It's something I can't afford, and I can't believe I did it.'

'Let's see it.'

From the hall closet, Hyacinth brought out a roll of multi-colored, patterned cloth, unrolled it and hung it from her arm to display.

'It was in a decorator's window,' she explained. 'Upholstery fabric. Feel the weight. But it's no heavier, really, than a genuine Scottish kilt. I thought, what a fabulous skirt it would make. And the colors! Don't they remind you of stained glass, all those cobalts and rubies?'

'It's certainly different.'

'You wouldn't like it?'

'I don't know. When would you wear it, and with what?'

'Wear it any time you want to. With boots and thick sweater, or in the evening with a silk shirt and a ruby-and-diamond necklace out of the family vault. But in that case, you should be accompanied by a detective.'

There was something about those colors that made her feel good in spite of herself, and Hyacinth laughed. 'I bought some grass green silk the other day, too. I happened to be downtown and found it on sale.' She did not say that she had bought it at a textile wholesaler's near where she had been living. 'It's cheap stuff to start with, but the color is wonderful, and I thought it would be good for cutting practice. I like to practice at home.'

'Let's see it.'

'Look. Isn't it lovely? It reminds me of a lawn after a good rain.'

'And what would you do with this?'

'Drape it very simply. But not so simply so that it looks like underwear. Too many things look like underwear, or else like Halloween costumes.'

'Go on. Tell me more.'

'Well of course, it would take a woman with a marvelous figure to wear a simple dress in such a vivid color. A woman with a figure like yours. Would you let me try out the drape on you?'

Francine was amused. 'Why not?'

'All right. Let me get some pins. We had a lesson in draping technique yesterday. It's really hard. I'm going to try Grecian folds. Stand perfectly still.' Through a mouthful of pins, she kept on talking. 'A plain dress like this ought to be hand-sewn. People don't realize, at least I never did, that hand-sewing is what makes all the difference. It's what you get at the couturiers in Paris. It's what you pay for. Granny could have worked in a place like that. I never realized it until now.'

'How on earth can you talk with that mouthful of pins?'

'Easy. It makes me feel professional.'

Concentrating, she fell silent. For an instant, she saw herself at the easel with a brush in hand; she felt the same peaceful absorption in creating a shape, making a something out of a nothing. She pinned and took out and pinned again. The material slithered under her fingers. It would go more easily with a firmer, better fabric. The line of the skirt below the hips would be more crisp, like the diagonal of a triangle. Still, this was not going to be too bad.

'There's a full-length mirror in the bathroom,' she said at last. 'Go in and tell me how you like yourself.'

In a second, Francine returned. 'I don't believe it,' she cried. 'Putting a dress together in no time. You, Hyacinth.'

'Well, we have big name designers coming to teach. If you pay attention, you can learn something, that's all.'

'You had this skill before you went there. Don't tell me everybody in the school picked this up from a few lectures.'

'It's not quite like that. There's a lot of hands-on work, too. Would you like me to sew this for you? Would you wear it?'

'Why darling, I'd put a sign on it with your name. I'd be as proud as Emma was when you made the rose dress for her.'

At the mention of Emma there was an instant silence. Francine's sigh was barely audible before, with obvious intent, she spoke cheerfully.

'I see now how art led you into this. Everything's carried over, hasn't it? The sense of form and proportion – it's all there. You know, I have to apologize, Hyacinth. You were right about making this career choice, and I was wrong in objecting. I told myself I had no right to an opinion because I don't know much about art yet the truth is – well, what you're doing now is really brilliant. This seems almost effortless. This time it's the real you.' She stopped. 'I hope I haven't hurt your feelings,' she said softly.

Francine and Will Miller. Two people who never knew each other and never will. She had kept her opinion to herself, and he had bluntly thrown his into her face.

'Do you still go into any of the R. J. Miller stores?' she asked.

'No, the one at home closed two years ago, and now the one where you used to live, in fact the whole chain, has been bought out by some conglomerate. They were old and nice, but behind the times, I guess.'

Hyacinth felt like a fool for remembering a man with whom she could not have spent a total of more than six or seven hours. Yet now and then on the street, she would see somebody who for some trivial reason, long strides, horn-rimmed glasses or a ruddy face, reminded her of him. There was no reason for it.

'I miss you,' Francine said. 'At least I used to be able to get in the car every couple of weeks and drive over.'

'So now you can take the train and be here just as quickly. Isn't your room nice?'

'Very. But I didn't know you'd have a room for me. I left my bag at the hotel.'

'You didn't! You went to a hotel? Oh, I'm sorry. I thought you understood.'

'No problem. Next time I'll know. At least I've seen where you live, and I feel better.'

'I pay half nothing for it, too, remember.'

'You don't really believe Arnie's story, do you?'

'Why shouldn't I believe it?'

'Because this is a very expensive building, and people scarcely do things like this for their own brothers, let alone for a friend. No, dear, Arnie is paying for it and giving you a handsome present.'

'Dad would say, "Francine, you're off the deep end again." Can't you hear him?'

'Oh, really?' Francine's eyebrows rose. 'Well, we'll see. What are you going to say when he asks you to marry him?'

'He won't,' said Hyacinth. 'I've told you that. It's ridiculous. I'm not his type, and he's not mine.'

'Well, we'll see. It would be a tricky connection, anyway, too close to Gerald.' For a moment Francine paused, frowned slightly, and then impetuously burst out, 'What are you going to do about your children? I don't understand you. When are you going to tell me what this crazy business is all about? Am I a stranger whom you can't trust? Am I?'

The black wave came back and swept over Hyacinth. Determined not to drown again, she fought back.

'It's not a matter of trust. It's a matter of privacy. Yes, you're my mother and I'm your child, but I'm not *a* child.'

Last week they found a man who, ten years before, had set fire to his estranged wife's house. They found him in Oklahoma. How they found him, Hyacinth didn't know. She didn't want to read the whole article. Somebody must have seen him or heard something – what's the difference? It seemed to her that hardly a month went by without her reading about somebody who thought he was safe and wasn't.

'All right. Maybe you'll think better of it someday.' Francine stood up. 'It's late, and I've got a day's worth of errands tomorrow. I don't get to New York that often.'

Hyacinth, too, stood up. And pleading now, said, 'Don't be angry. Please. It's very hard—'

'Yes, hard and sad, and I'd best drop it. I'm sorry I brought the subject up because we never get anywhere with it, do we?' Francine put on her jacket, belted it smartly around her narrow waist and took her handbag. 'I guess we won't be seeing each other for a while. The Child Welfare League is sending a committee to Mexico, and I'm to be there as a volunteer observer for six weeks. I thought I'd stop off in Florida on the way. One thing that's good about knowing Arnie is that I can call him when I want to see Emma and Jerry. I'll give them your love.'

'I speak to them almost every day, you know.'

'Even so. Well, I'll be going.'

They kissed, and Hyacinth said, 'I'll really make the dress if you want it. And if I can manage, you'll have it in time to take with you to Mexico.'

'Thanks. I'd love that, but don't push yourself. Take care of yourself.'

'You do, too.'

The elevator came. Francine stepped in, and vanished. Another cool leave-taking. Discreet, polite and cool, thought Hyacinth. I think all the time about the way it used to be when the children were babies, and how fresh and jolly and close we all were.

Gerald had thrown a stone into the pond, and the ripples are still spreading.

Time, she read. And again read Tennyson's old words, old but still true, and so befitting to her own condition.

> *And Time, a maniac scattering dust,*
> *And Life, a Fury slinging flame.*

Flame! How apt, she thought, and closed the book.

It was late. From where she sat, on an evening some weeks later, the city existed as a scattered sparkle against the night sky, itself stained faintly pink by the sparkle. No sound carried fourteen stories above the street, so that the room was filled with silence. In the summers of her past life, the nights had been loud with cricket chirp, interrupted on occasion by a dog's bark or the slam of a screen door.

At the end of the hall, the children were asleep. Tomorrow they would be going home, back to Gerald's house. Magnanimously, she thought with a bitterness so sharp that it pained her chest, he had allowed her these two weeks. In a way it was more painful to have Jerry and Emma so briefly and to part with them, than it was to speak on the telephone; the intervals between visits were too long, but the telephone, thanks to Arnie's intervention, was always there.

Thanks to Arnie. He had predicted that the apartment would bring luck, and it had indeed brought much improvement. At least the children knew they had a 'place' with their mother; the loss of the old house had disturbed them even more deeply than she had expected it to. And she reflected now upon the influence of 'things,' for it had seemed plain that they had missed the house more than they missed her!

Gran's clock bonged eleven times. It was too loud, but the children slept soundly through every stroke. The reverberation died away, and still Hyacinth sat, wide awake, thinking that she ought to go to bed. There were only a few hours left; tomorrow, Jerry wanted to go to the Museum of Natural History to see the dinosaurs again. After that they would have lunch, and after that, late in the afternoon, Arnie, who had taken advantage of this weekend for one of his business trips to New York, would fly back to Florida with them.

He had come to seem almost like family. Often it was easier to talk to him than to Francine. He never *questioned*. And the children has so much fun with him, not that Francine ever failed to be wonderful with them, but Arnie was different.

He and his horses were now a big part of their lives. It was amazing to watch Jerry's relaxed handling of a creature so much larger than he, or to hear him talk about the Thoroughbred and the Tennessee Walker. Arnie would chuckle and encourage him.

'You'd better keep up,' he would tease Jerry, 'because in a couple of years Emma's going to trot right along with you.'

'Then I'll canter,' Jerry would retort.

'I suppose I should learn to ride,' Hyacinth said once, and Arnie had agreed that she certainly should. But what for? For these occasional trips to Florida? Let them enjoy their horses with Arnie.

Let them be the beneficiaries of his kindness. We, my children and I, she thought, are only one among all his charities. He was an extraordinary giver, Gerald had told her, one of those rich, childless men who love to give of their money and their time.

Francine, of course, had a different explanation, and although she had not said as much, Hyacinth had an idea that she would actually welcome some attachment, marriage or otherwise, between Arnie and her daughter.

'Now that you're free,' she had counseled more than once, 'you should be getting out more. A young woman needs some emotional attachment' – meaning obviously, 'You are too young for a celibate life.'

As if anybody in good health was ever too old! But it wasn't all that simple. She longed to be loved! But there is no one, she thought. I work all day among students younger than I am, or else they are already committed to someone else. Or else they are not – and many of them are not – interested in women at all. There is no one.

The clock bonged midnight. On stockinged feet, she went to her children's beds to stand in the hall's pale beam of light, just gazing at them. Life. Life and Time.

'Don't you know I always like to do things in style?'

Arnie made a joke of the question, but he meant it, nevertheless. And he knew that Hyacinth knew it, too. He had hired a limousine to take them to the airport.

Emma and Jerry were tired and half asleep. They had tramped through the museum from top to bottom to top and back, and then walked through the park to the apartment and fetched their suitcases; now they had what Hyacinth told them were 'museum feet.'

'You'll sleep all the way on the plane,' Arnie said. 'And when you arrive, the attendant will wake you because this plane doesn't go any farther.'

Hyacinth was startled. 'Attendant? Do you mean you're not going with them?'

'I have to stay over and meet a guy tomorrow morning about some property. They'll be fine. That's what I was talking about just now with the attendant.' And when she looked dubious and distressed, he assured her that thousands of children all over the country traveled between their divorced parents these days.

'Signs of the times. I phoned Gerald this morning and he

approves, and nobody could be more careful of his kids than he is. You'll have to give him that much, Hy.'

Still anxious, she asked Jerry, 'Do you mind flying back without Uncle Arnie?'

'Aw Mom, I'm nine years old,' said he, jutting his jaw and stiffening his small shoulders. 'I can take care of Emma.'

'You will not! I take care of myself!' Emma shrieked with such an air of insulted dignity, that Hyacinth had to laugh.

So Hyacinth watched until they were out of sight at the end of the jetway. Jerry was carrying both suitcases, while Emma, perhaps forgetting her dignity, trotted behind him holding closely to his jacket. If it had been permitted, their mother would have run and clasped them both again.

'You angry at me?' asked Arnie as they turned away.

'A little. You should have told me.'

'Then you wouldn't have let them go alone.'

She had to admit that was true. Sometimes he annoyed her with his way of giving advice and taking charge. Absurd as it would sound if it were put into words, she had a feeling that he was treating her possessively, as a husband might, for her own good.

'I've reserved a table for us at my hotel,' he said abruptly.

Having planned to go home and get into bed to read, she was not entirely pleased. And thanking him, she very tactfully said that she had to get up early and would love to do it the next time.

'You're not going to bed at eight o'clock,' he insisted. 'I'll have you home early enough. Don't disappoint me.' And he gave her his very attractive smile, part coax and part plea.

Through gathering darkness, the heavy car rolled smoothly down the highway. Lulled after a while by the gliding motion, she willed her shoulders to relax their tension. The plush, comfortable little space in which she was sitting gave her a feeling of safety and protection. It was a long time since she had been aware of such a feeling; she had grown unused to it. And silently, to herself, she repeated, relax, relax.

The dinner, as expected, was the best, as were the surroundings, softly rose and gray with flowers in harmony, and unobtrusive piano music in the distance at the far end of the room.

Arnie was watching her. He was amused when she took out a palm-sized notebook and scribbled something beneath the protection of the table.

'Working here, too?'

'Sorry. It's become a habit. The thing is, if I don't get something down on paper when I see it, I risk forgetting it. And you never know when some little thing will catch your eye. It might be something on the street or at a costume movie.'

'What did you see just now?'

'Don't laugh. A man came in wearing a dark blue suit. The woman with him was wearing chocolate brown, and the colors were perfect together. I want to remind myself of that.'

'You really like what you're doing, don't you?'

'Well, it's not exactly what I wanted to do with my life, but that's the way things are.' She stopped. Then, having had no previous intent to ask this question, she did ask it. 'Does Gerald ever say anything about me? Does he really know how much you do for Emma and Jerry?'

'He never says anything about you, Hy. I would tell you if he did. We don't get a chance to talk much, anyway. We've a busy office, a madhouse some days. When we're not working, we go our separate ways. Maybe that's why our arrangement works out so well. Gerald's got his own social life.' Winking at Hyacinth, he added, 'He's younger than I am. But yes, he does appreciate the fact that the kids like me.'

Hyacinth was touched. If anything were to go wrong, Arnie's shrewd insight would recognize it. The nanny was all right enough, but you couldn't have the same faith in her judgment. She would still take any problems to Gerald, not to me, she thought. The nanny does not approve of me.

'I'll never know how to thank you,' she said. And raising the wineglass to her lips, thought to hide the moistening of her eyes.

'It's been a hard day for you, Hy, having to see them leave.'

He laid a kind hand over hers. 'Buck up, Hy. You're doing great. You're a great girl. You've got heart and stamina, like a great horse. Come on, I'm kidding you. You're no horse, you're a damn handsome woman, and you need another glass of wine. Don't argue with me. And eat. You've lost too much weight. Don't you do any more cooking in that nice kitchen you have?'

The mention of 'kitchen' brought something to mind. For a while, Francine's idea about the apartment lease had seemed foolish, and Hyacinth had dismissed it, but now in an odd way as she felt the warmth of Arnie's hand, it did not seem quite as foolish.

And she said suddenly, 'My mother doesn't believe that the apartment rents for so little. She doesn't believe your story that your friend reduced the rent as a favor.'

'No? And so who reduced it, if not my friend?'

'Nobody. You pay the balance every month.'

'Well,' he said. 'Well.'

'I was stupid and childish not to have guessed that you were doing it.'

'For a childish woman, you aren't doing too badly.'

Now his hand was stroking hers. His nails were immaculate, and she liked that; too many men were careless about their black-rimmed nails. His wristwatch was a sculptured gold band, like a bracelet; tiny diamonds were imbedded in his gold cufflinks, and she did not like that. But the second glass of wine was beginning to buzz in her head, and what difference did it make, anyway?

'I wanted you to have a decent place for the kids, Hy. And for yourself, too. You're a lovely woman. The women I meet are all the same, interchangeable, you know what I mean? They look the same and they talk the same, mostly nonsense. You're a bookworm, and still you're never boring. I've never felt this way about anybody. You're probably too good for me to get any idea about you. I guess I've told you this before. If I haven't, I meant to.'

Hyacinth switched the subject. 'You're too kind to me, Arnie. As soon as I finish up and get a job, I'm going to pay you back for everything.'

'Don't be a fool. Do you think I'd accept it? Drink the wine. It's a hundred and fifty dollars a bottle, for God's sake; don't waste it. And caviar — eat it up! I won't even tell you what that costs.' *He sprinkles money*, Gerald said. You'd think it was water. Well, he's got no wife, no children, no house . . . that makes a difference.

'When we're through here, I want you to come upstairs a minute, Hy. I want to show you something.'

'Not your etchings?'

She was not sure whether her remark was witty or merely stupid. But at any rate, he laughed and explained that, no, the things were only some toys he had bought for the kids and hadn't wanted to entrust to their care on the plane.

Upstairs in his room, he displayed a fancy, expensive calculator for Jerry and a marvelous doll in riding clothes, complete from helmet to jodhpurs, for Emma. When these had been whole-heartedly admired, he brought out a small velvet box.

On seeing it, Hyacinth felt a shock. Could he possibly have in his head what Francine always swore he had? But no. It was only – although 'only' was hardly the right word – a very fine gold chain holding a pendant made of two cherubs, female and male, with large diamond eyes.

'Turn around. Let me put it on for you,' he commanded.

In the mirror that hung between the windows, she beheld herself. Her cheeks were flushed. Her dark hair gleamed, her eyes gleamed, and the pendant gleamed on the white skin above her cleavage.

'Oh, Arnie,' she cried, 'it's lovely! Lovely. But—'

'But I shouldn't have done it,' he mocked. 'And why shouldn't I, please?'

Because, she wanted to say, *and did not say, I am already too obligated to you, and I don't want to be.*

'You do too much,' she murmured. 'It gets harder to find words to thank you.'

'You can at least give me a kiss.'

Obligingly, she moved toward his cheek, but he, moving faster, pulled her to himself and found her mouth instead. Her first impulse was to resist, but as he increased the pressure, her strength rushed away, and they stood there, firmly attached from mouth to hip. Now her will rushed away, and thoughts raced through her agitated mind: It's the wine, I'm weak, it's been two years since I've felt anything.

His fingers were undoing the buttons of her blouse, which

opened in front. His skin was fragrant with pine, or spices, or sweet hay. He was strong. Her thoughts kept repeating: It's been so long. How good not to resist, to float. Close your eyes. Let him . . .

They were in a suite, and when she opened her eyes, she saw past a door that was ajar. She saw a bed already turned down for the night; it was white and crisp. There he would take off her clothes and lay her down . . .

Oh, no! What are you doing, Hyacinth? You wanted *somebody*, but not just *anybody*. You don't want *this* man. You'll be sorry five minutes afterward if you do this. Oh, no!

'What is it?' Arnie cried.

She was so ashamed! And he would be terribly angry. He would think she was a common tease, one of those despicable women who lead a man on and then deny him.

'I can't. Arnie, I can't,' she whispered. 'Please don't be angry at me.'

Like hers, his face was flushed. He had been ready, and she had hurt him, had hurt this very decent, kindly man.

'I'm sorry. Oh God, I'm sorry. It isn't you, Arnie, it's just that suddenly I got scared. I don't understand myself. I guess I'm just not ready yet.'

Absurdly, they were still standing there, only inches apart. For a moment, neither spoke. Arnie's eyes had narrowed, his face hardened.

'What do you think you're doing?' he began, and stopped. 'No. You didn't start it. I did. I'm sorry, too. Button your blouse.' And he turned away, for her breast was exposed. And he repeated quietly now, 'It's not your fault. I started it.'

Some women would say that a night in bed was little enough to give him for all the good he had already done her. But she was just not one of those women, not able to do it.

He must have read the doubt and regret on her face, because he tried to comfort her. 'You have no trust left. That's what it is. I understand.'

'Yes, you do understand, and without knowing half of it.'

Her knees were so weak that she had to sit down. She trembled, and he saw that. He saw everything.

'Am I unstable?' she whispered.

He came to sit next to her. 'What? Unstable?' he asked.

'Gerald thinks I am. Am I?'

'Well, if you ever were, Hy, you sure as hell aren't now.'

It was wild, it was utterly reckless and senseless, this need that all of a sudden possessed her. It was jumping off a cliff into midstream, throwing her life away. But she did it now. She did the unthinkable.

'I was in the office that night. I've already told you that Gerald thinks I did it. He isn't altogether wrong. I was in the office that night, and I lied to you before, I guess I didn't know you well enough to trust you with my life.'

And she continued, 'I was smoking. You remember that I was almost addicted then? Haven't you noticed that now I never touch a cigarette? I made a vow: Oh God, never again.'

'Jesus, I'm sick!' Arnie said, and he looked it, sick and aghast.

'I went crazy, you see. I trashed everything and walked up and down, smoking one cigarette after the other. That's how the fire started. It was all on account of that girl, and now here I am!' she cried. 'Here I am. That's the reason he has my children. That's what it's all about. I had to sign them away, don't you see? Or else, or else—'

'I do see,' he said gently. 'I do.'

'Even now I'm not out of the woods. And I never, never will be. I shall never have my children. I shall never forget the innocent man who died because of me.'

When he put his arm around her, she laid her head on his shoulder; no passion now, no desire was in the contact this time, only the will on his part to give some comfort, and on her part the need to receive whatever he could give.

'It was an accident, Arnie, I swear it was. The curtains must have caught fire, and so it spread. Do *you* believe I did it on purpose? Tell me honestly, do you?'

'Knowing you, I'll say absolutely not. I don't see why he should make such a charge and be so upset, anyway. It wasn't even his building. I owned it.'

'He was tired of me,' she said simply, 'and that gave him an excuse. Now he has all the pleasure of his children without the nuisance of me.'

'You, a nuisance?'

'It happens all the time.'

'It wouldn't happen to me if you would – I don't know whether you ever would consider – no, now's not the moment.'

Suddenly, a terrible fear surged through Hyacinth's blood and chilled her very bones. What had she done? Clutching his arms, she stared into his face, crying wildly, 'Arnie! You would never let anything of this slip, would you? Not by accident? I trust you, Arnie! It's my life! My children's lives, too, if the worst should happen to me. I haven't even told Francine. I'm afraid she would get so enraged one day, that she would go to Gerald, and that would be the end of me. She despises him.'

'Hy, put it out of your mind. I've already forgotten it. I never heard it. You never told me anything.'

Perhaps she had been naïve. Naïveté was her major flaw, Francine said, and Gerald had said it often enough, too. Yet sometimes in this life you have to trust somebody.

'I trust you, Arnie,' she repeated.

He stood up. 'I'm going to get a taxi and take you home.' He kissed each cheek. 'I'm here for you, Hy, and I'll wait for you. I won't rush you right now. But think it over.'

Chapter Thirteen

For some months, on weekends and in the evening after classes, Hyacinth had been sewing, saving her work and showing it to nobody. It had become her habit to listen to music while she worked. I've gone through ten operas, she calculated, and enough clothes to make a small collection.

The upholstery-fabric skirt still hung in a closet. Out of the same cobalt-and-ruby cloth, she had made a jacket to be worn with a finely pleated chiffon skirt, in either of those two colors. These also hung in the closet. The apple green dress that she had made for Francine, who had worn it on her trip to Mexico and loved it, had now been duplicated in green satin of the finest quality and was naturally, she thought, twice as successful. The same closet held a plain black dress with a modified seventeenth-century ruff of superb white lace, a suit of gray menswear woolen piped in scarlet, a flowered linen suit, and various knee-length pants and blouses.

One day she stood looking at them all and wondered what they were for other than to give pleasure to her while she created them. She had not the least desire to wear them. The clothes she already owned were more than adequate for her lifestyle: classes, the weekend afternoons with a few of the women she had befriended in the apartment building, along with Francine's occasional visit to New York. Francine's social life was far busier than was her daughter's.

When she went to Florida, it was never for more than two days at a time. The children came north, but also briefly. Arnie, whenever he came to the city, took her out to dinner, but never above the ground floor of his hotel . . .

It was as if that evening had not even occurred. A complicated set of emotions was hers: gratitude and a deep affection. What his feelings after her rejection of him might be, she could only guess. Obviously, he wanted to see her; otherwise, why would he come to her? Surely he had other women who gave him what she would not give him. Perhaps it was simply a case of being sorry for her, and more especially so now that he knew the whole story.

As she stood ruminating about her life and absently gazing at her work she decided one day that it really would make sense to try selling it. If it should turn out not to make sense, nothing would have been lost. So before fifteen minutes went by, she had swept the closet's contents into a large flat box and gone downstairs to call a taxi. Not ten minutes later, she arrived at one of the city's most fashionable Madison Avenue shops, there to exhibit her work to the manager.

Is it possible, she asked herself as she watched him examine the contents of the box, that he is accustomed to such eccentric behavior as mine? For now, on second or third thought, she was shocked by what she was doing and would gladly have run out of the place if that would not have been even more eccentric behavior.

Apparently, this rather elegant gentleman was not shocked. On the contrary, he was even showing some interest. Silent minutes passed. Tissue paper rustled.

'I like the menswear suit piped in red with a lace blouse beneath it,' he told her, smiling a little.

One by one, he emptied the box, examined each article slowly and repacked them all with care.

'Well, I don't know,' he said, looking Hyacinth up and down.

She looked back, thinking, he doesn't know how to get rid of me nicely.

'Well, I don't know. Your work is interesting. You didn't expect a positive answer just like that, did you?'

Hyacinth wanted to say, Sir, I didn't expect a positive answer at all; do I look like such a fool? Yes, I suppose I do, or I wouldn't have come here in the first place. Look at the names on the floors below: every big wheel from Milan, Paris and New York is there. And she herself shook her head.

'How about writing your name here and your phone number and maybe a little bit about yourself. Give us some time to think. You'll hear from me, one way or the other.'

In a dreamlike state, not sure whether she was fooling herself or whether the gentleman was fooling her, Hyacinth picked up her box and took a taxi back home.

When, not very many days later, the telephone rang and she heard an unfamiliar voice, she thought at once that it must be that gentleman's secretary calling to tell her that Mr. So-And-So regrets that although he appreciates your coming to see him, etc., etc.

Instead, it was the secretary to a very, very famous name in fashion: Lina Libretti. What Chanel had been in Paris forty years ago, Libretti was today in New York – or if not quite a Chanel, she was – well, a Libretti. It seemed she had been told about the clothes that Hyacinth had displayed at one of the fine Madison Avenue shops. And would Hyacinth be interested in bringing them to the office tomorrow or the next day?

Completely overwhelmed, Hyacinth replaced the receiver. Of course she knew Lina Libretti, and not only because everyone else did, but also because on several occasions Ms. Libretti had come to speak at the Institute. She was a dark little dynamo of a woman, still with a strong European accent. So it was that on the following afternoon, Hyacinth set off for Seventh Avenue with the flat box under her arm again, and in her heart a mixture of fantastic hope along with some very realistic, cold-water common sense.

The room was large. Enormous windows brought in the sky, an enormous desk littered with magazines and sheaves of folders stood behind a large wall of shelves, and these were filled with photographs of famous people. In the midst of all this bigness, behind the huge desk, sat the tiny woman. In the classroom she had not seemed quite that small.

She stood up, giving Hyacinth a warm smile. Then speaking brusquely, she got immediately down to business. 'You needn't have lugged all that stuff with you. I know your work, your sketches. You don't remember that I was at your class?'

'I remember it very well,' said Hyacinth, thinking, how could anybody forget?

'Yes. I remember you, too. I had had it in my mind to talk to you at the end of the semester. I don't believe in distracting students in the middle of the year. But you beat me to it. You made an impression over there.' With this statement came a wide gesture toward Fifth Avenue. 'I do four collections a year, you know, and they buy heavily from all of them. But I suppose you've already heard that, too.'

Hyacinth had only a chance to nod before the flow of words resumed. 'And you made an impression on me, too. I have a feeling that you know something about art. Also, that you have a feel for nature. Am I right? Won't you sit down?'

Hyacinth was oddly affected. This woman was most out of the ordinary, certainly most intelligent, maybe a clairvoyant judge of people, and possibly possessed of a fierce temper.

'Well, am I right?' repeated Ms. Libretti.

'I do, or I have done, a great deal of painting. And I did grow up in a very small country town.'

'You see,' Libretti interrupted. 'I saw it in your work, all those leaves and shades of sky. The freshness. Maybe that sounds like a lot of nonsense to you, and maybe it is, but anyway, you're very good, my dear, very good. I'm an old woman, way over seventy, and I've seen hundreds come and go. They all think they have the talent, the touch, poor young things, because very few of them have it. They all think they're original, but how many are?' She laughed. 'I'm not all that original myself. Listen. Would you like to come work here with me? I can teach you twice as fast as they can teach you in a class.'

It seemed as if Hyacinth's heart was hammering in her chest, her ears, and possibly in her toes as well.

'All right. I see it on your face. You'll come. Now undo this box and let me take a look at your stuff. You practically knocked that poor man off his feet with it the other day.'

Looking back long afterward, Hyacinth estimated that it had taken about half a year for her to accept the full reality of events. For one thing, there had been so much for her to learn, that her first hour's euphoria had been completely squelched by the second day in Lina Libretti's establishment. At any moment, she had expected to be informed that she was, after all, not fitted for the work and that the whole thing was a regrettable mistake.

She had never before seen a workroom, where under ultimate strong lighting sat and stood rows of men and women sewing, cutting, pressing and finishing the objects of the designer's imagination. Except in fashion magazines, she had never seen a designer pinning and fitting a living model; the only such experience she had ever had was when she had fitted the green dress on Francine. She knew nothing about cutting knitted fabrics, not much about two-faced cloth and practically nothing at all about costs, or the whole price structure on which survival depends.

Her mistakes were discouraging, and she feared the reprimands that, like a whip, came cracking out of Lina's mouth whenever Hyacinth blundered or forgot. On one discouraging afternoon, she even went so far as to suggest that perhaps Lina would like her to leave. The response was another verbal whiplash of words, followed by a pat on the back and the words, 'Don't be an idiot. You'll be here long after I will – if you want to, that is.'

If you want to? Her head seemed to teem with ideas. She went to the costume museum, to the Chinese exhibit, to the Central Park lake, and all was fertile ground for her imagination. The lace on a baby's bonnet turned into a pyramid of flounces on an almond-colored ball gown, and a patterned sari became the flowing sleeves on a cream-colored sheath.

Lina nodded. 'Good. Now let's cut them. Watch me. Pay attention.'

When the same store to which Hyacinth had taken her early samples ordered several of the pieces and displayed them under the Libretti name, an article in a popular fashion periodical reported that the new designer was young, and that her name was Hyacinth.

Lina was generous. 'If you keep on as you've begun, I'm thinking about giving you full credit. You will work in a lower price range, not low, but lower, and we'll call your line "Lina Libretti's *Hyacinth* productions".'

It was interesting to see how individuals reacted to this sudden alteration in her life.

Francine was the loving mother. She made an immediate trip to New York, took her to a gala dinner at one of the city's grandest restaurants, and bought her a bracelet to go with her new celebrity. Yet, on her face behind the proud smile there could be discerned a slight, the very slightest, shadow of doubt or incredulity, as if to say that the whole business was unreal.

Arnie showed his typical boosterism and his typical skepticism. 'Great! Great! That's showing the world! But you're new at this, so take care, look around and find out what the going pay rate is. Don't let anybody take advantage of you.'

From Gerald there came a short, friendly letter of congratulation. Hyacinth threw it into the wastebasket and most certainly did not acknowledge it. Since Gerald had not been known to subscribe to fashion papers, it was surprising that he had even heard this piece of news.

'You told him,' she said to Arnie over the telephone.

'I swear I didn't. Face it, Hy, you're making a name for yourself. And after six months, too. But don't get a swelled head, kid.'

'Time assuages sorrow.' Out of silence emerged a tag end of wisdom, something Hyacinth had, learned in school so long ago that it might have been in another life. 'Time heals everything,' it meant. But for her it didn't. It only taught her to cover up and cope, to be grateful for work, for the health of the children, and for an escape, so far, from the storm cloud that still hovered overhead, ready to burst.

When I'm on the bus, thought Hyacinth, and I see a jolly boy with his bookbag, I must think of my own boy, who also is ten years old, and jolly. Then I think of Emma, a lanky little girl, sensitive and full of curiosity. She looks like her father, but also like Francine, and will be tall, like me. Unlike me, my children have both become accustomed to the way they live.

Everything has changed, or nothing has, depending on what you are looking for. Between Francine and me there is now an unspoken truce; she knows I will not tell, so she no longer asks. Arnie is still Arnie, lively, extravagant and faithful; between us two are things unspoken since the night when I broke away from his arms. Lina is still enthusiastic. Indeed, she is very pleased, because now, after just one year, the Hyacinth collection is selling out in eighteen of the most prestigious stores from coast to coast. I am having my first taste of trunk shows, photographers and interviews.

Yes, everything has changed, and nothing has.

'I have something to tell you,' Lina said. 'Come into my office and close the door. This is between you and me until next week, when everybody will know it. I am getting ready to sell this business.'

'Selling it, Lina? But why? What will you do with yourself?'

It was impossible to dissociate the little 'dynamo' from this building on Seventh Avenue or even from this room where she sat now like a queen behind that enormous loaded desk.

'Well, I'm not thinking about right away. I'm just preparing. Then I shall enjoy the millions that they are paying me.' Lina laughed. 'No seriously, I'm tired – oh, not too tired for a trip around the world or something, but I'm getting older and it's time for a change. That's where you come in, Hyacinth.'

'I? I should think rather that it's time for me to go out.'

'Nonsense. You happen to be one of the several reasons that these people want to buy me. They're a tremendous clothing manufactory, and like most of the world today, they're looking to expand. Frankly, although the gentlemen were too diplomatic to say so, they would like to inject some young blood into this firm when they take it over. You are the young blood, Hyacinth.' And Lina's black eyes twinkled as she waited for her words to take effect.

Hyacinth was stunned. 'You can't really believe that I'm competent to *manage* this whole place, can you?'

'Not by next Monday morning, nor even by Monday morning six months from now. Of course not. I shall stay on as advisor for as long as seems necessary. You will keep the same staff, sales managers, accountants, the whole lot of them, to help you. You will go on as you have been doing. Eventually, if you keep up as I expect, you'll sit where I'm sitting.'

Was it yesterday afternoon that she had left class and walked into this room, so vast and imposing, to meet Lina Libretti? Yesterday that, on her front steps she had said a sad goodbye to Moira? Yesterday that she had sat in the church at that poor man's funeral?

'I can't believe that this is happening to me,' murmured Hyacinth.

'I couldn't believe it either, when it happened to me. Yes, yes.' Lina tipped the chair back and gazed up at the ceiling as if a parade of her years might be reflected there. Then, tipping down again, she spoke briskly.

'This is a big outfit, this group, as I've said. Now they want to expand their market to acquire some upper-bracket luxuries like a name parfumeur, top-of-the-line costume jewelry, fine shoes and bags — well, that's the picture. I must tell you, one of their people saw your evening group in California, your ruffles and your bright flower colors. I'm sure that was one of the things that got them interested. You might keep it in mind, Hyacinth.'

'I still don't believe I'm awake and hearing all this.'

'Well, you are awake, and you'd better be awake, because they'll be sending some of their people to talk over details either tomorrow or the next day.'

'How thrilled your grandmother would be!' Francine exclaimed, which was a nice tribute from a woman who had never really liked or been liked by the grandmother. Then came the amendment: 'There is really not much comparison, of course. She taught you the mechanics, it's true, but her taste was dreadful. Those terrible pea greens and maroons! Like decaying grapes, they looked.'

'Better get a top-notch lawyer,' Arnie said when he telephoned, ostensibly to give his report on Emma and Jerry. 'You never know what can happen with these buyouts and takeovers. You need to protect yourself, Hy.'

She was idly recalling these two reactions when she walked into

Lina's office the next morning. There was only one man there, facing Lina, and so with his back to the door. As Hyacinth opened it, he rose and faced her. He was Will Miller.

The first thing she saw was the twinkle. It was all over his face, on his lips which were about to open in laughter, and in his eyes; she had forgotten how green they were.

'Well, well,' he said. 'Imagine meeting you.'

Lina was surprised. 'So you know each other?'

'Well, we did. But we had a bit of an argument the last time, didn't we, Hyacinth?'

She could not have described how she felt. In a way, her anger still rankled, for had he not been unnecessarily disdainful that day? But in another way, should she not feel pleasure in seeing him again? She had thought of him often enough! And in still another way, she knew that because it was impossible for her even to think of becoming seriously involved with anyone, his appearance now was only another complication. She had enough complications.

'You see,' she said with cool politeness, 'that I took your advice.'

'I had no idea when I gave it what marvelous advice it would turn out to be.'

This short dialogue was interrupted by the arrival of more people and not resumed until, at noon, the meeting ended.

'What about lunch?' Will asked.

'Sorry, but I mostly have a sandwich delivered here. We're rushing through the resort collection.'

'Then we can have a drink, and dinner.'

'Sorry, but I'm invited to dinner.'

'Today's Friday. We'll go to dinner tomorrow night.'

'I'm having guests. Some friends of my mother's,' she added quickly lest it appear that she was unkindly letting him know he could not be admitted to her party.

'Then we'll go for a walk in the park on Sunday afternoon. You're not going to get away with it, Hyacinth. Don't forget, you're about to become an employee of the corporation.'

There went the twinkle again! Defying it, she retorted, 'Don't you tell me that *you* own the corporation.'

'Not all of it. Nobody ever owns all of a corporation. What do you think *corporation* means, anyway? Go look it up in the dictionary.'

He amazed her, scoffing as if they had known each other for umpteen years. Or as if they were — they were intimate as — well, as Dad and Francine, who used to talk to each other like that.

'Well, what are you, then?' she asked.

'Okay. The R. J. Miller Company broke up when my father died, not long after I last saw you. It wasn't exactly a break-up, but a buyout, and now I'm one of the vice presidents in the new company. I'll be living in New York.'

Reaching into his pocket, Will brought out and put on a pair of horn-rimmed glasses. 'I've bought a new pair to use when I need to look older again. Do you remember when I needed to look younger? With you, now, perhaps I need to look older again. You'll have more respect for me since, thanks to me, you've become so important. Come on, Hy, smile. Here I am clowning, and you won't even smile at me.'

Ah, go away, she thought. Go away, I don't want you, I don't need you. I do want you, but I can't have you, it's no good, you don't know anything about me, it's not fair to you, this makes no sense, leave me alone.

'Sunday brunch?' he said.

Opals, she thought. His eyes are opals. And then, seeing that the glasses were only empty frames, a joke, she laughed and nodded. 'All right. Brunch, since you insist.'

'Don't eat any breakfast. I like a woman to have an appetite.'

'You're giving me orders already?'

'Of course. I'm the boss, executive vice president who's just bought you and paid plenty, too.'

'April. It's my favorite month,' Will said. 'Do you know why?'

'Because May is still to come, and then the whole summer.'

'That's right!' he cried. 'And how do you feel about September?'

'I don't like the fall that much. It's supposed to be beautiful, all red and gold, and I suppose it is. But still I feel that everything is dying. I like winter, though. In fact, I love it. Can you guess why?'

'That's easy. Because spring's on the way. The snow is falling and they're selling daffodils in the supermarket. Am I right? Is it the same with you?'

'Yes. Yes, you are, and it is.'

They were walking slowly through the park. This was the fourth hour; the brunch had taken two, they had talked all through it, and now they were still talking, as random thoughts that would seem to be completely disconnected were mysteriously connecting.

'You disappeared. I couldn't find anybody who knew you except people in the store, and they had heard nothing. I looked everywhere. You have never even told the Post Office where to forward your mail. Why?'

He was looking at her, and the look was so intense that you might think he was seeing the inside of your head. He had made just that impression upon her at their first meeting.

'It was the divorce,' she said. 'I had such bad feelings. I only wanted to get away, to forget everything and everybody connected with the place.' That much, at least, was entirely true.

'Understandable,' he said softly. 'Funny thing, Hyacinth. I have a particular reason for wanting to see you. Two reasons, actually. I wanted to make another apology for the rather rough way I had tried to get my point across that day. And the other reason was that while I was in Europe, I went to a Dufy exhibit and for the first time learned that he had done fashion drawing. I was amazed, though why I should have been, I don't know. His sketches were little gems in themselves, watercolors and pen and ink, for some famous Paris couturier back before the First World War. I thought immediately of you, and the connection between fashion and art.'

'So you really know more about art than you pretended.'

'I don't pretend. I really don't know much. I'm a learner.'

'So am I.'

All of a sudden, she had become so intensely aware of his presence beside her that she had nothing to say. Now their approach to the museum gave her something.

'Would you like to go in?'

'Some other time. Today I only want to talk to you. Tell me about yourself.'

'There's very little to tell. I work hard, and I like it. I've been lucky. You gave me good advice.'

'I wasn't talking about work. I meant, about you. Are you feeling alone now that it's over? Bad as a marriage may have been, people tell me that they often feel alone in the world after a divorce.'

She said quickly, 'I'm not alone. I have brothers, and my mother is only a few hours away. She's busy, a busy volunteer, and I'm busy, but we get together.'

He was not asking about her relatives, she knew that. In a roundabout way, he was asking whether she had a lover. And she knew, too, that if she were to say she had one he would, except for an occasional meeting at work, be gone.

She said only, 'I have a few friends, but nobody really close. I haven't had time.'

'Nobody really close? I'm glad. No, that's selfish of me. I didn't mean it quite like that. Not quite.'

They walked on past a pond and through a mist, a bare hint, of arriving green. Nearing a bridle path, they stopped to let some riders go through. There were children among them, a little one riding a pony not much larger than a toy, and another, an older one, sitting proudly and earnestly on his high perch.

'Nice,' Will observed. 'Shall we sit near the path and watch the horses for a while?'

They found a bench. For a minute or two they were silent, and she knew that his eyes were turned upon her with a smile in them. His face is passionate, she thought. It says everything and hides nothing. And this awareness was suddenly so troubling, contrasted to the secret that she carried, that her heart sank, even as she was compelled to speak.

'I have two children,' she said, very low; her voice sounded in her ears as though it was the voice of a stranger.

'You do? But why—' He was astonished.

'Why have I made a secret of them? I don't know. I guess because I don't want to think about how hard it is . . . the divorce . . . children don't understand.'

'How old are they?'

'Almost ten and almost seven. Jerry's the big brother and Emma is seven. It happened three years ago.' And she remembered that night after Christmas dinner and how, up in their rooms, they had wept together. 'It was awful for them,' she said.

'And awful for you. How are they now?'

'Better, as far as I can see. Still, you never know what's being suppressed, do you?'

'That's true. But having a strong mother like you, who's pulling herself up by what my grandfather used to call her own bootstraps, should be a big help.'

'I don't know about the bootstraps, but I hope you're right.' Hyacinth's voice began to shake, yet she continued, 'That boy on horseback reminded me of Jerry. He's crazy about horses, and I'm glad. It helps, it's healthy to have an interest of some kind. It means there's one part of your life that's really happy.'

'Do they see their father?'

'Oh yes, they're with him now. It's spring vacation. They spend vacations with him.'

Even as she spoke, she was thinking: Why am I lying? I've never been a liar. But you do know very well why. It's the old story: It's because a mother who gives up custody is a marked woman, she is *unnatural*; there is something terribly wrong with her. Isn't that what people say?

Needing now to do something *natural*, she opened her handbag, and having subdued the quiver in her voice, offered to show him a snapshot of her children. Let him write her off as a conventional bore and never see her again.

'Forgive me for boring you,' she said. 'Here they are.'

They were in riding clothes, standing in front of a paddock fence on the day that Emma had her first authentic lesson. Arnie had taken the picture.

Will was either interested, or being polite enough to seem so. She had a definite impression that the former was the case.

'You're not boring me at all. They're beautiful, both of them.'

'Thank you. Emma looks a lot like my mother, whose photo you saw at my house.'

'I remember. I told you she was beautiful but that I thought you were more so.'

If anyone were to have asked Hyacinth exactly what she was feeling at that moment, she would not have had an answer. 'Confusion' might be the closest to the truth. Again she had nothing to say, and neither, apparently, had Will. She wondered afterward whether either of them would have spoken at all at that moment if the wind, which had been rising, had not abruptly exploded into a chill gust and a fierce burst of rain.

'We ought to get back before it pours more,' she said.

'Of course.'

As if to prolong the goodbye at the entrance of the apartment house, he paused and mused. 'What a haphazard world it is. I caught a glimpse of you in the store that day and thought, "I like her looks, the long hair like a silk curtain, the way she strides off like a country girl walking on the road." Then I forgot you because one always sees interesting people whom one never sees again. But then I did see you again, crossing the square.'

She knew he was waiting to be invited upstairs. And again she lied, again she told herself that it was easier that way. It was better so.

'My mother's here with her friends, or else—'

'Another time,' he said, and looked at her as if, like her, he had been struck into dumb silence by the shock of knowing what was happening to them.

Riding up in the elevator, she repeated the tale he had begun. The package fell. He picked up the book. He quoted Stephen Spender . . . Suppose he were to ask her to marry him? It's plausible to think that he might, but it must not happen. Already it's gone too far. I am carrying dangerous baggage, she thought, locked baggage that, like Pandora's box, must never be opened.

He wanted to see her, while she needed to keep him away. Therefore, it became a question of being friendly in a cool way and of finding excuses both true and untrue, though mostly untrue. And so, whenever they met, she delivered the kind of message that every human being, especially the female human being, knows how to deliver: You are pleasant company and I like you, but only up to a point and no farther, in spite of anything that may seem to have passed between us that day in the park.

Almost always, Hyacinth was certain, the recipient of such a message becomes discouraged and is heard from no more. But Will Miller did not seem to be getting that message. It surprised her that so attractive a man was satisfied to accept a stroll through Chinatown or an evening at the movies, followed by a friendly goodnight on the doorstep, only to call a few days later. Surely, if he wanted to, in no time at all he could fill his address book with any number of young women.

What are we going to do, she asked herself, when we have explored the whole city? Foolish question, she replied. The city's pleasures are endless. Then she was troubled; if only he would move, be transferred to some place far away! But no, he was firmly planted here; had he not even showed her with pride the enormous, muddy excavation from which the company's great new building was to arise? Had he not spoken of his ambition to live in an apartment with a view?

As if he were content to keep their companionship just as it was, he persisted. It was as if he had never said any of those intimate things about his search for her, or about poetry, or about a curtain of dark silk hair. Most probably, she concluded, he must have an extensive collection of women, and she was merely one of them.

Yet she did not entirely believe so. And when in the middle of May, when Arnie came from Florida, she was truly glad to see him. Conversation with Arnie was easy. There were no long silences to be filled with neutral, noncommittal subjects. Their central subject was, naturally, Emma and Jerry. Arnie always had plenty to say about himself, his new racehorse Diamond and his business deals that apparently took him from Portland, Oregon, to Portland, Maine. In addition to these, he would have questions about her. It touched her to see that he was so proud and so encouraging about her success. So it was a blessing to relax with him, the one human being who knew her secret.

Yet even with Arnie there were complications. He didn't try very hard to hide what he wanted.

'I suppose you meet a lot of men now that you're out in the world, right?'

'Not many. I'm at Libretti's all day, and it's a long day.'

'But there are other designers there.'

'A lot of them don't like women, Arnie.'

Then, as if teasing but not really teasing, he would smile and tell her that he was still 'available.'

'Better grab me before somebody else does, Hy. Take a look at me. Not bad, hey?'

The lively face and the strong, athletic body were not bad at all. Yet something was missing. And a small pain darted across her forehead.

On the first of July, Lina made a decision: It was time for Hyacinth to see the fabric houses of France. This would be a start, and the next visit abroad would be to Milan. In time she would need to see handwoven tweeds in Scotland and embroideries in India.

'Oh, glamour!' exclaimed Francine when Hyacinth reported all this. 'French flowers, music, food, and of course the fashions – oh, lucky you.' She was in raptures. Then suddenly subdued, she added, 'I'm so happy for you, darling. You deserve it.'

She meant, of course, after all the trouble you won't tell me about.

Arnie, as ever, was enthusiastic. 'Great. If I didn't have appointments a month ahead in this office, damned if I wouldn't pick up and go along. Listen, have a ball. The kids'll be in school till the end of the month anyway, so you won't be missing any great visit down here. Have fun, Hy, but not too much fun, if you get my meaning.'

Ten days later she settled into the window seat. As she looked out at the activities on the tarmac, her thoughts turned to the last time she had gone overseas. The three years might have been three centuries ago in another life, or they might have been three days ago, so vivid was her recollection.

From the first-class section, one had a view of every face as its owner slowly passed. And as always, with her innate curiosity, she wondered how much a face ever truly revealed. So she observed the passing file, thinking about each one, and then about herself, until gradually, after many minutes had passed and the plane was almost ready to take off, she had reached a conclusion: I am stronger now than I was on my last flight to Paris. I am more able to endure because I've had to. It was, and is still, a case of endure or founder.

Without intending to, she sat up straight and tall. The seat was comfortable. On the tray lay a book, a Michelin Guide, and a cold drink. Below the dark blue cuff of her perfect suit, one of Lina's best, there shone the polished circle of Francine's gold gift. At her feet lay the perfect lizard handbag that matched the perfect shoes. And she smiled, recalling Lina's injunction: 'You are a walking advertisement now, and you must never forget it.' A sense of well-being, long unfamiliar, crept over her.

The seat beside her was still vacant. And she was thinking that, with luck, she might even have the benefit of its added space, when a voice cried, 'Well, imagine this!'

She looked up to see Will Miller preparing to take the vacant seat.

'I had no idea,' he said. 'Did you?'

His amazement was so ineptly acted, that the very absurdity of it increased her anger and dismay.

She replied sharply, 'No, not at all. Nor did Lina either, I'm sure.'

'Well, there's nothing much you can do about it now. They've pulled back the jetway, so you'll simply have to put up with me.'

She saw at once that another change had come over him. The impersonal, courteous manner of the past few weeks was gone. It had only been a studied reaction to her own coolness toward him. She had known that all along without wanting to know it. In its place there now appeared the man she had first known, a person determined and plain-spoken.

She had needed to be alone . . .

'You've been avoiding me,' he said.

Not wanting to argue, she tried to placate. 'No, no I haven't. We had a nice afternoon at the Morgan Library, didn't we? At least I thought it was.'

'When was that? Three weeks ago? Don't give me a foolish excuse, Hyacinth. All the rest of the time you've been busy. Always busy, you tell me, and I know very well you aren't.'

'What do you mean?' Indignantly she drew away toward the window. 'Who says I'm not busy?'

'Common sense says so. Lina doesn't work you to death. She told me.'

'She knows nothing about what I do after hours.'

'She knows more than you think.'

'Was this her idea? Yes, it must have been. Since you had left — oh, unexpectedly, of course — for San Francisco! What does she think she's doing? She has no right to interfere in my life.'

'I don't want to quarrel about Lina. In fact, I don't want to quarrel at all. Turn around and look at the Statue of Liberty. Have you been up at the top lately?'

'No.'

'Neither have I, not since I was ten years old. We'll go as soon as we get back from this trip.'

'What do you mean by "we"?'

'What I said. Listen, Hyacinth. You've been putting on an act. Hard-to-get. Don't deny it, because I see it. It's very feminine and old-fashioned and sweet, and all right for a starter, but we've gotten beyond it. We got beyond it on the day we saw that boy on horseback in the park and you showed me the snapshots of Emma and Jerry.'

'You don't know what you're talking about,' she said, very low.

'Oh but I do, and you know I do. You're saying one thing now, but your eyes are contradicting what you say. They're doing it right this minute.'

Her eyes, to her exasperation, had filmed with tears, and it was simply because he had remembered the names of Jerry and Emma. Stalwart, are you, Hyacinth? And she turned to the window, where far below the city was falling away. On the screen before them, the map showed their route, northeast toward

Boston, Halifax, Greenland – all those miles and hours locked into this seat.

'I won't bother you,' Will said abruptly. 'Read your book. I have one, too.'

She had been looking forward to the book, a new novel by a good writer; it had the fresh feel of untouched books, the glossy jacket immaculate, and all those tantalizing pages inside, enough of them to last until lights out and for two more nights alone in a beautiful room at the hotel. And now it was all ruined.

Her eyes read the opening sentence, but her mind made no sense of the words, and they had to read it again. Her mind had gone flat and stupid, repeating the overhead sign: *Fasten Seat Belts*. She read it in French and again in English, until it turned into a senseless refrain: *Fasten Seat Belts*. At that point, becoming alarmed, she tried to control her mind. Listen here, she commanded it. Listen here, Hyacinth. You're doing all right, or you were until he came. Now let's go all over it again: You're not hanging on to anybody's coattails or crying on anybody's shoulder. You're supporting yourself and doing it very well. You don't owe a cent to anybody now that you've made Arnie accept your repayment. It's true that you have your lonely hours when you're not working – God, how lonely – but you get through them.

Her mind faltered: Oh, if you could find a man for an uncomplicated relationship, he would be very, very welcome. He must be nice, like Arnie, only a great deal more – or perhaps only a little more – to your taste. But that sounds awful. 'Your taste,' as if you are some superior arbiter selecting a man as one selects a melon or a chair. Will is definitely not the person for any uncomplicated relationship. And part of it all is your fault, you know it is. There were several times, and you remember them well, when you could have said something that would have ended it. But you didn't say it. You didn't want to say it. So you encouraged him, and now here you are. You really don't want to get involved again, do you? So for God's sake, pull yourself together, get rid of him firmly when we land and go about your business.

The flight attendant came with the dinner menus. Will read his, she read hers, and each gave their order without any consultation between them. It seemed to Hyacinth that the attendant was looking at them with some curiosity, as if she were deciding whether they were strangers or a couple together. Not that it mattered what she decided.

Why am I like this? she asked herself with a touch of the original adolescent consciousness of self. Why do I care what anybody thinks? You are you, and if people don't like you, there's nothing else you can do.

They had both ordered the same hors d'oeuvre plate. Silently they ate and drank the aperitif that had come with it. After a few minutes, the silence began to seem unnatural. A pair of total strangers locked together a few inches apart for a long night would exchange a few cordial remarks.

'Delicious,' she said, catching Will's glance. 'You don't expect such food on a plane, do you?'

'On a French plane, you do.'

'Yes, they do know food, don't they?'

Now wasn't that a banal remark? Perhaps it would after all have been better not to start any conversation.

'If I remember, this isn't your first time over there.'

'No, it's my first time on business, though.'

'Ah yes, fabrics. It should be very interesting. Challenging.'

'I'm looking forward to it.'

Silence fell. Then, since heads normally move and eyes wander, their eyes met. Opals, thought Hyacinth, startled again by their extraordinary lucent color.

'Listen,' Will said. 'This is ridiculous. First you play the game, then I play the game. Men can play it too, you know. But you began it, always having something to do every time I asked. Your mother was in the city with your great aunt's second cousin's mother-in-law. Were you playing a game with me, or did you by any chance mean it? If you really mean it, please simply say so. Say: "Will Miller, I don't want to see you again. Leave me alone. Get out of my life." Say it, and I'll do it.'

She looked toward the window. It was quite dark, and they were so high, that no light of earth was visible. Everywhere was black. And where was the resolution that only a short while before had stiffened the spine of this brave little lady who was making a name for herself, owed nobody, and bore her tragedy in silence? A lump almost large enough to choke her rose to Hyacinth's throat and stuck there.

Will Miller waited. Time passed, perhaps only a minute or two that might just as well have been an hour or two before he spoke again, saying softly, 'I think you've given me your answer, Hyacinth.'

Still, she could not bring herself to speak, but putting a hand on his arm, let it rest there. He did not move until at last she spoke.

'I don't want to say "get out of my life." '

'What do you want to say?'

A felony-murder, second degree.

'I don't know.'

'I believe you do,' he said quietly now. 'I believe you're wary of a new relationship, and I can understand that because the old one was so painful. Am I right, Hyacinth?'

'Painful.' The word came out with a gasp. 'Oh, yes. Painful.'

'I won't hurry you. But do we understand each other this time? Are we on a straight road now?'

There was such conflict within her that she was physically racked with it. Deep shame filled her because concealment was a masquerade and a lie. And rage filled her that she, who had never meant harm to anybody on earth, should be so afflicted. This man here, so sensitive, perceptive, intelligent, proud and kind, was no object of an unlearned young girl's infatuation; he was the man for her belated womanhood, and she knew it.

So perhaps after all it would not be a wrong? It need not hurt him. How would he ever know, unless of course something . . . something should be discovered? But how was she, or how could anyone, let that possibility, or probability, control the rest of her life? If they could be happy together for however short or long a time, and then if the feared disaster were to come upon her, it would not harm him too much. So then, really, was she committing so terrible a sin in saying, 'Yes'? Was she?

'Straight road?' he repeated.

She nodded her assent, and he took her hand.

They slept in spurts as people do on a night flight. Waking from time to time, they felt the warmth of each other's shoulders. The touch was as intimate as if they had many times before shared the same bed. As the plane rushed eastward, they woke again at the same time to see the sunrise ahead.

'Look!' cried Hyacinth. 'It seems to be coming up out of the sea. Every day, faithful every day. It's a miracle.'

'Yes, a miracle. Like love.'

Lina, having one day asked Hyacinth casually where she had stayed before in Paris, had thoughtfully selected a different hotel.

'Now you're not annoyed with her anymore, are you?' Will asked, adding somewhat mischievously, 'You thought you fooled her, but you didn't. She's a pretty smart old lady.'

'You got her to plan all this, didn't you? Adjoining rooms and everything?'

'I can't say I didn't have a part in it. The adjoining rooms, though, were done for the sake of appearances. Looks more dignified that way, don't you think? More respectable.'

The rooms were decorated with fruitwood and toile, his blue and hers pink, which made them laugh. Suddenly, they were filled with laughter. You might expect to fall onto a bed for at least a short nap after a long and fairly uncomfortable night, but to the contrary, energized as if with oxygen, they ate an enormous breakfast and started out into a cool, sunny day. Turning toward the Tuileries, they walked hand in hand past the pond and on up toward an ice cream parlor where, at half past ten in the morning, they bought double cones. Seeing themselves reflected absurdly in a shop window, two adults burdened with two cameras, one map, one guidebook, one extra sweater, and ice cream cones, they had to laugh at themselves again.

'I'm walking on air,' Will said.

Yes, she thought, that's how it is. I could walk around the world, just start out now and keep on going. If I had wings, I couldn't feel any lighter. I'd go anyplace with him, anywhere at all. Just not to think, not to care.

'What shall we do with this day?' he asked.

'Let's just wander.'

'No museums?'

'Not today.'

'I'm glad you said that. This is the day we begin. It will be our anniversary. Let's simply feel it.'

So they wandered. They crossed a bridge and stopped for minutes simply to watch the boats. They passed the bookstalls, stopping to examine some books and buying two.

'It keeps you from forgetting the language,' Will said.

They went into a church. It seemed as if their feet always paused at the same places, first at the entrance here and then at a pew where, without speaking, they both sat down. For half an hour they listened to an organ fugue resounding through the lofty silence, and then, still without speaking, rose at the same time and went out.

The music followed them into the street. 'Was it Bach?' asked Hyacinth.

'No. Caesar Franck.'

Through the streets, the alleys and unexpected shady spaces of the old city, they walked on. The morning's laughter died away, and in its place a lovely peace wrapped itself around them.

When they stopped before a gallery window, it seemed as if by unspoken consensus they needed the same amount of time to look and were ready together to go on their way. At a café table under an umbrella on the sidewalk, they stopped for coffee and drinking slowly, still not saying much of anything, observed the scene: a fruiterer's magnificent display, a woman with three poodles on a leash, and a passing car bedecked with bridal flowers. They were both carried beyond words. After a while, Will touched her arm and asked, 'Shall we go back? Have we waited long enough?'

If he could hear her heartbeat! If a heart could speak!

'I don't want to hurry you,' he said.

She looked at him and smiled. 'But I want you to hurry me.'

Sliding between the louvered shutters, the afternoon light striped the carpet. Quietly Hyacinth stood in the center of the room and let him take off her clothes. His hands were firm and persistent; yet they were soft upon her. Neither of them spoke.

He kissed her, and still she did not move, letting the sweetness stream over and through her. It was as if she had never been desired and cherished; always the wanting had been hers. Hers only. And she had never truly known adoration until now, standing here in this room. Her ignorance had not been bliss. This was bliss.

After the first few days when both had taken care of their business affairs, their time was free.

'We don't have to rush home. I'll change the tickets and we'll take a few extra days. It's our honeymoon.'

He had already made a list of things to see: a monastery, the menhirs in Brittany, Mont St. Michel, and the Normandy beaches.

'Anything to add? Any changes you want to make?'

She had none except for one inn where she had stayed with Gerald on a rainy night of exasperation for him and worry for her.

'All that's past,' he said when she told him, 'and you are going to forget it.'

'I have already.'

Leaving the city, they turned the car toward the north, taking turns at the wheel. Often when the road was clear and Will drove, he held her hand. It seemed then to Hyacinth that strength was passing from one hand to the other, building a union between them. It was a marvel that they were so alike. When music came through the air, they both listened without interruption until the end. After so short a time together, they were able to foretell each other's quirks and habits; he liked his hot drinks hot, while she liked them warm; each of them wanted to read the newspaper undisturbed at breakfast; he had to sleep on his right side.

Their nights were splendid. At an inn where their room had a balcony, they lay one evening in a hammock, rocking under the trees until the stars came out. At St. Michel they opened the window to hear the enormous, terrifying tide come thundering in. Their days were splendid. In Brittany they took pictures of women wearing lace caps, they ate the famous pancakes, and wondered at the menhirs, those ancient, secretive stones standing in rows on their flat fields. Will wondered about their age and how they compared with Stonehenge. Everything interested him, whether swans on a pond, a small town's art exhibit, or a group of old men playing boules.

On Omaha Beach, he was extremely moved. 'My grandfather died here on June sixth in 1944,' he said. 'This is my second visit.'

From the top of the incredible cliff they stared down at the sand and the waves, then back at the Nazi gun emplacements, and walked away in silence. At the American cemetery nearby they looked at the white crosses stretching almost to the horizon, and found nothing to say, for Will's expression said everything. And Hyacinth, with a passionate gesture, put her arms out to hold him.

Now and again they had these emotional moments, but chiefly their mood was one of joyous calm. Their intimacies were unselfconscious. As though they had lived years together, they had their small routines: He brushed her hair, and she rubbed his back. Now and again they asked each other in mild astonishment how all this could have happened to them.

On the last night, in the formal setting of what had been somebody's small château, they dressed for dinner. Hyacinth's dress had short, black, lace sleeves.

'I hadn't planned to bring anything like this,' she said. 'I thought I'd be having dinner in my room, wearing a bathrobe. But Lina insisted.'

'Of course she did. I told you, she's a smart old lady. She had faith in me.'

'But me? She could only have been guessing about me. I never said a word to her about you.'

Will smiled. He was about to leave the room, with his hand on the doorknob, when he stopped to look at her. 'Wait a second. Just like that. Do me one favor, will you? Never cut your hair any shorter. Never.'

'I wasn't planning to, but why?'

'Because. I love the feel of it, on the pillow.'

Very happily she responded, 'Agreed. That's reason enough.'

Yet now, on the next to the last day, since in the morning they were to return to Paris, a thin edge formed itself upon this happiness. She had allowed herself, or rather forced herself, to forget during this enchanted week that it was deeply flawed. So it was almost uncanny that Will should choose just this moment of foreboding to say what he did.

They were at table when he remarked, 'You almost never talk about your children.'

'Don't I? I didn't realize it. I suppose I don't want to be boring, don't want to be one of those women who talk incessantly about how bright they are, and what the teacher said, or the coach at Little League had to say.'

'I'm not easily bored. And your children could never bore me. Will you see them before school begins in September?'

'I go down there to visit, and my mother does. Sometimes we go together.'

'Do they mind this joint custody arrangement? I suppose it's fair to the parents, but isn't it confusing to the children?'

'Well, mine seem to be fine. I think only time will tell whether they grow up with any scars.'

Hyacinth's heart had begun to race. And some change must have appeared on her face, because Will, always keen to observe, said quickly, 'I'm sorry. I didn't mean to bring up a painful thing that you can't change. Let's just enjoy what we have right now. Let's drink to us.' And lifting his glass, he touched hers. 'To us. To you and to me, always.'

Above the rim of her glass, she beheld him. So tender, so stubborn, wise and good! And again came that terrible sense of foreboding.

'What is it?' he asked. 'What are you thinking?'

'Only that this is our next-to-last day.'

'What of it? We have the rest of our lives.' With a quizzical smile, he waited. 'No comment?'

'It's the champagne. It always goes straight to my head.' She reached over to touch him. 'I love you, Will.'

'You'd better love me. Come on, let's eat so we can go to bed early.'

Needing to meet his cheerful tone, she bantered back, 'You always want to be in bed early.'

'Can you think of a better place?' he retorted.

Hyacinth's mind, unknown to Will, was already home long before they reached the hotel in Paris. It was therefore almost fitting that a fax from home should be awaiting her there. When the knock on the door came and it was handed in, Will took it, asking quickly, 'Shall I read it for you?'

'Oh, please.'

'It's fine, dear. It's nothing, no trouble, "Birthday greetings. Better late than never. All's well with everybody. Kids and I send love. How about dinner, usual place, Arnie."'

'That's all? Thank God.'

'You didn't tell me it was your birthday. When was it?'

'I have to count. It must have been – yes, last Tuesday. I'd never notice it anymore if it weren't for my family.'

'What, no celebration? Well, we're going to celebrate every birthday from now on. Mine's the fourteenth of January, and I want a proper cake. I want the works. Who's Arnie?'

'He's my former husband's partner, but a very good friend of mine.'

'He must be. Dinner? Usual place?'

'He comes to New York every month or so on business, and I often go to dinner at his hotel. He's very kind, good to Emma and Jerry, and I'm fond of him.'

'Oh. That's nice. How about a walk to stretch our legs before the flight tomorrow?'

She was grateful that *home*, rather than being a spoiler, had waited until now, at the end of the week, to reach out to her. On their walk they passed the shop in which she had seen the famous rose dress that had been the cause of so much change. It was unmistakably the place, and she could not resist telling Will.

'If it hadn't been for that dress, I wouldn't be here with you. I would never have met you.'

Never. The walls, the pavement, the very sky now fading into a melancholy gray, repeated the word. Never.

'And you wouldn't be a designer. Funny, somebody said to me that you don't look like one, however a designer is supposed to look. He meant it well, though, and I understood because I can just as easily see you pushing a baby carriage on a suburban street.'

'I've done that,' she said.

'Well, you can do it again. We could make a wonderful child. Smart, beautiful, athletic, artistic, good-natured, head of the class—'

'You forgot boastful,' she finished, pretending to laugh.

'Touché,' said Will. 'But seriously, be prepared, because we're going to have to talk.'

'Not now, for Heaven's sake.'

'No. But soon. I suppose I am a little hasty, although that's not unusual. We know each other as well as we ever could, and time's a wasting.'

Chapter Fourteen

The summer at home was long and hot. They said it was the worst heatwave in fifteen years, but Hyacinth, protected by air conditioning, was too busy to think about it, and far too concerned with her problems, anyway.

Libretti was preparing the fall line, with special attention to its Hyacinth productions, and the place was astir with buying and selling, viewing, fitting, and photographing. Hyacinth herself was to depart on a two-week tour with her trunk show to end with a splash of publicity on Fifth Avenue.

'This is your best work yet,' Lina told her. 'It's a new look for you. It's discreet and ladylike and very sensuous besides. Love must agree with you. Maybe I'm being too personal,' she added, as Hyacinth did not respond.

'No, that's all right, Lina.'

'You haven't said anything to me, although Will Miller has.'

'I guess I've been so swamped in the fitting rooms that I haven't had a moment,' she replied, which was at best a lame response, and at worst, a dodge.

She was making a stupendous effort not to think ahead. Will had this time really gone to California, where a long-drawn-out negotiation over some kind of merger was being held, and she was missing him to the point of pain. That very morning, another letter from him had arrived, and twice within the last few hours, she had taken it out of her purse to read it.

My Love,

Do you know you are everything to me? Wherever I am, alone or in a crowd, there is a part of my mind that is always aware of you. As clearly as if you were speaking to me, I hear your lovely voice. In the darkness, I see your brave eyes, and that one-sided curve of your lips when you laugh. We've had so little time together, only a few months, and yet I know you as if I had known you all my life. You have my total trust, and I hope, I know, I have yours. It's my last thought before I sleep, and the first when I wake.

Will

Total trust. And guilt, a thrust into the heart, a throb in the forehead, and a startle in the middle of the night.

What am I going to do? she asked for the hundredth or the thousandth time.

Then there was more. Although Arnie assured her by phone that Emma and Jerry were 'happy as clams,' she was not satisfied. Several times she had heard them in the background having a nasty, tearful quarrel; a few times they had also been sulky and snappy in their replies to her, so that she had afterward cried with frustration.

Meanwhile, her work had to go forward, and it did.

'I'm still in shock,' Francine whispered while the big Fifth Avenue show was being set up. 'Who could have guessed that you, in your jeans and T-shirt, you who never gave a darn about fashion, knew so much about stuff like this?'

'I always tell you, it's like painting.'

Still, it did amaze her when a customer consulted her as to what shoes to wear with this or that suit, or whether that dress was strictly 'after five' or might be worn at a noon wedding. It amazed her to watch the models make their smart pirouettes in garments that, not all that long ago, had been a mere sketch on the back of an envelope. There they came, parading in chalk white velvet with scarlet shoes, in yellow Turkish trousers with a beaded jacket, and in short black taffeta with a long, sky-blue petticoat and a naked back. There they came, and kept coming.

Lina was all smiles. 'Do you realize who's here?' she kept murmuring into Hyacinth's ear. 'Over there in the back row, he's from Texas. You mustn't skip their store next time . . . You don't know her? For goodness sake, she practically runs the patrons' list . . . oh, he always comes with his wife and buys half a dozen gowns for the season . . . You don't recognize her? She'll be on the cover of next month's issue . . . The short one on the left is one of the top European shoe designers . . . This is one tremendous success, my dear Hyacinth.'

At the end there was a babble and a jostle, with Hyacinth in the very center, everyone calling her name. She had a most surprising thought: For the first time in my life, actually, I don't mind the name. It's really not as silly as I've always thought it was. I should tell Francine.

'Hyacinth, remember me?'

Remember Moira? They spoke every week or two on the telephone, but there was still nothing like a hug and the sight of a kind, sweet face. There was no ease like that which you felt with a real friend who never put you on the spot with a tactless question or any reference to your troubles.

'Oh you look marvelous, Hyacinth! I'm so glad for you. One of these days I'm going to give myself some time off and take a weekend in New York. Maybe I'll treat myself to one of your dresses. Do you make any stylish stouts?'

Moira had the wonderful ability to laugh at herself.

'Hyacinth, remember me?'

Remember Martha? She could hardly have forgotten this nemesis of her girlhood.

'Of course I do. What brings you here?'

'Your mother told me about it. We're still neighbors, you know, and we pass each other on the road now and then. You look marvelous, Hyacinth.'

She was supposed to return the compliment, but somehow she did not feel like doing any more than answering graciously, 'Thank you. Thank you very much.'

'I've thought of you often since you moved away, about how we all used to be sort of mean to you in school. And in college, too, I have to admit. You must remember, although I hope you don't.'

Well now, wasn't that an apology? And wasn't this an awkward time to make it? How should she reply? She could say coolly something like: *Naturally I remember, though it was never all that important to me.* But since, in a subtle way, Martha had a beaten look, she said instead, 'It was a long time ago. What's been happening with you?'

'Not much. I never married, so I live at home. I work in town.'

Martha was still standing there and would have extended the conversation if Lina had not come rushing up with a message.

'It's about the velvet dress. They're asking whether you'll do the same in black.'

'I'm taking your time,' said Martha. 'I'd love to buy one of your dresses. They're beautiful, but I can't afford them.'

For an instant, Hyacinth watched her walk away. What happened to the teasing eyes, the proud, curly head and the toss of it? She acted as if she were stunned to see what has happened to me, while I feel the same about her. What a mystery it is all of it!

Will said, 'You did this whole dinner, fancy chicken, fancy vegetable soufflé, and fancy dessert? No take-out, now that you're in New York?'

'Why are you so surprised? You know I can cook. You said the same thing that day when you came to lunch and broke my heart right afterwards.'

'I don't know. I just am.'

People had always been surprised, first that such a bookworm should spend so much time in the kitchen, and now that a designer and a moneymaker should do it. People clung to their stereotypes.

Her feelings for the last twenty-four hours had been dreadfully mixed. She had been disturbed because Emma and Jerry had come unexpectedly on a short vacation just at the time she was filling some last minute, ultra-important orders, so now they had gone to spend a part of their time in the country with Francine instead of with her, their mother. Their father had simply found it convenient for himself to send them someplace without even asking whether it was possible for her to take them.

But last night Will had called to say that he was coming home on the 'red-eye,' and she had been gloriously excited. At work in the perfect little kitchen, she had had fantasies of a house and a dining room with all her beloved faces around the table, his at the head. Then, as the clock moved toward the hour when he would walk in, she had been shaken by panic, really physically shaken. This time, surely, he was going to pin her down to specifics. Something told her that this was to be the night for really serious talk. It had been postponed until the hectic showings were over, and until his return from California, but now it was here.

Under the concealing napkin, her hands were actually knotted together, the gold ring digging into her palm.

'That last showing was a triumph, I hear. I wanted to get back for it, but there was a lot of last minute delay, too much red tape,' he broke off. 'I missed you terribly, so terribly that it hurt.'

'I know,' she said weakly, with her eyes on the corner chair: navy blue with scattered snowflakes in two clusters, skip a space and there were two more clusters.

'I want marriage, Hyacinth. I want you to say when.'

Foolish words escaped her. 'Don't we need to know each other a little better, Mr. Miller?'

He stared at her. 'Don't be absurd. Don't be coy, for God's sake. Don't tease me.'

'I'm sorry. I didn't mean to.'

'Well, then?'

'You know I love you, Will. But we have to— to plan. My children – this apartment – it's not all that simple. I can't rush.' With every intention to sound natural, she heard her voice pleading. 'We've been so happy this summer, so can't we go on for a while until—'

'No. I don't understand what you mean by "not all that simple." There's room enough for the children and me in here until we can find a larger place. I'll find one. Give me a couple of weeks, that's all. You wanted to be fairly near their school, I know, and I'll keep that in mind. Where do they go now?'

She sighed. 'I may be changing their school, and that's another complication.'

'These complications are of your own making, Hyacinth. I think I know what it is. You're having a vision of the first time, all the wedding fears that turned out so badly in the end, and the thought of another wedding depresses you. It's affected your nerves. Isn't that so?'

For a full minute, Will sat still. Aware of his eyes upon her, she cast hers down and fiddled with a water glass.

'I know you love me, Hyacinth. Then trust me. Just close your eyes and jump. We'll make a small, quick affair of it. City Hall, if you want. Ten minutes and over. Painless. Nothing to it.'

'Then what's the difference? We can go into that room right now, and it will still be wonderful without any—'

'No.'

By now she was well enough accustomed to that decisive 'no' to see without looking at him exactly how his mouth had closed upon his even teeth, upon the word and upon the subject.

'I want to marry you, not only live with you. I'm not as "modern" as I've liked to think I was. I've had enough temporary stuff. I'm ready for something public and permanent, ready for a child of my own. I'm ready for your children, too. You need have no worries about that. That bothers you a bit, doesn't it? But I want to love them because they are yours. When am I going to see them?'

'Soon.'

'You should be getting them back after Labor Day, I suppose.'

'They're with my mother. I'm going up there tomorrow to spend a few days.'

'Then I'll wait till you come back to go over all our details.'

He stood up, and pulling her to himself, held her close to kiss her hands, her arms, her throat and her mouth.

If only we were alone on that beach in Brittany, she thought while he held her, with the tide racing and the mind racing and nothing to think about, nothing . . .

'I'll take care of everything, Hyacinth. Leave it to me. Now undo these buttons of yours. I can't seem to manage . . .'

The buzzer sounded.

'Dammit!' he cried. 'Who's that?'

'I can't imagine.' She said and then, replying to it, heard from the lobby that it was Arnie, already on the way up, A moment later there came a knock on the door.

'Open up, celebrity, it's me, Arnie. Remember me? Don't look scared,' he said as he stepped in. 'Everything's fine. I'm here on a quick two-day trip to see a guy in this neighborhood, so I thought I'd take a chance on finding you in.'

He had never done anything like this. And with the merest touch of coolness, she said, 'You scared me. I wasn't expecting anybody. Will Miller, Arnold Ritter.'

The two men, having made the usual acknowledgments, there remained nothing to do but to sit down and say something.

Hyacinth began. 'We've just had dinner. Can I get you anything? A piece of pie?'

'Thanks, no. Just ate with this guy. But you had a good dinner, I know that,' Arnie said, addressing Will. 'This lady can feed a man. Many's the good meal I've had at her table.'

Will said something, but Hyacinth was in such turmoil that she barely heard what it was. Every nerve in her body was electrified, ready to spark. What to do if Arnie should say the wrong thing about the status of Jerry and Emma? When time came to tell him, she, not Arnie, must be the one to do it. She ought to have told Will before this. But she had been dreading it so, dreading the questions that would follow.

'I thought at least I could cool off coming up north in September,' Arnie said. 'But it's as hot as Florida.'

'I've just come in from California. They seem to have escaped the heat there this summer. Weather's always a gamble, you never know.'

Weather, thought Hyacinth, is always a safe subject when the air is filled with tension. And she said inanely, 'Come January, with ice in the streets, we'll remember this and wish it back.'

The men agreed. And Hyacinth was saying silently, Arnie, why don't you just get up and go, when suddenly he drew an envelope out of his pocket and handed it to her.

'Have a look at these,' he said with a broad smile. 'I took them last week at the gymkhana. Emma's taken to horses like a duck to water.'

There they were, side by side in their fine habits on their fine mounts, looking like children in some glossy magazine. Her babies.

'Matter of fact, I think Emma's going to outdo her brother. Wait till you see,' he added, sounding like a proud father.

There was nothing to do but hand the photos to Will. He took rather a long time over them then, returning them, remarked that he also had some pictures in his pocket.

'I meant to give them to you before this, but I took them to California by mistake.'

And there *they* were, Will and Hyacinth, in Paris with the obelisk in the background, in Deauville, in Brittany, in front of the Louvre, in a garden, and in front of a pond with swans in the background. Wearing her usual jeans and top she stood with her hair blown like a ribbon in the wind; in the dress with the lace sleeves, she was elegant. And finally, she was on the beach wearing the bikini that Will had bought because she had not packed a swimsuit. In every scene was Will with his arm around her, making them unmistakably a couple, no casual friends on a genial outing, but a couple.

'Let's see,' said Arnie, reaching his arm out. Slowly he flipped through the collection and handed it back, remarking pleasantly that it looked as if they had been having a grand time over there.

'It was a business trip,' Hyacinth explained. 'Lina wanted me to look at French fabrics, and Will's firm has bought Lina's, so we're all one now.'

She knew each of these two men so well that she had no doubt about what each was thinking. Will, of course, was annoyed at this intrusion on their night, and Arnie was simply jealous. With a touch of wonderment she reflected that this was her first experience of being in a room together with two men, both of whom desired her.

Will broke the uncomfortable pause. 'Do you live all year round in Florida, Doctor Ritter?'

'Oh yes, I'm well settled. I'm in practice there. Surgery.'

'Then you're a native, the real thing,' Will said pleasantly.

Arnie laughed. 'Nobody's a native there. No, I just gave up my practice in Hyacinth's town a few years ago. Her former town, I should say. That's how we met. We're old friends by now.'

'That's how we met, too. My family had a store there, R. J. Miller, on the square.'

'That right? Used to buy my stuff there all the time, ties, sweaters and things. You had nice merchandise. You still there?'

'No, we sold out. They've torn our place down to put up a ten-story office building. The town's growing fast. When I think of what my great-grandfather paid for the land a hundred years ago and what we got for it — it's unbelievable.'

Now that they've got onto a subject, Hyacinth was thinking, I suppose Arnie will never leave.

'I know what you mean. I built my office, let's see, it's seventeen years ago, and the difference in cost is also unbelievable. I had a beautiful little white building, a fortune's worth of limestone, not big, just two stories, but the location couldn't be beat. It was just three blocks off the square.'

'That wasn't the office that burned down, was it?'

'Yeah, that's it.'

Arnie's glance passed over Hyacinth. The glance was neutral. Then he coughed.

Perhaps three seconds, no more, went by before Will sociably continued the conversation. 'I was in a rush that day and got into town not long after dawn, so I passed through all the excitement. It was still blazing. Terrifying, with the hook and ladder, the broken glass, the crowds, the flames and the smoke, a war zone. Fire and human flesh — it's an age-old terror.'

'Sure is,' Arnie said. 'Pretty tough.'

As always, when she was in distress, Hyacinth's hands clenched together in her lap. Now, willing herself to appear relaxed, she placed her hands on the arms of the chair.

'I heard talk that it might have been arson,' Will added.

Arnie shrugged. 'There's always talk,' he replied.

Will, agreeing to that, went on to explain his interest in the subject. 'We had some big trouble like it in one of our stores about twenty years ago. I remember all the talk every night at the dinner table. They did a lot of investigating. I guess everybody but the FBI must have been called in, and finally they narrowed it down to an employee who, after first denying anything, finally admitted that he had been smoking and must have been careless. My father never believed him, though. The fellow had a grievance against the company, and everybody knew about it. He had a clear motive.'

'So what happened?' asked Arnie, showing interest.

'I don't recall the details because I went away to college about that time, but I know they got him and he served a couple of years.'

'Was anyone hurt?' Arnie asked.

'No, fortunately nobody was, though it's a miracle. The place was an inferno.'

'He would have served a hell of a lot more if anybody had died in it,' Arnie said. 'That's a felony-murder, probably second degree.'

Hyacinth did not look at him. Why is he prolonging this conversation? Why is he doing this to me? He could easily turn it to something else, like real estate values or where Will had gone to college.

'It makes you wonder, doesn't it, how anybody can let a grievance turn into such rage. It makes you wonder about people, about whom you can ever trust. He looked so innocent, my father said, the kind you never suspect.'

This was unbearable. Her very heart and soul were exposed. She might as well have been sitting here naked between these men. And hoping that her face was not as bloody red as it felt, Hyacinth rose and moved to the television set, observing that it was time for the eleven o'clock news.

Arnie jumped up. 'Eleven already? I've got some day tomorrow, enough to break your back. So I'm going to run along, Hy. I'll be in touch. Say, Will – don't mind if I call you that, I hope – we can share a cab. It's tough getting one in this neighborhood this time of night, and we're lucky if we find one, let alone two.'

Now there was nothing to do but see them both to the door. How adroitly Arnie had pried Will loose! But it was just as well, for she was now in no condition for the night of love that had just begun when Arnie had intruded.

It makes you wonder about people, about whom you can trust.

What shall I tell him? He will want to know why, for all this time, I have hidden the truth. At the very least, he will doubt me. At most, he will despise me. I would, if I were he.

In an odd way, she saw herself stunned and mentally immobilized by terror. She walked the length of the living room and back. Back and forth. Midnight struck, and she lay down, hot and cold by turns, and too paralyzed to weep. The night passed.

The telephone rang twice in the morning, the first call being Will's.

'Your friend threw some cold water on us last night, didn't he?'

'I should say so. Funny, he's never visited without calling first.'

'Tell me about him. He's what you call a "character," isn't he?'

She knew by Will's voice that he was displeased, which surprised her, because he seldom allowed things to displease him seriously.

'There's nothing much to tell. He's never had children, and he's one of those people who should have them, so he's been very attached to mine when— when they're in Florida. He's horse crazy, and he's made them horse crazy, too, which is very healthy for them.' She was babbling too much. 'So that's about all,' she concluded.

'He's jealous Hy. He didn't enjoy those pictures of us in France and he showed it as if he didn't give a damn whether he offended you or me. Especially me.'

'No, no. Arnie's not interested in me. I'm nothing to him. He's got women all over the country, pop singers, starlets, gold shoes in the daytime, piles of makeup, glamour types. Not me.'

'I don't agree. A man sees other men more clearly than a woman ever can. He wants you, Hyacinth, and if he were your type, I'd have reason to be jealous. But since he's so obviously not your type, God bless him and good riddance to him. He interrupted our fun last night.'

'I know, but he really is a good sort.'

'Well, okay, but what about our important discussion? Can we continue it tonight?'

She was not ready. She must get away to think. She must figure out how to tell him about it all, the divorce, the children, the fire . . . She had a mountain to climb.

'You forget that I'm going to my mother's house for a few days. I'm leaving this afternoon.'

'Well, hurry back, will you?'

'Of course I will, as fast as I can, you know that.'

'While you're gone, I'll go apartment hunting. Want to bet that I'll have found a great place by next week? Have a good time. Say hello to your mother for me, and to Emma and Jerry. I'm waiting to meet them all.'

Not five minutes later, Arnie called. He was abrupt. 'I want to see you tonight, Hy.'

She did not want to see him and was beginning to say so, when he insisted, 'Tonight, Hy. It's important. In the restaurant at my hotel at nine.'

'Arnie, you're worrying me. Is anything wrong?'

'Yes, and then again, no. But we need to talk.'

At least the children, at Francine's house, were all right. Obviously then, this was to be all about Will.

In the evening she came prepared to upbraid him at once for last night, but first sight of him showed that he was troubled, and she did not. His silvery, lavish hair, always so carefully tended and waved, was tousled, and his hand-painted imported tie was askew.

'I didn't sleep last night,' he announced as he took his seat on the other side of the table. 'It was one of the worst nights I've ever had, and I don't mind telling you.' He waved away wine and waved away the menu. 'Order something, Hy. Whatever you want, I'll eat. I don't feel like eating, anyway. Haven't had a thing in my mouth all day except coffee.'

'I haven't felt very well either, Arnie. First, before we say anything else, tell me why you kept harping on that subject last night? You must have known what you were doing to me when you said that about felony-murders. I could hardly believe it was you saying it.'

'Did you know what I was feeling when your boyfriend showed those pictures? I went into a rage. I couldn't help it. I'm sorry, Hy.' And as he leaned forward within inches of her face, Arnie's familiar, friendly eyes became hard, copper-colored slits. 'He's your lover, isn't he? Level with me.'

'We love each other,' she answered simply.

Now, drawing back, he gave a low whistle. 'Right here under my nose! I was waiting for you, Hyacinth. Didn't you realize that? I thought we had a – an understanding. A relationship, or whatever you call it.'

The light revealed a drop of sweat on his forehead. And because he had never seemed to be a person whom one would associate with suffering, it astonished her that he should be feeling it so deeply. Then, ashamed of having made so superficial a judgment, she felt both guilt and pity.

With a break in her voice, she answered, 'I'm sorry too. I thought we were just very, very good friends. I never meant, I never would deceive you.'

'You knew we were more than "good friends"! You can't tell me you didn't.'

On the fifth floor, directly above this table, was the room with the bed. It flashed now before her: a fancy cream-colored head-board against striped wallpaper and a pair of lamps with pink shades on either side. She had been standing not more than fifteen feet away from that bed and far less than fifteen minutes from lying in it. They had been two warm, eager bodies, she with her breast already bared. Of course she had known!

'You never made it clear to me,' she said awkwardly.

'I saw how confused you were, and I gave you time to get over your troubles. You had the kids, your work, and the other business on your mind.'

The other business.

At the piano across the room a young man was singing one of those old love songs from the thirties that never seemed to go out of fashion. Somebody at the next table was humming along. A cork popped. Did anybody ever have, or could anybody here in the midst of all this velvety comfort, imagine something like 'the other business'? Her thoughts had already strayed from Arnie, so she brought them back to him, repeating, 'I'm sorry. I never meant to deceive you. Believe me.'

When the dinners were placed before them, he took a mouthful and laid down the fork declaring, 'Fact is, after your friend brought up the subject last night, I kept it going on purpose. I wanted to hear how he might deal with you if he ever should know, God forbid that he ever should.'

'God forbid? But I have to tell him. The trouble is that I don't know how, or else I haven't got the courage.'

'You really want to marry him, Hy?'

'Yes. Oh, yes!'

'I'll be damned, that's all I can say. I'll be damned. I can't get it through my head. Close as we've been, and the kids and all. Oh, I know I'm not like him, Hy. He's good-looking, not that I'm so bad, but he's more your age, and – oh, I know his type – high-class music and books, the stuff you like. But I'd do all that, too, to please you. You bet I would. And with me – well, there are no secrets. See? You're scared to tell him, and you should be. You damn well should be, Hy.'

The emphasis alarmed her, and she cried out, 'What do you mean?'

'I mean,' he said, lowering his voice to a secretive tone, 'because he won't like it. You heard him talking about that case of theirs. It was a case exactly like yours. He'll hesitate, or maybe he'll be scared away right off the bat. And he's got family, hasn't he? He'll talk it over with somebody he trusts. He'll want another opinion, and he'll get it. You'd better believe he'll get it. Take my word, Hy. If there's one thing I know, it's people. Nobody fools me.'

True enough. Arnie had all the marks of a man who knew his way about the world.

Nevertheless, she spoke bravely. 'Then I'll marry him without telling him.'

Arnie frowned. 'Oh, no. You'd never last more than a couple of weeks that way. People can't live together and keep things like that buttoned up inside. The secret would torment you. Every time you looked at him or touched him in bed, you'd feel you ought to tell him. And what then? Do you think any man would appreciate getting a hell of a present like that one dumped on him after he's just put the ring on your finger? What kind of a marriage do you think you'd have then? Or would you have any marriage? You want another divorce? And with the secret out? Once it's out, you know, it's out, let me tell you. And then there goes everything, big job, good name, kids, the whole works. No, you're better off the way you are, Hy. Take it from me. I wasn't born yesterday. And neither was your friend Will. He's on the way up in the world, and he doesn't need to carry your troubles in his luggage.'

'Why don't you stop this? I never knew you could be so cruel,' she cried angrily.

Yet, when she took out a handkerchief to wipe her eyes, Arnie looked away. For a man so blunt spoken, he also had unusual delicacy.

Why do I love you? Why do you love me? the man sang at the next table. People were laughing.

She took a forkful of mashed potatoes. She needed to be home in her bed in the dark with the blanket drawn over her face. She needed Will. Yet not right now, or until there was some light at the end of this tunnel. Her thoughts were raging and battling in her head.

'Either way, it's not easy,' Arnie said.

She did not catch his meaning until he continued, 'I hate to tell you, but you've got something else to think about beside love right now. The kids aren't happy. There've been changes.'

'Changes?' she whispered.

'Gerald's had a visitor all summer, one of his singers, starlets, or whatever you want to call her. She doesn't get along with the kids. Maybe it started because they don't like her. She takes Gerald's time – when he's not working – and that means less time for them. He plays tennis with her, for instance, instead of with Jerry. That kind of thing. Look, I'm no psychologist, but that's what I think. And a couple of weeks ago, they had a big run-in, something about Charlie, the dog, you know. She hit it, and Emma went wild and hit her. Then Eareen – some crazy, inventive name – no, Arveen – slapped Emma and Jerry pitched into Arveen. It's a mess. I heard about it from the nanny. Now the nanny's quit the job. Too much for her, she said.'

'Arnie, why didn't you tell me this before?'

'What would be the use? What can you do about it? It's not child abuse. You can't notify the police.'

Quite so. Gerald was the custodian. She had signed away her rights, and now she was helpless, sitting here speechless and limp while he cavorted in Florida.

'I told Gerald to get another nanny. The first one was kind of a pill, but she was good to them. The kids want her back, but she's already got another job. Looks as if the starlet's there to stay a while. He's attached to her, the way a woman gets attached to a piece of jewelry and wears it every day, even on the beach.' Arnie gave a sardonic chuckle. 'Well, well, I was his age once. Now I've learned enough to look for quality in a woman, not tinsel.'

Hyacinth's mind had been racing ahead. Her anger at Arnie had evaporated. 'Arnie,' she pleaded, 'you've been so good, so wonderful, you've acted like a father. So do you think you could call an agency down there and find another nanny? You'd know what to look for. Will you?'

'They don't really want another nanny, Hy. What they want is you. That's the long and the short of it. They want their mother. They tell me. Out on horseback and jogging along, we talk. I hate to hurt you, but you might as well know the truth.'

'What am I going to do?' she wailed, so bitterly that the waiter who had come to refill the coffee cups was startled.

'I don't know. You've got too much on your plate, that I do know. I will say this, though: If you were down there with me, I could probably influence Gerald. In fact, I'm sure I could put a little pressure on him. We get along fine, I don't mean that. But money – contracts, real estate, mortgages held in common – well, you see how it is.'

What she saw was a long path leading from herself, to Will, and to her children. The path was crooked and dark, filled with obstacles. And seeing no way past them, she sat across from Arnie with nothing to say. Evidently he, too, had nothing more to say.

At last he spoke. 'You're going to Francine's this week?'

'I hadn't planned to leave till Thursday, but I need to go sooner. I'd go tonight if it weren't already so late.'

'Why don't you confide in your mother? She might suggest something.'

Hyacinth shook her head. 'No. She's had enough with the loss of Dad. She's had enough on her mind. I don't want to crush her.'

'I didn't mean telling her about the fire. You didn't think I meant that, did you?'

'Of course not.'

'I meant the kids. And you and Will. Ask her what she thinks.'

It was quite clear to Hyacinth that Arnie wanted Francine to plead a case for him. And grasping his hand, she spoke from a full heart.

'There'll never be time enough to thank you, for everything you do,' she said.

'You thank me too much, Hy. Just don't forget that I'm here for you. And you ever fall, I'll pick you up.'

Arnie had been right about the children. Hyacinth had not been long at Francine's house before she saw that. The dog Charlie had come with them, and one of the first things they had to tell was about the day Arveen had hit him.

'Mommy! She wanted to kill Charlie,' Emma said. 'Do you know what I'll do if she does? I'll kill her. I'll buy a big gun and I'll blow her head off the way those boys do in school, the ones on TV.'

Emma's face, distorted in righteous anger, was unfamiliar. Every time I see her, thought Hyacinth, she looks unfamiliar, and it is not only because she is a few weeks or even a few months older. Experience and emotion have left their marks. Right now Emma looks as she may after four or five more years are added to her age: vindictive, with tight lips and narrowed eyes. Her little fists are clenched.

And trying to soothe, she explained, 'I'm sure she didn't mean to hurt Charlie. She was probably sorry she hit him. Sometimes people lose their tempers and afterwards they know they were wrong.'

'She wasn't sorry. You don't even know her, so how can you say she was sorry?'

'She's a bitch,' Jerry said.

'What?' cried Francine. 'I've told you a dozen times this week not to use that word any more.'

'Everybody uses it. You're old-fashioned. Everybody's grandmother is old-fashioned, and everybody says bitch.' And Jerry, giggling, was so pleased with his own wit, that he had to jump up out of the chair and upset his jigsaw puzzle.

'Oh damn, damn, damn!' he said. 'Son of a bitch, I've worked on this god-damn thing ever since we got here, and now look.'

Francine's silence was in deference to the children's mother, and the mother was astonished. How could Gerald, as precise and formal as he was, allow this language?

So using the two words she most avoided, Hyacinth quietly asked Jerry whether 'your father' ever heard him speak that way.

Jerry laughed. 'He can't stop us. Arveen says worse words, Mom, but he can't make her stop, either. Arveen is the boss.' Once launched on his speech and in possession of an audience, he continued, 'And do you know why? Because she's stacked, that's why.'

'Stacked?'

'Yes. Like this,' said Jerry with a knowing leer and the appropriate rounded gesture.

Something had gone terribly wrong. And the two women stared at each other as if asking what was to be done.

Perhaps nothing, and better to ignore it for the time being? You couldn't keep a ten-year-old boy in the nursery. And once he left it, he moved ahead into a world where he saw and heard things you didn't like. It was only to be expected, and more so than ever these days. On the other hand, must the world move into the home and take it over? Arveen, whoever she is, should not be a model for *my children*, thought Hyacinth. The repetition thundered in her head.

The dog got up, shook itself, and went to lie down again near Emma's feet. The softness of the little creature, only a heap of silky hair over fragile bones, moved her to pity. It was so innocent in its trust, so vulnerable to any cruelty that might come its way. It was like Emma.

'Charlie hasn't had his walk today. This is a good time to take him,' Francine suggested.

If they've been like this all week, she must be exhausted, Hyacinth thought, but she would never let me know it. And a wave of memory came over her here in the house where she had grown up: the cheerful sound of Francine keeping order in a roomful of noisy boys, her own three and the neighbors'; the good, hot smell of broiling on the grill, while from the farthest room came the reverberation of Jim's music. What an easy time she had had growing up in this cocoon of love and safety! But of course she hadn't know then how easy it was.

'Let's go. Get Charlie's leash, and we'll go down to the woods. It's lovely there.' It was important to sound enthusiastic. 'There's a little pond where I used to watch frogs.'

The children were wild with exploding energy as they raced ahead. The woods were indeed lovely, quiet and dark, with spots of light, a large circle of it around the pond where Hyacinth had used to sit on a log.

'Sit down and be very still,' she said now. 'Maybe we'll see some.'

After a minute or two with no frogs in sight she knew she must hold their attention, for both of them, disgruntled, were fidgeting with impatience. And she so much needed to have this time alone with them, to have their attention and to feel the closeness of their bodies.

'Do you know where frogs come from?' she began. When no answer came, she went on eagerly, 'Out of eggs, just like chickens.'

Her voice was high, nervous, and too eager. She wanted them to love being with her, to give them a store of memory so that one day they might look back and say, *We went to the woods with Mom and she told us about frogs.*

'Yes, like chickens, but not exactly because their eggs are tiny specks that they lay on twigs or leaves in the water. They lay them in the spring.'

There being no response to this either, she produced a fact that might be more interesting.

'Did you know that some frogs can climb?'

'That's not true,' Jerry said crossly.

'Oh yes it is. They're even called tree frogs because they live on trees and bushes. In the spring you hear their beautiful, loud chirping around you, and then you know that winter is really over.'

'Who cares?'

Deciding that it was probably best to ignore the response, Hyacinth continued. 'Don't you think it's odd that they can climb? Don't you wonder how they do it? Well, they have tiny pads on their toes so they can hold on. Other frogs don't have those pads.'

Emma announced that she was tired of sitting, so Hyacinth stood up and led the way back. Their feet, crackling over the leaves of many past years, were loud, as was the silence. A queer contradiction that was: loud silence.

'Look!' cried Emma. 'Look what Charlie has. It'll make him sick.'

'It's only an acorn, dear, and he won't eat it. Squirrels do, not dogs. Let him play with it.' And making yet another determined attempt to clear the atmosphere, she said pleasantly, 'Can you imagine? If you plant an acorn in the ground, it will someday be an oak like that one over there, twice as high as a house.'

Jerry mumbled something. Inaudible as it was, there could be no doubt that it was rude. He had really gone too far, and she was desperate. Perhaps, though, Jerry was desperate too? And although he resisted, she drew him to her.

'Tell me,' she said softly, 'why you're so unhappy today.'

When he shook his head, she continued. 'You're angry because you're unhappy. Won't you tell me?'

'I'm unhappy, too,' cried Emma, beginning to sniffle.

They were all feeling the solemnity of the moment. Something real, something deeply felt and not the easiest to express, was trembling among them.

'Is it because of Arveen and Charlie?' asked Hyacinth, knowing quite well that it must be far more than that.

'We don't like it there anymore,' Emma blurted. 'And Tessie says you're bad mother, and you are. You didn't let us stay in our own house, and I liked my room and the dollhouse.'

How to explain all this? There was too much to explain, that the dollhouse had been a built-in piece that could not be moved, and that Tessie was not to be believed. That dour person must be a marvelous cook, thought Hyacinth, or Gerald, who sought beautiful people, would never be keeping her sour face in his house. It was all too complicated, and she hardly knew how to begin.

Big brother was correcting little sister. 'Mom doesn't have that house anymore. Don't you know where she lives all the time? It's in New York, where we stayed in the apartment and she took us to see the dinosaurs and I had lobster for dinner and stuff like that.'

'Well then, I want to live there all the time,' Emma protested. 'I want to.'

Tactfully, gradually, Hyacinth approached the heart of the matter. 'Don't you like your school anymore?' she asked, meaning, *Don't you like, or love, or get along with your father anymore?*

Jerry answered, 'It's a new school. We haven't even been there yet. We'll have to stay all day till dinnertime. Then Tessie will put Emma to bed because we have no nanny. I put myself to bed, and I don't need any nanny. I'm too old.'

It's three years now, and going on the fourth. Time is racing, while I stand still.

'Aren't you going to get another nanny?'

'Dad's getting somebody to be with us on Saturdays and Sundays, to drive us around and stuff. Dad's always busy.'

Hyacinth could not resist a question. 'Because of Arveen?'

'Yep. Her and lots of people. He goes places when he's not working. He goes to parties with girls, out on boats and stuff, Bruce says.'

'Who's Bruce?'

'Bruce is my friend. You never remember my friends' names. His yard's next to ours. But he lives with his mother, not like us. His dad's no good. He hates his dad.'

Hyacinth said quickly, 'That's very sad. People need a dad and a mom. You mustn't hate your dad. I hope you don't.'

'No, but we don't have fun anymore. And I don't like being the only person who doesn't live with his mom. Well, I'm not the only. There's one, Buddy, but that's different because his mom is dead. But you're not dead.'

'Then why don't we live with you?' demanded Emma. 'You could live in our house. There's lots of room.'

'No she couldn't, stupid.' Jerry was exasperated. 'Dad's already got a woman, hasn't he? What do you think, that he wants two women? Or maybe he does, but mom's not one of them.' And he concluded laughing, 'You don't watch cable TV, or you'd know.'

Quietly, Hyacinth put the next question about when he watched cable TV.

'At night when Dad's out and Tessie's in her room, I get up sometimes. It's fun.'

She must keep her tone level. This was something that Arnie must take care of. Surely he would be able to. And she said, still quietly, 'It's not good for you, Jerry. I really don't want you to do it anymore.'

'I don't live with you, so I don't have to obey you.'

'That's a mean thing to say to me, Jerry.'

'No, it isn't. You're the one who's mean. You should let us live in that apartment where we stay. We could see the dinosaurs and go ice skating and stuff.'

Caught and tied. She must struggle to loosen the tie. 'I have to work,' she said, 'for right now, anyway.'

There was a pout on Emma's pert little face. 'You don't have to make those dresses.' And then, with no plausible connection between the two, she made another accusation. 'You don't even go riding with us.'

'I don't know how,' Hyacinth said weakly.

'Uncle Arnie can teach you. He always says he wants to.'

'All right. Next time I go to see you, I'll take my first lesson.'

'You promise?'

'Yes.'

'And you promise to come live in our house in Florida?'

'I told you she can't—' Jerry had just begun to shout when Hyacinth stopped him.

'Enough promises for today. First, I'll go riding with you and—'

Emma burst into tears. 'You don't love me,' she sobbed. 'You don't. You don't.'

They had returned to the frog pond. Hyacinth sat down on a log and opened her arms. 'Come sit here with me, one on each side. I want to tell you how much I love you. Then we'll all feel better.'

'Are you crying, too?' asked Jerry. 'You look it.'

'I am, a little.'

'I'm not. Boys don't cry,' he said with his voice cracking.

'Who says so?'

'Dad does.'

How like him to hold Jerry to his fantasies of perfection! And she said strongly, 'Dad's wrong. Boys certainly can, if they need to.'

'I wouldn't need to if you'd say you'd live with us.'

'I'll try. Now how about going back to the house and we'll all make a cake for supper?'

Persistent as always, Emma said, 'You didn't promise. You only said you'd try.'

'I will.'

It was an evasion, but no one caught it, and they started back home. Heaven forgive her for the lie, but it was the best she could do.

'So it's been a pretty hard week,' Francine concluded, as they were talking over coffee after Jerry and Emma had gone to bed.

'I'm sorry I wasn't able to spend more of it with you, but all of a sudden, there was a huge pile of work to get out.'

'I'm not complaining, Hyacinth. I meant that it was hard for them. They've changed, and it's very troubling. I've tried, but I haven't been able to find out very much.'

There was no sense in providing Francine with the clues in her possession. It would only awaken a sleeping dragon; ever since that impressive debut in the Fifth Avenue store, Francine had stopped harping on the disgraceful conditions of her daughter's divorce. It was almost as if she were experiencing a touch of awe at her daughter's unexpected triumph.

But on this evening, Hyacinth was not to be spared, for Francine was overwrought. 'These children are not doing well at all. They're secretive, they mope, they're impertinent at times, and then they're sorry. In short, something needs to be done about them.'

'You can be sure I'll look into it.'

267

'I can't be sure of anything,' Francine retorted. 'You don't tell me anything. For three years I've been kept in the dark. It's an outrage. You don't trust me? Me? You don't know that I would fight for you, or my sons, or any of my grandchildren? I'd fight with my last breath, Hyacinth.'

'I know that.'

'Well, then! There's something rotten about Gerald, something even worse than I ever suspected, though I resented him at first glance. For God's sake, tell me what this is about, and I'll get the best lawyer in the U.S.A. I've told you a hundred times at least. You'll never do it for yourself. You're too timid. You were born that way, and it's not your fault. I'm not blaming you—'

Hyacinth put up her hand. 'Please,' she murmured.

Francine was not to be stopped. 'I'm so proud of you, proud of your success. But I'm baffled, totally baffled by this other side of you—'

The telephone rang in the adjacent room. When Francine returned after answering it and reported that Will was calling, Hyacinth's first emotion was dread. Too many things were piling onto her all at once. When she picked up the telephone, Will's happy voice set up a buzz of conflict in her head. He was telling her that he had accomplished the miraculous and the impossible: he had found the perfect apartment in New York City. True, it was expensive, but it would be a lifetime city home, and between the two of them, they would be able to handle the mortgage. Of course, she must see the place and approve, but he was sure she would because it was only two blocks from the park, which would be wonderful for the children, and by the way, had she decided on their school? It was high time. He hoped it wasn't too late.

As all these words poured into her ears, Hyacinth's brain rang with the everlasting, terrifying question: what to do?

'Who's Will?' asked Francine. 'I was surprised. And he seemed surprised, too. "You mean that Hyacinth hasn't told you about me?" he asked. And when I said no, he said, "Well, ask her now, and she'll tell you how nice I am."'

If this question had been asked while she was living the idyll in Normandy, her answers would have poured out in joy and song, or if she had not chosen to answer right then, the joy and song would have been bursting within her. At this moment, she hardly knew how to describe what was bursting within her. Concealing a sigh, she began nevertheless the story of her first sight of Will, their mutual recognition of love, and the time in France during which the total awareness of their love revealed itself beyond doubt. She described him, his person, not storybook handsome, but attractive and strong; his thoughts and tastes, discerning and sensitive; his character, forthright and highly honorable; his manner, courteous and sometimes a trifle opinionated – this she said with a smile.

To everything, Francine naturally paid complete attention. At the conclusion, she inquired, 'Is he to be a husband or a "significant other"?'

'I hate that silly term, but I don't hate the idea. Will does. He wants marriage. He insists on it.'

'And you don't agree?'

'I don't disagree. It's just that – things get complicated. My days aren't long enough anymore.'

'What you're not saying is that you're worried about Emma and Jerry and how they will fit into the plans.'

There was a great lump in Hyacinth's throat, too large for her to give an immediate reply. After a moment she managed to say, 'That's no problem. Will loves children.'

'Does Will know that you don't have custody of them?'

'No.' And she met Francine's eyes, which were so keenly fixed upon her that the very working of Hyacinth's brain must be exposed to those eyes.

'In all this time you've never said a word? When on earth are you going to tell him? And what on earth are you going to tell him?'

'I don't know. Yet I'm thinking.'

Francine's lips tightened in disapproval, as she remarked that she was, to say the least, appalled.

'What can there be to think about? You can't possibly be intending to marry a man without telling him everything about yourself. My God, you've just been saying how honorable he is.' Francine's anger mounted. 'I asked you, what are you thinking about?'

That's just what Arnie she said . . .

Hyacinth stood up. 'I have to go to bed. I've had enough talk for one day.' She spoke abruptly, as Francine had done. 'We can talk again tomorrow, or maybe the next day if I'm able.'

As it happened, there was no time on the following day because, shortly before noon, there came a distress call from Lina. An important midwest shop had sold out the last shipment, important customers were in a hurry, and three important people on the Libretti staff were out sick, so would Hyacinth come back immediately?

'I have to take the next train,' she explained to Francine. 'It's an SOS, and I can't take Jerry and Emma with me. What would I do with them while I'm working? Unless you can come, too?'

'I can't leave until the roofers are finished here. They'll be through by Friday, I'm sure, and then we'll join you.'

'I'm sorry to leave them with you while they're in a bad mood.'

'When you love people, you put up with their bad moods, don't you? And these two are darling most of the time, anyway. They're simply puzzled.' Francine sighed. 'Lord knows, they have enough reason to be puzzled.'

There being no way of answering that without renewing the previous night's argument, Hyacinth made no answer, kissed everyone, hugged the beloved Charlie, and left.

On the train, and through two busy days and wakeful nights, she wrestled with herself. In the end, still not at perfect ease with the decision, she made it: She would tell Will that she did not have custody of her children. There was no other possible way.

But still, that was only half the problem. How to answer the obvious question: why? At worst, he would not believe her, while at best, say what you will, he would have doubts about her. She would have changed at once before his eyes. Gerald was, after all, a responsible man, a respected physician. Would such a man behave as he was behaving without good reason?

On the third day when Will telephoned, she was still distressed and unsure. He was annoyed. No, he was angry. Francine had told him that she was back in the city, and he failed to understand why she had not let him know. To say that she was working late was a strange excuse for not getting in touch with him. Hyacinth tried to mollify him by admitting that she was wrong, by apologizing, and by saying over and over how much she loved him. And she fabricated a touch of illness that was not altogether a fabrication, there having been many moments when her breath had seemed to fail.

At the end, Will forgave her, told her never to worry him like this again, told her how he loved her, missed her, and would be at her house tomorrow evening to talk about the apartment plans and dates.

Because her head still spun with worry about Will and worry about the children, Hyacinth determined simply to try for a good night's sleep, to think positively, and let events play themselves out.

On Thursday, Hyacinth left work an hour early, intending to relax in a long bath and change into something to please Will: a flowered lounging coat with very little underneath. Overnight her spirits had obligingly risen. When two people wanted each other and understood each other as intensely as they did, surely even the hardest problem would somehow be solved, she reasoned.

Thinking so, she turned the key in the lock, entered the hall, and there, she found Emma, Jerry and Francine sitting in the living room.

'Mommy! Mommy!' cried Emma. 'We came in the car because they didn't let us take Charlie on the train.'

She was stricken. 'But you said— you said you were coming on Friday,' she stammered.

'The roofers finished early,' Francine explained, 'and there seemed to be no reason to hang around. Jerry and Emma look forward to doing things in the city.'

Anger paralyzed Hyacinth, blocking thought. The dog jumped on her legs, Jerry said something about a boat ride around New York tomorrow, and Will was due in two hours. What was to have been a gradual, measured discussion between the two of them would now be a – a circus. She wanted to scream.

Francine was puzzled. 'Is anything wrong?' she asked.

'Well, just that I had plans for the evening, and I'm trying to think how to change them.'

'We got lots of food for dinner,' announced Jerry. 'We thought maybe you wouldn't have enough for us, so we bought good things at that store near this house. Lots of barbecued chicken – the man let me taste the sauce, and it's great. And some shrimps, especially for me because I'm the only person who wanted any. And those brown rolls with raisins in them. I love rolls with raisins. Do you, Mom?' Apparently, Jerry was turning into an epicure. 'When we live here, I could go to that store all the time, couldn't I?'

Oh please, she begged silently, don't let us get on that subject again, not now.

As if she had not heard his question, she went to the telephone in the bedroom, saying, 'I'll have to make a call.'

Will would be really angry this time, and no wonder, but she would have to make and risk some excuse; a sudden attack this afternoon, a cold and fever would be the most believable. And then stay out of work tomorrow and 'recover' the next day after Jerry and Emma had left. Even as the tricky plan took shape in her mind, she was stung with the shame of it.

Will's secretary told her that he had just left. She tried his home number. What she heard was the answering machine, on which she left a message: 'Call as soon as you get in. Not feeling well.'

Rarely had she felt so desperately cornered. Here was no question of a week's, or even a day's postponement; this was immediate. How was she to discuss or explain, or communicate to Will in the presence of Francine and the children?

Francine was standing in the doorway, looking anxious, and could not be ignored.

'I'm expecting Will,' she whispered. 'This is about the worst thing that can happen. I had intended to talk about things when the children leave, and – well, how am I to do it with an audience? Tell me that?'

'Come, come. He knows they exist, doesn't he? Don't get

hysterical. As for me, I'll get out of the way if you want me to. I'll go to the movies. No problem.'

'No, no, it's not you. Oh, it's too complicated. I left a message. If only he gets it!'

'Well, let's eat right now and have them go to bed early because we're getting up early for the boat ride. Tell them you have company and they must stay in their room. Come on.'

Francine had already set the table. The bought food was arranged on platters and the coffeepot was on the stove. Her thoughtfulness was touching. I am so brittle now, thought Hyacinth, that anything can break me, this little kindness or a cross word.

Fortunately for her in this condition, nothing was required of her during the meal. Both children were in good spirits, for Francine had let them take turns in the front seat and they had stopped at lunchtime on the way for pizza. All this discussion passed like distant whispers over Hyacinth's ears, attuned as they were to the ring of the telephone. There was only an hour to go, and it had still not rung.

'I'll tidy the kitchen while you talk to the kids,' Francine offered, and with marked sympathy gave counsel. 'Don't make yourself sick. It'll work out fine, you'll see. Just tell them to say a polite hello and then to go read or watch the small TV in their room. Anyhow, your man may not even come.'

But 'her man' did indeed come, and for an instant, did indeed seem very surprised to find Francine and two children there.

'An unexpected visit,' Hyacinth explained as she made the introductions, 'in from the country.'

Hoping that Will would see that this was an intimate family evening and cut his visit short, she remarked that they did not get to see each other very often, so that even a day was a treat.

This hint had apparently not been understood, because Will at once opened a friendly and what could be a lengthy conversation.

'By now I'm sure you all must have heard about me because I've heard about you, and I've been wanting to meet you,' he said, and turned to the children, who by now, in their neat bathrobes, sat properly on straight chairs, leaving the comfortable chairs for the adults.

'Do you know how I met your mother? She was carrying a beautiful dress she had made for you, Emma. It had roses on it. I hope you liked it.'

'I did like it,' Emma said earnestly. 'But I don't like it anymore because it's too small for me.'

'Well, that means you've grown, and that's very good. I'll bet, if you ask her, she'll make another one for you.'

'Of course I will,' Hyacinth said quickly.

Conversation must move fast; no empty space can last longer than a few seconds if the silence is not to deaden the mood.

And Francine, always alert to every nuance, jumped gracefully into the empty moment to say something about the talent that Hyacinth had kept hidden.

'Why, she had never in her life made a dress before that one for Emma. And now, look at her, with her name on a label.'

'I'm looking,' Will said, 'and I'm as proud as can be. I only don't want her to get too busy.'

'Oh, I'm not,' Hyacinth protested. 'These last few days – well you know how no matter what your work is, there's always a little rush, a small emergency, now and then. That's what's happened to me this week. But you have to expect it.'

'I have a feeling that you're pretty overtired right now. Working in New York under pressure is famous for doing that to people.'

'No, no,' Hyacinth protested again. 'I'm fine.' And then suddenly dismayed, she remembered the message on Will's answering machine. 'But since you've noticed, I have to admit I have a slight fever. Maybe I'm coming down with something. I don't know. I left a message on your machine.'

'Then you should be in bed,' Will advised. 'People don't walk around when they have a fever.'

Francine gave a fond laugh. 'You don't know her well enough yet. She's indomitable, a real workhorse.'

Intensely uncomfortable at being the subject and the center of discussion, Hyacinth sat with a fixed smile on her lips. Her mind was churning. Tomorrow or the next day, after the children were gone, there could be no more postponements or evasions; he would have to know that they lived with their father, and he would have to know why.

Why? If only everyone would stop talking, then Will would go home and she could go into her quiet room, alone! There in the stillness, surely a plausible answer would come from somewhere in her head.

'My family always laughed at me,' Francine was saying, 'and I suppose it was rather silly of me, but I always adored anything French. Anything. It seems to me that they really know how to live, don't they? So I know what you mean.'

Will obviously had been talking about their time in France. And hastening to catch up with the conversation so that she would not appear as uneasy as she felt, Hyacinth remarked that yes, she too had loved seeing Brittany.

'But we were talking about the south, about the wild horses in the Camargue,' Will said with a puzzled expression.

'I know! I mean that— I mean, I'm sure they're fascinating, but I meant that I still loved Brittany the best.'

Wondering whether there was anything too strange about this blunder, she glanced furtively at Will. He seemed to be enjoying himself, which was not surprising because Francine was interesting, elegant and poised; surely too, Francine was enjoying Will, who was equally interesting. If my mind were clear, she thought, I would be happy just to watch them together, happy that they must approve of each other.

All this time Jerry and Emma had been quietly observing the scene. They too must be making a fine impression upon Will. If he had had any doubts about how a pair of strange children might affect his life, he couldn't have many now. Touched to the heart by the picture they made, she gave them a wink and a smile.

'Maybe Mr. Miller would like some candy,' Emma said. 'Shall I get it, Mom?'

Francine laughed. 'That's very thoughtful, Emma. Tell me,' she teased, 'maybe you want some candy, too?'

'Yes,' said Emma. 'It's fudge, my favorite kind.'

Now Will stepped in. 'Isn't that funny? It's mine, too.'

And Jerry spoke up. 'Maybe you like rolls with raisins? We had some for dinner, but that's a long time ago. We could have more now if you want to, Mr. Miller.'

'Why, that's nice of you, Jerry.'

Francine proposed coffee. 'If you'd like some, Will, and if I may call you "Will"?'

'Yes to both. I certainly want you to call me "Will," and coffee would be just fine along with one of Jerry's rolls. I have an idea you have a good appetite, Jerry. Do you play lots of sports?'

'I'm pretty good at tennis, and everybody plays soccer and baseball, but mostly I like riding. I have a great horse. His name's Charlie, like our dog.'

The dog Charlie, who had been asleep in the corner, was awakened by the sound of his name, or perhaps by the general movement to the table in the dining ell. Now he followed and lay down under the table.

Rather solemnly, the children put the plate of rolls and a silver candy dish in front of Will. He was amused. His eyes had a twinkle when he looked toward Hyacinth, as if to say something like, *See? I'm already taken to these kids, and not only because they belong to you, but because they're really cute, really nice.*

So, as the little group sat comfortably together there, a new and welcome warmth began to creep through Hyacinth's veins. And with it there appeared, unbelievably, the solution to her tormenting problem.

How simple it is! she exclaimed to herself. All she must do is to say that the children want it this way; they love the Florida house, the beach life and the freedom. Considering, too, her own confinement at work, it did make some sense, although in another way it almost broke her heart. Nevertheless, to deny them their wish would have been all wrong.

Add to all that, she thought now, the fact that she was not the only woman with a busy career who had turned her children over to her former husband, and you have an answer to your question. You may not like the answer, but it is at least plausible.

'We really should give something to Charlie,' Emma said.

Hyacinth reminded her that he had had his dinner, but Emma persisted.

'He does want something so badly. Only a little bite, Mommy. He's begging. See his eyes.'

Will looked toward Hyacinth. 'Perhaps just that little bite and no more?'

It was probably the plea in Emma's eyes that had moved him, and overjoyed by seeing that, Hyacinth agreed. So Will broke off a piece of his roll, carefully removed the raisins, and fed Charlie. Oh, it's going to be good, she thought, and gave thanks. Yes, it's going to be good.

'So you both like to ride,' Will resumed sociably. 'Your mother showed me some great pictures of you on horseback. You should have one enlarged and framed, Hyacinth.'

'Uncle Arnie's doing that for us,' Jerry said. 'He's the one who took the pictures. Sometimes we even go riding with him, but he's much better than we are. He jumps, and we don't.'

'Well, I guess I'll have to learn to ride so I can go along with you too,' Will remarked. 'And you should, too, Hyacinth.'

'Uncle Arnie keeps telling her,' Jerry said earnestly. 'He even offered to buy her a nice easy mare for her birthday.'

'That's a very fine birthday present, I should say.'

This conversation was becoming too personal. Nothing wrong had been said, and Jerry was really being quite delightful, yet Hyacinth felt uneasy. Once he got started, it was almost impossible to know what he might in all innocence say next. So remarking that it was getting late, she asked him and Emma to say goodnight and be ready for tomorrow's boat ride around Manhattan. Obediently, on their best behavior then, they rose.

'Yes, and you people need to get back in the habit of waking up early for school,' said Will, sounding a bit like a father.

'Not as early as last year,' Jerry replied. 'We have a new school this year.'

Now desperation seized Hyacinth. 'Bedtime. Right now,' she insisted.

But Emma, already at the door, was not finished. 'We don't want to go to that new school. All my friends go to the old one, but Daddy won't let us. This one makes us stay till five o'clock every day, and I don't like it. I'm in third grade, and I'm old enough to go where I want to go.' All her grievances now suddenly rising to the surface, she poured out her lament. 'What I want is to live here. I don't want to live in Florida anymore. I want to stay here with Mom, but she won't let us.'

An odd stop occurred, a halt to momentum, as when a machine or an organism breaks down without warning. Three glances fled around the room; each of the three adults touched each other's eyes and sped away.

Hyacinth, whose heart had plunged in her chest, spoke first. 'That's enough, Emma. We don't want to hear any more. I said go to bed. Now.'

Mercifully, Francine got up to take charge, leaving Hyacinth alone with Will. They had both risen and stood now looking at each other, she with a violently burning face, and he with a puzzled, shocked expression. She was not sure whether or not it was also angry. After a few moments, he spoke.

'You're not feeling well. I won't keep you right now. Go in to your children. I was glad to meet them.'

Following him to the door and to the elevator in the outer hall, Hyacinth fumbled for words. 'You don't understand. It's complicated. I meant to explain it to you tonight, but they came, and — it's a long story — not too long, I mean, but when we talk, you'll see what I—'

'Yes,' he said quietly, 'we'll talk. We need to.'

When the elevator stopped, he said goodnight, and stepped in. With a soft whir, it descended.

Francine asked anxiously, 'What did he say?'

'Nothing. My God, why did you bring them here without telling me first?'

'I'm dreadfully sorry, but I never thought about it. There's nothing extraordinary about taking your daughter's children to your daughter's house, is there? I had the key, and we came, that's all.'

'But in the circumstances—' Hyacinth wailed.

'What circumstances? I see you've got big trouble written all over you, my heart aches and I hate to say this, but it's what comes of your absurd secrets, of this crazy, unnatural situation, and— Oh,

I don't know what to make of it, Hyacinth! What about Will? What's going to happen? Do you really think you can go on living like this? Do you?'

'No. But must we talk about it right now? I want to give the kids a good day tomorrow before they leave, and I don't want to have red eyes from crying. What I need is to go to bed.'

'All right, dear.' Francine's vexation drooped into sadness. 'Get some rest. Get some sleep.'

And another night passed.

'Has everyone gone?' asked Will when he entered.

'Yes, my mother has gone back to the country, and the children have—'

'Gone back to their father?'

'Yes, but listen, let me clarify everything, so you'll understand.'

'I already understand. I've thought of nothing else since I left your house the night before last. I understand that you have consistently lied to me. What I don't know is why.'

His sorrowful, keen gaze confronted Hyacinth. Scarcely knowing how to begin a reply, she labored. 'I haven't lied exactly. I do admit that I have avoided telling the entire truth, Will, and—'

'It wasn't an outright lie that you left on my answering machine? I found it when I got home. Not feeling well, you said.'

'I did that because they had come without telling me, and I wanted to see you alone.'

'I think you were afraid that the children would divulge the truth, which is just what they did do.'

'It isn't that simple, Will. Most divorces aren't simple. You don't know, you can't imagine it.'

'Then tell me.'

'We were very angry. I mean I was. I told you about the other woman. So you see, when he wanted the children and they said—'

'No, that was wrong, completely inside out. Begin again.'

'When I wanted the children, of course I did, then they wanted to live in his house, my parents had taken them once to Florida and they had loved the beach and remembered it, they wanted his house, they're only children and that meant so much to them, so I didn't want to deny them, it would have been harmful to force them, so I—' She stopped. This was absurd. How could she have thought that anyone would believe this tale that she was rattling?

Will's sorrowful, keen gaze still faced her. 'But they don't want to stay there now,' he said.

'I know, that's the awful part of it. I signed something, I didn't realize what I was doing, I was so confused and miserable about everything, but now it's signed and nothing can be done about it.'

Again she stopped, these last words echoing. Words of an idiot they were, not those of a woman smart enough to have earned half a million dollars for herself in this last year.

'Surely you must know that a divorce document signed under such emotional stress can be re-examined. Unless it was a court order. Was it?'

'No, just between Gerald and me.'

'It can be re-examined. You must take it to court.'

She had arrived at the impassable mountain. Here it loomed, a grim stone wall. Pressed now with her back against it, she paused, constructed a little steeple with her fingers, steadied her thoughts and tried to speak with reason and calm.

'It wouldn't work. I've inquired. I would have to show that I was completely irresponsible when I agreed to let him have custody. Nobody would believe that about a woman who works as I work. Incidentally, that's one of the reasons the children are better off with their father. I work long hours, as you know.'

Will did not answer. Without looking toward him, she was yet aware that he was examining her. Afraid of seeming foolish by wearing the usual silk robe with its promise of a long sweet night, she had dressed carefully and proudly; her feet, in high-heeled pumps, were crossed at her ankles, and her small diamond studs glistened in her ears. The significance of all this would not have escaped Will's critical and subtle mind. She knew him well.

But perhaps not well enough? He was tapping the wooden chair arm as he spoke. 'It won't do, Hyacinth. It's not good enough. What is the true reason that he got away with this? What did he threaten?'

'Threaten? No, no! He loves the children and they wanted to be with him, that's all there is to it. I guess they love the beach house more than they love me,' she said ruefully, and then with an easy smile added, 'Oh, I don't mean that exactly, but they're only children and it's more fun for them there than here. So even though it hurt and still does hurt, I do what's best for them.'

'A case of maternal sacrifice, then. Very touching.'

'Please don't be sarcastic, Will. I happen to be telling you the truth.'

'No, Hyacinth. It's simply not true, if it ever was. You'd better think up a new one. You heard Emma right here in this room. They want to be with you. Why won't you have them?'

She was beginning to sweat. He was driving her in circles, and she said so, protesting, 'You keep making me repeat myself. You know I work long hours, and I have to do some traveling. I just told you that a minute ago.'

Will shook his head. 'There are too many holes in your story. This whole thing is just so sad . . . I can't believe I'm sitting here listening to this, or saying what I have to say. There's so much . . . Who is this man "Arnie," anyhow? I don't like his type. To hear him talk, you'd think he was your children's father. Why these regular dinners you have with him? And the fine presents, the mare? Some casual present! Hardly like handing a person a Hershey bar.'

'To begin with, I didn't accept the mare. And as long ago as when we were in Paris, I explained who he is. Don't tell me you're making this fuss because you're jealous of Arnie.'

An instant later she knew she had made a mistake because he saw through her intent.

'You're trying to divert my anger by confusing the issue, and it won't work. Yes, your so-called friend Arnie is a part of this lie, and until you tell me the whole thing, we can't—'

When he got up to stand at the window, she followed. Down below, life crawled; a shrieking ambulance snaked through traffic; like huge beasts, buses lumbered along the curb, and walkers darted for safety before the light should change. No one down there knew or would have cared if he had known what was happening in this room where her heart — and surely Will's heart, too — was going to break. A terrible fear ran down her spine as if she were lost somewhere on an ocean or in a jungle without a path.

She could hear his breathing. And laying her head on his shoulder, she pleaded, 'I love you, Will. And you love me. Does anything else count?'

He did not move, nor did he put his arm around her, but speaking as if into the air or to the street below them, replied.

'Do you remember the time I told you about my affair with the married woman? I told you not because I wanted you to think I'm some kind of saint, which God knows I'm not, but because I wanted to come clean about myself, to keep nothing of myself away, or have secrets from you. We can't live together in a house where the closets are locked and only one of us has the key.' And pulling away, he looked down at her, straight down into her eyes. 'Now I see why you never talked about your children. I thought it was strange, yet when you gave me some sort of explanation, I accepted it. But there's too much concealed here. Even your lie about having a fever,' he said with sudden scorn. 'You wanted to make the children happy, so you let your husband keep them. Can you expect me to believe anything you say?'

Although he had not moved toward her, she shrank away. She was helpless before his power, and her tongue did not move.

'Your husband – your former husband – is a physician. He has a respected position in the world. He may also be a scoundrel, that's possible, but still, he could never have claimed this advantage over you if he hadn't known he could get away with it, that you were unable to prevent him.' Will's voice rose. 'What is it that you are not telling me, Hyacinth?'

He was ten feet tall, and his eyes were like sparks. Still unable to speak, she had to look away.

'What is it that you are not telling me?' he repeated.

'Nothing.' She managed to murmur, so low that Will stooped to hear her. 'Nothing. I've told you what I can, and you won't believe it.'

That keen ear heard every syllable. 'What you "can"? Then there must be things that you can't.'

God help me, she thought, and murmuring still, said, 'Please.'

She thought that his eyes were wet now, but since her own were blurred, she was not sure.

'Don't you see that we can't go ahead like this? That there's no future for people who can't be honest with each other at the start?'

She parted her lips, but no sound came.

'You won't say any more?' Will asked.

'Please,' she repeated.

Stunned as if all senses had fled, she still sensed his departure, the door's closing, and the stillness. After a long while, she went back to the window and looked down. Lights had come on, and the sky, like a warm blanket, smothered the city. She wanted air. She wanted to open the window, to let herself out into the air and down. How many seconds would it take to reach the street, simply to plunge into that night and feel no more?

But then she did feel: Oh Jerry! Oh Emma! And turning away from the window, went back to lie down alone in the darkness.

Chapter Fifteen

Dear Hyacinth,

This is the most painful letter I have ever had to write. This is the saddest experience of my whole life. I have been wondering whether it is the saddest for you, too, and I have to conclude that it cannot be because if it were, you would, weeks ago, have given me the only thing I ask of you, a truthful account of your past. I have written to you, we have spoken twice over the telephone, and still you deny me, although I have told you clearly that without perfect honesty, we cannot continue in life together. Surely you must see that.

At this point, I have to give up. I have to say to you what I dreaded to say, what I never dreamed it possible to say, and that is: goodbye. I am trying to find peace again for myself, and with all my heart I wish the same for you.

Will

In a black, upright script, these few searing sentences marched across a single page and trembled between Hyacinth's two hands.

In her room, lit by a weak lamp, the lonely night stretched without end through the apartment, out into the street and the world. Light, cheer, hope, love, sun – all of them were faded. What was left? The children, who were in truth not really hers anymore? The glittering 'career' that, for her at least, had lost its glitter?

'You need to work,' Francine had warned. 'Work is the antidote for heartache.'

She had telephoned almost daily since that night when Will had met the children and everything had fallen apart. To her credit, she had asked no further questions. Well, thought Hyacinth, she hadn't really needed to; anyone could have predicted the course of events. She had only offered help (but there was none), and spoken kindly platitudes about keeping busy. Francine herself was always busy with her projects; three scholarship college girls lived in the house; she liked giving personal charity, and besides, 'they were good company.' Francine knew how to adjust and cope.

From Arnie, too, had come well-meant advice. When, after a few days, she had not answered the telephone, he had become worried, called Francine, and had learned what had happened. If Hyacinth were not feeling so ill, she would even now be amused by the fact that behind his consolation lay a certain satisfaction with the disappearance of Will.

It was midnight. And reminding herself that tomorrow was to be another busy day and that she had already skipped more than enough days' work, she laid the letter aside and switched off the lamp.

'You don't look well,' Lina said. She had been scrutinizing Hyacinth for the past few weeks and making these comments.

Also well meant, thought Hyacinth, like Francine's and Arnie's comments, but also to no avail.

Unfortunately, Lina refused to let the subject alone. 'I'm truly, truly sorry, Hyacinth. I thought you were wonderful together, a perfect match for each other.'

It was not clear whether Hyacinth was supposed to agree or not. And Lina continued, 'Fortunately, he seldom comes here. There's really no reason anymore for him to come, since we'll be meeting once or twice a year at corporate headquarters. So you won't have to see him here, which makes it easier for you, I'm sure.'

Unquestionably, she was waiting for an explanation of events, such as who had dropped whom and why, but since it was not forthcoming and Hyacinth's vague gaze was directed toward the gray sky beyond the window, she switched to practical matters.

'Do you realize that you've been mentioned in almost every major magazine by now? And even featured in three? Do you realize what you've accomplished?'

What good is it, thought Hyacinth. It has no meaning. I'm ill. I have no energy.

'I'm not worth much to you right now,' she said. 'I've even been thinking that you may not be wanting me any longer.'

Lina's black eyes rounded as she cried her amazement. 'Not want you? Why, you little fool, you can go anywhere. Anywhere. Do you know that? In one hour you could get enough credit to walk out of here and set up your very own business. Whenever you want to, you can.'

'I would never think of doing that, Lina. Never. Why, you're the person who gave me my start. Would I do that to you?'

There was a sad touch to the older woman's little smile, as she looked at Hyacinth.

'Not many people are that loyal, my dear. Not any more. You're from another age and another place. I don't mean that as a disparagement, not at all. It's a fine innocence that you have, a lovely naïveté, for all your talent.'

'That's what they always say about me. I'm naïve.' And Hyacinth gave a rueful laugh.

The fall days straggled like a beaten army. First summer, not entirely finished, burned through a stifling smog. Then came fierce autumn rains to batter the city's very stones and bones, and give further emphasis to Hyacinth's defeat.

Now she began to work as she had never done before, all day and half the night at home, forcing the last shred of her unwilling energy. She worked because there was nothing else.

One day Arnie telephoned. He had not been in New York since the night he had met Will. She would never have expected to feel such a glow of gratitude as the one that came with the first note of his voice.

'Hello, Hy. I'm in town. How about dinner? Usual place? Usual time?'

He was enthusiastic, intimate, and he wanted to see her. Anticipation, in one instant, drew the scene: lights, warmth, music, and a person, a human being, who *wanted to see her.*

'I'll pick you up at work, and if you feel like doing it, we can walk uptown. Okay?'

'Very much okay. Six forty-five?'

'You work late!'

'That's nothing. That's early. We're getting the spring showings ready.'

She was sitting at her desk when Arnie arrived and stood for a moment in the doorway, taking in the scene. His eyebrows were raised in frank surprise. She understood that he must not have expected such a scene: the room, much smaller than Lina's and much more simply furnished, it must nevertheless be fairly impressive, its desk piled high with papers and its bulletin board tacked solidly with photographs and clippings.

He kissed her fondly on both cheeks, then glancing around in his usual quick way, exclaimed, 'Wow! I had no idea — but of course, I don't know a damn thing about this business except that women are damn fools enough to spend a fortune on a rag to cover their backs.' He laughed. 'No offence meant. If you can make a fortune out of rags, go to it. Say, what's this? This is you.'

In a newspaper clipping at the top of a pile, he had seen a style page from which half a dozen faces smiled: an Englishman's who was making a name for himself, a midwestern woman's who specialized in knits, and Hyacinth's.

'Hey, look at yourself. Those eyes, and the hair. Damned if it doesn't look like silk.'

A silk curtain, Will said. I love to feel it on the pillow.

'Picture doesn't do you justice, Hy. Damned if you don't get prettier every time I see you. What is it, some special vitamins or something?'

'Oh, just hard work, I guess,' she said, forcing a laugh.

'And in Canada — this paper's Canadian.'

'We do a lot of selling there.'

'Hard to believe all this. Gee, I still see you the day you drove up from Texas. Jerry was just out of diapers and you were only a kid yourself.'

'Twenty-six.'

'Well, that's still a kid. And you still look like one, only better dressed.' He grinned. He marveled and made a wide gesture encompassing not only the room, but past the window, all the stone towers in which lights were beginning to twinkle as far as the Hudson and beyond. 'How did you do it?'

Hyacinth shrugged, meaning, *Why go into all this?* First it had been Gran, who taught her to sew, and at her death had shown by her life's history how to persevere. And second was Will, who had directed her . . . Best not to think of that.

'I'm starved. How about you? Let's get moving, if you're ready.'

'I'm ready.'

There could be no mistaking the season, colored as it was in harvest's yellow and plum, fading toward the year's end. Shop windows were decorated with blond sprays of wheat and chrysanthemums. With half a mind attentive to Arnie's observations and the other half making her own observations as they walked, Hyacinth drew pictures out of the past: first Halloween and pumpkin faces on the doorstep; then Thanksgiving (no turkeys on display in this part of the city); then Christmas, red, green and tinsel – but look, somebody has already arrived at Christmas with a display of stockings and glass balls. Hastening the season, rushing time as if time did not rush enough! How many years now? Going on four . . .

And she had actually been glad of this evening! Now if she could decently get away from Arnie and go home alone, she would do it. But it was too late.

'Yes, you're an eyeful,' he began as he unfolded his napkin. 'Let's order, and then I'll tell you about the kids. It's hard to go into things over the telephone.'

Suddenly anxious and tense, she said quickly, 'I'll have whatever you have. I don't care what I eat. Is there anything special about the children? Anything different? They sometimes sound fine on the phone, and then again I get the same complaints that I can't do anything about.'

'Nothing's changed except that Arveen's gone and there's a new friend in the house. Name's Buddy, this time.'

'Buddy? A boy?'

Arnie laughed. 'No, none of that. Buddy is five feet ten – could be a model, but she's a singer. Natural blonde, but had a bad nose and he fixed it and she's in love with him. Or he says so, anyway. Cock-eyed names these dames figure out. Buddy, for God's sake.'

Lead in Hyacinth's chest seemed to drag her down so that she sank back in a chair. So cheap, so – so vile! Without shame.

'But she's good-natured and the kids get along with her. So don't worry about that.'

There was a moment of silence during which Arnie thoughtfully refrained from looking at her. When he spoke, he kept busy buttering a roll.

'As I always tell you, you mustn't think Gerald neglects them. He's still crazy about them, but he's too busy with— with other stuff. And you see, they're not cute anymore. Women don't stop and gush over Emma, or over Jerry when he still wore grey flannel short pants, all dressed up, you know, that kind of thing. They're getting independent, talk back, you know, the way kids do. Not so much fun.'

She could not speak. And considerately, Arnie prattled.

'Nothing much to tell you since I last saw you. I've been sending Diamond to a couple of races out of state, and he's doing well. A gorgeous-looking horse. Got prospects. Major, of course, I ride, lots of times along with your kids. But you know all that. Let's see. What else? Oh yes, I've been looking at some land. I'm sick of living in apartments, so I may build a house for myself. Why not?'

He was telling her that she had only to say the word. Yet, with kindly tact, he sensed her state of mind and was not about to press her right now. And then, as if to confirm this judgment of hers, he asked very gently the inevitable question.

'Have you seen him since we last talked?'

There was no need for any agonizing details, so she said simply, 'It's over. Completely. He wanted an explanation that I couldn't give him. That's all.'

Arnie whistled. 'I expected it. I believe I told you so.'

'You did.'

'So where are you now?'

'Here, as you see.'

'No chance of starting up again?'

'How could there be? I'm not out of the woods yet. Will I ever be?'

'To tell you the truth, Hy, one never knows. Of course, the more time goes by, the better. Yet you read the papers, you see how stuff is found out years after the event. And this isn't even four years yet.'

'I know. It was a silly question.'

'I'm sorry. I'd like to see you get past all your troubles. I hate to see you so hurt. If I could take the hurt away, I'd move a mountain to do it.'

Quite moved, she said only, 'My mother calls you a "prince," and I guess I have to agree.'

'How is your mother? How's she doing?'

'She's as busy as any two people could be. Also, she's just met a very nice man, and I'm glad about that, so I don't see much of her. But we will be going down to Florida together for Thanksgiving with Jerry and Emma. Why – what's the matter?'

Arnie's face had clouded. 'I wanted to let you enjoy your dinner before telling you. Gerald is taking them on somebody's yacht for Thanksgiving weekend, and he's taking them someplace else over Christmas and New Year's. Acapulco, I think.'

Hyacinth's fork clattered on the plate. 'I don't believe it!' she cried. 'He can't do that.'

'I'm afraid he can. I've tried to talk him out of it, but he's made his plans already. You'll have the February school vacation, he says, and that's a promise.'

'His promises! A beggar at a table, that's what I am, waiting for crumbs. And what if he says "no crumbs today, lady, there's nothing left for you"? What then?'

'Hush, Hy. That won't happen,' Arnie whispered, for in her outrage, her voice had risen.

'Oh, can you guarantee that?'

'I never guarantee anything. But I don't believe he will. He never has, has he?'

'Not good enough,' she said.

'Eat something, Hy. You haven't touched a forkful,' Arnie reproved, for the fork still lay on her plate. And when she still did not touch it, he turned jovial. 'You need food. Men don't like skeletons.'

'Men!' she cried bitterly.

'You're scared to death and you're angry, aren't you? And no wonder. I know this is lousy, but what can you do? Gerald's probably already sorry about this, but he won't admit it. So take the ten days in February. Come on down, and you'll have a great time.'

Arnie's smile was meant to be encouraging, and his eyes were almost pleading with her. He was comfort and warmth. Most of all, he was *there*. And that being so, Hyacinth owed him a bit of cooperation by way of thanks.

'All right. I'll settle for February. I suppose there's no sense banging my head against a stone wall, is there?'

'Ah well, Hy, you have to look at it that way. It just wasn't meant to be. And you're going to be just fine.'

It was one thing to take valiant resolve, and quite another to hold that resolve; through days of work one had to be alert and quick to smile, but at home alone the visions crowded, the past full of mistakes, the present full of confusions, and the future unfathomable, all merged into a kind of steaming brew.

And one night before Thanksgiving, which Hyacinth was to spend, and did not want to spend, with Lina's glittering guests at her splendid East Side house, she lost her resolve. Francine had wanted her to go along out west to visit the family there, but since even Lina's party would be preferable to that, Francine was going by herself. Flying from New York, she was to spend tonight with Hyacinth; inevitably their talk would be about Gerald, the cruelty, the outrage, the mystery and the usual: *Why in Heaven's name will you not tell me what this is about?*

It was too much. And springing up from her chair so abruptly that she almost tipped it over, she ran to the telephone and called Gerald's number.

'Yes, it's who you think it is,' she cried. 'What are you doing to me? Does it make you happy to torment me? Do you know you're a devil?'

There came the voice, the rich, melodious voice that had once enthralled her. 'A devil? I don't know about that. Isn't it a matter of opinion?'

Smooth, he was, and ever so slightly amused besides. If he had been in the room now, she would have struck him.

'Does it makes you happy to keep my children away from me? They're mine, do you hear? It's I who gave them birth. I nursed them, and you— you—' She was unable to finish.

Gerald's deep sigh came over the wire. She knew it well; it represented exasperation and sophisticated patience.

'You are, as I've said many times, Hyacinth, an over-emotional woman, given to hysteria. I do not keep the children away from you. You have nothing to complain about. You say I torment you. Why? Because of a change in vacation plans?'

'That's not the whole of it. Not nearly. Those disgusting women you have—'

'Disgusting? Who tells you that?'

She had no intention of betraying Arnie, her benefactor, her lifeline. 'Emma and Jerry,' she said, 'mostly Jerry. Do you know, does anyone know or care, that he watches pornography on cable television late at night? Did you know that?'

'No, I didn't, and I'll certainly look into it. You might remember that I have a busy practice and I can't be everywhere at once.'

'I'm busy, too, and I—'

He interrupted. 'I've heard about your success, and I'm impressed, but—'

She interrupted. 'Success or not, I would manage to watch my children. That's why they belong with me.'

'The children aren't suffering, Hyacinth. They're healthy and cared for. Take a look. Anybody can see it.'

'They are suffering, Gerald. They are. They want to live with their mother, as most children do.'

'Well, these children can't, and there's no sense in going all over that again. You signed something voluntarily, the price you paid for my silence.' Now the mellow voice turned harsh. 'You should be grateful because I didn't have to do it that way. I didn't have to return the evidence to you after I found it on the lawn.'

'What kind of a world is this where there's no forgiveness and no understanding?' she screamed. 'There should be some way, some human being who can get at you—'

He did not allow her to finish, but thrusting his words upon her with a force almost physical, retorted, ' "Get at me?" Just try to take legal means. You know what'll happen to you.'

Who of them hung up first, Hyacinth did not know. She knew only that her head was bursting with a rage so anguished that she might have been close to a stroke. In a flood of tears, she threw herself down upon the bed.

When, hours later, the doorbell rang, she was still lying there, quiet now and exhausted. Only when the ringing persisted did she remember that Francine was coming to spend the night. And getting up, she stumbled to the door.

There stood her mother, trim in a proper travel suit with her neat suitcase in hand and a look of absolute horror.

'What in the name of God is the matter?' she cried.

'It's nothing. I've been crying.'

'I can see that, can't I? What's happened? Look at yourself!'

Out of the mirror in the hall there stared a sorry, pale face between straggled ropes of ink-black hair.

'I talked to Gerald just now,' she said.

'Well? Well, what?'

'I want my children, and he won't listen to me.' She was too tired to speak. 'That's all there is. Please don't ask me any more. You know it all, anyway.'

Francine went into her usual room, where in her tidy fashion she removed her jacket and arranged her few possessions for the night. When she reappeared a few minutes later, Hyacinth had lain down on the sofa and was staring at the ceiling. Francine sat down nearby and with troubled eyes regarded her daughter.

'I don't know it all, Hyacinth. But of course there's no use in asking you for the thousandth time to explain this to me.'

Hyacinth looked up into the troubled eyes. The pity in them brought a fresh surge of tears. If Emma were feeling the pain that I am feeling now, she thought, it would be unbearable for me. What would I not do to take my daughter's pain away? And here my mother is begging me with her pity.

But no, it is impossible . . .

Francine inquired, 'Does anything hurt you beside your heartache?'

'My head. It feels twice its size.'

'That's tension. Sit up a little and let me rub your neck.'

The fingers were cool and strong. And as they soothed, queer thoughts passed through Hyacinth's sick head: She used to annoy me, she was not serious enough, she said foolish things, I loved Gran much more than I loved her, she must have known it, she did know it, and she forgave it. I was arrogant and young for my age. She is the only one who foresaw what Gerald would finally do. No, not finally. Not all of it.

Just try to take legal action. You know what'll happen to you.

Felony-murder, second degree.

Tears slid down her cheeks and under her collar.

'Oh, what is it?' cried Francine. 'I can't bear this anymore. Do you hear me? I can't.'

And Hyacinth heard her. Lying back on the pillow, she closed her eyes, and whispered.

'Don't look at me. Just listen.'

It was almost midnight, and they were still sitting up. Francine, with a ghastly face, was staring at the wall.

'Now I feel better, but you feel worse,' said Hyacinth.

'That's true. I would feel better if I could think of something to do, but I can't seem to think of anything.'

'Because there is nothing.'

'You couldn't tell Will,' Francine murmured, as if thinking aloud.

'And bring as my "dowry," ' Hyacinth said in mockery, 'a threat hanging over my head? Don't you see?'

'Yes . . .' Francine spoke reluctantly. 'Yes, even if he were willing, and no man, lover or not, no man with any brain, no man you'd want, would undertake it. Yes, I see.'

And then, after a silence, she said suddenly, 'No man except Arnie. Do you realize how exceptional he is?'

'Of course I do. I always tell him how grateful I am.'

'He wants more than gratitude.'

'I know that, too.'

'Is there no chance for him?'

Hyacinth smiled sadly. 'You want to see your daughter securely settled, and I understand. It's only natural.'

'So you're still thinking of Will?'

Thinking? Remembering. Longing. In an elevator the other day I heard his voice, and I didn't dare turn around until I saw that it wasn't he. Every time the telephone rings, she thought, my hand trembles when I pick it up, although I know it won't be Will.

'I'm sorry, Hyacinth. You need some peace.'

'I need some sleep. Right now I want to go to bed.'

Whether for good or ill she had spoken; she had revealed everything to Francine, and now it was too late to take anything back. Like an incoming wave, a tremendous tiredness swept over her.

Chapter Sixteen

At the lunch table on the hotel's terrace, Hyacinth, looking about at her family, saw new light in their faces. These few days of Florida sunshine together had been like medicine.

The wait for February had been daunting, as each succeeding day seemed longer than the one before it. The children had been waiting for her too. They had clung to her and again, to her despair, had been asking when she was going to take them back with her.

But at this particular moment, all was well. Emma was fascinated by the charms on Francine's bracelet. Jerry was talking baseball with Arnie, who had come this noon to join them at lunch; his loud, authoritative manner was amusing Arnie.

Happiness is only an atmosphere created by your mind, she thought. This grass is brilliant; this sky is blue as a robin's egg; the fruit on the platter shines like porcelain, and all the laughter ripples. When she caught Francine's glance, it told her that a day like this was worth ten times more than the trip to London that Francine had given up for this visit to her grandchildren.

There were only two more days before school would start here, and the spring collection would call Hyacinth back to work. But she must not think of that. Think, rather, of the now and here. At long last she had begun some riding lessons, which had delighted her children. They had all played ball on the beach, had gone deep-sea fishing, swum in the pool, eaten enormous meals, and not wasted a minute.

'What are we doing this afternoon?' asked Jerry. 'Are you going riding with us, Mom?'

Hyacinth was about to say yes, when Arnie spoke.

'I was going to ask you to do me a little favor, Hy. Maybe sometime today while the folks here go out to the stables you would spare a couple of hours to go along while I look for some property that's for sale? Maybe give your opinion? Would you mind?'

'I don't know the first thing about real estate,' she replied.

'I'll take my chances on that. You've never seen this part of the state before. It'll be interesting. No beaches and no tourists.'

It did not need a detective to see that something more personal than real estate was in Arnie's mind. There was no mistaking what it was. Francine's expressive eyebrows had risen in pleased surprise, and there was no mistaking that, either.

'I want to come, too,' cried Emma.

'Not today, dear. Some other day,' Arnie said.

His gentle tone, along with the child's ready acceptance of his direction, affected Hyacinth. He really was fatherly, no doubt of it. It was a pity that he had never had children.

'Let me run upstairs to get a hat and my sunglasses, Arnie, and I'll be with you,' she said.

To anyone accustomed to packed commercial highways or to royal palms on a pastel oceanfront, the landscape was unrecognizable. Flat as a tabletop lay the fields on which the sugarcane grew; there was not a tree in sight, and in the hot air, no breeze stirred. Irrigation canals at intervals cut through the fields, and at longer intervals wherever roads met, a shabby, unpainted hamlet would cluster around a filling station and a soft-drink stand.

Arnie was being instructive. 'These fields go on for miles. This is one of the largest cane areas in the country. I'll bet you didn't know that.'

These remarks were so unlike him who rarely spoke in general terms, that Hyacinth wondered how long it would take for him to get to the reason for this rather aimless expedition. It did not take very much longer because at sight of a soft-drink stand, he stopped the car.

'I could use a coke. How about you?'

'Yes, thanks.'

The owner of the stand, having accepted his pay, went into his house and slammed the door, leaving them to stand beneath his single sparse tree drinking the cokes in a total silence. Hyacinth's tingling nerves caused her to break it by saying something, anything. 'You surely aren't looking at any properties out here, are you, Arnie?'

'No. I only wanted to get away with you where there was nobody and nothing.'

He was looking not at her, but away down the vacant black tar road. Free then to look intently at him, she did so. What she saw was the same familiar figure, dapper and confident. Yet at this moment, there was something else; perhaps it was his stance, or the pose of his head, that brought to her mind with a shock that evening at the hotel where the bed, turned down for the night, was on view beyond the door.

Suddenly he turned and spoke. 'I've been waiting for you, for the time when you'd be ready. I hoped – I was pretty sure I wouldn't have to wait too much longer. So how about it, Hy? We aren't gonna live forever.' And with a strangely old-fashioned gesture, taking hold of both her hands, he made his appeal. 'Marry me, Hy. I've wanted you almost from the time I first saw you.'

She was helpless, held by his hands and by his eyes, which were glistening with emotion.

'You'll be safe and loved. I'll give my part of the practice to Gerald in return for that paper you signed. He'll take it. It's worth a fortune.'

'You'd actually give it to him, Arnie? That doesn't make any sense.'

'Why not? I'm very well fixed. Plenty of great real estate and plenty of ready cash too. I can retire, take you and the kids anyplace in the world. You just name the place.'

'I didn't – didn't expect—' she began.

'Yes, you did, Hy. Don't play with me. You knew I'd be asking

you soon. Listen to me: Could it be any nicer? These few days —
why, we've been like a family, you, and the kids, and even your
mother. Ask her what she thinks of me, especially now that you've
told her the whole story. She'll be the first to say, go to it, take the
guy. I know she will. He's smart, he's not bad looking, she'll tell
you; he's good to your kids and he's crazy about you. What more
do you want?'

His questions pounded her. His hands still gripped her, and he
kept on pounding.

'I'm no womanizer like Gerald. You know that. You'll be able
to count on me. You'll have a steady life instead of running around
trying to make yourself fall in love with some man who'll only
bring you the same problem you had with that fellow Will.'

Releasing her hands, he put his arms around her, and as if he
sensed that she was not ready for anything more, he kissed her
forehead and her cheeks with great tenderness.

'I'd really like to set us up in France. You love France, and you'd
be out of harm's way over there with the children if anything
should turn up.'

'Turn up? Oh, God. Is this to go on forever?'

'You can never be sure, Hy. We've talked about that often
enough, haven't we?'

The chronic fear was weakening her legs so that she needed to
sit down. 'I want to get back into the car,' she said. 'I don't feel
well.'

Alarmed at once, Arnie opened the car door and helped her in.
'We'll head right back. Oh I'm sorry, I didn't mean to upset you.
Are you all right? Are you sure?'

'It's a headache, a thunderclap — so much all at once, this whole
lovely week, and now these thoughts starting up again.'

'Lay your head back,' Arnie commanded. 'We won't talk.
You'll be all right. I'll take the short way this time.'

She gave him a faint smile. 'So there is a shorter way?'

He smiled in return. 'Of course. I was making the trip last as
long as I could.'

Her nerves, unstrung, were quivering. Peeking through eyelids
almost closed, she observed him, a robust and muscular man

appearing much younger than his years; his face, in the coppery afternoon glow, was Indian tan against the silvery crest of his hair. If she were to move any closer to him, she would smell his pine lotion. He was supremely fastidious.

In one week he could find a dozen desirable women who would want him. And he wanted her. He would be good to her . . .

To go away somewhere and have her children all to herself again! Wouldn't any woman in her position – if there ever was any other woman in this crazy position – accept him in a minute? Francine the practical, the almost-always-right, would approve on the principle that in this world you cannot have everything . . .

'We're here,' he said as the car stopped at the hotel. And he went around to her side to open the door.

Palms soared above her head. The breeze was fragrant, and from somewhere came a tinkle of music, leaving a rich sense of expectation as it passed.

'You slept,' said Arnie. 'A psychologist would say that you were escaping a decision.'

He was, of course, also supremely intelligent, which had been obvious from the beginning.

'How long shall I wait for the decision, Hy?'

She heard herself replying, 'Emma and Jerry have to finish this semester.'

He nodded. 'That's only a couple of months away. Understood.'

This time his kiss was full on her mouth. When he let her go, his eyes were happy.

Upstairs in the room, she opened a door and stepped out onto the balcony, where a pair of lounge chairs faced the ocean. Again the weakness overcame her, and she fell into one of the chairs. She was ill, but the fact that the illness was obviously psychosomatic was of no help at all. So she lay still and blanked out her mind.

After a while, when her mind came back to life, she began to reconstruct exactly what had happened during these last few hours. She had actually allowed his embrace! Yet could she, should she, have pushed him away? She had said something about the end of the school term. Had she given him any promise? All was a whirl and tumble in her head: her children, the fear, the threat, the responsibility of her job, Arnie's promises, and again, the children.

She stood up and gazed out over the railing. High up here the wind rushed through silence. From this height the ocean lay as if no wind disturbed its flat calm, but if you were down there below, you would see the great green swells and hear them crash as they broke onto the land. For a long time she stood there, her hands gripping the railing, just gazing and sensing the vastness of the sea.

Once on a night not very long ago, two people had lain in a hammock watching the dark waves until the moon came up and turned everything white. They say you forget . . . But when? When you're ninety, maybe, and past wanting anything? I hurt him, she thought. I've hurt Will. It would have been better for both of us if we had never lain in that hammock, or if we had never met.

It would have been better, too, if I had not let Arnie leave today with the wrong impression. He has given so much of himself to me; it's true that I never asked for that gift, but neither did I refuse it, and I'm sorry. Still, I can't pretend love, even to purchase peace, even if a part of me is tempted. No, I can never do that. And I will not.

Dear God, isn't there any way to straighten out this life of mine?

'Handsome children,' remarked the man on the neighboring bench.

An elderly man with a pleasant manner, he had been watching Francine as she took a picture of Jerry and Emma, and was watching them now as they walked away toward the stables.

'I think so, but of course I would think so, I'm their grandmother.'

'I come out here a couple of times a week, and I often see them. They both do well on horseback. Very well, I should say.'

'They're excited about the show on the fairgrounds next month. That's why they wanted to try out their new outfits today, new velvet caps, new boots, the works, for "dressage," they told me, not that I know anything about it.'

'Dressage is a parade around the ring, and a beautiful sight it is. My wife's going to be in the show, too. In fact, she's here now, rehearsing. But I had to drop out on account of this broken leg.'

Only now did Francine observe the crutch propped against the bench.

'Oh, too bad,' she said, murmuring sympathy.

'Well, it's a lot easier for a man to break a leg than for a horse to do it. They're delicate creatures, horses, although you might not think so when you're standing next to a stallion sixteen hands tall.'

'I guess not,' said Francine, murmuring again, but this time reluctantly because the man seemed to be prepared for a conversation that for all she knew might last another hour until Jerry's and Emma's return.

So she picked up her book, but not quickly enough, because a question was thrust at her: 'Have you heard about Diamond?'

'Diamond?'

'The horse. The famous Diamond. Or was famous, but now he's dead, poor fellow. He stumbled over a gopher hole and broke his leg. Had to be put down. They were all shocked here yesterday. The owner boards him here sometimes between shows and races, and everybody was glad that the accident did not happen on these premises.'

'Oh, you don't mean Arnie— Dr. Ritter's horse?'

'I'm afraid I do. Arnie – Dr. Ritter – was always a good judge of horseflesh. We used to ride together years ago in Texas. It's amazing, when I saw him here yesterday, he hadn't changed a day's worth since then.'

'I'm awfully sorry. But he never said a word about it to me.'

'I guess he was too upset yesterday to talk anymore. Well, I see you want to read your book, and I'll go back to my paper, learn what's going on in the world.'

The afternoon ticked by as a hand moves around a clock, always too slowly when one is in a hurry and tense with waiting for a crucial decision. She could not stop worrying about Hyacinth's country ride with Arnie. And yet, was there really so much to wonder and worry about? For the children's sake, if for no other reason, Hyacinth would surely do the sensible thing.

After a while, Francine got up and walked to the field, where a small class was practicing. 'Handsome children,' that man had said, and indeed they were: Emma with the fat, shining braids and shining eyes under the velvet cap, Jerry already alert and prideful like the man he would become. They're so much older than they were only a few months ago, she thought. It's come about suddenly, as when you look at a plant, noting that yesterday it didn't reach the windowsill, and today it does.

For obvious reasons, even though she loved all her grand-children equally, these two held a particular place in her heart. Always she had the sense that they felt themselves abandoned. They clung so much to many small, far-back memories. Jerry still knew the telephone number at their old house. Last summer at her house they both remembered, despite the fact that the strawberry patch was now overrun with wild grass, exactly when and where they had picked strawberries long ago with Jim.

Yes, it was a good thing that Hyacinth was doing at last. She needs peace and protection, Francine thought. I don't know how she has managed to stand up under all her burdens, the guilt over that poor man's awful death, and the loss of Will – for which you can't blame him, you really can't – and of course, most of all, the children. But now they can be with their mother, I'm sure, Arnie will see to that. I am still not over the shock, if I ever do get over it, of what Gerald did to her. And I finally do see why she kept it from me for so long: It was too hard and too terrible to put into words. She was terrified. But Arnie understands, and he will be good to her. They will all be safe with him.

In Hyacinth's ears, the airplane engines thrummed and throbbed. Across the aisle a woman with a maddening whine had been talking for the last half hour, while during that half hour Francine had not spoken a word. She had already said enough to make herself quite clear. Now she was simply staring out into blue space.

Then suddenly she turned to Hyacinth. 'You're a responsible person, and this is your life. I don't want to nag you, but I'll try once more. I don't enjoy throwing things up to you, but I have to do it. You're making a mistake. You didn't listen to me about Gerald, and now again you're not listening to me. I don't know what more I can say to convince you.'

'And I don't know what else I can say to make you understand how I feel,' Hyacinth said gently.

'I'm just so sorry about everything. Sorry for you and the children, and believe it or not, for Arnie. Between you and the horse, I'd say he must have had quite a week.'

'The horse? What horse?'

'His prize. His racer.'

'What happened?'

'It had a fractured leg and had to be put down. It's dead. There was a man at the stable yesterday who told me about it. Arnie was really broken up, too.'

'But he never said a thing to me! How did this man know?'

'He saw Arnie yesterday. They knew each other anyway, years ago, in Texas.'

'Well, I'm sorry. I'll phone tonight.'

Francine made a tight mouth. 'It's very nice to sympathize with him about the horse, but what about the other business?'

'That's not something to talk about over the phone. He'll be in New York in a month or two, and then I'll tell him as kindly as I can. I'll always be very, very fond of him, I'll be his friend, but I can't— Oh, you know.'

'Yes, yes, I know.'

Her mother was disappointed and even disgusted by what to her was a stubborn resistance. It's a sad thing to feel your mother's anger, thought Hyacinth, especially when you have a mother like Francine. When I think of how I misjudged her when I was young! She was so right about so many things . . . It's hard to disappoint her again now. Yet it can't be helped. They traveled the rest of the way in a silence broken only by an occasional neutral, necessary remark.

In the taxi from the airport, Francine asked to be let out at Grand Central Station. Hyacinth had expected her to stay overnight before going home, but she preferred to leave then, so they kissed quickly, and parted.

Francine was angry.

The telephone rang just as Hyacinth walked in at her door. When she picked it up, the familiar, enthusiastic voice rang out.

'It's me, Arnie. Just wanted to make sure you folks landed safely.'

'Yes, we're fine. It was a lovely week. But Francine told me something sad about your Diamond. Why didn't you tell us? You never said a word.'

'Didn't want to spoil the party. What's the use of doing that?'

'Well, it's an awful pity. That horse was your pride and joy.'

'I can't say it doesn't hurt. That was some gorgeous animal. Happened in Kentucky. I'm glad I wasn't there to see it. He had a ruptured intestine. Blew up like a balloon, they told me.'

'Oh! Francine heard it was a broken leg, a bad break.'

'Who told her that?'

'Some man out at the stables. Somebody from Texas who's known you for years.'

'Who was he?'

'I don't know his name. I don't think Francine knows it, either.'

'I can't imagine who it could have been, shooting his mouth off about my horse when he doesn't know a damn thing about it. Well, enough of that. What's done is done. I'll tell you what's on my mind. I had a brainstorm last night. You know what? The kids only have a few more weeks in the term. What are we waiting for? We've waited long enough, you and I. How about packing a couple of trunks and going. The kids can make up their work, and besides, they'll love it. Seeing the world — it's more educational than a few weeks in school. I'll send you a stack of travel brochures. In fact, I'll send them by express mail tomorrow. You pick the place, anywhere at all. You pick.'

Hyacinth's heart sank. This nonsense was exasperating, so late in the evening and after a long flight. But forcing good humor, she replied, 'I can't get over how fast you move. Slow down a bit, will you?'

'Why should we? Nobody lives forever, Hy. So once my mind is made up, I get moving. That's the way I am.'

The mental traffic, she thought, is becoming congested. Better glide out of it quickly onto a side street. And sounding a long sigh, she said that she could hardly keep her eyes open.

'Somehow this flight wore me out, so I can't think straight, Arnie. I feel like going straight to bed.'

'Well, you go right to bed. I wish I was in it with you. I'd show you a thing or two.'

All of a sudden, these words distressed her more than she had ever imagined possible. The reality of being in bed every night with Arnie was truly shocking. Had she ever *truly* considered it for more than an instant?

No, not *truly*. No.

The fact was that, far from being unable to keep her eyes open, she was unable to close them and sleep. She could scarcely describe the sensation that was keeping her awake. Something was bothering her. She was at the same time flustered and very vaguely uneasy.

Arnie was – he was *different* tonight. This rush and tension were so unlike the easy-going person she knew. Naturally, he must be thinking about his proposal to her and the inevitable changes it would bring to his life. Yet, since he had not yet been told that she was going to refuse him, he should in theory be in calm good spirits, shouldn't he?

So, when on the following day she came home from work to find him waiting for her in the lobby, she was not totally astonished.

Greeting her with a perfunctory kiss on the cheek he explained, 'I couldn't sleep last night after our talk. It just didn't get anywhere. I kept thinking, feeling, that we're floundering. You keep pulling away from anything definite. Or am I wrong? Stop me if I am.'

'Come upstairs and let's straighten out the confusion.'

This reply sounded braver than Hyacinth felt. And she thought of her father, who would go far to avoid an argument. Unfortunately there was at the moment no place to go.

They sat down in two chairs near a window, with Arnie's flowery plant in its rather gorgeous porcelain tub, between them.

He remarked it. 'Nice, hey? I've learned a thing about taste from watching you, Hy. Was a time when I thought anything was top stuff if it was expensive. Now I know that expensive isn't enough. This pot's an old piece, you know. Did I tell you?'

'No, but I could see that it was. It's very lovely. I've enjoyed it.'

A feeling of pity crept over her, simply because he felt it necessary to remind her that his gift was expensive. Besides, he did not look like himself; for the first time he looked his age or perhaps even more than his age.

He caught her glance and smiled. Apparently doing the brief ride up in the elevator he had rethought his approach, for making no mention of any concern, he drew some folders from his pocket and handed them to her.

'A picture is worth a thousand words, right? Take a look at these. There's France, of course, also Tuscany, not far from Florence with a load of art museums for you, and I've got more on the way, places in the Cotswolds, lots of atmosphere with thatched roofs, kind of stuff you'd go for. Take a look at these.'

As she leafed through pictures of sumptuous villas, of terraced gardens, statues, balustrades and carved ceiling beams, her spirits sank at the thought of the coming struggle. Arnie was going to be a tough adversary.

'See this that I marked in red? A plus? It's a French beauty. For rent furnished, with an option to buy, and we can move in tomorrow. And it's in the neighborhood of a first-rate riding school. Miles of trails through the forest.'

She needed to collect herself. And for lack, at the moment, of anything else to say, she faltered. 'These – these places – cost a fortune – a country place for an aristocrat—'

'Oh baloney, Hy! I can buy and sell half of your aristocrats! Stop worrying about money, will you? I guess I know what I'm doing.'

'I know, but Arnie, I never agreed to all this. I never really promised anything. You're taking too much for granted, making these plans. I even told you that Emma and Jerry have school.'

As if a hand had swept it away, the light went out of his face.

Once before, at the door into a hotel bedroom, she had seen that hard look and those narrowed eyes.

'There are some weeks of school, I know that. But I'm talking about years, Hy. What are you talking about?'

She took the bold step. There was no choice. 'Years as your friend, Arnie. As long as either one of us lives, a dear, dear friend.'

Abruptly he stood, and with his hands in his pockets caused a furious jingle of coins, after which he took one hand out and pounded a table with a fury that caused a heap of magazines to slide to the floor.

'Damn it! I'm not playing games. What the hell do you mean? You promised, you said not four days ago in Florida—'

'I promised nothing, Arnie! Don't put words in my mouth!'

'When I took you back to the hotel and kissed you there in the driveway you damn well did!'

'I know you kissed me. What should I have done? Pushed you away?'

'There are names for a woman who leads a man on and then dumps him. You want to hear them?'

'No, I do not. I never led you on, Arnie. I was confused that day. You rushed me. I was – I am very fond of you. Perhaps I should have made it more clear that "fondness" is not deep love. If I didn't make it clear then I'm sorry. I apologize. But I never promised anything, no matter how often you hinted.'

'What a bitch you are! After all I've done for you!' he cried, waving his hand to indicate the apartment. 'You knew how I feel about you. Your mother knew. And this is my thanks, is it?'

'I have thanked you a thousand times, Arnie. Nobody could be more grateful, than I am.'

'Then show it. Am I so hard to take?' His voice rose. 'Am I?'

'Not at all. But marriage is something else.'

'Something else, is it? Sure, I get it. I'm not your high-flown friend who romanced you all over France, am I? I don't quite fit in, do I? Do I? Who the hell do you think you are?'

'Don't shout at me, Arnie. I don't like it and I won't stand for your temper. There's no reason to act like this.'

'Oh my, oh my! You've done a helluva lot more than shout

when you're in a temper. Smashing computers, setting fires – but that's okay, isn't it? Now you're a big success, aren't you? But don't let it go to your head. You're hardly in a position to be so independent and don't forget it.'

She was appalled and shaken. At the same time her native temper, so rarely used and so hot when used, rose to the surface.

'This is my home. I paid you back for what you put into it, and now I'm ordering you out of it. Get out, Arnie,' She opened the door. 'And when you're in a better mood, you're welcome back.'

At that moment the elevator stopped. Three people got out and glanced toward Arnie and Hyacinth. Taking advantage of their presence, she closed the door, shutting him out in the hall. Then bolting the door, she stood waiting for him either to take the elevator or to pound on the door. When all was quiet, she collapsed into a chair, and began to calm herself. Her fear, she decided at last, was unfounded. The implied threat of betrayal was really nothing to worry about; Arnie, no matter how angry he was at her, would never hurt Emma and Jerry in that way. Of that she was certain. Yet something was terribly wrong.

He was a highly intelligent man and he knew quite as well as she did that all through these years she had never in any way led him on. Why, then, was he so agitated? Why in such a hurry to go away? Was he having some sort of breakdown?

After a while she got up and went to bed, her thoughts still rolling in her head. That odd business about the horse kept bothering her.

An intestinal obstruction, he had said. Or rupture, or infection, something like that. But Francine, though, had said it was a broken leg, and they'd had to 'put him down.' Fancy words for a bullet, most likely.

She sat up, pounded the pillow into a better shape and rolled to her other side, wanting to sleep.

Still far from sleep, her thoughts nagged. Arnie had said one thing, and Francine said that man had said another; so why the discrepancy? One of them was either making a very odd mistake or else not telling the truth. But why?

That horse meant so much to him. He talked about sugarcane all afternoon and never even mentioned its death. Also, later on, he said he couldn't imagine who the man was who had talked to Francine. Yet he must have talked to him, else why would the man say Arnie hadn't changed?

In the morning she awoke with a need, almost compulsive, to question Francine. Telling herself again that her behavior was probably eccentric, she nevertheless made the call to ask Francine's opinion of the man whom she had seen at the stable.

'The one who told you about Diamond's broken leg. Was there anything strange about him?'

'Strange? No. He and his wife, whom I met later, were perfectly ordinary, solid, conservative people. Why do you ask?'

'I only wondered . . . Did he definitely say that Arnie's horse had a broken leg?'

'Yes.' Francine was becoming impatient. 'He caught his foot in a gopher hole, I told you.'

'Did you get the impression that he was hiding anything?'

'Not at all. What should he hide? What's this about?'

Having no proper answer to give, Hyacinth made an excuse, hung up, and in spite of being late this morning, sat on at the telephone for several minutes as if she were trying to assemble the scattered pieces of a disturbing puzzle. The trouble was that there were not enough pieces to work with.

Yet the longer she sat there, the stronger grew her conviction that something was very definitely wrong. Granny would say, 'I feel it in my bones.'

On the third day after these events the feeling grew even stronger; for returning home toward midnight after a long day at work and a late dinner with Lina, she found four messages on the answering machine. They were all from Arnie.

'I'm terribly sorry, Hy. I said things I didn't mean. You know me better than that—'

'Sometimes in a business deal you come up against a tough character who wants to upset the cart and dump all the apples on the street—'

'I was all worked up and took out my temper on you. God, I only want the best for you, so can't you please—'

'Call me, no matter what time you get home—'

She was torn. A part of her dreaded an emotional appeal, an apology, a long explanation, and another description of another lavish European retreat. There was no point in any of it; her answer stood as it had been given. But the other part of her heart reminded her of the many calls — how many hundreds of them? — that she had made to him about Emma and Jerry, beside those he himself had made to soothe her worry. And she went to the telephone.

'Hy, I want you to reconsider. Come away with me. I can't go into all the details now, so just believe me. I've never failed either you or the kids, have I? Have I?'

'No, Arnie, you haven't.'

'Well, then listen to me. I can fly back up there again in the morning and straighten this out in your mind. The telephone is no good. You'll never regret it.' His voice shook. 'Okay, Hy? Listen, you can do your work, you can design wherever you live, if that's what's worrying you. Listen, I'll be there tomorrow.'

'Arnie, I can't!' she cried. 'I'm going to Texas for a couple of showings.' This was the truth. 'I'm not sure yet how long I'll need to be there.' This was not the truth. She was fearful, without knowing why, except perhaps that she merely needed time to prepare herself for a stormy session.

'Good God!' Arnie groaned. 'Haven't you any idea when you'll be back?'

'A week or so, I guess. I'll call you as soon as I am.'

So it stood. All through the three days in Texas, where in artless joy her adult life had really begun, Arnie accompanied her, a heavy weight at the back of her mind. And home again, after two days, she was still steeling herself to call him, Tonight for sure, she promised. Just grit your teeth and do it, Hyacinth.

If she had not happened to catch a glimpse of Will Miller coming out of a seafood restaurant with two other men at lunchtime, the course of events would have been very different. She barely saw any more than his back as he walked away, but there was no mistaking him. He has probably had fish chowder, she thought irrelevantly; it would have to be very hot, with toast on the side.

She had intended to do an errand before returning to work, but the unexpected sight of Will, whom she had not seen since September, was more disconcerting than she had thought it could be, and she turned back to Libretti's instead. There at her too splendid desk, she sat with her drawing board propped against a pile of books, a pencil in hand, and not an idea in her head. In one instant, all her vivid images had flown; the plans that had been taking shape while she was in Florida were gone. In their place were nameless dread and a need to tell somebody about it, somebody who would understand. And again she had a sensation that had come to her only a few times during the crises in her life — such as that moment when Gerald had demanded the abortion — a fear of being without direction. An hour passed, and still she sat holding a pencil. Between the battle . . . with Arnie and the sight of Will, she was lost, back on that street in the city where nobody spoke her language.

And yet there was one person who spoke it well, or had once done so . . . Truly the thought was bizarre! Still, had it not also been bizarre to take the suitcase full of her samples to that grand Madison Avenue shop a few years ago? She, a mere nobody of a student? The worst they can do is to ask me politely to leave, she had argued with herself. So she argued now.

It must have been well into the second hour before, without actually willing to do it, Hyacinth sprang out of the chair. Before a long mirror in the lavatory, she took a careful look at the plain dark blue dress, the small lace scarf at the neck, and the pearls that appeared when her hair fell away from her ears. She had no wish to charm, for that was out of the question; she knew that well and was only concerned with being dignified and in control. This whole business made no sense. Nevertheless, perhaps it did. And she was about to do it.

* * *

She stood smiling before him. When Will gave her no answering smile, she understood what she ought to have known, that her smile was an embarrassment and only a nervous tic at best.

'I haven't come, as you are probably thinking, to make any plea,' she said quietly. 'I'm not asking you to come back because it's clear that you won't. This is nothing personal. I've come because I have a problem. I need advice, and I don't happen to know anybody else who can give it as well as you can.'

'Not your friend Arnie?'

'No. Please listen to me. But if you're not at all interested, I'll leave. Maybe I've done an unforgivably foolish thing in coming here.'

'Sit down,' he said.

He had risen when she entered the room, and both of them were still standing. Now, as he drew a chair up for her, they both sat, separated as is usual in a professional office, by an oversized desk. He looks tired and stern, she thought before turning her eyes away.

'What kind of problem is it? If it's medical, I'm not a doctor. If it's legal, I'm not a lawyer.'

'I'm not exactly sure what it is. That's part of the problem. It may be somewhat legal, but I don't really know that, so—'

Will interrupted. 'A lawyer would know it.'

'I can't go to one. I don't want to mention an innocent person's name to a lawyer if it isn't necessary.'

'That's being overly scrupulous, I should say. In fact, it's absurd.'

'I don't think it is. Not if a person has been a close, loyal friend. You'd want to be careful how you used his name.'

'A close, loyal friend. That wouldn't be Arnie again by any chance?' Will spoke with scorn in his voice.

'Yes, I'm sorry to say so, but it is.'

'He's your lover, isn't he? So why do you come to me?'

'To begin with, I've told you before that he is not my lover. He never was. It's true that he would like to be and that he has asked me to marry him, but I will not marry him because I do not love him. I like him very much, though, and I believe he may be in trouble of some kind. That's the whole truth.'

'You haven't answered my other question. Why do you come to me?'

'I thought I answered it. Because I trust you.'

She sat up straighter and waited. There was silence in the room. He was looking at her without revealing any judgment or any feeling at all.

He has someone else by now, she thought, and I have become a curiosity. He was a stranger. The crisp speech, the formal posture with folded hands resting on the desk, the eyes that refused to meet hers, all these were strange.

She wanted suddenly to be out of the room, away from this unnatural atmosphere. But he was waiting for her to say something more, so as quickly and clearly as she could for he tended to be impatient with long-winded descriptions, she related the events that disturbed her, the affair of the horse and the troubles with Arnie.

'Maybe there's no sense in all this,' she concluded. 'Maybe I'm frightened about a burglar in the house when it's really just the wind rattling the window.'

Will was looking over her head at the opposite wall and did not answer. The ruddy color that had once so become him had bled away; in the dimming light of the late afternoon he looked gray.

'I don't want to hurt this man who's been so good to me and my children,' she said. 'Yet when a person acts so out of character—'

He interrupted. 'I'll speak to someone. The man I have in mind is discreet, and no one will ever know that you were here. When I have something to report I'll call you.'

Understanding that she was being dismissed, Hyacinth rose and thanked him. The interview had been dignified and correct, as she had determined it would be. It had even been somewhat helpful, as she had hoped it would be. It had also been so cool, that no witness would ever have guessed that this man and this woman had once loved each other.

Yet as she put her hand on the doorknob to leave him, she could not help but turn to ask, 'And how have you been?'

'Getting along. And you?'

'Getting along. And thank you again.'

It began to snow. The slow, thick flakes of earliest spring made wet spots on Hyacinth's smart Libretti coat. From her equally smart red handbag, she drew a collapsible umbrella. Then, fearing that she might possibly pass somebody who knew her, she put on her sunglasses. Surely there was no glare coming out of the dark sky, so it was not for that reason; it was only to hide her eyes, which suddenly were overrun with tears.

The waiting time was wretched. Every day for the next week, Hyacinth fended off Arnie's insistent arguments and pleas as best she could. Every day she went through an argument with herself: Had she stirred up a hornet's nest? Or perhaps a nest in which there were no hornets, thus making herself more than ever into a foolish meddler? Not that it really mattered . . .

Francine, making her weekly telephone call, was evidently frustrated by Hyacinth's unwillingness to take her advice, because she had obviously decided to let the subject drop. And Hyacinth, when their rather timid conversations ended, was saddened, for the mother, the good mother, had only been planning – mistakenly, as it happened – for the daughter's benefit.

At last, on the second Monday, there was a message. 'I now have a full report and can see you at my office tomorrow afternoon, or can bring it to your house this evening, whichever you prefer. Will Miller.'

Will Miller, instead of *Will*. As if, without the full name, I would not know who he was! A little thing like that speaks volumes. Expect nothing, it means; I am merely doing you a decent favor. Suddenly, she did not want to see him again, especially in that forbidding office. Let him come here then, to her own territory.

When she opened the door to him that evening, she felt the very air of his last departure there: the sound of the door's soft closing, and the silence afterwards. She wondered what, or even whether, he might be having any remembrance of that moment.

He gave no sign of anything but businesslike efficiency. With his slight frown and his refusal of coffee, he made it clear that he was in a hurry.

'In this computer age,' he said, as he withdrew a notepad from his pocket, 'you would expect to learn something in hours, but this business, as it turns out, became somewhat complicated. These are my personal notes. I definitely did not want to own anything in writing.'

With her hands clutched together in her lap and her nervous heart already racing, Hyacinth fastened her eyes on the paper from which Will read.

'I'm going to start in the middle,' he said, 'beginning with the death of the horse. It happens that its death was already under investigation before you came to me. Insurance companies are very suspicious when a valuable horse dies. There used to be too many cases like that. In fact, the moment you told me about the death I thought of a case that happened in my home town where a prominent society leader – very fine lady but not too fine to murder an animal for the insurance – well, no matter. But in recent years there have been very few such cases because people are afraid now. However, some daring souls still try it, and sometimes it's successful. But then sometimes, other things happen. A righteous person finds out or suspects, and goes to the authorities. At the same time the partners in the conspiracy can have a falling out, probably about splitting the money. And there you are. And then, then—'

She could not help but interrupt. 'You can't mean Arnie?'

Will nodded. 'Yes, I consulted a private investigator whom we employ, and I do mean Arnie. The clues were mainly the conflicting causes, one a broken leg and the other an internal rupture. The truth is that the horse was simply shot to death. And the excuse that was officially given was the broken leg. But apparently there was a falling out, and somebody talked.'

Hyacinth gasped. 'I can't believe Arnie would do anything like that! There was no cruelty in him, not at all. How could he—'

'Well, at least there was no pain, except for the insurance company,' Will said wryly. 'Many a respected business finds it very convenient from time to time to have a fire sale. It's nothing new.'

'I can't believe it's Arnie,' she repeated. 'It doesn't fit him.'

Will grimaced. 'You can't always judge people by their outsides, can you? Are you feeling all right? You look faint.'

'Not faint. Just sick.'

'Are you sure you want to hear the rest? It's not a pretty story.'

'Go on,' she whispered. 'They have a lot of evidence, Arnie's signature on a falsified certificate, the man in Florida, probably the one who talked to your mother that day, and somebody else who went back twenty-five years to when Arnie Ritter was Jack Sloan.'

'They're both his name. Jack Arnold Ritter-Sloan was his name, but he hated it. He always said, "Hell, I'm no hoity-toity aristocrat who needs a double name."'

'It seems to have come in handy for a while, though. He had a fire when he was a medical student in Texas, insured under the name of Sloan. It was a big fire, his whole apartment went up in flames, and he lost all his valuables, rare books, very costly, or so he claimed. It looked suspicious at the time, but they could never prove it, so nothing happened.'

'Twenty-five years ago,' Hyacinth repeated in horror.

Had they not said he left Texas in a hurry?

'Yes, and but for this horse affair, nothing would be happening. Now it's all come to life.'

Neither spoke. Will seemed to be studying her now, and his scrutiny was so unbearable that she had to look away, down at her own feet.

'It's a terribly painful thing to be disillusioned when you thought you knew a person,' he remarked.

No doubt he meant that for her, but she let it pass, saying only that she wanted to thank him.

'I'm very, very grateful to you, more than I can say.'

He inclined his head in a formal acknowledgment. 'I'm glad I was able to help. But it's all about to come out in the news pretty soon any way.'

What are we waiting for? The kids don't have to finish the last few weeks of school. Let's go now.

'Arnie,' she said again. 'I still don't understand. He was so kind, so loving to us all.'

'Tell that to the insurance company.' Will's tone was grim, 'That man who died in the fire—'

'What!' cried Hyacinth. 'What fire?'

'The medical building, Arnie's own building.'

'He burned it down? Arnie did it?'

'Indeed he did,' Will said, still grimly. 'He's had to confess. I learned it this morning. Of course he didn't have a leg to stand on, what with the Texas affair and now the horse.'

As, after long darkness, a person's eyes are struck by a shaft of brilliant light, so now Hyacinth was pierced by pain. Her life, the life of these past years, went whirling, and seated there in her own room the very walls went whirling.

'My children!' she cried. 'They took them away from me and now they are mine again! Mine!'

'What is all this? What are you talking about?'

She was unable to speak. She was too stunned to find words and yet her thoughts were flashing.

Such relief! Such unspeakable relief! Emma and Jerry . . . And I'm not responsible, not even through the carelessness of a dropped cigarette . . . not responsible for anything . . . I can explain it all: to Moira, my friend, to my brothers and above all to Francine . . . poor Francine . . . she suffered . . .

Will was staring at her. And all at once she saw that his cool, formal courtesy was nothing more than a defense. She saw his painful effort to contain his pain within himself. And bowing her head into her hands she broke into sobs.

The next instant brought him to his knees before her. 'What is it? For God's sake, tell me,' he cried, forcing her face up toward his own.

'You see— You see,' she stammered, 'they thought I did it, that I burned down the office because I was in a rage about a woman and Gerald found my things on the lawn, and it was a murder, you see, because the man, the poor fireman, died and that's arson murder, a felony-murder, and I— I—'

'They thought it was *you*?'

'Yes, yes, they thought it was, and Gerald, he said—'

Will got up and took her into his arms, while she, with her head on his shoulder, cried out her story.

'Take your time, take your time,' he whispered, kissing her head, stroking and holding her. 'Who dared to accuse you? Who dared?'

'Well, Gerald. I told you—'

'He ought to be drawn and quartered. Or is he insane?'

'No, no. He really believes that I did it.'

'Oh God in Heaven, why didn't you tell me all this before?' Will's cry was agonized. 'Didn't you trust me? Why?'

'I was too afraid. I was terrified. They would say I had a motive, and I did have one. So I had no defense, did I? You don't know what fear like that can do to you. Every hour of every day I thought of my children. And all the fear was locked up inside me, sealed like a vault in a bank. Sealed. I felt that if I talked about it, it would come true. You see how things do come out after twenty-five years, don't you?'

'But me! Me. You knew I loved you. I would have done anything—'

'I wanted to live with you, Will. But you wanted a wife. How could I do that to you? If all of a sudden I should be accused and very likely convicted, how could I do that to you?' she repeated. 'You were, you are, a man rising in the world. To put you at risk to share my trouble – how could I?'

'Who gives a damn about "rising"? Do you really think that would have stopped me?'

'Are you saying you wouldn't have cared? Will, be truthful with me.'

'I have always been truthful with you, even about those half-baked pictures you used to paint. Yes, I would have been very worried, very worried for your sake. But that would never have kept me from taking you as my wife. You were, you are, for me as close to perfection as one can ever hope to find in this world.'

Perfection. And lying quite still, Hyacinth felt his heart as it touched her own, the thumping beat upon the beat of her own.

'Did you ever think about me?' she murmured.

'Yes, the way one thinks sadly, while trying not to, of someone who has gone away or died.'

'I never went away, but there were plenty of times when I wished I would die.'

'But you came to me when you needed help.'

'I knew that if anything should be revealed about me, you wouldn't hurt me.'

'I didn't like Arnie, you know. I told you so. The only time I was with him, riding away from your house in the cab, I felt something concealed behind the friendly grin. It wasn't because I was jealous, although I admit I was. I simply didn't like him.'

'You don't know him, Will. He was – is – the kindest soul on earth, and I can't make any sense out of what he's done.'

'Contradictions. We all have them. Only his were extreme.'

'I pity him. Of course I also despise him for letting me suffer as I have. I suppose that's my contradiction.'

After a long minute, Will spoke again. His voice was very soft, and breaking. 'I'm remembering the hammock and the crashing waves. Those nights keep coming back and back again.'

'Do you remember that day in the park when all of a sudden we looked at each other and both of us knew and neither of us said it?'

'And before that there was the day you dropped the bag of books on the sidewalk.'

'And I'm remembering—'

Will raised his hand. 'Enough. Enough of remembering. We have lost time to make up for.' He was kissing her, and now at the same time, laughing a little. 'Get up, so I can carry you inside.'

Chapter Seventeen

'Yes,' Gerald said, 'you could have knocked me over with a feather. I'm still in shock.'

Hyacinth had been bringing the last of the children's belongings down the stairs, when Gerald had appeared. Having hoped to avoid him, but caught now at the foot of the stairs, she stood there surrounded by boxes and bags.

'How a man as smart as Arnie can mess up his life like this is beyond me. Who ever could have imagined the things he's done?'

And who could imagine that Gerald would be talking to her as naturally as if they were in the habit of holding daily conversations? Here, in his tennis whites, cradling his racket and shaking his head in astonished disbelief, he continued his narration.

'Cashed in all his securities and emptied his bank accounts to the last penny, but didn't touch our corporate account, which of course he could have done. And now he's vanished, God knows where to. How's it going to end, do you think?'

'I have no idea,' she said, sadly.

'Oh, they'll get him eventually. They always do. Always did. But now, with the World Wide Web and Voice of America's Crime Alert, it's even easier. Another thing' – and Gerald's face took on an expression of wise judgment – 'a man like him who likes to show off his wealth, a flamboyant type, you know, won't be able to stay inconspicuous. You should see what he's done with this office downtown. Arnie's always been a big spender. He makes it and spends it.'

Hyacinth was thinking, you don't do too badly, either. She was looking past Gerald's shoulder through the hall and the rooms beyond. They had been changed since the single visit she had made here before. New influences had left their mark everywhere in hideous artificial flowers, in heavy gilt and thick, dark satins, all expensive and unsuited to the climate. There was a time when he would have rejected such a gaudy display.

Gerald was telling her, 'He left me a note. Came yesterday, postmarked here, probably just before he left for wherever he went. It's an apology to me, and some stuff about you: *"Don't blame Hy. She had absolutely nothing to do with the fire in any way. Nothing at all."* He underlined it.'

For a moment, overwhelmed yet again by the sadness of everything, she was silent. Arnie. How to explain him? Was there ever any real explanation when decent people transgress?

'I have a note, too,' she said. It was none of Gerald's business, and yet for some reason she wanted him to hear it. " 'Forgive me, Hy, for all the terrible hurt I caused you. I've tried to make it up to you. Please try to remember that I really loved you, and still do."'

At the last words, when her voice cracked, Gerald exclaimed with heated indignation, 'I can imagine how you'd like to shoot him through the heart. I know I would if I were you. I'd want to destroy him.'

'No,' she said. 'He's a tragedy. All the goodness in him gone to waste.'

'What? You're not enraged? You're an unusual woman, Hyacinth. Amazing.'

'Oh, I'm angry at him, very much so. But far, far more so at you.'

It was Gerald's turn to be silent, and she saw that her words had struck home.

As he turned away from her, she took the opportunity to examine him. There it was, the face with the slightly tilted, teasing gold-brown eyes, the face that women loved, not a day older than it had been on the afternoon when she had rescued him from the rain storm, she, the delayed adolescent, ignorant and infatuated. Even now that face still spoke of humor, pleasure and passion. Even now it promised nothing. It had never really given anything, nor had it ever loved.

Well, yes, she corrected herself. He had loved the children; after all, they were extensions of himself.

'I really thought you did it, Hyacinth,' he said now. 'I really thought you were jealous enough to have done it. That's God's truth.'

'Then you never knew me. If you had loved me enough, you would have known me better. You would have known that I was no arsonist. If you had loved me, you would not have taken my children away.'

Gerald threw up his hands. 'God Almighty, I'm sorry. The whole thing's been an awful mistake, a mess. And I was terribly wrong. But I still don't see how you can be more angry at me than at Arnie.'

'Arnie had a heart, you see. The only people he hurt were the insurance people, which is certainly a terrible crime, but I also must remember that he paid off the fireman's mortgage for the widow and gave her four years of college for each of her children. That's to say nothing about all his other kindness, and especially his goodness to Jerry and Emma and me. He's a sick man, I think. He must be. And so I'm terribly sorry for him.'

'Well,' Gerald conceded, 'you do have a point. He was a gambler, and from there, I suppose, it's not too big a step to worse things when you happen to be in need of cash. Yes, it's pitiable, the way you put it. It's an addiction, like alcohol.'

'Or women. By the way, how is Sherree? Or was it Cheryl? The one after Buddy, I mean.'

Gerald's smile was followed by a flush that rose to the roots of his hair. 'That's all nonsense. With a little serious will power, addictions can be overcome.'

He was admiring her. Suddenly, she was conscious of her dress, which was the color of ripe apricots, of her shining black sandals and the ribbon band that she had worn to keep her hair from blowing in the wind. And suddenly she was aware too that never before when in this man's presence had she felt such confidence, or even such superiority. A picture flickered for an instant before her eyes and flickered away: Jim at the little dining table in Texas had just talked about giving them the big house when Gerald was finished with his training, and Gerald was almost visibly discarding any thought of abortion. With hindsight now, it was all too clear.

'I've been reading and hearing so much about your success,' he said. 'I've wanted to congratulate you, but since you wouldn't even talk to me—'

'There was no point in talking to you.'

She was restless. The conversation had gone on too long, and Will was waiting outside in the rented car. She had not wanted him to come in. And moving now to depart, she was stopped by Gerald's quick yet somehow tentative question.

'Now that we have talked, I was thinking that – well, that possibly you might give some thought to maybe trying again.'

Two suitcases dropped from Hyacinth's hands and thumped onto the floor.

'Trying again? You can't mean what I think you mean?'

'Well, yes I do. You and I – after all, we were – I thought, seeing you, and with so much cleared up in our minds—'

'You can't be serious, Gerald. You can't be. Why, I'd as soon adopt a cobra.'

As if in alarm, he withdrew as if he were expecting her to strike him. 'All right, all right. Forget I said it. The only thing is, I don't like to see you go away with so much hatred toward me, Hyacinth.'

'The fact is, I'm not going away with all that much hatred toward you. I've just realized that, actually, I don't have it. Well, maybe I still do somewhat, because what you did to me was unspeakable. But at least I'm not going to waste too much time and energy over it. I'm far too happy.' Pausing, she looked straight into his eyes. 'Now if you'll ask Tessie, please, to help me with all this stuff, I'll appreciate it. My mother is waiting with Emma and Jerry at the hotel. We're flying home tonight, right after an early supper.'

With sudden force, Hyacinth was affected by Gerald's relative lack of emotion now that his children were departing from his house. Yes, as he had said, he would miss them, he hoped they would like their new school, he would keep in regular touch with them; but with all of that he seemed to feel nothing that compared with her agony when the situation was reversed. But had Arnie not remarked that they were no fun for Gerald anymore? Yes, that's it, she thought. He has grown vaguely tired of being constantly with them, just as he grew tired of me. The very model of a man, he is.

'One more thing,' she said briskly, for at the other door, Tessie had come partially into view, wide-eyed, dying of curiosity and suddenly very respectful of 'that crazy woman.' 'One more thing. I want you to know that I do not intend to poison the children's minds against you in any way. I have never done it, and that's because of their welfare, their mental health, not yours. Also, I want you to know that you may see them whenever it is convenient for me, assuming that it is also their wish, and I'm sure it will be, because they love you, and should love you. Oh, and the last thing! Good Lord, I almost forgot the dog. Will one of you please get Charlie for me?'

'One second, Hyacinth. First let me take these things to the car.'

'Thank you, but no. Tessie and I can manage them. It will be less awkward that way, given the circumstances. My husband is out there in the car, you see.'

'How was it?' Will asked.

'Not as bad as I thought it would be. It was really more pathetic than anything else.'

'Francine thinks you had a lot of spunk to go by yourself, or to see him at all. We were talking about it last night. She was afraid he'd be nasty and that there'd be a bad scene.'

'It was just the opposite, not that I would have minded either way. He even suggested that maybe he and I could get together again. Can you believe it?'

'After the story of your friend Arnie, I guess I could believe anything.'

'The tragedy of Arnie, you mean.'

'A tragedy and ·a mystery. Nobody's ever explained and probably never will explain what makes a Gerald, an Arnie, or – or any of us.'

'Francine can't get over how wrong she was about Arnie, even to hoping I would marry him. She isn't used to making such a huge mistake, having been so right about Gerald.'

'Francine's a "character."' Will chuckled. 'She told me she's given up going into the fortune-teller business.'

'Did she tell you she's leaving on a cruise to South America with her new man? I haven't said anything yet, but I'm surprising her with all the clothes for it, a Libretti wardrobe.'

Will corrected her. 'The Hyacinth line. Yes, she told me about the cruise. She also had the nerve to tell me that she hopes you'll be pregnant by the time she gets home.'

'She still has a good sense of humor, I see.'

'No, no, she was serious. She was in earnest. And I am, too, in case I haven't already mentioned it.'

Deep, endless blue lay between the beach and the horizon, on which three sails were moving westward toward the afternoon sun. And there, running on the wet sand with their backs to the sun, were the children, Hyacinth's own.

'Look, darling,' Will said. 'They've been waiting for us.'

She was filled with the most wonderful lightness, so that she had to cry out.

'I feel as if I could fly!'

He looked down at her. His eyes, those humorous, kind, honest eyes that missed nothing, understood her completely. They smiled, and his arm went around her.

'We'll both fly,' he said.